The Picture Book

Jo Baker

W F HOWES LTD

This large print edition published in 2012 by
W F Howes Ltd
Unit 4, Rearsby Business Park, Gaddesby Lane,
Rearsby, Leicester LE7 4YH

1 3 5 7 9 10 8 6 4 2

First published in the United Kingdom in 2011
by Portobello Books

A CIP catalogue record for this book is available
from the British Library

ISBN 978 1 40749 554 5

Typeset by Palimpsest Book Production Limited,
Falkirk, Stirlingshire
Printed and bound in Great Britain
by MPG Books Ltd, Bodmin, Cornwall

*One generation passeth away, and another generation
  cometh.*
*All the rivers run on to the sea, and yet the sea is
  not full.*

Ecclesiastes 1:2, 7

The Electric Theatre, York Road, Battersea,
14 August 1914

The lights go out. The cheap seats erupt in shrieks and roars, as though the dark has changed everyone into wild animals and birds. It's hot. The stench is terrible. Amelia fumbles for William's hand.

A mechanical whir and clatter starts up behind her. She twists round to look over her shoulder. All she can see is a saturating flood of light, which makes her blink, and then the light begins to flip and flicker.

'It's starting,' William says.

Amelia turns back in her seat and cranes to look between the heads in front, through the twists of tobacco smoke.

A man snaps into existence. The audience cheers. He bows, blows kisses. He's framed by rich, draped curtains, and wears an elegant morning suit. He is very handsome. He is soft shades of porcelain and charcoal, silky-grey.

'That's Max,' William says. 'Max Linder.'

1

Amelia's hand squeezes William's. 'What's the story?'

'He's on stage,' William says. 'Taking a curtain call.'

The miracle of it. A gentleman like that, bowing to them; to the audience crammed there, two kids to a seat, all of them jabbering away as if this was nothing. The place smelling of old clothes and boots and sweat and bad teeth and disease.

'What do you think?' William asks.

She just shakes her head, smiles.

The image changes: she sees a husband and wife now, talking. There's a title card: the lady wants to meet Max; can the husband send a note? The kids in the cheap seats gabble out the words, translating or just reading out loud for their parents: a tangle of English, Yiddish, Italian. It's like bedlam in the theatre, but on the screen everything is beautiful: the husband is in evening dress, and the lady's wrap is just the loveliest thing Amelia's ever seen, the silky drape of it. It would feel so good on the skin. But the husband is jealous. You can tell that by his eyebrows, his fists.

The man in front of her leans to talk to his neighbour, and she moves closer to William, shoulder against his shoulder, to peer round the obstacle.

In the dark, William draws her hand into his lap, unbuttons her glove and peels it off. She repossesses the empty glove, smoothes it flat on her lap. He twists the narrow wedding ring around her finger, then strokes her palm with his thumb, the calloused skin grazing and snagging on her hot skin. It's distracting, but she doesn't pull her hand away. Tonight he is allowed.

She glances round at him, at his angular profile. His eyes are on the distance, watching the screen; they catch the flickering light and flash green. Then he laughs, creases fanning, and she looks at the screen to see what made him laugh. The maid lays out a china coffee set, and Max is charming, and the husband seethes, and, while the wife and Max are turned away to admire a painting, the husband pours a dose of salts into Max's coffee!

The audience roars. Amelia claps her gloved hand over her mouth.

The husband dodges over to join his wife and Max, and, when all their backs are turned, the maid, who is also beautifully dressed in hobble skirt and high heels, goes to take away the tray. Seeing the coffee is undrunk, she sets it down again, but has, by chance, turned the tray around, so that the tainted cup is set before the husband's seat. The audience roars again. Amelia's hand drops away from her face. And then, for good measure, the husband dodges round and pours another dose into what he thinks is Max's cup, but it's the wife's. They're all going to cop for it now!

'Oh my goodness!'

On screen, the three of them sit down at the coffee table, but then there's an exchange of

3

courtesies, of sugar lumps and cream that just goes on and on and you can't bear it because you know any moment they're going to drink, but it keeps on not happening, and not happening until the husband, dainty for his bulk, smug in the expectation of Max's humiliation, lifts his china cup and sups long on his coffee. He doesn't know what's coming! A moment later, he grips his stomach and rushes for the door. Max and the wife look on, bemused. Then Max drinks, and grimaces, and has to rush out too! And then the wife! They return, with accusations, and then there's outrage, confusion, revelation, and then a caption: the wife isn't in love with Max – she just wants to be in one of his films!

A wave of laughter, and the kids are gabbling again, and there's a second wash of laughter afterwards.

On screen, everyone shakes hands, kisses cheeks; they resolve to make the film together. All troubles are over, all discord is resolved: no-one loves the wrong person or wants something they can never have, or has to face something they simply cannot face.

The reel ends with a clatter, empty white panels flipping up and away. The lights come up and Amelia blinks, staring down the length of the room towards a blank white screen, between the greasy heads in front. The heavy curtains are kept pulled tight, and the electric light glares uncomfortably, and the man in a huckster's suit, who took the money at the door, walks the length of the cheap seats, spraying the crowds with scent. That she is here, in a place like this, where the audience has to be perfumed – disinfected? – halfway through the show, is testament to her feeling, her resolve. Amelia gets a whiff of the spray – sweet violets but with a sharp tang of ammonia. It makes the kids laugh and jostle, and even the adults down in the cheap seats don't protest or really seem to recognise the shame of it: one woman raises her face towards the spray, eyes closed as if in enjoyment. But she and William are all right where they are, up in the sixpenny seats. No-one will spray them here.

The lights flick out again, and the clattering wheel of the bioscope starts up, and the huckster slips out of the way, and the scene is of the sea, a fleet of proud grey battleships nosing across an expanse of iron-grey waves.

'Can you see your ship?' She peers in hard at the murky grey-on-grey. 'Is the *Goliath* there?'

He peers. 'Those are the new ones. *Goliath*'s getting on a bit.'

Then there's a title card: *The Gallant Navy Boys*. And there's a clutch of them on deck, three lads in their rig, joking and laughing, eyes bright white against dark weathered skin. She feels again for William's hand, and squeezes it, and feels a flush of pride. And then from somewhere towards the front, a young woman's voice breaks out into song.

5

'Tis the Navy, the Fighting Navy,
That will keep them in their place
And other voices join her, and Amelia tries, but the words come out thin and husky.
For they know they have to face
The gallant little lads in Navy Blue.
She reaches up to touch the wet away from her eyes.

'All right?' William asks.

She nods. 'I know you have to,' she says. And that's the only thing that makes it bearable at all.

When the lights go up at the end, he tugs on her hand, and they're on their feet ahead of the crowds, and they slip past the projectionist who is crouched and fiddling with his machine, and they're out through the front doors and into the busy evening of York Road, and he's spinning her round on the pavement like a child, whirling through the warm thick summer air, and making her protest and laugh.

Then he stops her, and holds her waist. She's smiling dizzily.

'Thank you for coming,' he says.

She inclines her giddy head.

'I know it's not really your cup of tea.'

She straightens her hat, remembers the handsome Max, bowing to the stinking, roaring, shrieking crowd. 'If it wasn't for that spray—'

He grins, turns her lightly, side to side, at the waist.

'But just think: they can film anything,' he says, 'and show it anywhere. It's amazing. Anything. Japan. America. The whole world—'

'The whole world in a little room.'

He stills her, lets his hands fall from her. 'I suppose so.'

She takes his arm, and they walk. William tucks her arm in tight to his side. He doesn't speak. She wonders if she's offended him, but can't work out quite how. An omnibus passes by, the horses dragging along tiredly, lamps glowing, making her realise that the light is fading.

'Do you want to go somewhere else?' she asks.

He clicks his tongue, shakes his head.

And that's true enough. There's nowhere else to go. Too late for the park; music halls and pubs are vulgar. So, by rights, is the bioscope, though she's let that pass for once. And it's not like you can just go for a stroll along the riverbank; it's not that kind of river in this part of town.

'He might be in bed by now,' she says.

'You never know.'

They are nearly at the corner of Plough Road; nearly home. They turn down the road, and it's quiet now. For a moment they are alone, and a sparrow chitters along the length of a back wall, and you can hear the clattering of cabs and drays down the York Road behind them. William stops and pulls Amelia to him, holds her, making the edge of her corset dig into her flesh, so that when she undresses later there are red marks on her

7

skin. She catches her breath, doesn't protest: she wants him to be happy.

He dips his face into her neck, and almost lifts her off the ground, and says, 'Oh my sweetheart, Oh my girl.'

She could have had anyone, her mother always said. Edwin Cheeseman, from the grocer's. Lionel Travis, who's doing so well at Price's. Mr Bateman, a senior clerk in the city, who'd been casting eyes at her ever since she was fifteen. A whole host of good, sound, solid men who'd've been only too happy to have her as their wife. So why on God's good earth did it have to be *him*, William Hastings, a scruff from the wrong end of Battersea with little to recommend him but a job on the factory floor at Price's and a bold manner, who clearly thinks he's better than he is? And Amelia would dismiss her mother's objections, dismiss the whole world and all the sound solid men in it with a toss of her head, and turn back to the window, to look out for him, so that she could see him from the moment he turned down Edna Street. Watch him walk all the way to her front door.

The old man's clinking and clattering in the kitchen; William leads her instead into the cool dimness of the front parlour, propels her gently towards the seats by the window.

'Sit down.'

She sits. The summer sky is a deep blue strip

above the houses opposite; little light reaches into the narrow street. She watches as William goes over to the cabinet and lifts a package from the top. He brings it over to her, puts it in her hands. It is neatly wrapped in the stationer's striped paper, tied with creamy soft cotton tape. There is substance here, heft. She feels an unaccountable prickle of apprehension. She has to fight an urge to hand it straight back to him.

'Open it.'

He sits down on the arm of the chair. His arm presses against her shoulder. She teases the knot undone, conscious of the brush of her sleeve against his thigh. The paper peels apart.

The book's cover is a deep inky blue. A flowered plant twines up the left side, curling round the black embossed word *Album*. She runs her fingers over the skin-cool board, tracing the lines and shapes, the dents and ridges of its patterning. She doesn't know what to make of it.

'It's beautiful,' she says.

He shifts eagerly on the arm of her chair, leans in to lift the cover. Inside, the page is cut with little angled slips.

'It's for postcards,' he says.

He touches the four cuts where you would slide in the corners of the cards. He lifts the page, turns it, shows her the spread of two pages, blank too, the whole book of it waiting to be filled.

'Wherever I go,' he says, 'every country, every city; I'll buy postcards, and send them to you.

So that you can see the world, see everything I see.'

She runs her hands over the cool paper, feeling the snag of the corner cuts. She smiles up to him.

'Like a picture book,' she says. 'Lovely. Yes.'

The sheets feel damp on her skin. She can see, in the narrow strip of evening sky, a single bright star. It is still not quite dark. The room is humid, hot. She can hear her father-in-law in the next room as he moves around, getting ready for bed. The chink of his collar studs on the washstand, the sucked-in breath as he undoes his belt. The walls are thin. Everything about the house is thin: the rooms, the corridors, the curtains and the floorboards and the brick and mortar and the lath and plaster. Everything is permeable: damp seeps in, and smoke oozes out of the chimney, and the fog slinks in from the street and leaves oily dirt on the windowsills. Whenever a door is opened or closed, a step climbed, a curtain drawn, whenever someone sits down, stands up, coughs, the shift is felt throughout the house, by everyone.

She lies still as she can, and breathes, 'Hush, love, please.'

He grunts in reply, too occupied in himself, in making the springs jangle, making the bedframe creak and the bedhead tap the wall. His body slithers on hers in a film of sweat. She hears the old man step out of his trousers and the huff as he bends down to pick them up. She can feel the neighbours in the rooms either side, can almost hear them breathe. She misses Edna Street, she often does. Things were more solid there.

William is done. He presses his face into her neck, and kisses her. It's ticklish. After a moment, he pushes off her, and gets up and pulls on his shirt and goes to the window and lights up a cigarette, and pulls the sash up high. He sits on the windowsill, holding the cigarette outside, out of courtesy.

She tugs the sheet up to her shoulders and watches him, the soft creases of his shirt, the lean muscle of his naked legs. The way he leans down to the gap to blow the smoke out into the night. At moments like this, he seems so foreign to her, almost unknowable. Like a fox met on the turn of a lane – encountered for a moment, and then gone.

He looks round at her. Grins. She swallows down the fear, and smiles back.

HMS Goliath, *Grand Harbour, Malta,*
14 April 1915

The post comes in as William is scrubbing up after the forenoon watch. He's bone tired, his back burning, his palms raw, and what he really should do is eat something, slump into his hammock, read her letter, sleep. But he has shovelled coal and slept and eaten, turn and turn about, for days, and now there is a whole new island out there. A whole new country. He has dug his way here through mountains of coal.

As he climbs up from the mess, daylight dazzles him; he crosses the deck half blinded, stunned by sun and noise. Coal thunders into the hold, crates swing, ropes creak under the strain, gulls wheel and cry. He reaches the far rail and he leans there, and looks down and down the curving flank of the ship into the giddy depths, coloured flares swimming across his vision, and he breathes in the unfamiliar air, the smell of harbour water, coal, drains, bread and oranges, deal, the dusty smell of hemp. He sucks it in.

Below, fishes flicker in the glassy water. Strange fishes, new fishes, Maltese fishes now. There'd been sea snakes off Africa, slithering through the waves. Flying fish scudding across the surf. His eyes adjust, and he looks up, across the harbour, where fishing boats sway at their moorings. They look back at him with blue painted eyes. Behind them, the harbour wall sweeps round like a protecting arm, and buildings straggle up the hills from the quayside. Above it all, on the clifftop, stands a vast building, quiet and empty. It must be a cathedral, he thinks, or some kind of ancient temple, to have that scale, that prominence.

The colours are so clean, so simple here: just golden rock, just blue sea and sky.

He recalls the letter, dangling from his hand. He opens it. There's something about her letters – the neat, closed handwriting, her careful sentences – that's just like her. He reads the words, and it's like her voice is speaking them. It's an uneasy feeling.

I was able to speak to Mr Travis, and he assured me that you can have your old job back, at Price's, when the war is over, and we have you home with us again. It is great news, that we can have that to look forward to – your return, and our security as a family.

He closes his eyes, and the redness pulses and flares with colour. He tries to imagine her. Her pale curls, her grey dress, her buttoned collar, the alien swell of her body beneath her clothes. It is all so far away. In the damp and chill of Battersea the workers stream into Price's in the dawn dark, stream out again at twilight. He tries to see himself amongst them, another dark figure in a dark coat in the dark winter evening, the way he used to be.

The baby is due in May.

'Drink, Billy-boy?'

Sully. He leans in beside William, elbows on the rail. Sully is an old hand, leading stoker, and a bad penny. It's hard to say no to him.

William folds the letter briskly, slips it into his pocket. Notices Sully notice it. Sully grins, and it reminds William of something, but he can't quite place it. It's like his skin is somehow too tight for his bones.

'Seriously. Drink.'

'Postcard first,' William says.

'Everywhere we go, you're off looking for post-cards.'

'For the missus.'

'She must be quite something.'

William inclines his head. Once, when they were courting, he'd caught a glimpse of her coming down from the offices at Price's; the swirl of her skirts, a flash of ankle, the neatness of her waist: before he'd even realised it was her, his chest had tightened with desire.

'Drink first though. You can buy a postcard after. It's young Paveley's birthday.'

'It's always someone's birthday.'

Sully shrugs. 'You've got to take your chances when you can.'

Of course you do. Because who knows what's going to happen next, or if you'll ever get another chance at all? Sully nudges closer, conspiratorial. He smells of the boiler room. Coal dust. Sweat. Damp. A smell like old mattresses.

'We're off to Spiteri's,' Sully says. 'You'll come to Spiteri's. You'll like it there.'

William looks out across the harbour, where the little boats rock on the little harbour waves. The blue painted eyes stare back at him. Above them stands the quiet temple. He'd rather go – just walk out through the streets. Climb up to the temple, its shadowed cloisters. See the city.

'What d'they do that for?' William nods towards the fishing boats.

'Eh?' Sully squints out along William's sightline.

'Those boats. Why do they paint those eyes on them?'

'Oh,' Sully says. 'That. It's for good luck. Safe return. They think if they paint those eyes on their boats, they can outstare the evil eye.'

Valletta wrong-foots him. He feels queasy, liverish. It's like nowhere else he's been, or rather it's like everywhere: it seems caught between Africa, Arabia, and Europe. It's like stepping into an imagined city, into someone else's dream.

There are five of them, climbing through the city streets. Sully, Paveley, Dwyer and Spooner.

Him. The letter swings in his pocket as he walks, the corner of it pressing into his thigh with each step. It is cool and dim in the city: the buildings are high and the streets are narrow, cutting out the sun. The men pass by ornate carved stonework and under balconies and beneath a crisscross of washing lines slung high above. They jump up onto doorsteps and skip along their length and leap off the other end; they run fingertips along the heavy wooden doors, over the cold metal stare of doorknockers. Everything is grand, but also somehow faintly shabby, like a girl in evening dress with bare and dirty feet. The men talk and laugh and shout, but the houses stand shuttered, silent, and as they make their way deeper into the city the silence begins to prickle into William's skin, and makes him rub at the cropped hair on the back of his neck, and he falls quiet too.

Something lands hard on his shoulder, making him jump, and it's only when he touches it and brings his hand away wet that he realises that it's water fallen from the dripping linen high above.

He watches his step then, moves round the wet patches on the pavement. He becomes mesmerised by the progression of his boots over the flagstones, the way they keep taking him on and on, even though he's not himself certain where he's going, or that he wants to go there. Then, sudden and familiar, birdsong bubbles from a shuttered window. He looks up, looks round for the source of it.

16

'You hear that?' he asks.

'Yes.'

'Is that a nightingale?'

'Think so,' Dwyer says.

'At this time of day?'

'They blind the birds, to make them sing all day.'

Sully tosses this information back over his shoulder as if it's nothing. William rubs again at the back of his neck, trying to rub away a shudder. When he was a boy, back in Kent, there'd been nightingales in the fields behind the house. He'd lie awake at night, crammed in between his sleeping brothers, and listen to the birds sing.

They wheel round into a cross street and three women are coming down the far side. He feels it in himself, sees it instantly in the other men, the way they register the women's presence. Go quieter, watchful. The women come towards them, wrapped in dark Maltese capes, the hoods arched high with ribs of whalebone, shadowing the face, concealing even the shape of the head. Passing the open door of a Roman church, William catches a glimpse of candlelight, hears the mutter of mass, catches the smell of incense smoke. Then the women turn silently and drop into the church, leaving behind a scent in the air, smoky and sharp, with a shade of roses. Their passing makes him acutely aware of himself. Of the hair bristling from his upper lip and the sweat gathering in his armpits. He pushes his hands

17

into his pockets. The coal dust never quite washes from the skin.

They turn a corner in shadow and climb a flight of stone steps. The streets are busier here. Market girls pass, barefoot, carrying baskets of scarlet tomatoes and sheaves of green herbs on their shoulders, heads in determined profile. On the pavement, men in blue workclothes crouch to play dice. They glance up as the seamen pass, but then look back to their game, barely noticing.

'There,' Sully nods.

There's a bar right up at the top of the street. It's painted green; its windows are dark. Spiteri's.

'C'mon,' Sully says.

They march on up towards it. Their footfalls echo back from the quiet buildings. They reach the door. William slows his pace, lets the others filter in ahead.

'Whatcha waiting for, Hastings?'

'I'm not . . .' William says. 'I'm going to . . .' He gestures out along the street, up ahead. See the city. Buy a postcard. Write home to my wife.

Sully jerks his head at the dark doorway. 'They sell postcards in here.'

Of course they don't. And up along the street there is a flight of stone steps, and a carriage clattering along the street above, and an archway that opens onto darkness, and a whole city just aching to be seen. But William can't afford to put Sully's back up. He steps up to the doorway of the bar. Sully grins.

'I'll just have the one.'
'Course, son. Course.'

It's dark; it smells of dungy foreign cigarettes and old wine and spice. William's heart lifts at the strangeness of it. Mr Spiteri waddles over, arms open, pretending to remember Sully, happy to be introduced to the new hands, calling them his boys, ushering them across to a huddle of chairs round a circular table at the back. His apron is long and stained and his belly is as big and round as a horse's. They order the local red wine, which is cheap. Spiteri's delighted with their order, and off on his way to get it, still talking, commending the menu. William finds himself smiling: this is not the Prince's Head, with his dad and his workmates playing dominoes and smoking and watching him through their pipe smoke. No-one knows him here.

There are, as he's already well aware there always are in harbourside bars, whores. They sit at the counter, in satin wraps, their legs showing right up to the calf, the bulge of flesh like a soft unfamiliar fruit. One woman turns and catches William's eye, and he smiles instinctively in reply to her smile. He hadn't meant to look, but he finds himself caught, until she drops her gaze and turns away. She's pretty, in a rough sort of way. Ragged curls, bitten dirty nails. Skin like milky tea.

Not like Amelia.

He drinks. The wine is both harsh and sweet. The first mouthful makes him shudder. Sully proposes Paveley's health; they tip back their little tumblers and empty them down their throats. Paveley is nineteen; he had his birthday while they were at sea. It makes William feel old. He is twenty-four next birthday. He is going to be a father. His job at Price's is waiting for him, when the war is over.

The bar fills quickly, becomes dark with men and noisy. He'll have just one more. Then he'll go and find her a postcard. Something pretty. You can't say very much on the back of one postcard. You can't be expected to.

Sully tilts the bottle towards William's glass. William nods. He watches the liquid tumble in, watches the dark level of it rise.

Mrs Spiteri emerges from the kitchen. She carries a plate of warm pasties, glistening with oil. Mrs Spiteri's face is round as an apple, shiny and damp. She sets the plate down and smiles at the men as they eat, enjoying their enjoyment, and when she catches William's eye she nods to him, asking his approval. He smiles back, nods, *It's good*. And it is – the filling is a kind of pease pudding, spicy, peppery – and she smiles broader, and nods again, more vigorously, saying something in Maltese, and when she nods her body shakes – unsupported breasts, soft belly, no corsets on – and William drags his thoughts away from her soft giving

20

flesh, the clear satisfaction she seems to find in others' pleasure.

The lads are talking, but their conversation is trailing, loose-knit: they are distracted by the women at the bar, who glance round every so often to catch an eye. Then the pretty one turns round in her seat, and recrosses her legs, and her wrap slips away to show a smooth knee and a glimpse of thigh, and Sully's on his feet, heading over to her, drink left unfinished on the table.

William watches. He shouldn't. Sully lays his hand on the whore's hip, on the silky wrap. She doesn't flinch, doesn't stiffen. She just turns to him, then leans in towards him, serious, big eyes looking up at Sully's face. He talks, confident, sure of what he's doing. She gives him a smile, but the smile doesn't reach her eyes. She slips down from the stool and takes his hand; she leads him over to the stairs.

William watches them until they move out of his line of sight. He downs his drink. He thinks he can hear them. Hear their tread cross the landing above, hear their talk, their creaking through the upstairs room. It's not really possible, not with the noise of the bar. He wishes he could be like Sully. Just for a bit. Just for the next half hour or so. Then forget what he had done.

Paveley downs his drink, gets to his feet. He brushes his hands off on the seat of his trousers, grins to the company, and heads over to the women. The one in the mauve wrap turns towards him, and when he stands talking to her she touches his chest, laying her hand flat there and as she talks to him, looking right up into his face, like she knows him. Everywhere they go, the whores can always speak English.

The two of them go upstairs. William pours himself another glass of wine.

There's no talk now. He sits and drinks with Dwyer and Spooner. They're all locked into their own thoughts. The women.

Then Dwyer gets up, his chair scraping back, his cheeks red. He goes over to the bar, just touches the remaining girl on the arm. She looks round at him and smiles. She's not a girl; she must be knocking on forty. The agreement is made briskly. He follows her to the stairs, following her broad backside in its silky wrap.

William downs his drink. There's an ache in his belly. He wants.

Boots thunder down the stairs, and Sully bursts back to the table, stuffing his shirt into his misbuttoned kecks, grinning like a baboon.

'Be so kind,' he says, nodding to his glass, so William fills it, then fills his own glass too, and drinks it down. The wine is inky, sweet and dark, and it is not working, not softening or warming him at all.

The bar has filled up with soldiers now; a few of the Scottish Borderers and the Welsh, and more seamen off the *Goliath*. It's full and dark and noisy.

Dwyer is engaged to be married. Earlier in the

voyage, on shore leave in Simonstown, in that bar near the market, where the women with their glossy skin and their blue-black eyes lingered, a few drinks over the eighth, William had told Dwyer what he'd never told anybody else, what he only said to Dwyer because he'd thought their circumstances were similar, what he'd never dream of telling Amelia; though if he could tell her it might make her understand what the world was like and how he had to live in it now. That he'd made a promise to himself, that whatever else happened when he was away, he wasn't going to go with a whore. He wasn't going to bring home a disease, he'd told Dwyer, head drooping low and heavy over folded arms. Much less leave some poor half-breed bastard to starve in a foreign gutter. And Dwyer had nodded and agreed. William was just right, good man, good for him. And he, Dwyer, he'd do the same, because he had a girl at home who was worth the waiting for. *Skin like cream, skin like the finest Welsh cream,* he'd said, shaking his head, thinking of that skin and of the wedding night to come. But two bottles of rum empty on the table, and Dwyer had gone out the back with one of the black glossy women, and William had drunk on alone, chin on folded arms, tilting the glass to his lips.

Sully empties the remaining wine into his glass, and Spiteri sets down another bottle with a flourish.

Which is the difference, of course – the waiting

23

for, William thinks. When it's still all possibility, when it's all still in the imagination. When you dream of plucking open those little pearl buttons on her blouse, of pulling the ribbon of her camisole bow to make it come undone, of her breath quickening, of pushing up her skirts in creamy folds of cotton to stroke her milk-white thighs and kiss her sweet, clean, legitimate wifely cunt. Before it's real.

He pours another glass, looks back to the bar. Sully's whore is back. She sits on her stool, calm, unruffled, and the barman hands her a glass of something and stirs a spoonful of something into it. They chat easily; old friends. The way the satin slides over her hips, the way it hangs around her peach-soft calves. She lights a cigarette, and her lips are a fleshy mushroomy pink. At the table, Sully drinks contentedly, sucking down the wine between his teeth and leaning back in his chair, sated. He will sleep tonight, slung in the hammock above William. While William lies awake and wanting.

Sully starts to talk about this new campaign in a distant, unbothered way, like it's going to happen to someone else. This is the swift strike that ends the conflict; that Churchill fellow is sharp, you know. It won't take much: they won't be expected there, in the Dardanelles. They'll ship in the Tommies, the Tommies will have a pop at old Asiatic Annie, and Annie will run squealing like the bunch of schoolgirls that they are, and Sully, himself, is going to watch it all from the safety of

Goliath while the guns boom out overhead and pummel anything that's left of the fleeing enemy.

'You sure she's safe?' William asks.

'*Goliath*?' Sully asks. 'She's sweet as a nut.'

'She's getting on a bit.'

'Give over. She's well-seasoned, that's all.'

Nodding, William rolls himself a tickler, his fingers thick with drink. 'Not quite got the turn of speed, though, of the newer ships.'

'Bollocks,' Sully says, swigs his wine. 'Shovel faster.'

William laughs, lights his fag, making the tobacco strands flare and fall into ashes.

'Might head up to that temple in a bit,' he says.

Sully just looks at him. 'Eh?'

'That building up above the harbour. You know. Saw it today.'

'Temple? No. You mean the hospital.'

'Hospital?'

'Military hospital. Left over from the Crimea. That's what all them crates are for. Medical supplies.' He nods towards the cluster of men in their greyish-green uniforms; the pimpled pink faces of the soldier boys. 'For them lot. Just in case Annie gets in a sneaky one.'

A sneaky one? Just in case? William's eyes blink shut. The bar noise just flares hard and loud, the voices, the shouts and calls and laughs and curses and coughs of the men. He thinks, the trade in carnage that must pass through this tiny island, to make them need to build a hospital like that.

25

He opens his eyes, watches Sully drink; expression bland, not a flicker. Sully does this: makes him laugh, makes him like him, then makes him shudder. He's a dog. That's how come he can do what he does and then just forget about it. A dog doesn't think, it just does, it just is; sometimes good and sometimes bad, whatever suits it at the time. A man, a good man, doesn't behave like that.

He loves Amelia. Of course he loves her.

But.

The stream of dark-coated men, trailing through the candleworks' doors, and him in his dark coat walking up to join them, and disappearing into the black and white and grey, into the dark.

Hush, love, please.

His eyes narrow, head heavy, the smoke twines around him. The scent somehow reminds him of the hooded women: they ghost past through his mind's eye; and the market girls, their eyes skimming over him as if he wasn't there. And the men in their blue workclothes, who played at dice; who looked up, and looked away, as if just a breeze had passed over them, a breath of air.

We're just shadows here, he thinks. Shadows. We come and go unnoticed as the gulls.

He lifts his head and watches the whore. The pretty one. The one Sully had. The way she sits, elbow on the counter, cigarette lolling from her hand. She turns, catches someone's eye. Smiles. William glances along her eyeline, to see who she's looking at. It's one of the Scots. A young lad: he stares back at her slack-jawed, hungry; hands in his pockets. There's a rash of spots across his chin. The lad's pasty fingers will be grubbing around in his pockets for money; in a minute he'll be counting out the coins on his palm. William looks back to the woman. There are deep lines down from her nose towards the corners of her lips, and they deepen as she smiles.

He wants her. He can't help wanting her.

But he can leave. Buy a postcard. See the city. Write.

She tilts her head. Runs a finger down one edge of her wrap, where it lies over the curve of her collarbones and dips down between her breasts. He tries to think of Amelia, how he'd imagined her before they were married, when she was the girl that he was waiting for. But he just recalls the red lines pinched into her skin by stays. The way she turns her head away.

There's a grain of guilt; a gritty nub of it. That's all. He stubs out his cigarette.

'Give me a thing, Sul,' he says.

Sully stills his glass, looks up at him. Gives him a slow grin. 'Well I never.'

'Just give me one, eh?'

'Not brought your own?'

William swallows dryly. 'Please.'

Sully raises his eyebrows, reaches into his pocket, draws out a chalky disk of rubber. Skims it across the table to William, who pockets it.

'Wash it out after, eh.'

William nods, drains his glass in one swallow. He feels the scrape of his chair as he pushes away from the table, and as he stands up his head swims. He turns and walks steadily towards her. She notices him. She turns towards him, and smiles. Not at the eyes.

Upstairs it is bright. High windows with dusty white curtains. It seems strange that it is still day. She speaks in English, but her accent is strong and he is blurred with drink.

'What you want?' she asks him.

'You know.' He juts his chin at her, at her body.

'You want the whole business.'

He nods, swallows, takes out a handful of sterling, and she looks it over, scoops it into her dry little hand.

'That's good. We can fuck.'

The word makes him harder, clears his head. He watches her backside as she crosses the room, clatters the money into a tin box on the dresser. Her feet are slim, beautiful, dirty on the bare boards.

She comes back. Moves in close. She smells of Parma Violets and tobacco and other men. She unties her wrap. Underneath she wears a whitish slip. She takes his hand and leads him over to the bed. She sits him down and he sinks into the mattress and lies back and his head spins. She steps astride him, and the bedsprings jangle but she doesn't seem to mind. Underneath the slip she is naked. She lets the straps slide down her shoulders and the slip crumples down and her breasts are small, her nipples dark. His calluses snag against her skin. It is a miracle, a simple perfect miracle, that money can buy him this. He heaves himself up and kisses her breasts. She lets him. He dips his fingers into the wet of her, and she doesn't stiffen. She lets him.

'Thank you,' he says.

She is busy unbuttoning him.

'I've got this,' he says, remembering, rifling in his pocket.

'Okay good.'

She takes the rubber from him, scrolls it down his cock. It's as much as he can do to stop himself spilling in her hands.

The cathedral is long and dim and smoky with incense and candles. He walks down the aisle, holding himself upright, attempting discipline, though his head reels with drink. Black-clothed women kneel at the front, heads covered; he can hear the mutter of their rosaries. He stumbles, grips the back of a pew. The noise is loud in the hollow of the nave. One of the women lifts her head but doesn't turn to look. He shuffles into the pew, sits down.

He ducks his head down, grips his hands together.

God.

Dear God.

He really tries, articulating each word carefully in his mind.

Forgive my sins. Forgive my weaknesses. Forgive me.

His head spins worse with his eyes shut. His mouth is too full of spit. He's going to spew. He swallows, opens his eyes. The air seethes with the dim flickering lights of the candles, and the women's muttering and the smell of incense. Then his eyes shift into focus and he's looking at the pillar just beside him: a stone skull grimaces at him above crossed bones. He tries to look away but his eyes snag on the empty sockets of another carved skull, and then another. A whole column of them, writhing and grinning and staring and rising up and up and up into an arch, high overhead, and his head whirls and reels and he closes his eyes, and he thinks, *Amelia.*

He gets up from his seat, rushes for a side door, wanting openness, air. But he stumbles into a smaller room, empty, ringing out with his footsteps. Up ahead is a painting. Figures pooled in light. A struggle. He finds his balance, swallows down the greyness in him.

Vast, dark, the picture fills a whole wall of this side chapel.

His head swims to a standstill. He looks at the painting.

He stares at the figures; at their positions, drapings, flesh. St John the Baptist, the poor bleeder. His neck is slit wide open. They're going to take his head clean off. Of course they are. They have to.

It's their job. He steps closer, peering. Even through the blur of drink he can almost feel the resistance of the flesh to the knife, the hot blood on the dust, the slackening, trailing limbs. He feels the queasy wait of the maidservant, and the fascinated jeering horror of the other prisoners. He sees the way the blood trickles out from its pool to spell out a name. He peers closer. A capital *F.*, and then what looks like *Michel*. And then the blood just trails away.

This is not a holy picture, William thinks. This is not a holy place. There's too much dirt and dark and blood: this is all too human.

He thinks, there's no God, no guidance, no forgiveness to be found.

From where he sits, in the Barrakka Gardens, he can see the fleet riding low and grey in the Grand Harbour. The shallows are pop-bottle blue, the deep harbour water's blue as medicine bottles where it's shadowed by the ships. In the afternoon heat, boys are swimming naked in the harbour, basking on the rocks.

His head bangs. His mouth tastes of wine and Parma Violets and acid. His fingers still smell of her.

He looks at the picture postcard. A hand-tinted photograph of the Grand Harbour, with inked-in blue sky and yellow stone. The old Crimean hospital in the background. He's already stamped it, addressed it. He just needs to write something now.

He knows she'll like it, though. It's pretty.

He licks the pencil's lead.

Thank you for your letter, which came in today's bag. I am well, thank you, and

Movement makes him glance up. A boy is splayed in the air, like a frog in mid-leap. He crashes into the blue water between the *Beagle* and the *Goliath*. The boy surfaces, shouts something in Maltese at his friends, hauls himself dripping out onto the rock and shakes the water from his hair. As though the ships are barely there. As though the fleet is just a drift of clouds, darkening the water for a time, and then gone.

longing to see you, and the child

I am glad to hear what you say of the offer of work

The pencil leaves grey lines on the clean white. Acid rises up his throat.

I thought you would like this picture. I am sitting now, looking out

I promise you I will work six days a week with the hot wax and moulds and wicks and the stink, and on Sundays take a walk in the park, and watch the Thames roiling past on its way to the sea.

over this particular spot. I think you would

And once a week spend sixpence at the flicks, and maybe sometimes you'll be persuaded to come too, and at night I'll look up at the strip of sky above Knox Street, and you will lie still beside me, your face turned away.

The world will be cold, narrow, will be shades of grey.

find it quite beautiful.

Give all this up.

Yours ever

The wide blue distances, the scents and the cries of gulls and the new land on the horizon, and spindrift on the waves, and the cities peeling back from the blue harbours, full of everything, of possibility, of difference.

William

He tries to swallow it back, but his stomach heaves, and he stuffs the postcard into his pocket, staggers up from the bench, stumbles over to the low Barrakka wall, and vomits. Red wine and mashed pea-pastry and stomach acid wrench out of him, fall through the empty air, down a hundred feet and more, to crash onto the stones below.

He wipes his mouth, wipes his eyes. He turns, and shambles away from the wall, and down the path, and out of the gardens, and back down towards the harbour, and his ship.

The Tows, off Y Beach, Gallipoli, 25 April 1915

The water phosphoresces as it ripples away from the keel. The sky is growing pale. He can see the dark lines of the other tows, the boats strung out behind the trawlers like beads. He can hear the trawlers' muffled chug. He hopes the Turks can't.

He's near the prow; there's only Sully behind him. He can pick out the hunched figures of the other seamen, their oars tossed, waiting in their places; he can see the dark mass of soldiers sitting in the belly of the boat. Earlier, when the dark was perfect, he had felt he was entirely alone, passing in the night from one world to the next. But now it's clear that he's in company.

There's no joking, no ribbing, not even any complaining, the usual army–navy rivalry over-ridden. Everyone is chilled by the night. There is just the occasional creak or shuffle as a soldier eases the discomfort of sitting still for too long.

Then the towlines go slack: the trawler's

stopped. It seems too far out from shore. He twists round to look, but then the order comes to unhitch; he feels the change in the cutter as it's released, like a horse that's slipped its harness; in the grainy half-light he watches as the trawler's coxswain spools the rope into a coil, dragging it through the waves, a flickering snake. Beyond, he can make out dark cliffs, blue sand; and where the waves lick up onto the shore, they glimmer. Still quite a way to go.

They lower oars carefully so as to make no splash. They heave, and glide across water smooth as glass. William moves with the oar. His palms heat with its friction. He drops into the rhythm of it. He can see the soldiers clearly now, though leached of colour. They adjust chin stays, sling their rifles. He thinks, I am lucky, I am immeasurably lucky here.

The cutter lurches, then grinds forward a little way. A shoal, or a reef; something underwater.

An army officer on board gives the order. There is a moment's hesitation – the soldiers just not shifting – and then the first stirrings as they get to their feet. The boat is beached and so barely rocks. William feels the warmth and breath of the men as they crowd past him. The boat lists as the first chap clambers over the gunwale, and drops into the water. There's a splash, and then the catch of the breath as he hits the cold. It's deep. And then another goes, and then another, each time the same caught breath: each body's identical response to shock. He can feel the way the cutter lightens, and sits more cockily on the water. They should have no trouble shifting her once they've unloaded.

William twists in his seat to get a good look at where the boys are going. It's like an image on a bioscope screen, all shades of dawn grey. He gazes at the slope of sandy beach, the gully with its low rocky cliffs. The other boats are dotted out at a distance from the shore: they've all hit the same line of reefs. And from them columns of men push on through the water, towards the beach, and as William watches the first of the soldiers is into the shallows, dashing up through the spray, and onto the sand.

It's so quiet. An offshore breeze brings the scent of dust, and wild sage, and pine. They shove off from the reef, and begin to bring the cutter about to head back to the trawler, and as they're turning, parallel to the shore, the sun clears the horizon and everything is suddenly brilliant and the drips from the oars are diamonds. Just the space, the joy of it – the milky white light and the new warmth and there, just yards away, the land: pale gold, hazed with scrub, plumed with dark green cypress – and if it wasn't for the war, if it wasn't for the dark trickle of soldiers onto the beach and up towards the gully, like trails of ants – if he could do what he wanted, William would leap in himself and wade to shore and climb up that gully and walk out into the empty spaces, towards the desert cities, in the wide space and the rising heat.

And then the air rips itself apart. A shot crunches itself in a flower of splinters just by William's arm. Then another bullet hisses past his shoulder, hits the water like a hot horseshoe.

'Sniper!'

'Fuck!'

'Get moving!'

There is a horrible slowness and fluster as they complete the turn. The bullets arrive almost silently, sometimes a soft huff, sometimes a buzz like an insect. The cutter turned, they heave through the water. William's teeth throb. His head throbs. His eyes throb. He drags then lifts and pushes on his oar. He doesn't think. He doesn't consider Amelia. Or the baby. Or anyone else, or what will happen afterwards. He is just his body and it's determined to live.

He sees Dwyer jerk back, slump onto Silcock's oar and Silcock shove at him to get him off. The bullets whine, hiss. They crump into wood, sear flesh. There's a yell from right behind him – Sully's hit – but he can't turn round to look. Loosed oars skip over the water, clatter against the live ones. William, swinging through his stroke, sees the scrub on top of the gully in the pink-gold glow of dawn: sniper, up there, in the bushes. Sully's cursing behind him, low, short of breath: *Fucking bastard Annie, fucking evil bastard Turks.* Someone else is screaming.

But the gunfire's stopped. William doesn't know how long for. But no more insect whine, no more searing bullets. The screaming, though, continues.

They slacken off the pace, but still row on, making distance, uncertain of their safety. The blood pounds through his head. No more bullets. Still there are no more bullets. William scans round for the trawler, they should head back, get help, get orders; then he coughs, and is taken over by coughing, wracked with it. Sweat drips off him. But he is sound, still; unbroken. He spits over the side. He wipes his face with a hand, looks round, taking stock.

Dwyer is slumped forward over his oar. The blade's forced dripping up high into the air like a signal. His cap has fallen into the boat and his right arm is dangling as if he's reaching down for it. There's a dark red hole in the side of his head, and there's dark blood dripping onto the boards. *Skin like cream*, he'd said, *skin like the finest Welsh cream*. Spooner's pale, with a bloody right hand pressed to his left arm. It's a lad called Clelland that's screaming. Writhing on the boards at the stern. Two men crouching at his side, holding his arms; morphine ampoule, syringe. William turns round, feels sick. Checks on Sully.

Sully's face is a twist of fury, his hand clamped to the side of his head. There's blood running between his fingers, blood down the side of his face and neck, soaking into his rig.

'You all right?'

Sully just narrows his eyes.

'Let's have a look.'

Sully hesitates a moment, then he lifts his hand away. There's just a raw weeping stump, blood.

'Blimey.'

'Bastard fucking bastard Annie.'

Clelland stops screaming. The morphine taking effect. They're shifting Dwyer now, taking him by the armpits, making the boat rock. Someone is leaning over Spooner, examining his wounded arm. William turns back, nods towards Sully's ruined ear.

'Dress that for you?'

Sully shakes his head – then winces, stops. 'No. Fuck off.'

Sully reaches his unbloodied hand into a pocket. He takes out his cigarette case, clicks it open one-handed, but then can't pick a fag out, not without getting the papers bloody.

William reaches out for the case. 'Give it here.'

Sully hands it over with a grimace. William picks out one of the smokes and holds it up. Sully dips his head down, takes it between his lips. He juts his chin towards the case, offering William one. There's gunfire from inland, and the sound of waves chopping against the hull.

William takes a cigarette, and lights both, shielding the match with a hand. The cigarettes flare quickly and crumble away: Sully always rolls them too loose. William drags the smoke deep into his lungs. They feel raw as butcher's meat.

'Could have been worse,' William says.

'Fuck off.'

'An inch to the right and it would have killed you straight.'

Sully lets out a thread of smoke. 'Six inches to the right and it would have hit *you* smack between the eyes.'

William turns away. He watches the ratings struggle with Dwyer's body. He feels sick. They're just boys, the two of them, all raw bones and sunburn. He should help them.

'Blame the sniper, eh. Not me.'

Sully is silent.

William gets up. His head spins, but he steps out of his bench and makes his way over to help with Dwyer, nudging the ratings aside, taking him under the arms. Dwyer is solid, weighty with death. His jerkin is soaked with sweat and blood. His head rolls back. Pale blue eyes stare up at the pale blue morning sky.

He has dealt with the dead before. But never a friend.

William lays him down on the boards. The boy has the ghost of the boiler room about him, the film of grey around the fingertips, around the nostrils and mouth. His head lolls over to one side. He lies where the soldiers had been sitting. It seems like days ago. Another world.

That poor girl back in Cardiff. His poor mother.

Some kind of shabby order is restored. Wounds

are dressed, rum dished out. William returns to his place, sliding in so his back is to Sully again, and his face towards the shore. He takes up the oar. His hands hurt. He looks out at the beach, the rocky gully, the scrubby clifftop where the sniper must be hiding; all is now sharp and clear in the cool morning light. Then he spots movement. A clutch of men scrambling and jostling through the bushes. Then the knot untangles, and sunlight kicks off a bayonet, and one man is being held, and fighting against it, struggling, desperate: the sniper, they've got the sniper. There's no sound, no scream to be heard, not from this distance. William doesn't see the blade go in, but he does see the man jerk back, and then crumple forwards as the steel sinks deep and twists up and through his guts. The man goes slack. His captors let him fall. They stand around him, looking down. Then bayonets flash again in the morning light as they dig them down into him.

That is good, William thinks. It must be good. But he feels sicker now.

The men lean down and lift the body. It hangs limp from their grip. They carry it to the edge of the cliff, and swing it out over the edge. For a moment it seems to sail out into the air, but then gravity catches it and it falls; the body glances on an outcrop, rolls and slides and falls again, then catches on a patch of scree and slithers down it, streaking blood on the golden stone, losing momentum, coming to a halt and lying still, at an angle, feet higher than the head, the waves lapping at the rocks a few feet below.

Behind him, he hears Sully's dry lips tack apart, but he doesn't speak.

William says nothing. After a moment, he nods.

This is the end, he thinks: this is the end of everything. He closes his eyes and the colours swim and flare. How can there be anything after this?

But the day goes on. It heaves itself forward in lurches.

They crawl their way back to the trawler, returning with the wounded and the dead. The guns pound out from the battleships; the *Goliath* is hammering the Turks' inland positions. Shells scream overhead making the men in the cutter flinch and duck. Killed by the percussion, dead fish rise to the surface, form a slick upon the water. They make the work heavy. Flies buzz and settle on the fish, and on the dead and wounded men, and the spilled blood in the boat.

When they reach the trawler, they hoist up Clelland, who's barely clinging onto life, and Spooner pale with loss of blood, and then Dwyer slack and heavy and unmanageable, his body shunted onto the higher deck from their shoulders. The cutter rocks beneath them as they work. Then Sully elbows his way in, blood streaking all his left-hand side, and two able seamen lean down to grab his arms and help him up on board, and as he's scrambling his way up William hears his voice:

'Where's the fucking rum?'

The gaps in the crew are filled with what remains of another shattered crew. They are given rum, and coffee, and biscuits. They are given new orders. To head back for the shore, to retrieve the wounded, to begin the evacuation.

The dead have been laid in a tideline across the beach.

From inland come the whizz and thump of artillery, and the whistle of shrapnel. The barrage is constant and huge and it makes the air shudder.

The boat approaches the jetty: a snaking raft of lashed-together pontoons, thick with wounded soldiers. They look like one great long straggling creature: a green-grey, bloodied, sullen thing, unsteady on its feet, hunched under the noise of battle. As William's cutter comes alongside and moors up, the creature gathers itself together, presses forwards. Then men spill out from its flank, like maggots bursting from a skin.

Bloodied bandages, a sling, a man limping along with his arm around a fellow's neck, another carried on a stretcher. They step down into the boat, settle in whatever space they find. A sergeant with half his head covered in field dressings picks his way between the bodies and takes his seat near the prow. William finds himself searching faces, wondering if he landed any of these men earlier. But all he has to go on are the pale ovals in the morning dark, the sound of their breathing. There's no way of knowing.

Stretcher-bearers set a lad down just near him. The boy lies there, his blue eyes open, his head bandaged. The dressings are dark and wet with blood. There's a pimple on his chin. It's this, an angry Vesuvius of a pimple, which makes William's chest tighten so that he can hardly breathe. It could be the lad from Spiteri's, who fancied that whore, that woman, and the memory is vague with drink and sharp in moments and makes him flinch inwardly. That postcard, written, addressed, stamped, unsent. It's in his sea-chest, slipped into the gap between his folded clothes and its battered tin flank. There was the garden, he remembers, and before that, the cathedral. His thoughts loop back to the picture: the soldiers, the prisoners, the executioner, the blood in the dust, the woman standing, waiting, to carry the severed head away.

The boy's head rolls a little as the boat sways. William wants to say something, to offer some comfort, but can't think of anything.

They pull away, low and heavy in the water. The boy blinks every so often; he looks puzzled. He doesn't make a sound. He doesn't look like he's in much pain: he just frowns up at the bright

Mediterranean sky, as if he can't quite remember something. William's mouth is dry, and he's short of breath.

'Where you from?' William asks, but either the boy doesn't hear him, or he can't. William remembers, from the action at Ostend, that the shelling can blow out their eardrums. All they can hear is a muffled roar, the sound of their own blood.

The boat heaves out into the clear water, heading back towards the grey shapes of the battleships. The sounds of gunfire fade over the distance. Close to, there's the creak of the oars, the grunt of tired rowing, and the moans and whimpers and the hard breathing of the wounded.

Then somebody laughs.

William blinks up, looks round. Just catches other men looking round too, or men so deep in their own pain that they can't register anything else. Then William spots him. A private, sitting near the stern, facing towards William. He's shaking with laughter. His cap is hanging low over his eyes, his mouth is open, and his face in a spasm; the laughter is shaking him like a fever. His arm is wadded with field dressings, but he's really laughing. William can't make sense of it. Has he completely lost his marbles? And then he realises: it's a Blighty wound. The lad knows he's taken a lucky shot – been hit badly enough, but not too badly – and that he'll be heading back. Shipped off to Malta, to the hospital like a temple on the golden cliffs. To be given tea and bread and milk and oranges. To take the air on the clifftops, to sit in the cool whitewashed rooms, the sunlight through tall windows.

One of the army officers snaps a command – *Act the white man, son* – and the laughter stops, but the quiet that follows is almost as bad.

Down by William's feet, the boy's look has gone somehow blank. A long moment passes, but he does blink, slowly. William's skin goes cold and numb, his face feels like a mask of wood. It's like he could take his razor and cut deep into his cheeks and not feel a thing, not care a bit.

They heave on through the water, all of the seamen moving in practised perfect unconscious rhythm, crawling back out towards the big ships, *Goliath* and her cruisers, some of the soldiers moaning, some quietly conferring, others sitting blank with shock, and others lying still and slowly slipping into darkness. William tries to just be his body; he tries not to think. He tries to live in just the movement of muscle and the effort and the rough surge and squeeze of air as he sucks in and heaves out breath, and not be in his head at all. He doesn't notice the wounded boy's last blink. When he looks back down again, the eyes have somehow silvered over.

He mutters the old words, out of instinct.
Our Father
Who art in heaven
But the words are faint and dry and carry no freight of love; they bring no comfort. They are

alone, William thinks: they are insects crawling across the water's skin. There is no afterwards. There's just this.

When they reach *Goliath*'s hulking keel, he wipes his wooden cheeks, and they are wet.

HMS Goliath, *off Cape Helles, 3 May 1915*

William lies in his hammock, his chest bare. He didn't sleep last night; he can't sleep today. They've sustained some damage, *Goliath* was hit by Turkish guns yesterday, and now it seems too risky to sleep. You don't want to close your eyes in case you never open them again.

He watches the bulge of Sully's hammock writhe above him. Can't get comfortable because of that ear. Sully's on light duties for the time being, spared the heavy work of stoking; it's left him itchy with unspent energy. From here and there around the mess comes the sound of low voices. Card games, conversations. The men are exhausted.

William reaches round underneath his hammock, and into his sea-chest. He fumbles for his cigarettes. His fingertips catch instead on the corner of the unsent postcard. He pushes it further down inside the chest. But when he drags his cigarettes out, her letter comes too. He lifts it, turns the envelope round in his hands. Doesn't need to open it or read it.

when the war is over, and we have you home with us again.

Even if he could somehow travel over all that space – sail all the way back out of the Med, along the coast of Spain, cross the Bay of Biscay and round into the Channel, plough up the Thames, moor up at Plantation Wharf, dodge down the alleyways between warehouses and walk the broad sweep of York Road, and off into the cobbled damp, and through the rows of narrow houses to Knox Road – he still wouldn't have come home. It will never end, he knows: not while any of them are left alive. It will cling to them, like coal dust works its way into the clothes and hair and skin. *When the war is over* no longer seems to mean anything at all.

Perhaps, he thinks, the child is born by now.

He runs his fingertips over the tidy folds of the letter. He tries to think of the baby. Of what he will be like. But all he can bring to his imagination is one of those photographs of children who can't sit still. Featureless, unfocused; a pale blur above a tiny sailor suit. He can't make it come clear.

Sully swings his head down over the side of the hammock. Winces as the blood floods into his wounded ear. He clocks the letter. William fumbles it guiltily into his pocket.

'Smoke?' Sully asks.

William nods.

They sling on their rig, filch two cups of tea and find a nice spot behind a bulkhead where they can lurk unnoticed and unbothered for a while, protected from the breeze. They sit back, leaning against the warm grey steel. It's sunny, and there is salt on the air, and a dusty, scrubby smell blows from the land, and there is the distant thump of artillery. Sully's thin tongue flicks out and licks his lips, and William realises what Sully reminds him of. A lizard. Resting on a wall in Simonstown, the flicker of its tongue between dry lips, the only thing moving in the midday heat.

Sully lets smoke drift from his lips and breathes it up into his nostril.

William rests his palm on the deck. Below him, the ship hangs hollow in the deep water. He thinks of Amelia, waiting, back in Battersea, for a postcard to drop through the letterbox. The one he hasn't sent, can't send. It's still stashed in his sea-chest. Her letter, in his pocket, presses its edges into his skin.

'You've been at sea a while, haven't you?' William asks.

'Ten years,' Sully says.

'And you've seen the world?'

'Pretty much.'

William nods. The steam scrolls off his tea: the air is cool despite the sun. They both stare out across the water, to the shore.

'Could you give it up?'

'Give what up?'

'After all this, after seeing what there is out there, could you settle down? Go home and just be there?'

'I don't know.' Sully bites at his lower lip. 'No-one's ever asked me to.'

A moment passes. William studies the glowing tip of his cigarette.

'She's beautiful,' William says. 'My wife is.'

'Good for you.'

'No, she is, really she is.'

'Bloody hell, Hastings. Leave off, will you? We can't all have your luck.'

Sully's cigarette is pinched between his lips; his jaw is set, his eyes are just dark lines in the sun. William wonders, for the first time, what it must be like to be him.

'She's having a baby.'

'Congratulations.'

William nods. For a moment he just teeters on the brink of saying it, and then with a kind of horrified relief, he says, 'I can't go back.'

'What?'

'Not after this.'

'This?'

'This.' William flicks his hand out to include the water, the coastline, the distance, the sun.

'This.' Sully tucks his chin in, raises his eyebrows. 'This fucking wasteland, this bit of camel-shitty desert?'

'There's so much more to see. It's beautiful.'

51

'All them postcards and then, what? Nothing?'
William bites at his lip.

'You'll stay on then, in the navy? If you make it
through the war?'

'I don't know. It doesn't matter. Just I can't go
back.'

'Well, if she's beautiful like you say she won't
be alone for long.' Sully takes a last long pull on
his cigarette, and the smoke puffs past William's
face. 'Someone else'll have her.'

Sully flicks the cigarette butt out through the
railings. They both watch its trajectory, watch it
drop out of sight.

'Don't you ever think about jumping ship?'
William says.

'Jesus.'

The bell chimes. They lift their heads like a pair
of whistled dogs.

'We take another shot like yesterday,' William
says, 'if Annie gets lucky, chances are we're going
to die here.'

Sully heaves himself to his feet. He shakes his
mug out over the water, flicking out the last drops
of tea.

'You'd be fucked, though, mate, if you did jump
ship. It's war, that'd be desertion.'

The bell chimes again. William takes a couple
of quick, final drags on his cigarette.

'And anyway, where'd you go?'

'Anywhere.'

'But it's all war, everywhere.'

William flicks his cigarette out after Sully's, over-board.

'We'd better shift,' Sully says. 'Unless you're planning to—' He swoops his hand through the air with a diving gesture, after the cigarette.

'No.'

'Coming?'

'Be down shortly.'

Sully turns and goes, heading round the bulkhead, out of sight. William gets to his feet and leans over the railing. He shouldn't have spoken. He shouldn't even have said it out loud to anyone, let alone Sully, because it's made it real. At least Sully is not the kind of fellow to hold a thing like that against you. He looks out across the sea, to the yellow-grey line of land, the sky spreading above, deep and blue and cloudless. He twines the letter between his fingers. Then he looks down and down the grey hull of the ship, to the deep shadowed water below.

He lets the letter fall.

It twirls down towards the water and slips onto the surface. It drifts a moment, and then begins to sink.

He pushes back from the railing.

It is not good, he knows. It is not good. But if he is to live through this, if there is going to be an afterwards, then he really has to live.

HMS Goliath, *Morto Bay, 12–13 May 1915*

T he gun fires. The ship heaves with the recoil. As he pulls himself up the steps, the air smells strange, but it's only when he's on deck and a searchlight's beam swings overhead that he is really puzzled. A kind of white glow. No moon, no stars. The light skims round again, searching out the Turkish trenches ashore, but its beam is clouded, dense.

Fog.

Fog, in the Mediterranean, in May. He stands for a moment, looking up and out through the night as the searchlights wheel and turn, blank, cutting across the dark tracery of the rigging, skimming the superstructure. The searchlight is from the *Cornwallis*, stationed on the seaward side of the *Goliath*. Visibility is two hundred yards, maybe three. Another of the *Goliath*'s guns pounds out a shell. The ship heaves beneath his feet. His ears buzz. His skin fizzes with unease.

They have to be here. The straits – the Dardanelles

– must be kept clear. The supply lines must stay open for men and materiel. For the boys from England and Australia and New Zealand and France. The boys who troop out along the pontoons, across the beach and up into the hills, and are gone. What they carry back from the beaches are not boys. What they carry back are rinds and husks. They have become grocers of men. They deliver them ashore full and whole, then come back for the empties.

He goes over to the seaward side. The air is clammy, thick with smuts and smoke. He leans out over the rail. He can make out the flank of the *Cornwallis*, and if he peers along into the dark, a glimpse of a destroyer, one of *Goliath*'s bodyguards – either *Beagle* or *Bulldog* – as the searchlight brushes across her. But he can't see a thing beyond.

His breath makes the fog tumble away in little eddies. This is just perfect cover for an attack. They have been hammering all hell out of the place for weeks; the Turks'll be just itching for a chance to give them a taste of it right back. And the ship is lit up like a West End show. You'd have to be an idiot not to give it a go. And whatever else you say about Annie and Fritz, they're not idiots.

'We're sitting ducks,' he says out loud, into the deadening fog.

The engines turn over. The power of them throbs up through the deck. One revolution, two, then stopped: they're in readiness to go, at immediate notice for steam.

So maybe they'll be off. He's got to swallow the fear. Get through it. Once they're under way, they won't be such an easy target.

But the fear comes anyway, getting him in the back of his neck, in the back of his knees. The unease of this aged ship, her fated name. She is too old, dragged out of retirement for this last fight. Her joints ache; a little pressure and the rivets would just come adrift, her panels peel apart in segments. There's just light Krupp armour between them and the dark water. Six hundred and some men. All those lungs sucking and squeezing the tired air. He becomes aware of the rail beneath his hand, the old weather-greyed wood. He digs his nails in, and the wood gives. She's just too old, *Goliath*. An old giant, just waiting for the boy to fling a stone.

The engines turn over again. But the ship lies still. It's too much: he can't wait, can't do nothing. He pushes away from the railing, turns back towards the deck – if he can speak to someone – then the officer of the watch comes down from the boat deck through the dirty fog.

'Get below, there.'

'Are we under notice, sir?' William calls.

The officer halts, and looks back. 'What's that?'

'Will we be shifting soon?'

'We're staying put.'

'Sir, we're sitting ducks.'

56

'Those are the orders.'

'But does Command know about the fog?'

The officer just gives him a look. 'Those are the orders.'

Then William's eye is caught by a movement: down by his side, the officer's hand is twitching. His thumbnail presses into the cuticle of his index finger. It scrapes at the skin. The flesh is raw and oozes blood.

There is nothing to be done, William realises. There is no getting out of this.

But he can't die here, not yet. He wants more. He wants spindrift off the Atlantic swell; he wants to know what ice is like when it stretches for thousands of miles. He wants to step off the ship and be in South America, Japan, Russia, Nova Scotia. He wants a lifetime of this.

'On your way now, Hastings. Get below.' And the officer walks off into the fog. And William has no choice. He heads back down below.

Down in the mess, Sully's hammock is swinging slightly, though the others all hang still. His eyes are closed and he's breathing heavily. William looks at him with a mixture of guilt and sympathy: maybe he's asleep at last, maybe he's just braced against the pain. He doesn't think of disturbing him, warning him: what good would there be in that? And sleep is so hard to come by nowadays, you don't want to waste a drop.

William strips off his jerkin, getting ready for his

stint in the boiler room's swelter. He ducks down to stow it in his sea-chest. But something's wrong. He peers closer at the lock. It's broken.

'What the hell—' William heaves the lid up and back. The sudden noise makes Sully stir.

'Sorry,' William says.

'What's up?'

'Someone's been at this . . .'

Sully leans up on an elbow, peering sleepily down over the edge of his hammock. 'Oh balls.'

William leafs through the contents: spare rig, underwear, shaving gear, cigarette box, matches, playing cards. The postcard's not there. The last, unsent postcard. He peers into the chest; it's too dark to see properly. He shoves a hand down between the folded clothes and the side, and runs it up and down. The bell starts to chime. He feels hot. He glances round the crowded, fuggy room. No-one's even stirring.

'What happened? Who was it?'

Sully shrugs. 'I was asleep.'

The bell chimes. William straightens up. 'Really?'

'Yeah.' He rubs at his eyes. 'I was sleeping like the dead. What did they get?'

'Not much.' William's jaw tightens. 'Nothing.' Just that last postcard, with his wife's address.

'I'll sort it for you, if you want. Fix the lock.'

The bell chimes. Six bells.

William looks him over. The wiry muscle of him, the thin flicker of his eyes. We can't all have your luck, he'd said. Would he take the card?

'Thanks.'

'It's not like I'm good for much else at the moment.'

'I suppose not.'

'You go on,' Sully says. 'If it can be fixed, I'll fix it.'

Eight bells.

William has to go. There's no choice. 'Right,' he says. 'Thanks.'

He has to descend into the belly of the ship, to where the boilers gape and the air is thick with heat and the dark water swells just inches away. The shovel will be damp from the last man's hands. The coal dust hanging in the air, sticking to sweating skin, working into the pores, blackening the nostrils and making that catch in his breath that makes him see the dust glittering like crystals in the hollows of his lungs. Just keeping the boilers fed, keeping the engines turning over. He'll swallow water from a shared tin cup, and if he's lucky, if they're all lucky, he'll do his shift and lean his shovel up with the others, and climb back up towards the mess, and wash, and eat, and sleep again, and then wake to do it all again, the day after, and the day after that. And that is the best that he can hope for, and now it seems impossibly wonderful: that time will still keep ticking by for him, and will not stop.

He wishes that she had got the postcard. That he'd promised her everything she wanted. That he had lied.

★   ★   ★

When the first torpedo hits, a few minutes shy of 1 a.m., William is stripped to the waist, sweat darkening the waistband of his trousers and forming a V shape down his backside, hair pushed back in a dark, sweat-soaked slick. Coal leaps from the blade of his shovel; flames flicker up to devour them. His back and shoulders are knotted with muscle. His arms are like twisted rope. He is all body, all movement, lost in the mechanism of his work.

The impact of the first torpedo makes him stagger. The explosion bursts his eardrums. He hears just the rush of his blood.

He rights himself, looks to the next man, Paveley, red-lit from the boilers' glow; his mouth is moving, he's shouting something. William can't hear.

When the second torpedo hits six seconds later, he doesn't hear it either, he just feels the thump of impact, the shudder through the body of the ship. The deck beneath him bucks, and it's too late now to think about anything because the ship is tilting, and William's slithering, trying to get purchase; he yells, *Head for the stairs*, but can't hear himself either, and the heaped coal is slithering too, rolling out underneath his feet and the ship tilts further, and then there's nothing but the horror of burning coals pouring from the boilers' open mouths, falling around him like a punishment from God; his hair burnt through to his head, the scalp seared, his hand burning as he scrabbles the coal away; his shoulder burnt and as he whisks round to brush the burning embers off, his cheek kissed by a glowing orange coal and there's water round his feet, coals hissing as they land, and Paveley is there, he didn't make it to the stairs, and they are thrashing and scrabbling through the fire and the water with the others, trying to get to the stairs, and the water's round his knees, up to his waist, his chest. A third impact. A crunch and then a massive jolt as the torpedo finds the ammunition store and explodes. Water up to his shoulders, and now he's struggling to keep his face above the water, and the hissing falling coals and the smoke and steam, and the water rises to his mouth, his nose, and it's bubbling, sooty and harsh, in his nostrils, and he can't keep his head above the water.

Knox Road, Battersea, 14 May 1915

The old man opens the door. She hadn't even reached the handle. He must have been looking out for her. She doesn't need him to say anything. His face, and his presence there, a strong, squat shape in the door when he should be at the factory, say everything. He brings with him the smell of that place, the hot waxy reek.

She drops her basket. It spills onto the flags. Lengths of lemon and mauve ribbon ripple along the pavement. A cotton reel bumps down into the gutter.

He holds out a stained hand to her. He takes her by the elbow and helps her into the dark parlour. He sits her down in the best chair.

'I'll get the—'

He leaves the front door open and gathers up the spilt things, rolling up the sprawling ribbon, chasing down the cotton, placing them thick-fingered back into their paper wrappings. He brings in her basket, sets it down on her lap, in front of the hard bulge of her belly. She takes the basket handle in her hands.

'I'm sorry, love,' he says.

She nods. Thumbs at the weave of the basket handle. She looks up at him, at the pitted skin.

'Is it certain? Is it absolutely certain?'

He nods.

Her mouth is dry, and the words come out dry as husks: 'All hands?'

'Five hundred lives lost.'

'So there are survivors?'

'They've fished out a couple of hundred, that's what they're saying.'

'Then it's not certain – he could be—'

He takes her hand, squeezes it. 'He was on duty.'

She knows what this means. That he was below, trapped in the boiler room. In the heat and dark and water.

'I'll make you tea.'

She sits in the good chair in the cold parlour, holding onto the basket balanced on her knees. He goes into the kitchen. She listens to him clattering clumsily with the range, stoking up the fire. And then quiet, as he stops, as he muffles his sobs.

She rests her forehead on the arch of the basket's handle, looks down at the clumsily rolled ribbon, the cotton reel with its thread wound untidily on. The tiny things, tinged grey from the street and the old man's handling.

It is her fault.

She should never have asked Mr Travis about the job, never have spoken or thought or planned for afterwards. She jinxed him: she has jinxed them all.

She picks out the thin yellow ribbon, scallop-edged, and unrolls it carefully, then twists the end round her fingertips, and begins to roll again. Then she does the same for the mauve. The basket tidied, she sets it on the floor. Then she lifts her picture book off the green baize of the card table. She turns the pages, touches the glazed surfaces of the postcards. These past months the cards have fallen through the letterbox like waymarkers, like pebbles dropped in the woods, marking off distance and time. A confirmation of his continuation in the world. A reminder of his love.

The track stops here. The final pages are empty. There is no way forward.

She has no photograph of him. This comes with a flash of sudden utter panic. It is too late now ever to have a photograph.

What if she forgets what he looks like?

Hand shaking, she turns back through the pages: blue-washed sky and mountains and women in native dress, a foreign street with camels clopping down it, a rowing boat drifting in a blue grotto. Trying somehow to put him together in her mind. She remembers the flash of his green eyes in the bioscope, the touch of his hands on her waist. The brush of his arm against hers as he leant across and opened the empty book, showed her the blank pages they would fill between them.

She could have had anyone, her mother always said. So why on God's good earth did it have to be *him*?

Because he was everything. He was necessary. He always will be.

She won't forget. She won't let herself, ever. She insists on remembering.

Knox Road, Battersea, 27 May 1915

She leans down in her chair to button her boot, and there is a sudden hot trickle of liquid between her legs. Oh Lord. She stands up and twists round to look at the seat of her blue shift-dress, and there is a dark wet blot there. Oh goodness. She flushes. Is this something that happens? Do women in her condition just wet themselves sometimes? She doesn't know, but it always seems that other women manage the whole thing so much better than she does.

At least she is alone. At least there is no-one to see.

Flustered, she steps back out of her boots, and goes to climb the stairs. Her thighs chafe in the wet. She tries to hold it back, but can't: the water oozes out of her in a steady seep.

She doesn't know what's happening. Has she damaged herself somehow? Has she harmed the baby?

She is halfway up the stairs when the first contraction hits, making her gasp, stop, and grab the banister; and with it a burst of wet that runs down the inside of her thighs.

Shaken, she climbs on up, and in the bedroom pulls off her dress, and her shift, which is wet through at the back. The smell is not ammonia, but warm and brackish. Not urine. Hands shaking, she pulls aside underwear to find the long-unused rags at the bottom of her drawer. Sort herself out, then she'll go next door, and speak to Mrs Clack, and try and bring herself to ask her if this is normal, if this is what is supposed to happen – and what she is supposed to do about it.

As she stands at the dresser lifting out her clothes, the child shifts itself around inside her. She feels the sudden urge to make water, and tugs the pot out from under the bed, and squats, naked, to urinate. The other water still seeps out of her too. She watches as the taut skin of her belly shifts, a small angular bulge pressing out, riding along inside the skin, and then softening away.

And then another contraction hits. It knocks the breath out of her. Makes her grab the edge of the bed and hold there, squatted on the pot, looking down, so that she can see the way her belly squeezes tighter with the pain, and the way the steam from the urine rises from the pot, and then a sudden gush of liquid from her.

The peak of pain is gone, but it leaves a dull ache behind, like a monthly pain, like a warning.

She drags herself up, clinging to the side of the

bed. It hurts more. She can't quite stand upright. She crawls into her dress, wads her drawers with rags. With her foot she pushes the pot under the bed. She makes her slow way down the stairs.

The pain comes again in the street. She crumples in on herself, a hand on the gritty downpipe of the guttering. It takes her a couple of minutes just standing there, breathing, assuring herself that it is safe to move, and that she won't just fall into a heap, before she can take the three more steps to the Clacks' front door.

Mrs Clack answers with little Francie on her hip.

Amelia can feel how strange she must look – hunched, sweating, shivering, her walk a painful waddle.

'I think something's wrong,' Amelia says. 'I don't feel quite well.'

Mrs Clack just looks at her. 'You're all right, ducky,' she says. 'You're going to have the baby.'

Then Mrs Clack reaches out for Amelia's hand, and helps her up into the house.

Mrs Clack has four children of her own. She explains what's happening carefully, not wanting to scare the girl. Still, Amelia blanches and shivers.

'I would have told you sooner,' Mrs Clack says. 'Only, I thought your ma would've said something.'

Amelia nods. When she'd first got her monthlies, her mother had told her she must have injured herself playing out with her friends. So she wasn't allowed to play out any more. It's not the kind of thing she could speak about to her mother, even when her mother was still speaking to her.

'Don't worry,' Mrs Clack says. 'It's just like shelling peas.'

They drink tea, and then more tea. Amelia makes her painful waddling way to the lavatory at the end of the yard. When she sits there, nothing will come but the slow seep of water – the water, Mrs Clack said, that the baby has been sleeping in all this time. She looks down at the tight aching drum of her belly. It must be like a frog, cold and slippery, to have lived in water all this time: she hadn't known. She thinks of what Mrs Clack said, about it being just like shelling peas. The baby is the pea, and she is the pod, and the pod gets split in half and thrown on the midden. The pea is what it's all about: you don't care what happens to the pod.

When the Clack boys get home Amelia goes back to her own house, which will be empty till the old man gets back from work. She doesn't want to see anyone. Her unsettled, leaking, waddling state seems shameful. She climbs up to her room, and tries to lie down, but the pains make her heave herself back up from her bed, and lean over it, clenched, gasping.

At six, the old man taps softly at the door. Mrs Clack must have waylaid him in the street, because he already knows.

'Do you need anything?' he asks.

69

'No.'

'Shall I go for Mrs Bradley?'

'I don't know.'

Mrs Clack comes by at nine, after the children are in bed. By this time, the pains have subsided, and the midwife is not fetched, and Amelia sleeps.

She presses her forehead down onto the top rail of the bedstead. The iron is cool and hard. Mrs Bradley tells her to breathe. Mrs Clack rubs her back and says keep breathing through it, honey, keep breathing. Amelia wants to punch her. All she can do is clamp down with the pain, squeeze her eyes shut, feel and think about only the pain. The pain is everything. While it happens, there is nothing else. When it fades, she flings herself up and away from the bed, and crosses to the wall. Four steps between the bedstead and the wall. She is in just her shift. She is sweating. The fire is lit. She comes to the wall and stops. Four steps between the bedstead and the wall. Four steps between the pains.

She has no idea of time.

She rests her forearm on the wallpaper, rests her head on her arm. Closes her eyes. The pain builds. She braces herself, stiffening. Behind her Mrs Clack and Mrs Bradley talk, too quiet for her to hear. Mrs Bradley costs money. The pain screams, roars, and then it softens, aches and fades. She pushes away from the wall. Four steps back to the bedstead.

'What is it?' Amelia demands. 'What are you saying?'

Their faces turn to her. But then the next pain hits, and she grabs the bedstead with both hands, and cries out. When she opens her eyes again, there is blood on the floor.

'Sorry,' she says to the doctor. The doctor costs more money. His shining things are laid out on a cloth on the bedside table.

He shakes his head, dismisses this with a tut. Mrs Clack has gone. Mrs Bradley stands ready, arms and hands bare and scrubbed. The doctor wets a wad of lint with chloroform.

She wants to ask him, Am I worse at this than other women? Do I make more fuss, have I made more mess than everybody else? Are there other women who don't work properly too? Do other women fail so miserably at the first hurdle?

He screws the lid back onto the chloroform bottle, drops the lint into the apparatus. He slides a hand under her neck, steadying her. His hands are clean and cold.

'Now,' he says, 'breathe deep.'

The apparatus over her mouth and nose, she heaves in a spirituous, strange breath. And the world collapses into darkness.

When she surfaces again, she can't think what has happened.

A light has been left burning. There's an oily,

mineral taste in her mouth. She thinks for a moment that she has had some kind of accident – that she's been hit by a 'bus – she feels sore all over. But then it returns to her – the hours compacted down to an eternity of pain, the failure, and then nothing.

She turns her head and sees the baby in the crib.

For a long time she just looks at the baby. Its skin is a reddish-pink colour, and there's a sticky tuft of dark hair on its scalp. It looks raw, underdone. Its head is squashed into a strange shape, like it's wearing a skullcap made of its own skin. It's not pretty. It is very far from pretty. But it is there, and it is real, and it lives. It sleeps there with a kind of quiet prepossession, as if entirely sure of its place in the world.

She reaches out to touch it, to smoothe down its sticky hair. The movement makes the bedsprings creak, stabs her belly, sends a flicker of pain down between her legs. She sucks in a breath. Breathes it out. The pain fades. She reaches out again. Her back and shoulders ache.

She touches the child. It is warm. Its skin is dry.

I have to love you, Amelia thinks. Whatever else happens, it is my job to love you now.

The old man must have been listening out for her, because she hears him come into the room now, tentatively, but without knocking. She doesn't look round.

'Are you all right?'

She nods; the movement hurts. Even her neck is sore.

He comes round the bed, and sits down beside her. He reaches out and touches the clean new cheek with his blackened hand.

'What'll we call him?' His voice is choked.

She didn't know that it was a boy.

'Don't bother him. Let him sleep.'

The old man hesitates, lifts his hand away.

'He'll be William,' she says. 'After his father. William Arthur Hastings. His son.'

Knox Road, Battersea, 15 November 1925

A ladder descends into the dark. He pulls himself down, hand over hand, deep into the water. He flips round into a flooded corridor. The corridor leads on and on, sloping downwards. He swims deeper and deeper. He reaches a door, and heaves it open. Beyond, the space opens out into a cavern. In his dreams he is not afraid of water. In his dreams he can swim.

He sees him, where he always is. A dark shape hanging in the water, the water clouded with soot.

And this is the moment when it could all happen. This is the moment when change is possible. He could just grab him and swim hard. The two of them. If he can get him back to the surface, he will have a father, and his mother will be happy. And he will have saved him, the man who matters most in the whole world.

He reaches out to take the arm – in his dream he can see his own hand reach out, pale in the darkness, and he knows what is coming next. He sees his fingers sink into the flesh as it gives like moss, cold and sodden. The corpse turns slowly in the water, turns to face him. Its eyes are black, empty sockets.

Billy

And then he can't swim. The skill's gone. Legs twisted in the water and then the thing reaches out for him. Its hand is white and spongy. Its touch will kill him. The hand lays itself on his chest, over his heart.

Son

He jumps awake, tangled in the sheets. She's there, looking down at him, her hand resting on his chest. Mother. Billy struggles up from under her hand. She sits on the edge of his bed, her hair tied up in soft rags. He rubs the dream out of his eyes. He knows better than to mention it to her. His father is a hero, that's what she says. He died protecting them from bullies. Billy's dreams of him should not be like this.

'Good morning, Billy,' she says.

'Morning.' The word comes out gluey with sleep.

'Come on then, time to get up. Special day.'

When she's gone, he dresses in the dark, shivering, pulling on his drawers, shorts and shirt, and his sweater. Yesterday's socks hold a glossy imprint of his toes. His boots are waiting downstairs in the scullery.

In the kitchen it is stuffy-hot. The range is glossy with black-lead; she has stirred the fire up and boiled the kettle and made porridge. Sometimes there is sugar, sometimes salt. Today, because it is a special day, there is jam. A dark blob of it sinking into the centre of the bowl as he sits down at the table.

'Thanks, Ma,' he says.

'Mother,' she says.

She leans down and offers her lips for a kiss. He stretches up and touches their soft coolness with the dry scratch of his own. Then she puts her arms around his neck and holds him and he waits until she's finished, smelling her clean cool smell. When she lets go, he starts to pull the blob of jam apart with his spoon, teasing out the scrolls of plum skin that look like little quills.

'Eat up,' she says. 'I've had mine.'

She gives him a pat, and then a rub of the hair, and then tidies it for him with her fingers as she watches him eat. She murmurs the kind of thing she always says, but with the added emphasis of the day: such a big boy now, starting his morning job, his very own delivery round before school, and who'd've thought it, all grown up, and how proud of him his father would have been. All that kind of thing. He concentrates on the spoon, on the careful portioning of jam to each mouthful.

He doesn't mind the hair-fussing, though from the way she pauses from time to time he knows she's considering whether a bit of scurf might be a nit, and he hopes to God she won't find any because that means a day stuck at home with his head wrapped up in paraffin and cloth, and his hair raked through a million times with that scratchy little comb because she won't buy the powder from the chemist's because then everyone will know that he's got a dirty head. She's telling him about when he was tiny, and he loves to hear about when he was tiny, it gives him that little bright coal in his chest, the sense of his own story weaving around other stories in the world. She tells him about the time she set him down on his feet when he was ten months old, a prodigy for standing and walking, never seen the like of it with such a tiny child. She'd set him down on the kitchen floor and turned her back to fetch his bread and milk, and when she turned round again she found him sitting on the tabletop, poking at the butter, having climbed up there from the seat of the chair: only ten months old, what a little marvel he was, just like his father, a busy, active man. Then she reminds herself of something, and takes her hands off his head, and goes to reach a little parcel down from the mantelshelf.

'That's for you, Son.'

She puts the small cardboard box down in front of him. He lifts it, tilts it. The thing inside rolls down the slope and hits the end of the box with a satisfying thunk. He knows what it is and a grin spreads across his face. He smiles up at her.

'Thanks, Ma.'

'Mother,' she says. 'Go on.'

He unpicks the end panel and lets the car slide

out onto his palm. Racing green; a Jaguar, long-snouted as a lurcher; and with its little driver there, all gauntleted and goggled. The yellow-painted headlamps are tiny and perfect. Straight from Atkinsons' window. He runs it across the tabletop. He picks it up and studies the ripples in the India rubber tyres, like the creases in tiny lips. The undercasing is unpainted lead.

He reaches up to kiss her.

'It's smashing, Mother,' he says. 'Thank you.'

He traces it around the table one-handed as he finishes up his porridge, trying to swerve the car round his teacup as the soft grains and swirls of jam spread out between his tongue and the cave-roof of his mouth. The car's axles are fixed, so it judders at the corners. He wonders if he could do anything about that. He picks at a screw with a thumbnail. He'll have a bit of a tinker after school.

The sound of the water hitting the enamel bowl makes him look up. He watches as she tops the bowl up with water from the kettle to take the chill off. She's saying that he has to remember to stand up straight and say his please-and-thank-yous and she knows he'll do all that, because he's such a good boy, a wonderment.

'Well,' she says. 'Well. Come on then.'

He scoops up his last spoonful of porridge, with its faint trace of sweetness. School dinner on Monday is liver and onions and potatoes and you can pick out the green bits and purple bits and black bits in the potatoes. And then plain cake for pudding. It's good the way you feel full afterwards. He rolls his sleeves as he gets up from the table. Leaning over the bowl, he slaps the lukewarm water to his face, puffs and blows; she leans over him and scrubs at his neck with a wrung-out cloth.

When he is washed and dried, she buttons up his jacket for him. She looks him over.

'I'll be good. I'll do my best.'

'I know you will,' she says. 'My little man.' She does up his top button, tucks his canary muffler in around his neck, kisses him. He scoops the car up off the tabletop, slides it into his pocket.

It is still dark. At the corner, under the lamp, Mr Bell's horse Rosie stands steaming between her shafts, the milk churns clustered cold and grey in the fog on the flatbed behind her.

'Hello, my lovely.'

Billy runs his hand along her flank as he comes up beside her, his knuckles bumping over her ribs, and she turns her head and looks round at him, blinks her great glossy eyes. The lovely warm smell of her huffing breath. He rubs at her jaw, and she blows with pleasure, great clouds of warm steam in the cold fog. He gives her a kiss and her nose is so soft and warm and alive, greyish-velvety, blotchy-pink, bristly.

'Morning, Mr Bell.'

The dairyman clambers back up into the seat and offers him a lift, but Billy says no and thank you, that he's off to Cheeseman's, starting work

79

today, and Mr Bell asks after Freddy who used to do the deliveries, and Billy says he's started work at Price's, so – and Mr Bell wishes Billy good luck, and Billy says thanks, and he's near the end of the street now, keeping pace with Mr Bell and Rosie, and then waving goodbye as they turn into Battersea High Street and he ducks down the back alleyway, boots clattering along the cobbles, his arms wrapped round him and his horse-scented hands tucked under his armpits and his lips faintly tingly. He bumps his way in through the back gate into Mr Cheeseman's yard.

Mr Cheeseman is at the back door of his shop. He has a box of parcelled groceries held out from his hip. There's an oil lamp hung from the wall. It casts a warm orange glow, filled with grainy fog.

'Ah, Billy,' he says. He sets down the box by the back step.

Billy stands up straight. 'Good morning, Mr Cheeseman.'

Mr Cheeseman brushes his hands. 'Your mother well?'

Billy nods. 'Yesser.'

'Good good. Well then. So. You can ride a bike, then?'

'Yesser.'

In fact, he's only had a couple of goes, standing up on the pedals, on this very bike, Freddy having marked him out some months ago as his successor. Freddy himself had set him going with a hand under the saddle, then a final push and laughing when he let go and Billy looped round in the street and found he couldn't make the turn and couldn't stop and yelled and wove about, and then banged the front wheel on the kerb and came off sideways and took the skin off his knee, which made Freddy dash over all concerned and examine the solid tyre and go phew with relief when he found it was undamaged. Billy'd also had a ride from time to time in the grocery box when he was small, but you're not supposed to lark about with Mr Cheeseman's bike.

'Well this ol' girl won't give you any trouble.'

Mr Cheeseman heads over to the lean-to shed and drags open a door that needs its hinges redoing; the bottom is scraping itself away against the flagstones.

'Let's see you give it a try.'

He reaches into the dark space and half lifts, half pulls out the bike. Billy feels a fierce delight.

It's an Alldays & Onions. There's a wooden box fitted above the front wheel; and down the side of the box the words *Cheeseman's Quality Grocer's* and *Established 1873* picked out in gold and white lettering against the black. That's where Billy'd sat, knees buckled up, backside numb, rattling over the cobbles with Freddy cruising along and singing behind him.

Billy crouches down, admires the mantrap pedals, thumbs at the solid rubber tyres. He rests a hand on the sprung leather saddle. His face breaks into a grin.

Mr Cheeseman shifts in his nice boots, he has to be getting on. Billy stands up. He brushes the dirt off his hands, rubs the oil away.

'Give her a go, then?' Mr Cheeseman says.

The smile spreads further, making Billy's cheeks bunch up, ache. This is a *job*. This is *work*. Mr Cheeseman's going to *pay* him to do this.

'She weighs a fair bit herself,' Mr Cheeseman says. 'So we'll try it first without a load.'

Mr Cheeseman holds the saddle while Billy punts along with one foot, and then hops it up onto the pedal and Mr Cheeseman lets go. Billy dips back and forth through the frame like a wind-up toy.

'Watch it,' Mr Cheeseman calls. 'Try and stay upright. If you had a load on that, you'd topple right over.'

A few more yards, passing the backyard gates of the houses, and he's picking up speed, whipping through the cold cobwebs of fog. The pedals taking him up and over and down, up and over and down, his back up straight and the cold needling in through the weave of his jacket. The sheer breathless joy of it. Then the alley ends – opens out onto Simpson Street, a pool of lamplight – and he careens out, swings the bike round. He's taking it too wide and is going to hit the kerb – he tightens the turn, slows off, but he's lost it, balance almost gone, and he's going to fall, crunch the bike onto the cobbles and wreck it, splintered wood and bent spokes and scored paintwork. He can't let that happen. Billy drops a foot off the pedal, and clatters his boot toe over the cobbles, slowing, dragging the bike round, finds his balance, and he's got away with it. He's back between the backyard walls, into the alleyway, all the world is good. The wet fog whips past him and whistles through his teeth, gritty and wet and sour, and he is happy.

Mr Cheeseman stands by his back gate, his hands stuffed in the pockets of his duster coat, his muffler pulled up over his chin. Billy slows down. He drops a foot and drags it bump bump bump over the cobbles, bringing him to a stop at Mr Cheeseman's side, in the edge of the backyard lamplight. He slips down off the pedals, stands astride the frame, not ready to get off yet. His face glows. His fingers throb with cold. He doesn't want ever to get off.

'Good chap,' Mr Cheeseman says. 'But watch those boots. Your ma will have both our hides.'

Billy steps off and wheels the bike, following Mr Cheeseman into the yard. He leans the bike up against the wall, and cranes to look at the slip of paper Mr Cheeseman's taken from his pocket. It's an old Lifebuoy soap wrapper, still smelling of soap, with a list of addresses pencilled on the inner side. Billy knows the addresses – they are the streets that crisscross between Westbridge Road and the railway. Mrs Goldman is the lady that his ma doesn't say hello to, though she always smiles at Billy. She has a blue overcoat. Mr Clovis rides a Marston Sunbeam to work.

'This all make sense to you?' Mr Cheeseman asks.

Billy nods.

Mr Cheeseman pockets the list and lifts the first package from the crate by the back door. He dips the package so that Billy can read the pencilled name and address.

'Right,' Billy says.

'Last one on your list,' Mr Cheeseman says, brandishing Mrs Goldman's package of rolls, butter and cheese. 'So it goes in first.'

He places it carefully in the bottom of the box. Billy bends to help.

'Next time you can load it up yourself,' Mr Cheeseman says. 'And Mrs Cheeseman will give you a cup of tea and a bun when you get back.'

Billy stops. Mr Cheeseman continues loading. There is stubble on his chin, and his neck hangs loose above his collar. Mr Cheeseman looks up from his work. Billy offers his hand to be shaken. Mr Cheeseman's hand is thick and warm around his.

'Good chap,' Mr Cheeseman says, bumping his hand up and down.

Good chap. Billy likes this. He feels entirely happy. He doesn't like being called son.

Mrs Goldman gives him an Everton Mint. She leans out into the street in her red satin wrap and asks how Freddy's getting on down at Price's. Billy hasn't got a bleeding clue, but he grins at her, sweet bulging in his cheek, and says he's doing famously, thanks for asking. Freddy's day is over and it's Billy's day now, and the world is his lobster.

He pushes off, one foot on the pedal, one on the pavement. Inside his mouth, the taste changes from bed-sour and porridge and plum jam to cold mintiness. He pedals hard, building speed. There's a satisfying rasp at the edges of his breath, his chest just ever-so-slightly raw, and his legs faintly trembly. He'll get strong. He'll get great strong legs, strong chest, strong as a horse's.

The clock chimes seven forty-five, and he's due back at Cheeseman's at eight. Job done and fifteen minutes to himself. He rides in great looping curves, his breath puffing out into the foggy air. He is a locomotive. He pounds up the hill; ploughs slowing onto the crest, and then creeps up the final yards, his heart hammering, breath catching. He's almost stopped, wavering, a foot about to meet the ground, but then the slope catches him, the bike begins to roll, the weight of it and the pull of gravity and then it's downhill, in a long wondrous swoop, the cobbles rattling him, eyes wet, eyes streaming, the mist whipping past. His legs and his chest and his belly clenched for each push and he is just body and machine and it is good. He lets the speed cruise itself away – rounding the bend into Orbel Street clean and perfect. Then he's out onto the High Street and the fog is lighter here, and the new business of the day is unfolding – the joy and clatter of it, the speed – and Mr Hartley is unfurling the awning on the butchers, the new girl at Palmer's emptying a bucket into the gutter, Leibmann's clerk taking down the blinds. At the greengrocer's the boys are unloading sacks from the wholesalers' wagon, and the horses stand blinkered and half asleep and Billy turns his head to halloo the lads, to show off, but just then a man steps out into the street in front of him. Billy swerves, brakes. The man steps back just in the nick of time.

'*Little fucker.*'

For a second, Billy's eyes are snagged on the man's. But then he shifts attention back to the bike, balance, the road ahead. He cycles on.

He only had one ear, Billy realises.

But he doesn't matter: Billy's past him now, rolling off through a heap of horse dung, riding out along the High Street, back towards Cheeseman's, the day beginning.

He walks to school unpeeling the spiral of a Chelsea bun. It's one of yesterday's buns and a little bit stale but no less the welcome for that. No time to stop for a cuppa; he'd rather skip the tea than give up even a moment on the bike. Tomorrow he will shave another minute off his round. Another minute to dash out and away from the neighbourhood – see how far he can get. He whoofles the soft currants off the yeasty inner flesh, breaks off squares and rectangles of sweet dough and chomps them down. Spice and the sweet pulp of currants overlay the mintiness, erase it.

This is work. This is what work means. A bike. A currant bun. An Everton Mint.

Little fucker.

He flinches inwardly at the hard words. They don't have words like that at home, but you hear that kind of thing sometimes, from the rougher men. Forget it, it doesn't matter, over and gone now. He sucks the sugar off each finger, tasting both sweetness and the sourness and salt of skin. Could he borrow the bike on Sundays, or maybe in the afternoons? Would it be cheeky to ask? Maybe give it a week or two, settle in a bit first. He turns the corner into Cabul Road, sees the backs of Francie Clack and Mickey Peters and he dashes to catch them up. Hand in his pocket, cradling the toy car. The world is new today. He has a power, and it makes everything different from the day before. He can fold the world up into a concertina, roll it out into a ribbon, loop it into paperchains. He has a bike. He has speed. He can go anywhere.

He comes alongside them.

'All right?'

He ducks his head down and scuffs his feet along, and tries to keep his grin under wraps.

'Look at this.'

He shows them the car. They walk along, heads bent to examine it. They round the corner and there are more boys here, heading for school, traipsing down the pavement and kicking along the gutter in twos and threes and singly, delaying the inevitable. They're following the schoolyard wall now, the building looming rusty-black above them, with yelling and scuffling coming from the last-minute games on the far side – tig and football and British bulldogs – and the noise makes Billy pick up his feet, lift his head, hurry on, ready to run and shout with the rest of them, before school closes down around them for the day.

And then he sees them. Tim Proctor and Charlie Grover. Billy slips the car back into his pocket. Long legs with scabs on and long wrists and jumpers worn out at the elbow. Just leaning there by the gate. Francie and Mickey go quiet. But the three of them keep on walking. They might get past without notice; there are plenty of other boys: Tim and Charlie might pick on someone else.

There's a boil on the side of Tim Proctor's neck. It peeps up from underneath his collar. It looks sore. A nasty pinkish red, with a custardy crust on top. Billy blinks away, but it's too late – Tim looks round, right at them. The movement must make the boil really hurt, brushing the crust against the collar and at the same time making it twist with the skin. There is no real colour to Tim's face, Billy thinks: pale hair, pale eyebrows, pale eyes. The only colour is the rhubarb-and-custard of that boil.

They have to keep walking towards him, because it's the only way into school.

Tim pushes himself up, away from the wall. He nudges Charlie with an elbow, shoves his hands into the pockets of his shorts. Billy and his friends falter, stop.

'Aye aye, pipsqueaks,' Tim says. Charlie is moving into place with that uneven rickety gait of his, blocking their way.

This is how it starts: something said, and something said back, and the two big bony bodies closing in. And it ends in getting hurt. They'll just cut you off with a smack if you get clever and try to talk yourself out of it. You can't even run, because Tim's got legs like a lurcher's and can outrun anyone; and anyway school is starting. You could try and make a dash for the classroom, but then it's just waiting for you when you get out, and you've got a whole day ahead of you knowing what's coming at the end of it. Billy knows, now, for the first time, why they choose him in particular to poke at, prod, provoke. The boil on Tim Proctor's neck gives it away. It's because Billy has a clean shirt for school, and jam on his porridge and the new toy car that cost more than she can really afford and must have made a hole in the housekeeping – a hole from which everything could unravel into hunger and cold and dirt if it wasn't for her carefulness and watching and curbing and holding back, and stitching the hole back together for him, so that everything is safe.

Next time he will keep the Chelsea bun for her.

'Can we just come past?' Billy tries.

'*Can we just come past?*' Charlie mocks.

They are caught on the brink of it. Tim plus Charlie plus him and Francie and Mickey equals – getting hurt.

'Aren't we the proper little gent?'

'Whatcher got there, Billy-boy?' Tim asks, nodding at Billy's bunched hand.

Billy's hand tightens round the car. Rubbery wheels and silvery underbelly, cool as a stickle-back. He can't let Tim take it.

He doesn't think it any further. He launches himself at Tim's middle. Skull into belly, the big boy crumples over him, and the smell of dirty wool and unwashed skin is like an old brown blanket round him. Billy flails, blurred, banging his fists into the skinny sides, the bony back, and for that stunned moment it all seems to be going pretty well. Then Tim hits Billy. Bang. On the cheekbone. Everything whacked out of line. One eye blurred. Head jangling. And then another, an up-cut to the chin. The taste of blood. Someone has him by the belt and is dragging at him, and he lets himself be pulled away. He can hear the shouts and chants of the other boys, but everything is dizzy, swimming. Blood in his mouth. She will be disappointed. Blood on his shirt. She will cry. He wants to cry too. But he has his car. He still has his car. And he stood up to the bully; she should be proud of that. That's what you're supposed to do.

★   ★   ★

His cheek still throbs, and is tender to the touch, but the skin is unbroken. His lip, however, is split open and tastes stingy. If he tucks his chin in and squints down, he can see the dark blood stain on his shirt, just below the collar. He glances side-long at Tim Proctor. The big boy is upright, soldierish, stiffly staring at the sage-green wall, his skin grey in the indoors light. His kneecaps stick out like doorknobs. Tim's dad died somewhere in the mud. Probably. They mostly did.

Billy wants to say sorry, but he knows it's better not to.

The door opens, and the headmaster half leans out.

'Ah, boys,' he says, as if he'd forgotten them. 'You'd better come in.'

The headmaster is not a bad sort. Not half-mad with nerves like Mr Hilling, not mean like Mr Roberts, and he doesn't smell of drink. When he picks the cane up from his desk and runs his hand down its length, his face is frowny, as though he can't quite remember what he's supposed to be doing, or if he isn't entirely sure that it's a good idea. Although it's already half past nine, the day, outside the headmaster's window, is pale grey, dawnish, as though it will never quite get light.

'Right then,' the headmaster says. 'Assume the position.'

Billy turns back his cuffs. They are clean. He holds out his hands. There is dirt in the creases

91

from the bike. He feels guilty about that. Tim's hands are grey and long and bony, no flesh on them, and Billy wonders, would it hurt more or less for that?

Then the headmaster brings the cane down, swish, on Tim Proctor's narrow palms – one, and then the other. The hands are whisked back, tucked away.

The headmaster moves past Tim, and comes to Billy. Billy watches his own hands tremble. The cane whips past his face, hits his left palm. Then the cane flicks past again, and hits the right.

For a moment there is a kind of silence before the pain is felt, when it seems like it'll be all right. But Billy knows that it is just a trick of the nerves, and then the pain when it comes a second later is just astonishing – hot and bright and loud. He tucks his hands up under his armpits and squeezes hard. He wants the velvet of Rosie's nose, the cool metal of the bike. He wants the morning's washing water that slipped through his fingers almost unnoticed, the same temperature as skin. His eyes bud with wet. Like a cough or sneeze will make your eyes wet; it's not the same as crying.

Amelia steps off the pavement to let Jonnie Clements past. He's having a bad day, shaking so hard it's a struggle for him just to put one foot in front of the other. He takes up the whole width of the pavement, one arm outstretched for balance, the other running along the front walls of the houses to keep him going straight. She says hello; she's friendly with his sister. He seems to catch a glimpse of her through the nightmare, but she doesn't really know if he's nodding back, because his head is moving all the time anyway. He's not himself any more, his sister says so, but anyone can see it. He left himself behind somewhere in France.

She turns down Knox Road. The streetlamps are like dandelion clocks in the foggy dark. A man is making his way down the street ahead of her, through the haze of a streetlamp's pale glow, and then gone into shadow; but she doesn't pay him much attention, because she's not really there herself. She's in the old Electric Theatre on York Road, under the flickering grey light. William draws her glove off her hand, and strokes her skin with his calloused fingertips. She's watching the woman with the beautiful clothes and the jealous husband, and Max Linder charming one and then the other. That last, lovely night before William left.

Max Linder is dead. It feels like she knew him. If feels like a personal loss.

The newspaper is folded tight and wedged between the cake box and the parcelled-up potatoes. But when she'd bought it, she'd stood there reading it in the street, like a man.

Because now they're saying he killed himself. That Max Linder took his own life, and persuaded his young wife to take hers along with him. The paper's calling it a suicide pact.

The basket bumps against her hip. She remembers the cakes: they'll spoil. She lifts the handle from the crook of her arm and though it's chillier like this now she's no longer holding her own warmth around herself, she clasps the basket firmly, arms wrapped around its girth instead. Three more streetlamps and she'll be home.

He'd died before, of course, Max Linder had, during the war. She'd read about it at the time. And when he'd turned up wounded in a shell-hole in no man's land days later, it had seemed like rare good news. But all you had to do is look at a picture of him, a picture from afterwards, and you could see that he wasn't well, he wasn't the man he had been. He was shadowed, hollowed out inside.

He was infected. Why did no-one notice? He'd caught death out there on no man's land, as he lay out amongst the dead. They let him bring the contagion home with him, God help him. Let him, through no fault of his own, pass it on to his wife, like with the Spanish flu.

Which leaves their daughter, a tiny daughter. And it makes her think of Billy: Billy bounding through to the kitchen, bringing the smell of fog and wool and school. Billy sitting at the tea table, scrubbed up and shining and solemn, and his pleasure when she brings out the cake box, and lets him choose between a vanilla slice, and a cherry bakewell, and a macaroon. To think of the dark hollow eatenness of that poor infected man, of death worming through his young wife's heart, to think that they could find no solace at all, no joy that was worth the suffering for, even in their child.

She used to say things like, *when all this is over*, and, *afterwards*. She would think that if you had your man back then you were lucky, that it was everything you'd need.

Ahead, the stranger moves on down the street. Their twinned footfalls are muffled by the fog. He pauses under the second streetlamp. He wears a brownish coat and hat, she notices. He carries a small suitcase. He peers at a front door. The Clarys' house, halfway up the street from hers. He moves on.

There is tea to make, and the table to set, and the old man is going out later to his class, and she'll have a quiet evening with her knitting. Billy'll choose the vanilla slice, she knows. And the old man will have the macaroon, which leaves the tooth-jangling sweetness of the cherry bakewell for her.

She passes through the white glow of the second streetlamp and out into the blur of fog on the other side. She slips the basket back onto her arm, and rifles in her pocket for her key. Up ahead, under the third streetlamp, the man is peering at the front doors, picking out house numbers. A new rent man, she thinks as she gets closer; a tallyman. Or door-to-door salesman perhaps, with that suitcase. Whatever he's after, it's nothing to do with her. She's paid this week's rent already, she's not buying anything, and she doesn't owe anyone anything beyond what she can settle on a Friday. She's almost beside him now: he's checking the Hollidges' door, next door but one to home. She steps aside and off the kerb onto the cobbles to go past him, but he turns and follows her round, watching her. In the corner of her eye she sees his profile as she moves past him – a strange face, bony, taut.

The key presses hard through her woollen gloves. She steps back up onto the pavement and approaches her own door. He moves too, coming round behind her, and she knows he's checking the house number.

'Ah.'

She isn't going to look round. She's just going to go in and shut the door behind her and ignore him, and even lock the door behind her if she has to. She's not got time or money to waste. These people: what do they think they're doing, intruding like this? Hovering around a lone woman as she lets herself into an empty house. In the dark. Her skin blooms with perspiration.

'Madam?'

Despite herself, she glances at him. He stands almost directly under the streetlamp. His face is shadowed by his hat brim; her gaze drops down the length of his brown coat and lands on his boots. They stand out stark in the gaslight. They're old; the soles are scuffed thin at the toes. And the trouser cuffs above them are worn through at the edge. She sees what he probably thinks people won't notice – that he's snipped off the fraying threads of the hems in an attempt to neaten them. Her heart flushes through with unexpected sympathy: whoever he is, he has his struggles, she thinks; he has problems of his own.

'Madam?' He steps closer. 'May I trouble you a moment?'

No, she thinks, please don't trouble me. I've had trouble enough to last a lifetime.

'I can't help you,' she says.

She turns back to the door, peels off her gloves and slips the key into the lock. She wants to be indoors; she wants Billy home, the old man home, she wants cakes and tea and knitting and the evening to revert to its normal path, its ordinary harmony.

But he doesn't move. 'You are Mrs William Hastings, aren't you?'

The name seems somehow different when he says it, as though it stirs and shifts, coming alive again after all these years of ordinary use. She lets the key go, leaves it sitting in the lock, and turns to him again. He pushes his hat back. In the foggy light his face is all skin and bone.

'Do I know you?'

'I'm George Sully,' he says.

Her mouth is dry. She shakes her head.

'Ah, well, there we are then.' A quick grin. 'He didn't make this easy, did he?'

'What?' The word comes out thin as a fallen leaf. 'Who didn't?'

'William.'

In that moment, it is more than memory. She can feel William's hands rest on her waist. His face press into her neck. His calloused fingertips snag on the palm of her hand. Her body is haunted by his touch. Her stays feel too tight. She can't get her breath.

'I served with him,' he says. 'On the *Goliath*.'

She reaches out to the doorjamb.

'Back in the year fourteen, fifteen. We were—' He moves closer to her. 'Mrs Hastings? Are you well?'

But the world contracts, goes tiny. She feels him lift the basket from her grip, takes her arm.

'Mrs Hastings. I am sorry.'

She tries to shake her head, but everything spins and she just sinks. He puts his arm around her, turns the key. He lets them in.

She is in the parlour. Her head rests against the wing of the chair. He stands in the window, looking out, through the net curtains, the fog, the street beyond. She blinks, stirs herself. He turns at the sound. She goes to push herself up, but her head reels. He comes over to her, puts his hand over her hand, where it rests on the arm of the chair.

'Don't get up.'

She looks up at him. He lifts his hand away from hers, moves back a step.

'You've had a shock.'

The room is cold, dim, lit only by the cool light

98

from the street- lamp outside. Her basket, with its three cakes and newspaper and bag of muddy spuds, is set beside her seat. She sees his worn shoes on the green rug of the parlour floor. His suitcase is tucked in beside the card table, where they never play cards: the picture book lies on the green baize surface, with a red poppy, bought on Remembrance Day, laid on top if it.

He stands, looking at her, his hat still on. He smiles. It must be difficult for the men, she thinks, to just keep on going on, through the days and weeks and years, through the emptinesses, the absences, the threads left trailing off in mid-air. To know there are people looking at you, resenting you, angry that you're alive, when the man they love is dead.

Her hat is pushed askew by the high back of the chair. She reaches up to take it off. She stabs the pin back into the felt, lets the hat drop onto her basket. She touches her hair.

'Do sit down, please,' she finally thinks to say.

He looks round a moment, then sits down in the other chair, facing her across the window.

'You were with him, then,' she asks, 'on the *Goliath?*'

She is very conscious of the act of speaking, of forming the individual words.

He nods.

She leans forward and picks up the poppy. She rolls its wire stem between her fingertips, watches its paper head turn from side to side, a slow

99

negative. They fade so quickly, real poppies, if you pick them. They can't survive long indoors. They shed their petals, fall apart, dust the windowsill with fallen stamens, pollen.

'He said, William said, that if he didn't make it through, I should find you. He gave me the address, so I could come and see you, and pass his message on.'

'There was a message?'

Sully clears his throat. 'He talked about you a lot.'

The word comes out dry and dusty: 'Oh?'

A pause; then, 'He said that you were beautiful.'

Amelia blinks down at the poppy; it blurs and smears through the wet. 'Oh.'

'I didn't believe, him, of course.'

She looks up at him.

He smiles at her. 'I thought it was just the kind of thing people say.'

She tries to smile back.

'He missed you,' he says. He seems to hesitate a moment, rubs at the side of his nose. 'He was desperate to get back.'

He reaches into the inside pocket of his jacket, and takes something out. He holds it out towards her, and for a moment she just looks at it, a blur of bright blue and yellow. A postcard.

'He wanted me to make sure you got this.'

She puts her hand over her mouth.

'Go on,' he says, reaching it closer to her. 'It's for you.'

She leans forward and takes the card. It is a precise, piercing, miraculous pain. Her eyes swim. She looks down at the picture, the yellow city, the blue-inked sea and sky. Across the top, in neat small print, *The Grand Harbour, Malta.*

'When did he—?'

'On the way to Gallipoli. So . . .'

So he never got the chance. She turns the card over. His sloping, careful copperplate.

Thank you for your letter, she reads. She blinks away the swimming wet. The words fracture, fall apart—

longing

the child

I thought

you

you

Yours

She runs her thumb over the pencilled name. *William*. It smudges slightly.

'Can I fetch you something, Mrs Hastings?'

She closes her eyes.

'I'm sorry,' he says. 'It's been a shock for you.'

Her breath comes and goes, comes and goes.

'Mrs Hastings?'

She shakes her head, presses tears away. 'It's all right. I'm all right. I'm sorry.'

'There's no need for sorry, Mrs Hastings.'

'Won't you take your hat off, Mr Sully?'

He lifts off his Homburg and reaches round to set it down on the card table. It lands with a soft thump on top of the picture book. She is starting to her feet, about to protest, but then she sees, with an inward twist, the exposed stub of his ear.

He sees her see, and grimaces.

'Oh,' she says. 'You poor thing.'

When Billy bundles into the kitchen at teatime, his hands and face and knees are icy and he's grubby from playing out in the street. He and Stanley Dunlop have a ropeswing slung from the lamppost on the corner, and they've been scuffing round and round on the cobbles, and swinging up into the air. It hurt the sore bits on his hands, so he tugged his sleeves right down and wrapped his arms around the rope instead, and he got the wool all stretched and snagged and little bits of rope-hemp stuck in the knitting, and he's thinking he might just get away with it if he can stop her from noticing it today, because if you leave it long enough the sweater could go back to normal on its own account and he can brush the little bits out if he has to. The blood on his shirt is a different matter: he can't do anything about that. But he is so hungry – hungry as a lion – and she promised him a special tea since it was his first day of work, and that outweighs the worry about the clothes.

He hurries over to the sink to wash his hands before she has the chance to get cross about that too. He's half aware that there's someone extra in the kitchen, sitting on the far side of the table with his back to the dresser, but assumes it must be one of the Clack boys popped in for a lend of something from his grandpa. But even in passing he did notice that there was cold ham, and buttered bread, and mustard set out on the table. He scrubs his knuckles with the grey-green soap, eager for his meal, when he notices the way Ma's talking, all of a fluster and chatter, not like her at all, and that Grandpa isn't saying anything, has somehow taken a step back – sitting at the range and just looking at the flames, and not saying a word: so it's not one of the Clack boys.

Billy turns round, hands dripping, to see who it is.

The One-Eared Man, the nasty-mouthed man from the morning. He smiles at Billy.

'Hello there, son.'

Billy looks from him to Ma. She's looking at the One-Eared Man all smiling. Then she turns to look at Billy. Her expression is warm and bright.

'This is Mr Sully,' she says. 'He was a friend of your father's.'

Billy folds ham onto bread, and bites into it. His jumper is tickling his bare belly, because his shirt is soaking in the scullery. She's made very little fuss about it, considering. Hadn't even given him the look when he'd spun her a line – that he'd tripped on a paving slab and knocked his face on a lamppost. He can see it in his mind's eye, a Stan Laurel trip and teeter and thump, and him sitting on the ground, face crumpling, scratching his head. She hadn't even really seemed to listen. Just tugged him out of his jumper and shirt, dumped the shirt in the sink, and handed the jumper back to him.

Billy watches the One-Eared Man talking to his ma. He doesn't seem to remember Billy from that morning. And Billy's not going to bring it up – there are words that can't be said in front of Ma; there are things that she is better off not knowing. But he knows. He knows what the One-Eared Man said to him. The kinds of things the One-Eared Man will say, in certain circumstances, if he thinks he can get away with it.

He eats his vanilla slice, and the One-Eared Man has a bakewell, and Grandpa has a macaroon, and Ma says that she isn't hungry, and that is perhaps true, because she's all flushed and funny, maybe going down with something. He hopes not, because nothing's any good when Ma is ill.

The One-Eared Man has brought a postcard from his father. Billy's ma lets him hold it. The handwriting is the same as the other cards, but then that's how they teach you to do it at school: his own will be like that by the time he leaves. Grandpa holds the card a while, too. His eyes get shiny and he rubs at his nose like it's itchy. His ma gets the picture book from the parlour, and takes the postcard off Grandpa, and fits it into place, the final postcard, this one softened and worn from being carried around for all these years.

'And still there's so many spaces,' Ma says, turning the blank leaves till she reaches the end.

Then she stirs herself and has the One-Eared Man look through all the pictures with her, and he keeps telling stories, *Oh I remember, I remember*, but if you really listen they aren't really about Billy's father at all, they're about the One-Eared Man.

After a long half hour of this, Billy has run out of patience.

'Why didn't you die?' he asks.

His grandpa looks up, looks from Billy to his ma. His face is all grin apart from the mouth.

'Billy!' his ma exclaims.

'But why didn't he?' Billy turns to his ma. 'If Father died, then why didn't he?'

'For goodness' sake!' She turns to Sully. 'I'm so sorry.'

'It's quite all right, Mrs Hastings.'

'Amelia.'

'Amelia.'

Billy feels his cheeks go pink and hot.

The One-Eared Man fixes his gaze on Billy. 'I was rescued. Picked up out of the water by the *Cornwallis*. It all happened so quick, son, there was no getting out if you were below.'

Billy folds his arms. 'If my father was below, why weren't you?'

'I was on light duties, recovering from wounds.' The One-Eared Man reaches up to touch the stump of his ear: 'This, son. This saved my life.'

Grandpa sniffs, turns back to the fire. Billy's ma lifts the teapot.

'Tea?' she asks, to deflect attention.

But Billy thinks, this is not fair: if the One-Eared Man was a stoker, then the One-Eared Man should have been down there, with Billy's father, in the dark, stoking. The One-Eared Man should have died too, or they should both have lived. And if his father had survived, and was here, now, at home with them, Billy's pretty sure this Sully fellow wouldn't be.

Billy doesn't like it, not one bit.

His ma brings him up to bed, and says what a day it's been, him starting work and now this, and aren't they lucky to have Mr Sully here to see them? And even though she's right there, she's somehow far away too. She waits while he says his prayers. Billy clamps his hands beneath his chin.

As I lay me down to sleep
I pray the Lord my soul to keep

He squints up at her, one eye open, one eye closed, and says, 'When is he leaving?'

She's looking off across the room, towards the curtained window. 'What's that, sugar?'

'He's brought a suitcase.'

'Oh, he just came to tea. He's not staying here.'

Billy nods. That's all right then. Goes back to his prayer.

And if I die before I wake
I pray the Lord my soul to take.

'Don't you think it's wonderful, though? A post-card from your father, after all this time?'

He drops his hands. Looks up at her. She is all pink and glowy. She is never pink and glowy. It must be wonderful, if it makes her feel like this.

'Yes, Mother.'

She drops a kiss on his forehead. 'Now go to sleep.'

He stays awake though – listening to the voices through the floorboards. To his grandpa climbing the slow stairs, hours earlier than usual, and pausing at his door.

'You all right, old fellow?' the old man whispers.

'Yes, Grandpa.'

'Good, good.'

Billy listens to the old man make his way to his own room. He can hear the chink of the ewer, the clank of his belt buckle as he washes and undresses. Then the creak of bedsprings, and then again, as he turns to get comfortable. Lying down makes his lungs trouble him: he coughs hard, wet coughs. From downstairs, Billy can hear the dark rumble of the One-Eared Man's voice, though he can't make out the words. Next door the old man falls asleep – Billy can hear the thick, phlegmy breathing. He lies awake until he hears his ma and the One-Eared Man in the hallway – the man saying how wonderful, what a delight, though the circumstances of course, what a smart young man Billy has grown up to be, what a lucky man William was in this, if not in other matters. Quiet affirmations from his mother. The opening and closing of the door, and a farewell in the street. It is only then that Billy turns onto his side and lets himself soften into sleep.

The next day, after school, when Billy gets back from climbing trees in the park and being shouted at by the parkie, the One-Eared Man is there.

He stays to tea again, talking about himself, and eats three eggs and half a loaf of bread as Billy watches, biting his lip, wanting to ask what there will be to eat tomorrow.

In bed, Billy lies awake, hot and seething, listening out for the voices in the hall, the opening and shutting of the door that means he's gone. Why is she being so kind to him? Why is he allowed to eat up all their food? He can't make sense of it.

In the morning, loading up the bike at Cheeseman's, he yawns so widely Mr Cheeseman boggles his eyes at him and asks if he's been burning the midnight oil. Midnight oil must be really beautiful, Billy thinks; blue as ink and rich as treacle and full of shivering colours. He says sorry, shakes his head clear of cobwebs, and swings up onto his bike and lets the cold November morning clear his head, and for a while is lost in the joy of the bike, and speed, and the buffetting of the cold damp air. But on the High Street he spots the One-Eared Man trudging along, collar up, hat down, slumped over to one side with the weight of his suitcase. He looks like he could have been walking all night.

And that evening, while the One-Eared Man is pretending to read the paper, and Grandpa has taken himself out for a walk down to the wharves to see what ships are in, even though it's November and dark and freezing and he could have done that earlier on his way back from the factory, she gestures Billy into the hall and asks him quietly to give her the money from Cheeseman's round.

'No,' he says.

She looks startled. 'What do you mean, no?'

'I've not been paid yet.'

'When will you be paid?'

'Tomorrow morning, I think. I don't know, really.' In fact, he hadn't even thought about it. He'd forgotten that it was the point.

She turns to get her coat. 'I'll call round there and ask for it now.'

Billy catches her arm. 'Don't.'

She glances down at his hand, then back up at his face, her eyebrows raised. He releases his grip.

'Sorry,' he says.

'I should think so.'

He scuffs his toe into the matting. 'But, please don't, Mother.'

'Mr Cheeseman won't mind.'

'It's not that,' Billy says. Though it is partly that. But it's more that she doesn't care what Mr Cheeseman thinks of her going round there asking for wages before they're due, and she doesn't care because it's for the One-Eared Man. Billy shuffles, resentful, conscious of his smallness and youth, and queasy with the sense of not being quite so very important any more.

She slips an arm down her coat sleeve, tugs the yoke up onto her shoulders. 'Then what is it?'

'It's him,' he says, and gets suddenly hot and flaps his arms around. 'It's that man. He's, I don't know—'

'Shush.' She glances back to the kitchen door, leans in close to hiss. 'For goodness' sake.'

'Why'd you like him so much?'

'He was your father's friend.'

'Do you believe that?'

'What?'

Billy straightens himself up to her. 'I don't.'

'Do you think he'd *lie*?' She flinches back, coat still hanging half off. Her throat is going blotchy.

'He can say anything,' Billy says. 'How can we know that it's the truth? We only have his word for it.'

'No we don't, Billy. We have your father's word too; the postcard, you remember? He entrusted Mr Sully with it.'

'That's what he says.' Billy shrugs. 'He's a liar, though. Bet he is.'

She smacks him, open palm whack on the bare

back of his leg. Her coat swings round like a pigeon's tail, grey and shabby.

He rubs at the sting. It doesn't hurt, not really. His eyes water. It's just the suddenness, the shock.

'A little respect, Billy.'

'He just eats our food and drinks our tea and sits in our warm—' his voice is rising, almost a wail '—and I don't like it. I don't want it any more.'

'That's enough. I'm not standing for this.'

Her voice is like a water biscuit, parched and brittle. She fumbles her other arm into her sleeve, plucks the buttons through the buttonholes one after the other. Her lips are set. She doesn't look at Billy.

'Why now?' Billy asks. And it makes sudden, brilliant sense. 'It's been years and years. Why didn't he come before?'

Then she looks at him.

'I see him walking the streets,' Billy says. 'First thing, when I'm on my rounds.'

'So what? What are you suggesting?' But she's faltering now, he sees it, presses harder.

'That he's got nowhere else to go.'

Her lips press tighter. 'He's here because of your father.'

'He doesn't give tuppence, you know he doesn't. If he did, he would have come soon as he could; he'd could have posted the blooming card if he'd really wanted you to get it. If he cared, we'd know him already. We'd have known him for years.'

She blinks, shakes her head. But she's coming round to him, he sees it. He pushes his point home.

'He just needs somewhere to be, that's why he's here. One night, you'll let him stay, and he'll be here for ever. Or till it suits him to move on.'

She goes white. He actually sees the pink fade from her cheeks.

'How dare you.'

'It's *true*.'

'Go to your room.'

'I won't.'

'Right.'

She grabs him by the arm and yanks, clatters him up the stairs. He stumbles, his feet barely touching the treads; his shin bangs against a wooden edge. She pulls him to his room and opens the door, then pushes him in. He stumbles to a halt. It's angry crying, not sad.

'Don't let him stay, Ma,' Billy says. 'Please. Don't.'

She slams the door.

Amelia puts on her hat and goes out of the front door and walks to Cheeseman's through the evening dark. Her breath plumes in front of her. Her feet clip on the paving slabs and the cold air cools her cheeks. Her palm stings. It will freeze tonight, she thinks: when she gets into bed later, the sheets will have that faint slick of dampness about them, which never seems to go away no

112

matter how she washes and dries and airs the bedding.

The words worm through her head: *He's got nowhere else to go.* She can see him, in her mind's eye, standing in the lamplight, with his suitcase and his broken shoes.

One night, you'll let him stay. His suitcase tucked in beside the card table. His hat dropped on top of the picture book. Without a thought, without a word of apology.

When she goes into the shop, with its warm familiar smell of ham and tea and brown paper, Mr Cheeseman is at the door, just twisting the cardboard sign round to *Closed*. But when he sees her there he lets go of the sign and stands back and opens the door to let her in. He smiles, his face dimpling and folding, and rubs his hands together, and greets her and asks after her health and what he can do for her, and she replies without even knowing what she's saying, and comes into the shop, and watches as he moves back behind his counter and stands there, smiling at her expectantly, and she should ask him for the wages, for cheese and bread and maybe a pie, but instead she's marooned in the middle of the polished floor, not quite knowing what to do with herself.

He's a liar, though. Bet he is.

Billy couldn't know what it would mean, not the adult bedroom things that it would mean, that one night she would let him stay. But really, might she have done that, if it would have meant she didn't have to face the years ahead alone? What exactly is she capable of?

Mr Cheeseman is speaking.

'Sorry?'

'That boy of yours,' he says, and shakes his head in admiration. 'Legs on him like pistons, that boy has.'

She nods. Her head is full of twisting tangled threads, of postcards drifting across a bright blue sea, of a row of steady, solid suitors parading past for her to choose from; of Sully lying between her cold sheets, his pale freckled arms reaching out for her.

longing to see you, and the child

Her palm still stings. She hit Billy. She feels a jolt of shame: she never hits him; she never has to. Billy bounds through her days, bringing a cloud of cool outdoors; his skin is barley sugar and fog and soap.

'You must be very proud of him,' Mr Cheeseman says.

'I am,' she says. 'I'm very proud.'

'He'll go far, that lad, you mark my words.'

She smiles carefully at him. Edwin Cheeseman, who had been in love with her all those years ago. She wonders if he still is, a little bit. 'Thank you.'

'A great consolation to you, he must be.'

He nods complacently, rubs his fat hands together again. Maybe he thinks she regrets it, choosing William over him. Maybe he thinks, given a second chance, she'd do differently. But it is only

114

William, always William. That's what she should remember. It's the words he sent that matter, not the man who brings them.

She has been such a fool.

'So,' he says. 'What can I get for you?'

She glances round at the shelves, the jars and tins and packets. She realises that there is nothing here that she wants at all.

Back home, she drops the packet of tea onto the hall stand while she sheds her coat and hat. She had to get something, couldn't ask for Billy's wages of course, and an ounce of tea was all she could bring herself to ask for on tick. She will settle up as soon as Billy's paid. She sweeps her hands down her skirts, takes a big breath, and opens the door into the kitchen.

Sully is sitting at the table. He looks up expectantly, smiles. Shows his long yellow teeth.

'Everything all right?' he asks.

'Fine, yes, thank you.'

She sets the tea packet down on the table, goes over to the range and opens the burner, grabs the old singed pan-holder to shove the kettle onto the flame.

'Difficult age, that,' Sully says.

She flushes, not just from the heat. Was he listening? What did he hear?

'He's a good boy.' She folds the pan-holder, then folds it again, then unfolds it.

'A credit to you.'

'Thank you.'

'It can't have been easy.'

He means, bringing him up all by herself, without a man around. He is working his way up to something, she senses, towards some kind of statement or question or confession. She looks down at her hands, the snags and cracks from washing, cooking, cleaning. And her clerical work has left her fingers faintly crooked, flattened at the tips, from the hours spent every day hitting the heavy stenograph keys.

'There's his grandpa,' she says.

'The old man. Yes.' Sully flicks out the newspaper and folds it, then lays it down on the table, and smiles again, as though settling in for a good long chinwag, but Amelia just can't bear to look at him now – his strange bony face, his ragged ear, sitting where William could so easily have been. She turns away to the range, and ducks down to open the firebox. She pokes at the coals unnecessarily.

'And there's plenty of boys growing up without their fathers,' she says.

'But what a shame, though, don't you think?'

'Billy's father's dead,' she says briskly.

The kettle begins to hiss. She closes the fire door, straightens up.

'Still, it's not easy on you,' he says lightly. 'Shall I have a word?'

He shifts his chair away from the table to get up.

'No.'

The word comes out too quick, too sharp. It shocks her, how afraid she is. She turns away to the cupboard, to fetch the teapot.

'What did you do, Mr Sully?' she says, her back to him. 'After the *Goliath* sank?'

'Please, do call me George.'

'George. What did you do?

'Like I said, the *Cornwallis* picked me up—'

'No,' she says, 'I mean, after the war?'

She stands, hand on the open cupboard door, looking up at her scant array of crockery. She hears him creak forwards in his seat, leaning his elbows on the table. A pause. The kettle's hiss narrows to a whistle. She thinks, he will have known that this would come eventually. He will have prepared for it. Once the shock has passed, *Why now?* is, after all, the obvious question, if you think to question anything at all.

'I stayed in the navy, until the year nineteen. Then I went into the merchant fleet.'

'And you were at sea, all that time.'

'Africa, the East Indies, all over really.'

And you never passed a postbox, not once, in all those years, she wants to ask. Not once in ten whole years?

She reaches down the brown teapot. She is such a fool.

'This is your first time back in England then,' she says.

'Yes,' he says. 'No. I mean, a few days' shore leave, of course, yes. Sometimes Liverpool or

Bristol. But no time for anything, not really. Hardly been in London at all.'

She sets the teapot down on its trivet, on the table in front of him.

'So you've left the merchant fleet now, have you?'

The kettle's whistle builds into a scream behind her. She looks at the angular face, the white-rimmed stub of his ragged ear. She sees the calculation in his eyes. And she knows, with perfect clarity, that she has to get rid of him.

He nods. A pause.

'I tried to write,' he says. 'But—'

'There wasn't really time,' she says.

'No.'

'And it's not easy, to write that kind of letter.'

'Yes.'

'Even though you had years and years and years.'

The kettle rattles, shrills.

'Tea,' she says brightly, and turns to lift the kettle from the heat. He tucks his chair back in under the table. Sets the newspaper to one side. And when she brings over the heavy teapot, he smiles up at her – a quick, narrow little smile.

Billy sits on his bed and listens. He can't hear the words, but he can tell that the patterns of their conversation have changed. A series of dodging runs from him, like a striker dribbling a football up a pitch; and slight, brief comments from her, landing like a dropped cloth; soft, dampening things down. He listens till they come out into the hall. A lot earlier than before: his grandpa isn't even back yet. And they don't linger. She says a brief goodnight, and the One-Eared Man returns the farewell more fully, but indistinctly. And then he leaves.

His ma's footsteps come up the stairs. His bedroom door opens and she stands there, in the dim light from the streetlamp outside his window. She draws the curtains.

'D'you want some cocoa?' she asks.

Billy gets to his feet and wraps his arms around her waist and she squeezes him close.

The next time they see the One-Eared Man is on Sunday and he is heading down the far side of the street towards their house, carrying his suitcase, his collar up and his hat pulled low. So he hasn't given up yet, Billy thinks – but then it is a savagely cold day, he'd be tempted to try his luck again just to get out of this wind. Billy digs his chin down into his muffler, links his arm in through his mother's arm. He tries to drag her along past the One-Eared Man before they notice each other. But he feels her flinch: she's seen him. And then the One-Eared Man raises his free hand and crosses the road to them.

'It's arctic, isn't it?' he says.

Billy's ma murmurs something in agreement. The One-Eared Man says something more about the weather, but nobody is really listening, not even himself. He hasn't got any gloves on, Billy notices.

His knuckles, standing proud as he grips the suitcase, are white against the livid pink skin. For a moment no-one speaks, and Billy tugs discreetly at his ma's arm, thinking he should just get her to scarper before someone says something, and the other says something else, and before you know it the two of them will have slipped back into being all warm and cosy together.

'I shouldn't keep you standing in this cold,' Billy's ma says, eventually.

Billy looks up at her. Her face is pale and tight.

'Oh,' the One-Eared Man says. 'Are you off out?'

He glances up the street, the grey sky low overhead, the wind blustering. Of course they are, Billy thinks; that's why they were walking down the street. He feels ever so slightly sorry for him. But mostly he feels pleased.

His ma says, 'We'd best be getting on.'

The One-Eared Man stands there. Billy looks down at his ratty trouser cuffs, his broken shoes. He does try really hard not to smile.

'I'll call by later then,' the One-Eared Man says.

Billy's mother takes in a sharp little breath. 'I'm afraid we won't—'

Her arm squeezes tighter against Billy's arm. He squeezes back.

'That won't be convenient,' she says.

Her voice sounds odd. She tucks Billy in closer to her, and he lets himself be held tight against her side, his cheek on the thin roughness of her coat.

'Right-o then,' the One-Eared Man says.

Billy looks up from where he stands, leaning into his mother's protecting flank. The One-Eared Man is looking up the street, nodding slightly, as if working out what to do next. Then he shifts his case from one hand to the other, and looks down at Billy.

'I see how it is,' he says.

He knows. He knows that Billy made this happen. That Billy cracked open the happy, cosy little cocoon that the One-Eared Man had spun around Billy's ma. That it is Billy's fault that he is out in the cold again.

Billy shivers.

'Good afternoon, then,' his mother says. She pulls away, drawing Billy with her.

But the One-Eared Man just holds Billy's gaze. 'Be seeing you, son.'

Billy blinks up at him. He hopes not. But if it happens, Billy thinks, he'll be ready for him.

Then the One-Eared Man turns, swinging his suitcase out in an arc, and walks away, his coat flapping in the bitter wind. Billy's ma looks down at him, and he gives her a smile. She smiles slightly back, but her face looks kind of puffy and swollen. Billy gets the sudden feeling that he has been luckier here than he realised: that this is a skin-of-the-teeth escape.

In the park, the trees are bare and it is cold. He and his ma march along the paths, huddling against each other, her arm around his shoulder, holding him close to share their warmth. He feels giddy with success and with the blustering wind – he wants to run and shout and clamber up the skeletal, clattering trees. But instead he walks with her, soberly: he is all she has. He will be her man now. He will always be her man.

And the One-Eared Man: he can't worry about that. He's gone. Over time, he'll disappear from their thoughts completely, Billy tells himself, like a bloodstain left in the scullery sink to soak.

They pass the pond, where a few ducks sit looking cold and miserable. They sit down in a shelter, huddling into a corner of the bench. Her arm round his shoulder, the smell of soap and powder off her skin, and the faint trace of cooking and the candleworks off her clothes.

Billy feels, at this moment, quite content.

Knox Road, Battersea, 18 April 1935

Billy sits up. The water heaves away, crashes into the sides and end of the bath. He reaches for the shaving bowl.

As he stirs the soap into bubbles with his brush, his privates move in the tepid water; his cock is half-hard from thinking of her, but he ignores it: the feeling will fade away if unattended to, and right now he can't afford to waste anything. He lifts his left knee and presses his foot against the cold metal. His toes fan out like a fin.

From ankle to mid-thigh he brushes curves and spirals, sucking on his back teeth as he paints, reaching round to the hanging ham of his calf muscle, and up into the underside of his knee. Where the water meets it, his skin is puffed and pink; above the water line, it's hard with goose-pimples. He reaches out over the chilly enamel edge of the bath, dripping soapy water, and sets his soap bowl down on the rush seat of a kitchen chair. He lifts his razor.

He loves the feel of it, its weight in his hand.

Closed, the cutting edge is kept safe inside the bone handle. Tease it open and the handle fits snug in the crook of his palm, the blade gripped neatly between his thumb and forefinger. There's a perfect unity of form and function here, the kind of beauty you get with a good bike. He angles the steel against his skin and scrapes away a drift of foam and hair.

He has to keep his attention on the ritual, the routine. He can't think too much ahead, can't let himself. If he lets himself stop to consider possibilities, rather than do what needs to be done, he'll get lost in speculation, and not be properly prepared. But things are good, he thinks. Things are definitely good.

He can hear his ma moving around next door, in the kitchen, putting his silk sweater out to air. He hears the creak as she sits down. Then there's the sound of a bottle being unstoppered, and the rustling as she unfolds the newspaper across her lap. She'll be rubbing down his shoes for him, the soft chamois almost as flexible as glove leather. She'll do a good job of it, he knows; she always does.

He inches the blade up over the ribbed skin of his knee. There's a big shiny scar there, and smaller ones, hard dots and pits, down the side of his leg. He'd misjudged a sprint trying to take a jump on Seaton last year. Gone flying off the cycle track onto the centre, lost traction on the cinders, and come down hard. Even in the fall he'd heard the crowd's massed intake of breath. And that transformed everything. He didn't care about the pain, the damage done. The crowd had gasped for him.

God, but the ache in his shoulders and neck as he'd cycled home on his own roadster: he could barely look up to see where he was going. The impact shunted everything sideways: upper arm, collar bone, spine. Tore at ligaments. Took the skin off his knee. He stank of liniment, and was black and blue and yellow all down the inside of his right leg where it'd whacked against the frame. But he didn't care. It didn't matter. What mattered were those breaths suddenly caught. For him.

He'd been in the game for four years then, building bikes for Butler's during the week, racing them at weekends and bank holidays, and that alone was enough to leave him dazed with gratitude and a sense of his good fortune. Perhaps the pay wasn't that wonderful, but then it hadn't really felt like work to him, so he didn't mind. But after he took a jump on Seaton, even though he failed, even though he wrecked himself for the rest of the season in the attempt, things changed. He already knew Mr Butler to nod to and say good morning, but that was the first time that, when Mr Butler had come through the workshop, he had stopped at Billy's bench to have a word. And when Billy had stammered out his idea about the new cranks, about how they could take out one of the bearings and lose a little weight and a little friction too, Mr Butler, Mr Claud Butler himself, had patted Billy on the shoulder and said that was smart thinking: a little thing like that could make all the difference in the world. Could be the difference between winning and losing. And when Mr Butler had gone on, and Billy had blinked up, flushed and proud, he'd caught Alfie's eye, and Alfie had grinned at him and raised his eyebrows. *Good for you*, he'd said.

The injury had put him off form for the tail end of that season, when he should have been at his peak. He'd trailed; he knew he had. But he didn't care. Butler's didn't care. Because.

Tomorrow. Good Friday. First meet of the season. Billy's chest tightens at the thought.

The first leg is bald as India rubber. He unsticks his foot from the end of the bath, lets the leg sink down, only registering now the remaining warmth in the water. He heaves up his right leg, crooking it against the end of the bath. He soaps up again, shaves again.

In other sculleries, in bathrooms and in front of kitchen fires, other men will be shaving their legs. In Hoxton, for example, Vittorio Cinelli will be slathering his shaved legs in olive oil: he swears by it. In Canning Town, Patrick Hooley will be in his sister's bath, nieces crowded at the door, listening in on the splashes and shifts of their famous uncle, the track cyclist, over all the way from Dublin for the Good Friday meet. These are the men Billy has to measure himself against. He got close to Cinelli last Whit, but that was before he crashed out and messed up his shoulder. He rode against them both in the final meet last year, when his neck was cricked and his elbow still weeping and the scab on his knee cracked open. He held on well in the Miss and Out, but not conspicuously well, not noticeably well. Didn't make himself a threat. If they remember him at all, it'll be as nothing to worry about. They'll be matching themselves against each other, not him.

So.

So.

So.

He mustn't jinx it.

But he *knows* it's different now. He's changed. In training he just loosens his jaw and drops his head and breathes himself through the pain, breathes into the rhythm of the bike, breathes himself into the beauty of its perfect union; bike and body; muscle and metal; the peel of the rubber on the track, the swell and squeeze of his chest; the perfect circle of the pedal's orbit, the contraction and release of the calf and thigh. The other lads fall back, drop away. Head low, elbows in tight, eyes wet with speed, he is not Billy Hastings any more. He is out beyond himself.

He's got the new bike tomorrow. Mr Butler said he should have it. So he must stand a chance, a good chance. Mr Butler must think that he will make the gear look good.

He can't let himself imagine what it will mean

if he does win tomorrow, what opportunities will begin to open out for him. Trials for the Olympic squad that summer. Then next year, Berlin. Berlin. But he mustn't start to think like that.

He dips the blade into the bath, moves it under-water and casts adrift clots of hair-speckled foam. The water is cool, grey with soap, filmed with his body's oils.

Berlin.

You're not supposed to blame the Germans. It was the Kaiser, that's who you're to blame. A mad bully.

And afterwards. Turn professional. Frank Southall got eighty pounds for appearing at that Coventry meet last year. *Eighty pounds.*

He rinses the razor for the final time and reaches out over the side of the bath, dripping water, leaving a trail of wet across the cold scullery tiles. He lays it down damp on the chair. When he rubs himself dry with the small stripy towel from the nail, he finds a stray hair curving back against the skin of his right ankle. He pinches it hard between his fingernail and thumb, and plucks it out.

He tucks the towel around his waist. 'Ma!'

The door knob turns almost instantly; she'd been listening out for him. She pushes against the door just enough to let a wedge of firelight and a gust of hot, fire-dried air into the scullery, making its cold blue seem even deeper. She reaches round; his warmed pyjamas are draped over her arm, his slippers hooked onto her long fingers. He takes them off her.

'All right, my lovely boy?' she asks, as he knew she would.

'Yes,' he says. 'Thanks, Ma.'

The hand falls away, the firelight giving a flash to the gold wire on her finger. He drops his slippers on the floor, shakes out his nightclothes.

Tomorrow is the start of everything.

He steps into his pyjama bottoms, treads his feet into his slippers, lifts each foot in turn to hook the leather up over the heel. The prize tomorrow, it's a clock. No cash prizes in the amateur game, but the clock's worth ten pounds, Mr Butler said. Mr Butler had had them stop work yesterday to tell them about it, standing there in the workshop in his dark suit and his coat thick and tan-coloured, looking sharp and every inch the success he is. Billy'd been finishing a wheel, smoothing the edges of the bamboo veneers. He'd had the dust from that in his nose, making his throat dry, and the smooth feel of the sanded bamboo in his hands, listening to the boss talking about the rose-and-cream marble clock. The sound of it had started to make him feel hungry, and he was thinking he'd ask his ma to make a custard or a shape that night, and he was thinking of taking that clock down to Leibmann's, the bell dingling as he went in, and the warm yellow light through the bow windows, and the smell of leather, dust and polish. Mr Leibmann would unwrap it, eye the clock through his pince-nez, and realise its quality and worth. And then he'd look up and eye Billy, and he'd realise he was someone to be reckoned with. He'd unlock the cash box, and count out ten pound notes, and put them in Billy's hand.

Ten flippin pounds.

But he can't let himself think like that.

He tugs his pyjama cord tight around his narrow waist. For supper, bread and jam or bread and scrape. It'll do; it'll fill his belly. He won't be hungry, but he needs more than this.

Lightheaded, Amelia steps up into the omnibus. It is warm inside, and dark and airless after the bright, blowy April morning. And the noise! Loud voices and the crush of bodies and the smell too, of mothballs and old sweat and damp. The lower deck is very full, but then it would be, with the cycling on. She peers from side to side as she moves up the aisle, looking for a seat. Spring hats and cigarettes, and a young man leaning out to talk to the fellow on the other side. He has his knee stuck out into the aisle, his hat pushed back, an elbow resting on his offending knee. He leans back slightly to let Amelia pass, but he doesn't break off, just ducks his head to look round her as she steps through his conversation. What if she just announced it, calm as you like, *I'm Billy Hastings' mother, I'm on my way to see him race.* They'd be up on their feet and shaking her hand and offering her their seats.

There's a space. She brightens, quickens her step – two together, in fact, an unexpected joy – her soft face tightens as she makes her way towards it.

She's reaching out for the backrest when the driver heaves the engine into gear, and the 'bus surges forwards. Amelia sways. Just a cup of black tea in her stomach since she got up, and it's swilling around now queasily. These mechanical buses are nothing like the old horse ones. The 'bus jolts again as the driver changes gear, and she staggers. Someone catches her elbow, steadying her. She stiffens, looks round.

The young woman is beautiful. Dark, waved hair. Her face chalky with powder, smoke streaming out through pillarbox-red lips, eyebrows plucked to nothing and drawn back on.

'Steady,' she says.

The accent, the looks – a Jewess, Amelia's certain of it. So many of them nowadays, in this part of town. She can't imagine where they're all coming from.

'Thank you,' Amelia says, detaching herself from the woman's grip.

'Watch how you go now,' says the woman, and gives Amelia a long, assessing look that travels up to her hat and down to her shoes. Amelia flushes, touches her hat back into place. The girl's own hat is very much the *dernier cri*. A neat, nape-skimming cloche, mulberry-coloured, with a natty duck-egg-blue flower. Which means the girl is a milliner or has a good friend who is one, because it might look like the Paris fashion but that's not where she got it. Not a girl like her.

'Thank you,' Amelia says again, and turns away, and slips into the empty seat.

Her cheeks burn hot and she feels almost tearful. She expects the girl to burst into laughter at her any minute. Which is not, she thinks with a burst of passion, fair. Amelia is well turned out, all things considered. Her hat may have done her seven years but cloches are still in, aren't they, even if the style of them has changed a bit? She tugs her fawn-coloured jersey skirt down over her knees. Fashion's got so little to do with style these days, anyway: all these long wet droopy lines like you've been left out in the rain. She folds her gloved hands on her lap, over her bag.

The men in the seat in front of her are talking about the cycling. She finds herself looking at a neck, a line of white skin above the collar. It is fuzzed with fine pale hair. It looks warm, and soft, like silk jersey left to air above the range.

She fixes her gaze out the window and away.

She wishes she had been kinder to William. She just hadn't known quite how.

The men continue to talk; the one in front of her gets out his cigarette case and lights up. She watches the vague impression of the Common through the dirty glass – the green openness, the regular dark swipe of a tree as they pass by.

Still, it is good to be out, and amongst people.

She can't get used to the emptiness of the house nowadays, the quiet when Billy's off training. She half expects to hear Grandpa's cough of an evening, through the thin bedroom wall. Sometimes she half thinks the quiet is just the old man's breath caught before a fit. The ache he's left, the absence, still lingers. This was an unforeseeable love, bringing unexpected grief.

The 'bus turns off the Common, and rounds the corner onto the High Street, and she feels the slow in momentum, the change in the engine's pitch. They are stopping. There are no noticeable rustlings of coats or searches for packages or farewells made: it looks like no-one is getting off. They'll all be heading to the cycle track at Herne Hill, like she is. The bus halts and the suspension sinks slightly, and Amelia's heart sinks with it. The new passenger lumbers up the aisle towards the only empty seat, beside Amelia.

A large, dark-clothed woman sinks onto the bench, giving out a huff, making the wood flex and creak and lift up ever so slightly beneath Amelia. The woman's breath smells of onions. Her body is too much for her half of the bench, making Amelia shift away and press up against the window. She settles a large shopping basket on her lap, squashes a brown paper package between her corseted stomach and the basket's keel, then leans right across Amelia's lap as she reaches down to arrange the rest of her boxes and packages at her feet. The woman's hat, directly in front of

Amelia's face, is an old toque, not at all becoming, her hair is a fluff of greying mouse, and her cheek is thread-veined and innocent of powder. The woman straightens up, then smiles at Amelia. Amelia is trapped.

'I hope I'm not crowding you,' the woman says. She has bright small eyes and a flustered smile.

Amelia graciously inclines her head.

'Busy morning,' the woman says.

Amelia smiles uncomfortably. Her gaze dips to the shopping basket. It is very full. There is a cake box from Patterson's, and a number of small but weighty packages of folded paper, stained here and there with patches of grease and blood. Meat. Beef, Amelia thinks, and her mouth floods. She squeezes her hands between her knees and turns away, but she can't turn away from the smell: bloody, rich, raw. There had been meat on Sunday, a piece of mutton cut up for a casserole, but she'd let Billy have the most of it, and had potatoes and a little gravy herself. The hunger is easier to bear when she is with him. There's satisfaction in watching him eat.

Her eyes stray back towards the basket, fixing on the spreading stain of blood on the brown paper.

The woman has her plump gloved hands on the basket's rim, steadying. She's looking straight ahead, rocking as the bus rocks, her mouth set in a benign upward curve. Her thigh and shoulder touch Amelia's shoulder and thigh. This woman has a man at home; that much is clear: you don't get fat like that, you don't get beefsteaks on a woman's pay. Amelia studies the side of her face, the curve of the flesh from neck to chin, the soft round cheeks, the faint down of fur on her upper lip. The plump sheen to her skin. Then she turns away. Her stomach clenches like a fist.

If he wins, they'll go straight from the cycle track to the pawn shop and from there to the butcher's. They'll buy the biggest, fattest, finest beefsteaks that they can find. She'll fry them up with some onions, and cut some bread, and butter it thick, and she'll make enough so that they're both full to bursting and not able to eat another thing, and still there'll be leftovers for tomorrow's lunch. And a box of cakes, cream cakes from Patterson's. They will eat in silence, smiling full-mouthed at each other, eyes dreamy at the taste of cream and jam. It'll be the start of things, of things getting better. When he's winning races, winning prizes, doing her proud, they will eat meat every day. Bacon for breakfast and maybe a lamb kidney now and then; ham in his bait box, fried liver with onions for their tea; she will make steak and kidney puddings, boil tongue and serve it cold and sliced with piccalilli. There won't be this endless stretching thin of things, the constant worry that even when she can appease his hunger she can't quite give him what he needs. Because he won't win, no matter how talented or hard working, if he isn't properly fed.

They just have to clear this first hurdle. Once he has started winning, he will keep on winning, and all good things will come. She will have a new suit in the longer line, and a new hat.

Mr Rudd wheels the bike; Billy rolls along in his thin-soled heelless cycling shoes. The cycle track hides in a pool of secret green, surrounded by lawns, trees, the gardens of houses standing with their backs turned, looking out into the streets. Spectators flow in through the entrance lane like ants through a crack.

He's very aware of Rudd, his weathered beaky face and bristling white tache, the bike ticking along beautifully under his hand. Mr Rudd's put himself between Billy and the new bike, and is keeping a determined profile. No chat.

He shouldn't let his coach's moods bother him. All that matters is the race.

Up in the stands, the crowds are a dark mass, already noisy with excitement. Ahead of them Cinelli and Hooley roll along beside their coaches, ahead of them in turn march a knot of track officials; at the very front, Mr Wilson carries the starting pistol and holds himself sergeant-major straight. They crunch across the cinder athletics track, then step up onto the crook of the pitched cycle track. There's a burst of applause. The light dazzles; the sky is bright and pale. He looks down, watches his feet swing out in his oiled and supple chamois shoes. He doesn't look up at the stands: she is out there, somewhere, in the crowds.

Cinelli and his party peel off to the left and head towards their mark. Billy watches the hard, angled muscles of the Italian's calves, the meat of his thighs. And then he notices the skin. It creases into folds, is soft over the muscle. Cinelli's getting old.

The sound bounces strangely in the shallow bowl of the track: Billy moves through a patch of quiet where the crowd is just a hum, and then back into the roaring noise. They reach their own mark. The official stands aside; Rudd clicks the bike into the gate, then moves away to let Billy swing himself over the crossbar. He watches as, ahead, Hooley rolls on to his starting point.

He can't do this.

Billy stands astride the bike to make his final checks. Rudd's breathing is loud and whistles through his teeth. He's tugging at Billy's toeclips, then moving round to check the gate, while Billy adjusts the fastenings on his mitts, flexes his hands.

Good.

He reaches up to touch the foam-filled leather strips of his crash-hat, runs a finger round inside his chinstrap. No distractions, no irritations; there must be no pain other than that of the cycling itself.

He doesn't want to do this.

He settles himself back onto the saddle. He

wraps his mitted hands around the handlebars and glances down to tuck his toes into the clips, and lets the gate take the balance of the bike. He stretches out his back, eases out his neck and shoulders. Then he leans forwards from the hips, angling himself down along the crossbar, his hips higher than his shoulders, only inches between his concave belly and the steel tube. He tucks himself in. His nose almost touches the handlebar. Billy breathes. Mineral oil, leather, wood varnish: the smell is wonderful. And this bike is beautiful, a perfect thing. He fits it. It is right.

He keeps heaving in the breaths, flooding his lungs and blood with oxygen. Behind him, Mr Rudd gets into the starting position, poised, alert.

Billy lifts his head.

Up ahead, Hooley is ready at the hundred and fifty mark. Mr Wilson makes his way across the pitch. Behind Billy, another hundred and fifty yards behind, Cinelli waits. He might be getting old, but he brings a weight of muscle, tactics, experience. The thought of the Italian creeping up behind him, ready to pounce, makes the hair stand on the back of Billy's neck.

So the answer is – his thoughts shift and slot into place – he has to think it differently: there's no-one behind him, there are just two men ahead. First Hooley, then Cinelli. Simple. Clear. Perfect. Two men ahead. Two men to catch. No-one creeping up behind.

And a hundred and fifty, three hundred yards – they're too far away to think about for now. So don't look beyond the next ten yards.

Wilson is almost at the centre of the pitch, and it's only moments off, the crack of the pistol shot and the heave into speed. Billy closes down. He blinkers himself. There is no periphery. There is no crowd. Just the man ahead, and the man ahead of him, the handlebars in his grip, the pedals under his feet. Soon there will be only the pull and press of tension between these points, and the breath heaving into his body and flooding out again. The breath. Concentrate on the breath.

'You all right, son?'

For a moment, Billy can't believe it. He dips his head down to glance back between his legs; Rudd is crouched down behind the back wheel, he can't quite see him: just a tuft of white hair.

'I got to tell you something,' Rudd says.

What is the old man playing at? 'What?'

'Mr Butler, what he said to me. Just. Thought it might help.'

He should know better. He *does* know better. 'What?'

'This is your year, Mr Butler said; "This is young Hastings' year."'

Billy squints harder at the pinkish blur. The dark smudges of his eyes. His voice is constricted by the odd angle of chin curled down to chest. 'He said that?'

The blur nods.

Billy lifts his head. Tries to resettle himself. Chin to handlebars, elbows at ninety, breathe. Breathe. Breathe. He tries to push all other thought aside: there is just the man ahead and the man ahead of him, and the press and heave of his bike and body, and the next ten yards, and then the ten yards after that. He can't think about what it will mean if he wins. Not about the Olympic trials coming up, or what it would be like to ride for Britain in Berlin, or about after that, about World Championships and turning professional, about racing for a living and having money come in in handfuls and your picture in the paper. He can't think what it would be like to wear a sleek grey double-breasted suit and glacé shoes, and have people recognise him in the street and come up to shake his hand, and all the while have her arm looped through his arm, feel the smoky warmth of her beside him, to know she's his. To have all this, and to have it by doing the thing you love most in the world. He can't think about it now. That comes afterwards, if it comes at all: what matters now is the race. You don't look beyond the next ten yards. Rudd taught him that.

So Rudd should bloody well know that. Does know that.

He hears Rudd suck the air in through his gappy teeth: Billy grits his own.

'I'm just saying, lad. Just so's you know. Mr Butler's got that kind of faith in you.'

This is deliberate. He's doing it on purpose, the bitter old sod.

Back at Butler's, Rudd's picture's on the office wall, clipped from a paper: he's standing by his bike, an old drop-handled fixed-wheel roadster. Must be turn of the century, maybe late 'nineties. A white crewneck sweater with the Manchester Wheelers crest on the front. A brilliant look in his eye and his nose a great streamlined beak. Mr Rudd, twenty-odd, amateur champion in his day. Been coaching Billy ever since he was taken on at Butler's.

'Thanks,' Billy says. *Bastard.*

The linesman's ready: he reaches his flag up into the air. He'll drop it when the gun goes, whisk it up again if there's a foul start. Mr Wilson stands poker straight and to attention. Rudd takes a tighter grip on the saddle, rises to a sprinter's start, as if nothing's out of the ordinary, as if he hadn't said a word.

Billy feels his heart now, the slow determined thud of it. He has trained for this. He is prepared. He knows the track better than any foreigner can ever hope to.

He will do his best. He will get through the next ten yards, and the ten yards after that. He'll catch the man in front, and the man in front of him.

Mr Wilson raises the starting pistol. The officials stand aside. Billy's pupils dilate. The crowd sounds blur into a pulsing roar like blood, or waves on shingle. His vision saturates with light, the sky is a wall of white fire, the figures ahead on the track are stark and clear. Everything is diamond-cut, beautiful. The air splits. The flag drops. For just a moment Billy is in the crazy accelerating fumble of the push-off, heavy on his pedals, Rudd hammering along behind him pushing at the saddle, a waft of pistol smoke in the air, and his legs straining with the work, and then the launch and freedom as Rudd lets go, and the air streams and the world collapses down to just his body. His bike. His breath. The men ahead of him. The next ten yards.

They've reached the far side of the track. The afternoon sun makes her squeeze her eyes narrow. She can just see out between the dark heads of the men in front of her. That foreign man thunders on, his legs bunched with muscle, powerful; and he's taken the inside track. Amelia's teeth pinch her lip. Billy's skimming along on a wider loop, halfway up the banking.

He looks ever so slight, ever so vulnerable.

He presses himself smaller, harder, forcing the bike faster, dropping it down from side to side as he pushes each pedal through its circuit. A heaving, hard progress. But he is fast. Very fast. She thinks he's gaining.

Down on the thick spring grass of the central pitch, the ginger fellow has already dropped out. He bends double, hands on knees, desperate for breath. Billy caught him in three laps.

The cyclists blur along towards her now, coming round the far curve, closer, closer, the stand roars, and the dark man's past, and then for a moment Billy's profiled, sweating, gaunt with effort – and away – she follows his back as he pulls away. He's climbing up the outer edge of the track, high up the banking, just below the crowd, tilted almost against gravity, at an odd angle to the world. She knows what's coming. The crowd knows what's coming. They've seen this tactic before. The noise begins to swell. The dark man passes again, and then Billy – muscles proud, shirt dark with sweat – and she stands up to watch his back as it speeds away from her, her mouth open, shouting for him, bouncing, willing him on. And others are on their feet in the stands, hollering – and she sees it; a kick-up of speed, like he's dug his heels into a horse – the crowd noise breaks like a wave and voices yell, bellow, cheer her son on.

Hastings. Hastings. Hastings.

She sees the foreigner notice. There's not a glance up or round or a wobble, nothing as obvious as that, but it's there: from the crowd's reaction he knows an attack is coming. And then Billy dives down across the track, hurtling like a demon, using the slope and height to – it's dangerous, he risks a crash, will he – and then the older man catches sight of him, and there's a noticeable break in his rhythm, a kind of flinch. And that's it, Amelia knows. That's the failure of nerve. He could power on, try and squeeze out a little more speed from

143

the bike, try to clear the spot Billy's aiming for before Billy makes it there, risk a crash. But he doesn't. He's afraid. He slows off a fraction. It's lost him the race.

For her, the moment is calm and clear and silent and beautiful, as though she is standing alone on an empty hillside. Billy's front wheel clears the foreigner's front wheel, and he's slipping in front of the older man, taking the inside track now, and heaving the bike on ahead, faster still if you can believe it. He's done it.

Then Amelia's heart explodes in fireworks. She yells out at the top of her lungs. Billy. Billy. Billy.

He's coming back round towards her and she blinks and a run of wet escapes down her cheeks. Her hand's over her mouth and she is crying. *Billy. My Billy.* She's laughing behind her pressing hands, and her gloves are blotched with tears.

One of the men in front of her glances round at her, and she wants to say, That's my boy, my son, my Billy, but she just laughs and cries and shakes her head.

The foreigner slows off, shifting his hands up to the top of his curved handlebars.

Billy is upright now, sitting back in his saddle. He touches his crash-hat, courteous, as he passes the foreigner, and the dark man nods back. Amelia can see Billy's stomach swelling and sucking like a frog's throat. And as he passes her, there's an expression on his face that she doesn't recognise, that she has never seen before. She can't know how he feels. She can't really ever know, because none of this belongs to her. Five thousand people roar and clap and stamp for her son. She can't know how it feels.

She sits down. She folds her arms across her stomach. The men in front of her sit down too. She hears her son's name from all around. Hastings. Billy Hastings. Billy Hastings. The world reels, unsteady. She folds her arms tighter across her stomach's hollow, to try and stop its groaning. She smiles to herself, exhausted, her face wet with tears.

If your father only knew.

Billy crunches to a halt on the cinder track, fifty yards past Mr Rudd. He swings off the bike. His legs are hardly there and his knees buckle and for a moment he thinks he's going to fall. His ears roar; he doesn't know if it's the crowd or his own blood. The bike holds him up. Everything hurts. The sky's too bright and there is so much noise. He tries to gather himself, think himself into his knees, his thighs; tries to keep upright. Rudd's coming over towards him already, with Billy's jacket slung over an arm, pulling his mouth into a congratulatory smile.

'Told you, didn't I? Your year, Billy-lad. Your year.'

Rudd holds his hand out for the bike. His palm is pink and dry and creased. For a moment Billy doesn't move. The bike is Billy's, like his legs are his, like his lungs are his. It is part of him.

145

Rudd gestures for the bike. Billy reluctantly lets its balance tip to him, then looks up into those rheumy eyes. Rudd holds his gaze a moment, just a moment, doing his best to pretend that he had spoken in all innocence earlier. Billy feels a strange kind of exalted grief; he has moved beyond Rudd, out and away. Rudd failed as a sportsman, and now he's failed as a man too. And he, Billy, well. It looks like he might just be a success.

Then Rudd glances down to Billy's jacket which he's holding, and offers it to him. Billy takes it, shrugs it on, turning away from the older man. The movement makes him feel dizzy. There's a great big sore swelling in his throat, even worse than his lungs.

From across the pitch, people approach them. Soon there will be a crowd and distraction from the brokenness of things. Rudd digs his nail fussily into the handlebar tape; it's not loose and doesn't need adjusting.

'Mr Butler will be over,' Rudd says.

Billy nods. The crowds are a blur of dark suits, pale faces.

He picks out Cinelli and Hooley, standing some distance apart. Hooley's just slouching there, with his coach, fists in his jacket pockets and scuffing the grass with a toe. Cinelli's handing his bike over to his man, frowning as he talks, gesturing down to the wheel, as though it's some fault with the bike that's lost him the race.

The breeze cools the sweat on Billy's skin. He

146

does up his jacket buttons. He moves away from Rudd, from the bike. He reaches up and unbuckles the strap of his crash-hat, lifts it off and his sleeves feel strange and stiff against his race-cooled skin.

Billy heads to Hooley first. When Hooley notices him approaching, there's a moment's uncomfortable, indecisive flicker before he pulls himself together. He comes to meet Billy, his hand extended. The Irishman's face is the colour of boiled ham. He blinks out through spectacles, smiles. Billy takes his hand. Hooley squeezes it, jolts it down hard, then lifts it up again. Billy gets an impression of strength and solidness and damp.

'Good man,' Hooley says, and lets go of Billy's hand, and turns away.

Cinelli's palm is paper-dry. His face is stark. His black eyes, the ridge of his nose, the blue shadow across his cheeks and chin. Ten years Billy's followed this man's races. Cheered him. He was a kid when Grandpa first brought him here to watch the great man race; Grandpa always used to say Cinelli was unbeatable. Billy feels a deep ache at the loss of the old man, who'd brought him to the races here, and who'd taken him down to Butler's and insisted on speaking to the foreman, who'd told Rudd to his face that he'd be a fool not to give the boy a trial. Who isn't here to see this day.

'Congratulations,' the Italian says.

'Thank you,' Billy manages.

Cinelli's going to turn away, but Billy says, 'We've met before.'

He turns back.

'You beat me, last year.'

'Oh?'

'You shook my hand then too.'

Cinelli presses his lips together, as if remembering. He nods, frowns. He doesn't want this conversation.

'Thank you,' Billy says.

Cinelli dips his head, then turns away, back to his man. They slip back into Italian.

Billy looks round for a race official. In the stands, the crowd noise has softened to a buzz. Someone will come for him soon, and they will give out the prizes. But for a moment he is alone. The air is wet. The breeze is cool. He can smell hyacinths from the nearby park. He feels like he's a kite, sailing through an empty sky.

Billy teases the last fibres of flesh out of the crook of a chop bone with his fork, marshals them into a heap with his knife. He feels glossy, sleek, though his legs are stiff and his lungs still raw. He crushes the mutton together against the tines, raises the fork to his mouth and slides the meat off between his teeth.

The canteen is open to the sky. Outside the track, trestle tables and benches are laid out on the grass, like for a fete. Alfie has finished eating, has started up the company song:

Oh we'll pump up our tyres till they bust
And we'll grind up our pedals till they're dust
For we are the boys from Butler's
The best of British bikes.

Charlie and Ted shovel down their fuel. They are all red and shiny just like Billy, all wiped down and brushed up and back in their Sunday suits. The races have continued, but for the boys from Butler's there have been no further wins.

They're being very nice about Billy's success. Still, Billy doesn't want to rub their noses in it.

The clock stands off towards the end of the table, a layered confection in rose-and-cream marble, with an elegant bronze figure poised on top. She's dressed in a slip, arms extended like a swan's wings, leg raised, toe pointed, caught in the middle of her callisthenics. The boys have been squinting up her skirt. Alfie has persuaded him to wind the clock up, see how it sounded. Imposing is how it sounds, even in the breezy April open air: a great considered mechanical tick that would fill the whole tiny house, if he were to keep it. He has no intention of keeping it.

Because this is just the beginning. Everything is possible now.

'What's next then?' Alfie shunts his plate away, leans his elbows on the table. 'For our bold champion?'

'I don't know,' Billy says. 'I don't know.'

He crushes a chunk of potato onto the fork with it, and raises it to his mouth. He chews. He does know, and Alfie's a dunce if he doesn't know too. The Olympic trials are in June. And after that, Berlin. Wheeling the light-framed bamboo-wheeled bike tick tick tick through the German parks and gardens and out towards the track. It will be good to beat the Germans on their home turf.

'Try for the Olympic squad?' Alfie asks.

'Ride for Britain? I'd love to.'

'Bet you will,' Alfie says. 'Bet you a quid.'

'You're on.'

Alfie shrugs, grins. 'That way we'll both be happy, eh?'

They shake hands. The others talk, a tangle of agreement, encouragement, because they are good lads, they are the best. Billy reaches out a fingertip, and runs it along the grain of the marble. It's cool to the touch. The moment shops are open again after the Easter weekend he'll be down to Leibmann's with the clock and get his ten pounds.

There's a thread of meat caught between his back teeth. His tongue pushes at it, and at the sharp broken edge of the tooth there, and Charlie is asking if he fancies heading to the Half Moon for a couple, and he's thinking maybe not, since Rudd will be there with the old boys, and then he's thinking, sod Rudd, and beginning a nod, and glancing up, and raising his hand, index finger crooked, to hook into the back of his mouth and claw at that stuck meat with a nail. And he sees her. Her face powder white, her lips pillarbox red, and her eyes shadowed dark and smoky. The sun making her squint. A cigarette between her lips and smoke spooling up into the blue.

She's twenty yards away, moving between the Humber crowd and the BSA lot. They notice her. One of the boys glances idly up, but then his gaze clicks into place and slides down the length of her to her ankles, then back up again to rest on the swell of her breasts. A nudge to the next man along.

Billy starts to his feet.

She's looking for him. She's short-sighted.

Alfie twists round in his seat to see what Billy's looking at. Charlie cranes his neck.

'What, what is it?' Charlie asks.

'Ruby,' Alfie says.

And there's something in the way he says it that Billy doesn't quite like. But Alfie's stirring sugar into his tea, one spoonful after another, as if he's intent only on that. And he doesn't look up, doesn't offer anything else by way of comment, so Billy just turns away, leaving him to it, swinging one heavy leg over the bench, and then the other, then skirting round the table to her.

She's coming towards him. The effect she's having. That figure-skimming suit.

His cheeks burn. He's out past the end of the table, and into the walkway between the trestles. She peers at him, uncertain, for just a second. Then she takes a few tottering steps towards him – her heels are sinking into the grass – and a slow smile spreads across her face, pushing her cheeks into powdered curves like breakfast rolls.

His smile wavers, tense, as she approaches. Quicker now, on her toes, a little skip to her step. He wishes they were entirely alone.

'Darling,' she says, and there's that slight tint to her voice that speaks of the fabric shop, the lush mountains of cloth, the jewel colours, the scent of foreign tobacco and her dad behind the counter with his yellow skin and greyed curls, looking up over the rim of his little brass-rimmed spectacles, his eyes creasing in welcome.

She comes right up to him. They're almost of a height. The length of her body is parallel to his. He's aware of himself, his body – its rawness, his skin filmed with oil and salt, mutton fat on his lips. He can smell her scent: something sweet but overlaid with smoke and warmth and body. If only they were alone.

She takes his naked hand in her gloved hand. The press of kid leather, and beneath it firm, plump flesh. Her eyes are dark as black coffee. Her breasts are just inches from his chest. Her hips just there. He could reach an arm around her and crush her to him, make her feel what she is doing to him. He glances round to see if the Humber lad is watching, to see if the men realise. That she is his, and nobody else's. That she is his.

When she's explained who she is, the race official nods Amelia through. She makes her way along a

152

path worn into the grass between trestles and canopies and through the abrupt and concrete talk of men. It's something like a summer fair, something like an army camp. A bike lies on its back, a young man in track gear giving the front wheel a spin, an older man in a worn brown jacket crouched, frowning at its turn. There's a smell of cooking that makes her stomach twist, and of mineral oil and chamois and wool and sweat, and through it all is the throbbing sound from beyond, from the crowds. She passes a lad perched on a camping stool; a man kneels on the ground in front of him, the lad's sinewy bare foot on his lap, the calf muscle like dough in his hands.

Then she spots Billy.

For a moment she doesn't see the collision that is just about to happen, doesn't even notice the woman walking along the same path as her, just a few yards ahead. Amelia thinks Billy has come looking for her, is stepping over the bench and striding down the grass path to come and find her. His face when he sees her – already here, shoved and pushed and excused herself through the crowds and come to meet him! What a picture. She grins so broadly that it hurts. She raises a hand in a jolly little wave. Her pace quickens over the worn grass path. But then something about his face makes her hesitate. And then she sees. He's not looking at her, he's looking at that woman. He is going to her. They reach each other, stand facing, close. Amelia can't see much of him any more: the woman, with her back to Amelia, obscures Billy almost entirely. But she does see the movement as their hands join. Amelia's heart rises in her chest. Oh.

And then the woman turns, and they both come towards her, now arm in arm. The kohl-rimmed stare. The pillarbox lips. The cigarette. The Jewess from the 'bus. And for a moment she's so appalled that she doesn't notice the man in the brown Homburg approaching her son. But then she does, and it makes her heart stand still.

Billy tugs at Ruby's hand. He'll take her somewhere quiet – the lounge bar at the Commercial Hotel. She'll have a port and lemon in the dim mirrored room and he'll have a pint and no-one will look at her, no-one will stare, because it will be a different kind of a thing, not just men and sweat and skin, but buttoned-up collars and upright seats and someone in an apron behind a bar who polishes glasses and keeps an eye on things.

'Come on,' he says.

She takes his arm; they turn to go. And then he sees his mother. She falters, stops. Stands unsteadily on the worn-out grass. Looking at him and Ruby.

And then, almost at the same moment, someone taps his arm.

'Billy Hastings?'

'Yes—'

'Billy Hastings as I live and breathe.'

The man reaches out to shake his hand, and, dazed but gratified, Billy lets his hand be shaken. Then his hand is released, and a race programme is thrust at him. Billy doesn't look round, he just takes it, then the stub of pencil offered. He watches as his mother turns and walks away.

'You don't mind?' the man says.

'Not at all.'

'Been following you a while now. Knew you'd make good.'

'Thanks.'

'Impressive turn of speed you've got there.'

'Thanks.'

He peers after his mother. He should be enjoying this, but instead it's all got complicated and difficult. He should have mentioned Ruby to her sooner. He should have explained. The man taps the top of the programme with a yellowed fingernail, dragging Billy's attention back.

'Who's it for?' Billy asks.

'George Sully.'

He looks up. Ten years compact like a squeezebox and he shrinks back to a child. Billy'd told himself that he'd be ready, but he isn't. Sully's lips pull back, he bares his teeth. You might call it a smile. Billy swallows, glances back to his ma. She's moving away across the grass.

Billy looks back to the One-Eared Man.

'What do you want?' Billy asks.

155

Sully raises his eyebrows in mock protest. 'That's not very welcoming.'

Sully's gaze shifts to Ruby. Slides over her body. Ruby's attention is elsewhere. She shifts on her sinking heels, pulls on Billy's arm, impatient to be gone.

'Who's this then?' Sully asks.

'Doll, can you just give me a minute?' Billy says.

Ruby loosens her arm from his, gives him a look. But what can he do? The One-Eared Man is really staring at her now, his face spreading into a slow, real, unpleasant grin. His side teeth are missing on the left.

'Billy's terrible like that,' he says, leaning in, hand extended. She gives him just half a glance, not interested. 'Never thinks to introduce you, does he? I'm—'

Billy can't have this, any of it. Has to cut this off, cut it clean away. He is not a child. He has just won his race: he will not be afraid.

'Look, that's my ma,' he says, taking hold of Ruby's arm, drawing her away. 'That lady there, in the suit.' He nods towards Amelia's retreating back. Fishing in his jacket pocket, he picks out a sixpence. 'She looks all done in. Can you go and get yourselves a cup of tea?'

She takes the coin, hesitates. 'You're not coming?'

She means the both of them. She means him and Sully and Ma and Ruby all sitting down together for tea and scones and lighthearted chit-chat.

'Just a bit of business to clear up,' Billy says.

She raises a perfect narrow eyebrow. Business? With this old scruff?

'Won't be a moment,' Billy smiles. 'I'll come and find you.'

Ruby's not used to being treated like this. He wants to say sorry, he wants to say forgive me, he wants to say just go and get my ma away from here. She gives an almost imperceptible shrug, and she turns and walks away, and the One-Eared Man watches her go. Her jacket reaches mid-thigh, her skirt reaches mid-calf. He watches her legs, in their sheer grey stockings. Billy bristles.

'Right.'

The One-Eared Man drags his attention back, grins at Billy.

'What do you want?' Billy asks.

'Little chat.' The One-Eared Man jerks his head towards the exit from the grounds, starts fishing in his pockets for cigarettes.

Billy walks with him in silence, towards the backs of the big houses, joining the lane that leads out onto the street. He'll want money, Billy thinks, noticing the fraying edge of the older man's cuff, the greasy sheen at the turn of his collar. He's wearing a pair of ancient dress shoes, patent leather. They're worn and scuffed and creased, and one of the creases has split and shows a strip of grey sock. He walks like they're too tight for him – a flinching kind of walk. Sully is not

157

prospering. But he doesn't owe him anything, Billy tells himself. Nothing at all.

They come out onto the street. Clipped privet hedges and sharp looking rose bushes – all sticks and thorns. It's far enough for Sully: he stops here, rolls onto the sides of his feet, easing the discomfort.

'So,' Billy says. 'What, then?'

Sully tilts his head. 'Been following you a while, Billy-boy. Been impressed with you, my son.'

Sully lights his cigarette. He offers one to Billy. Billy shakes his head.

'No, I suppose not,' Sully says. He flicks out his match, draws hard on his cigarette, lets the smoke ooze from the side of his mouth. 'Tend to shorten the wind, don't they?'

The first spectators are beginning to leave, emerging from the laneway between the houses. The meet is ending. Billy tries to keep his tone light, not wanting to make a scene.

'Why are you here?'

Sully raises a brow, as if shocked at the indelicacy of the question. 'I take an interest.'

'You're not welcome here.'

'It's a public place.' Sully leans in closer, drops his voice. 'And anyway: friend of the family, aren't I? Friend of your father's. And your ma's. She had a soft spot for me, you know.'

'You were spinning her a line.'

Sully inclines his head, drags on his cigarette again. He holds it between thumb and first and middle fingers, cupped in the shelter of his palm. The tobacco threads flare and crumble into ash. He looks down at the cigarette, turns it, considers it. And the spectators keep coming, straying out onto the empty street, ambling across to the far pavement, others slipping past the two of them, glancing round, spotting Billy, whispering.

That's Billy Hastings, that is. That's the chap who won . . .

'Your ma. She's had a sad life, hasn't she? Really, when you think of it?'

'You leave her out of it.'

'But you wouldn't want her upset now, would you?'

'Just try it.' Billy squares himself up.

Sully smiles unpleasantly, shakes his head, as if Billy is no threat to him at all.

'It wouldn't take much. Just a word or two,' Sully says.

'What?'

'Your dad. I know a thing or two. A few choice gems.'

'My father was a hero.' The words come out without the need for thought.

Sully's bottom lip draws itself up in the middle, making his chin crumple. A kind of sympathetic smirk. 'Course he was, son. Course he was.'

It prickles through him: those stories Sully told, that never quite came to anything. His father just wandering across the background, not quite there: was it because Sully had had to leave out

159

so much? Was it because the truth, the detailed truth, was not retellable to the widow and the son?

'I'm not your son,' Billy says.

'True.'

'Why would she believe anything you say? She adored him.'

Sully rubs at his chin. There's the dry sound of his gingery stubble.

'True, yes. But you can imagine, can't you,' Sully asks, 'the way that kind of thing would eat at you? Hearing something terrible. Would you want that for her, after everything she's been through?'

Then there's a pause, and Billy feels the weight of it, of all she's sacrificed for him.

'Why would you do that, after all this time?'

'Why d'you think I came back for her in the first place?'

'You were chancing your arm.'

Sully narrows his eyes. 'See, we'd go drinking together, me and your dad. We'd go chasing after tarts. No great surprise there, of course, everybody does that, given half a chance. And you know some are worse than others and maybe your dad wasn't that bad. But for a woman like her, a decent woman, hearing about that . . .' He shakes his head.

Something in this rings queasily true; after all, Billy knows now what it's like to be a man. It would be terrible for her to know, even if it changes nothing. His head tumbles with fury and frustration. His first win, and it's being taken from him.

160

Not just the joy of it, but the money too. Sully is going to take it, or he'll take his mother's peace of mind.

'And the thing is, what you've got to see is that I was going to do the decent thing, take care of her, bring up her brat; but him, your dad, he couldn't face up to it. He was a stinking bloody coward, your dad was.'

The anger is straightforward. It comes in a great liberating rush: Billy's fist collides with Sully's jaw; the older man didn't even see it coming. His head jerks back, his hat goes spinning, and he staggers, and then hits the green cushion of the privet hedge and sinks slowly into it.

Billy shakes the sting out of his knuckles. Passers-by stare, move away, leave Billy standing in an empty pool of pavement.

Whether it's true or not just doesn't matter. It only matters that she never hears.

'You come near my ma—' Billy says.

Sully smiles. 'You sure cycling's your sport, son?' A pale tongue darts out and licks the narrow lips. He pushes himself up, out of the hedge, brushes down his suit.

'I'll kill you. I mean it. If I see you again, I will kill you.'

'Just give us a few bob, eh? You can spare it.'

Billy ripples his fingers, clenches them again into a fist. 'You're not getting a penny.'

Sully holds a hand up. 'All right, son. All right.'

Sully tugs his cuffs down straight with excessive

161

care, then leans down stiffly and picks up his hat.

'Used to think your dad was a bit touched. The beautiful wife, the job, the kid, not wanting any of it.' Sully cups the crown of his hat in his hand. 'Turns out the poor bastard had a bit of sense after all.'

'Just clear off.'

Sully tips his hat onto his head. He tweaks the hat brim, and then turns away and shambles off down Burbage Road. From somewhere nearby a blackbird begins to sing. Billy thinks, he just knows how to play me. That's all it is. He just knows the tender spots and prods right at them. Well, I was ready for him, after all. I was ready for him this time.

Billy becomes conscious of the voices around him – the spectators moving past him, staring, getting in between him and Sully's retreating back, blocking the view of him.

That's that fellow, that's Hastings, that's him. Did you see him in the pursuit? Did you see the way he—?

Then, through a gap in the crowds, Sully turns, calls back over his shoulder:

'Keep an eye on that girl of yours, my son.'

Then he grins, revealing the black gap in the side of his mouth, where the teeth should be. He blows a soft admiring whistle.

'Girl like that, shouldn't take your eyes off her for a minute.'

Portsmouth Docks, 3 June 1944, 2 p.m.

There are three squads in front of him, Alfie to his right, and the rest of his squad following behind. The heavy bike ticks along at his side. And behind them there's everybody else. The whole of Britain, it seems, pushing forward to decant itself into the sea.

From way back a few of them are singing an old song:

Wash me in the water
That you wash your dirty daughter in

But it's just a couple of voices, and no-one else joins in. The song peters out and the sound is of boots thumping on the road. He looks down at his legs in their green serge, the way they're swinging him along, like he has nothing to do with it. Like he's a raindrop on a window, racing down the pane to disappear.

Then Alfie sings:

Oh we'll pump up our tyres till they bust
And we'll grind up our pedals till they're dust

Billy catches Alfie's eye, and Alfie flashes him

a grin, and Billy blinks, looks away, and Alfie
sings on:
For we are the boys from Butler's
The best of British bikes.
They swing round past the harbour buildings
and onto the quay. You can't see the sea any more.
The boats are packed so closely together that they
hide the water, and move with a loose unease
against the quay. Some of the vessels ride low,
weighted with tanks and half-tracks and artillery.
The infantry craft, the LCIs, are still empty, and
ride higher in the water, waiting for their freight
of men.

His hand sweats on the rubber grip. He shifts
it, takes the cool steel instead in his palm. His
boots are landing on boards now; between the
planks he gets glimpses of the surface of the water.
It's dark, glittering, lapping at the tarred wooden
pillars that hold up the jetty. The craft rises up in
front of him, sheer-sided, grey, with a gantry down
to the pier.

The head of the column turns and slows; the
men filter into single file, begin to clamber up
onto the gantry. Alfie slips in ahead of him, Barker
in behind. Billy's mouth is full of spit. He swallows it down. His palms sweat and itch.

He looks up, at the gulls wheeling and crying
above, bastard gulls, nasty dirty shitting gulls. He
shuffles forward.

He bumps the bike up and steps onto the slope.
The tilt shifts the weight of his pack and he's off

balance. His foot moves backwards to steady himself; his bike rolls back and the rear wheel knocks into the front wheel of Barker's bike and there's a stumble and Billy apologises and Barker says something matey and helpful. Billy grabs the handrail, because that's what he has to do. He climbs. The walkway judders with the men's footfalls. He bumps the bike down and onto the deck. Gulls stand in a row along the rail, moving their weight from one yellow leathery foot to the other, eyeballing him. He fumbles in a pocket for a cinema ticket, sweet wrapper, something – he picks out a fibrous yellow bus ticket and skims it across towards the birds. One flaps awkwardly into the air, scaring the next one along – the third staggers ungainly along the rail, squawking, flapping.

'Hate fucking gulls,' he explains sideways to Alfie.

'You should stop fucking them then.'

They cross the deck together, their wheels parallel.

Billy wants to ask him what he thinks of all this. He wonders if it's as sore for Alfie as it is for him to be faced with this: the salt in the wound.

'How d'you rate these things?' Billy juts his chin towards the bike.

Alfie tips his cycle slightly, gives it a considering squint. 'It looks like a bike.'

'Yeah.'

'I mean, two wheels and frame and forks and

even brakes.' Alfie squeezes one, making the back wheel judder on the deck.

'I can't get used to having brakes,' Billy says. He can see the sea now, stretching out beyond the harbour wall. It seems to slope up towards the sky, grey, humped, somehow animal. 'It just seems like overengineering. Clutter.'

The men in front are peeling off to stow their bikes, then they're disappearing through an open doorway, heading below. Stepping down into the dark. Billy's skin bristles with goosebumps. He takes a breath, blows it out again, steadying himself.

'Seems to me,' Alfie says, 'it's like so much nowadays. Like powdered egg. And saccharin instead of sugar. And Robinson's rhubarb cordial instead of blackcurrant, and margarine not butter on your toast, and flippin parsnips in your cake.'

'What are you on about?'

'I mean, it looks like a bike,' Alfie says, 'and it feels like a bike, and it even sounds like a bike. And I'm thinking it'll do its job okay, you know, work like a bike. But it isn't what a bike used to be. It doesn't smell like a bike, not like a real bike. Not like it should.'

Alfie's right. He'd not thought of it like that before, but Alfie's right.

Alfie ducks down, laps his tongue across the handlebar. 'Don't taste right either.'

Billy laughs. 'You're daft in the head, mate.'

'But it matters,' Alfie says, fixing him with a

serious look. 'You've got to notice these things. You've got to remember. You get used to the fakes and you forget what the real thing is, and you can't tell the difference, and if you can't tell the difference who's to say that they're not going to keep on dishing out the same fakery for ever and you'll just keep on swallowing it down?'

'You might be onto something there.'

'Damn right.'

Alfie slips in ahead to stow his bike; Billy hesitates, moves aside and rolls his over to the railing. He leans the bike and squats down beside it. He tweaks at the brake cables, and tugs at the pads: noisy bloody things, slow you right down if you get them out of alignment. He tries its weight again. It's a heavy bastard.

'Get that stowed, Hastings.'

He wants to oil it, rub it down with a rag, check every joint and cable and tooth and link. It has to get him past sniper fire and gun placements and enemy patrols. They have a map, but the place names are blanked out; he knows the route though, knows their first target: they are to secure a crossroads. It's sheer bloody madness, when you think about it: a bicycle against the Nazi war machine. But it's not about going head to head, of course. It's about the speed. It's about getting free of the lumbering columns of tanks and half-tracks, about getting deep into enemy territory. It's about being there and gone before the enemy have even noticed that you're on the way.

But he's not convinced. This bike is a saccharin-and-parsnip thing. His Claud Butler track bike, now that would get him where he's going in half the time. Though in fairness it might buckle under the weight of his pack.

He shifts the bike away from the rail, and wheels it to join the other bikes, strapped down for the crossing.

Below deck, the men fill the room like peas rattling into a jar. A navy boy, a midshipman, is yelling orders – one bunk to every three men; sleep in eight-hour shifts.

Billy eases his pack off, and for a moment it feels like he's going to rise straight into the air, like a barrage balloon that's slipped its moorings. But he's sweating already from being below decks; the ceiling is too low, the deck below too hollow, his skin creeps with the old fear. He steps up to the midshipman, a kid in his early twenties, peers at the clipboard.

'Someone else can have my turn, if that's all right by you.'

'What's that?' The boy is nervous, expecting grief.

'I'd prefer not to sleep in the bunk.'

'Is there a problem?'

'If you don't mind, I'll stay on deck.'

'The whole crossing? We're expecting something of a time of it. Weather forecast's bloody awful.'

'Even so.'

'You want tablets?' he asks, patting down his pockets. 'I've been issued tablets for you lot.'

'Not sickness. Just can't stand to be below.'

The midshipman's got enough on his plate without arguing the toss on this. 'Get along then. Stay out of the way though; don't get under our feet.'

Billy climbs back up into the daylight, slipping past the downward flow of men. However long it takes, however rough it gets, he'll stay above decks. He's done it before. When they were shipped out to Africa he'd slept in a lifeboat. Even then the old nightmare kept on coming back: swimming down through the dark water, the feel of the soft flesh of a dead man's arm. He would wake up staring at the tarpaulin above his head, shivering and bathed in sweat. When he'd joined up it hadn't occurred to him that being a soldier would mean being at sea.

Alfie deals the cards. Billy stretches his legs out in front of him, leans back against the rail, sets his helmet down on his knees. It lies there, with its ragging of camouflage, like something old and drowned, something overgrown with weed.

Two thirds of the troops are on deck; the other third are on their shift below, sleeping or trying to sleep. There are just so many men – talking, sweating, crowding, close, smelling of tobacco smoke and leather and gun oil. And there's still the tramp of boots along the quayside as the

169

massed landing craft fill up with infantry, and the deck beneath Billy's backside thrums with footfalls as the men move around and find places for the crossing, set up little camps for themselves.

Things are all right for the moment. Things are, in fact, quite nice, he thinks, blinking up at the sky, pale with a high thin film of cloud. So don't even think about what's coming.

Billy slides his cards towards him, lifts them, picks through. If this is the way his luck is going, he thinks, then fuck this for a game of soldiers. But he keeps his poker face.

Gossum unbuckles his helmet, sets it down on the deck. Billy unwraps a pack of Allied francs from their waterproof covering. The first stakes flutter into Gossum's helmet, which rocks gently on its back, like an upturned tortoise. The money is easy-come-easy-go, handed out to them in bundles earlier today. No-one even knows if the Frogs will take it.

'Same old same old,' Alfie says, eyeing his cards, tweaking out one and placing it in a more appealing position.

Billy shifts his service revolver out of the way, loosening the strap. 'What's that?'

'"Hurry up and wait".'

Billy lays down a card, takes another. 'Well, there's a lot of men to shift. A lot of stuff.'

He feels again that strange sense of dislocation that comes with being made corporal, that he's explaining and justifying stuff he's had no say in, doesn't agree with, that annoys him as much as everybody else.

Barker watches them, doing a good impression of hearing what's going on. He's got good at lipreading. Never been quite right since Egypt, since that artillery barrage in the desert, the flares lighting up the pyramids.

'I don't mind waiting,' says Alfie.

'Right,' Billy says.

'I quite like it, in fact.'

'Glad to hear it.'

'Much prefer it to getting shot at.'

Gossum grins. 'You're going to be a happy man then, my son.'

'Eh?'

Billy looks up. With his talent for logistics Gossum is wasted as a private soldier. He should be a quartermaster. He's always gossum chocolate, gossum cigarettes, gossum of anything you might want but can't lay your hands on. And he's always got a handle on what's going on.

'As the man says,' Gossum continues, 'there's going to be plenty of it. The marshalling, that's going to take a while: men, loading, getting out to sea, getting into convoy.'

Gossum is right. There are minesweepers to clear the routes through, then destroyers and battleships and monitors and cruisers and troop ships and then the little craft, LCTs and LCAs with tanks and artillery and LCIs like the one that he is on, the little ships tagging along behind like a

171

bunch of kid brothers. All of them trying to make their way through the same narrow channels of safe passage. And then gathering at the far end, where they will shuffle all the ships around and get into their groups, and each group head off to their stretch of coastline, their particular section of the beach. And everything will have to be held back to the speed of the slowest ships – a colossal, creeping fleet. There will be hours spent at sea, with the cold deeps beneath them.

'He's been to France before.' Alfie jerks his head to Billy.

The men look at him. Billy glares at Alfie. Did he really have to bring this up?

'Is that right?' Gossum asks.

'When was this, Dunkirk?'

'No. This was before the war.'

It was 'thirty-five, it was Paris. It was a meet at the Vélodrome d'Hiver. He'd won a medal, but it'd meant nothing at all, because that summer he'd failed to make the Olympic team. He'd got drunk on the way there, and got drunk again on the way back, and had slept a couple of hours on a bench on deck, and woke up shivering at the misty sight of the white cliffs, the journey almost over.

'We went through Dover, that time,' he says.

Alfie's watching him as they speak, watching to see what Billy says. Alfie wants him to talk about the old days. Billy looks right back at him. The innocent expression doesn't shift. He is generally unshiftable, Alfie is. Acting as though the world hadn't changed entirely and for ever on the day Billy had come out of his interview with Mr Butler, and walked right past Alfie's bench, and all the other lads, and had kept on going, out through the workshop and into the street, and away, leaving his coat, his tools, a half-finished wheel rim behind him. Because he couldn't stay, not on those terms; he couldn't live with it. But that same evening Alfie had been round the house with Billy's overcoat and the last season's track bike ('Gift of Mr Butler, with his respects') and the easy expectation of a welcome. They were friends: Alfie insisted on it wordlessly, made it habitual, kept it ticking along throughout Billy's changing jobs and new addresses. And when the war came, they'd joined up together. But what Billy doesn't know, always wonders, is whether Alfie is aware of Billy's blistering sense of shame.

'Dover's the shortest crossing,' Billy says. 'S'only a few hours.'

'So how long's this one?' Barker asks.

'Seventeen hours,' Billy says, glad to shift the conversation sideways. 'Maybe eighteen.'

They explode, outraged.

'Once we're under way,' Billy finishes, and the protest kicks up a gear.

'In this fucking tub?'

'Stone me.'

'We could swim it in less.'

'I've fucking *seen* France. Seventeen hours? Fuck's sake.'

'You in some kind of a hurry then?' Billy asks.

He doesn't even want to think about this. He wants to play cards. He peels off another couple of notes, drops them into the helmet. Because when you think about it, that's when it gets to you. Seventeen, eighteen hours of chugging out across the water, during which time all it would take is one lone U-boat, one single solitary patrol plane, or just a fucking kid in a lookout post with a telescope, and they're spotted. And if they're spotted then they're done for. All Jerry needs to be is reasonably alert, and the fleet is in serious trouble. They'll be picked off like geese on a pond. He can see it, in his mind's eye, the foundering ships, the oil burning on the waves.

They won't even make it to the other side, he thinks. Their feet won't touch dry land. He'll die like his father died; at sea, at war. Lungs full of filthy water and the sea on fire. But whatever happens, he won't let himself be trapped below.

'You that keen to get stuck in?' he asks.

A universal pause, shrug.

'He's got a point,' Barker admits.

Billy watches as their attention returns to the game. He watches the fluttering of the Allied franc notes.

The orders keep coming from a distance: the Mad Bastard yelling for them to get a move on, to shift along, to budge up, to make some bleedin

174

room. Gossum makes a show of shuffling around on his arse without moving any distance at all. Barker shoves at his pack, pushing it upright, tighter against the side, but then letting it slide back again. Alfie slides his backside forward, but then leans back on extended hands. No quarter given, no territory surrendered. Not an inch. Billy feels a perverse kind of pride: they are cussed sods.

'My lucky day,' he says, of his cards, and taps them into a neat block, lays them face down by his leg.

Gossum snorts, shucks a cigarette out of his pack, tucks it in under his moustache:

'Getting crowded here, init.'

He wraps the pack up again in its waterproof cover, then taps open his matchbox.

'And I'll tell you something for nothing,' Gossum adds. 'I'm not having some fucker sitting on my knee for seventeen hours.' He drags hard on his cigarette, making the paper blacken and peel back with a tiny rustling sound.

A gull flaps down to land on the gunwales nearby. It strolls along on its yellow feet looking them over with an assessing beady eye. All it needs is a swagger stick tucked under its wing.

'Fold,' Barker says, and drops his cards into the centre of their circle, making the helmet rock gently. He looks away. Billy follows his line of sight towards the prow, where the gunner and his mate are going over the gun with oil and rags. Getting it match fit.

Ten yards. Don't look beyond the next ten yards.

'Raise you,' Gossum says, and drops down another pair of crisp never-before-used notes.

Billy flips through his francs. He flings another three notes onto the pile.

'See you,' he says. 'Raise you ten.'

They play until Gossum has filled his helmet with cash and the rest of them are cleaned out. Gossum bends his head, tips the helmet on. The helmet stands proud by a good two inches. Paper notes hang out round his ears. He grins, shakes his head from side to side, like Dorothy's Scarecrow.

'Dimwit.'

Gossum tips the helmet off again, starts to dig out the cash and divide it into piles. Billy watches his practised hands as he sorts the notes.

'Where you going to stow all that?'

'I can't,' Gossum shrugs. 'Not got a bleedin spare inch to stick it. Unless you've brought some Vaseline?' He rolls up a pile of notes, makes an upward thrusting gesture.

Alfie snorts.

'Don't laugh,' Gossum says. 'It's a bloody tragedy. Bloody tragedy of war.' He hands a stack of notes back to each of the men. 'Play again?'

When Billy is cleaned out a second time, he leans his head back to rest against the gunwale. It's noisy, and that's good, because it will help him stay awake. He doesn't want to fall asleep, not if he can help it. If he sleeps, chances are he'll dream, and he doesn't want the men to see that. See him shivering and sweating and afraid.

The talk is onto France. He keeps his eyes shut so that they don't ask him about it again. They're telling their dads' stories of the last war's egg and chips in small-town cafés, pissy beer and rough French wine and brandy that'd strip your throat right out, and though their dads didn't talk about the women there must have been women even back then, women that their dads got their legs over in some room above the egg-and-chips cafés. And who got, likely-as-not, once-in-a-while, up the spout, so that by the end of the last war there must have been dozens of half-breed little bastards running around these small towns in northern France, and as that's more than twenty years ago now they'll be grown up and some of them are bound to have been girls, and you know how these mixes are always better looking, like mulattos, gorgeous, so the worry is, isn't it, when you get your leg over a sweet little French whore it could be she's not so French as all that and is in fact your half-sister.

Roars of horror and disgust.

Gossum announces over the noise that he doesn't give a monkey shit, half-sister or no half-sister. The first thing he's going to do, once they've slogged their way through the German lines, before brewing up or getting drunk or getting a good feed or working out what deals there are to

177

be done, he's going to get himself a fuck, because he's spent too many weeks around you stinking men, and what he really needs is a nice professional girl all smooth and powdered and smelling of French perfume not sour boots and farts and bad breath, a girl who's ready to do anything for a few Allied francs – of which he's going to have plenty once he's won this game like all the others, because they're such a bunch of useless gets – or she'll maybe even do it for nothing, given that he'll be liberating her from the Nazi curse shortly before he fucks her.

The men yell in protest, tell Gossum he's a pig.

Billy runs his tongue round his teeth, picking up the sour debris at the back, snagging on a sharp bit of a molar. Do you ever think, he wants to say, that this is really the same war as before? Because here they are again, all over again, fighting the same enemy, and with the same men in command. Mr Churchill loves a good invasion. Gallipoli was his big idea too.

Mr Churchill killed my dad, Billy wants to say. And most likely he'll do just the same for us too.

Billy blinks his eyes open and reaches into his helmet and lifts out the photograph from the inner band. He unwraps the waxed-paper covering. In the picture her skin is white with powder, her lips dark; she's smiling, lips slightly parted on pearly teeth, but her eyes look vague, unfocused, dreamy. Although it's probably because she won't wear her glasses, it looks like she's gazing out beyond the camera. Like her eyes are on the photographer, not on the lens. Ruby. Ruby. That gentleman in pinstripes and bowler hat, his gaze catching hers as he passed, and she'd returned the look – or at least it had seemed like it. He'd see her smiling at the barman's smile. The lads at Herne Hill, the way they'd stared. And she had known, and she had loved it, loved to be noticed – but she had loved him more. When they were courting, and he was still in the game, he'd get stopped in the street: people would want to shake his hand. And she would stand back, arm linked through his, half a step away, her beauty, for a moment, eclipsed by his fame. And she hadn't minded at all; she had smiled and nodded hello at whoever it was, and waited. Somehow it'd seemed fair. They were both wanted, in their different ways. It seemed to even out.

And then he remembers. The last night of his last leave. The blood swells in him. And he can't help it, he's grinning. He's fighting it but it's spreading across his face and he can't help it any more than he can help that he's stiffening. Remembering her in that small back room, her hand gripping his belt, her naughty smile, pulling him back towards the bed.

He lifts his helmet and turns it over so that it's domed on his lap. He blinks, rubs his face, still smiling.

'What's that great shit-eating grin for now, boss?'

Billy shakes his head, still smiling, trying hard

not to, and laughing now too, and shaking away the thoughts of Ruby for some other time, not now, for a moment of peace and solitude, though God only knows when that will come. And through a brief new alignment of gaps and spaces between backs and shoulders, packs and helmets, his sight catches on someone on the far side of the deck. He's thin, dark-haired, a boy of maybe twenty; he's chewing on the side of his finger, right by the fingernail. Really gnawing at it, tearing with his eye teeth at the flesh along the side of his nail.

'Thinking about his bird—' Gossum says, of Billy's far-off look.

'That's his wife you're talking about,' Alfie says.

'Still a bird.'

The boy tears a strip of skin off his finger, then glances at the finger, registering the cut, while he chews the slip of skin. His face is all bone and shadows. Then he looks up. He looks at Billy. He just gazes a moment, then the gaze clicks into focus, and he stares. Frowns. Peers at him.

Billy doesn't recognise him; he's pretty sure he's never seen him before. The narrow intensity of the stare makes him look away, and when he glances back, the sightline is cut off: a couple of squaddies come up to join their friends, standing between Billy and the staring man, and all Billy can now see is the green-grey of their uniforms.

He catches Alfie's eye. Alfie squints at him through tobacco smoke, his brow creased.

'You all right, Boss?' Alfie asks.

Billy flashes him a smile.

'Peachy,' Billy says. 'Just peachy.'

Wind blusters through the darkness, whips round the deck, whistles through the stowed bikes, snaps the tarp he's slung from the rail to keep off the worst of the weather. Rain clatters onto it, just above his ear. There's a steady drip somewhere nearby that's driving him quietly mad. It's supposed to be June. Billy rubs at his gritty eyes. The deck is hard beneath his groundsheet, and his pack makes an awkward, lumpy pillow. He's afraid that his shoulder – still vulnerable with the old cycling injury – will be completely buggered up by morning.

He knows what the weather means. There is no way that they are setting off any time soon. They need calm seas if the smaller landing craft are not to be swamped. And they need high tide to clear the beach obstacles at the other end. And they need that high tide to happen early in the morning, so that for most of the crossing they are under cover of darkness. These are the necessary conditions; all three of them have to be in place at the same time.

It will be at least twenty-four hours before the next chance to land. That's if the gales die down soon. Twenty-four more hours on ship, twenty-four hours in which the Germans might just happen to spot something, to notice what's going on.

His hip creaks against the deck. He rolls onto his back. The tarp droops low over his face. He closes his eyes. He remembers, from the train journey to and from Paris, ten years ago, the way the countryside had spun past his gaze. A wide green landscape, with woods and spinneys, clustered villages, church spires pushing up towards the sky. He thinks, there is all this to come, on the other side: a whole continent, dim with woodland, green with flashes of silver water, patched with cities. Utterly unknown. It seems somehow comforting, strangely welcoming, to think of this, these distances.

After a while, he sleeps.

Time ticks by. Two hours, two and a half, three. He wakes to cold grey light and the shrieking of the gulls.

Denham Crescent, Mitcham,
4 June 1944, 1.27 p.m.

Ruby unclips her handbag, digs its contents out onto the kitchen table. A crack as her compact lands – damn. She tips the bag, shakes it: a slide of bus and Tube tickets; the soft tumble of her handkerchief, then a scattering of grit and dust and fluff. No lipstick.

She opens the compact, squints into the mirror; at least it's not cracked – seven years' bad luck would just be the marzipan on this. Her one day off, her chance to do something a bit special, and she's lost her bloody lipstick. Yesterday was Saturday; early shift, tea and sawdust cake at a Lyons Corner House with Evelyn moaning about some man, then the flicks. Lipstick slicked on in the work lavs beforehand, reapplied after the tea and cake. Then she dropped it back in the bag: she can see herself doing it, clipping the bag shut. She hasn't used the lipstick since. And now it's gone. And it's that feeling again, that her life is just a conveyor belt of days, stuff just keeps on coming for her to deal with, and she has no control, not even over the tiniest of things.

Mrs walks in, clocks the mess on the table, gives her a look, then heads straight for the sink: Ruby watches her narrow, neat, disapproving back.

'Lost something?' Mrs asks over her shoulder, twisting open that little brass sprayer, which looks, to Ruby, more like a perfume bottle than anything else: it's like she goes out there every day to spray the bloody flowers with scent.

'Doesn't matter,' Ruby says, separating out the tickets, scooping the rest of the things into her bag.

'What was it?'

Mrs twists on the tap, watches the water pummel into the brass container. Ruby brushes the tickets together and herds them to the edge of the table, easing them over the brink into the cup of her hand.

'Lipstick,' Ruby says.

'Oh no, what a shame.'

Mrs turns round, but her gaze is on the flower-spray – she's fitting it together, dipping the pump mechanism into the barrel, twisting the cap back into place. She can't waste anything, can't Mrs. Not even half a moment doing one thing when she could be doing two. Ruby can see what she's thinking as clear as if it were scrolling in ticker-tape above her head: *Better off without all that paint, ruins your skin, and it's just to get the men's attention, what she's thinking, tarting herself up like that, with Billy away, asking for trouble.*

'Still,' Mrs says. 'Count your blessings.'

'Mmm,' Ruby says. Count your blessings. I'm not dead. Billy's not dead. I have a roof over my head.

Actually it helps.

She lets the tickets fall into the compost bucket – a subdued confetti of soft greens and blues, murky yellows and tired reds.

'You meeting that Evelyn?' Amelia asks.

'No, not today.'

'A concert would be a bit high class for her, I'd say. Bit cultured.'

This may well be true, but still it gets Ruby's back up. *No better than she should be, that Evelyn; be leading her astray.* But the kind of straying Evelyn does just doesn't appeal to Ruby. Fumbling in the park. Grass stains on your petticoat and your hair like a jackdaw's nest. Can't see the fun in it herself.

Ruby gives up on the lipstick, thumps up the stairs.

Standing at the bathroom sink, she turns her head from side to side, studying the angles of her bones. She presses her fingertips up under her jaw, touches the soft skin under her eyes. Her gold ring glints thinly. When she smiles, lines radiate from the corners of her eyes. Her hair is still good, its thick dark curls teased out into a glossy wave, but she needs a bit of colour nowadays, bit of lippy just to

185

perk her up. She looks worn and tired and thin. But then, who doesn't?

She opens her mascara pot, spits. She rubs at the blacking with the brush, opens her eyes wide to comb the blackness through her lashes. She bites at her lips, skims them over with Vaseline.

Count your blessings. She's got three. That's not so bad.

She gives herself a smile. Cause that helps too.

Bransbury Park, Portsmouth,
4 June 1944, 2.21 p.m.

It is good to be on solid ground, Billy thinks. It's a damn sight better than being on board. If they have to wait, then it's better done here, in the canteen, with boards and cement and brick and deep chalky earth beneath his feet, and the exceptional pleasure of a proper Sunday lunch in front of him, for all it seems to mark a retreat before they've even started.

Above the hum of voices and clink of crockery, the rain clatters on the corrugated roof and the wind buffets the prefab walls, sneaks in through gaps, whines. Outside the window, the lilacs toss their heads like ponies. It is bloody awful weather for June, unseasonable. You could take it as a sign, if you were the kind of person to go looking for signs.

Behind the serving hatch, the catering corps boys are clearing up after the first course. Billy pushes his last scrap of meat around the plate, scooping up the gravy. The sauce boat is old and cracked and beautiful, with a gold seam that catches the light and Billy half considers filching it to bring back for his ma. She likes nice things.

'Good stuff that.' Gossum jerks his head at the plate.

'Oh yes.'

The potatoes were warm and firm and waxy, the skin peeling away from them in transparent curls. Briny French beans and carrots from a bottle. Across the table, Barker blinks up at them, pushes his mouthful into his cheek: 'Never ate like this before I joined up.'

'Slap-up feed,' Gossum agrees.

Alfie nods. The skin moves over the cables of his thin wrist as he reaches out for the gravy boat. He pours the last thick clots onto his plate.

Billy never ate like this either, not when he was growing up. Since he joined up the food's been sufficient, but not as good as this. And now, through the cluttered noisy air comes a faint whiff of something sweet and sharp. Stewed fruit, he reckons.

'Will there be custard, d'y'think?' Barker asks.

'You never know.'

Custard, not so long ago, was made from fresh eggs and milk and vanilla pods. Now it's made from powdered milk, water, and custard powder. And Billy likes it. It doesn't mean that he's forgotten that there were ever fresh eggs and vanilla pods; it doesn't mean that he'll never want to have fresh eggs and vanilla pods again. It just means that right now, as far as he's concerned, powdered custard is fine. It's far superior, in fact, to no custard at all.

He looks at Alfie, and considers outlining his theory of custard, countering Alfie's earlier notion about saccharin and parsnips and rhubarb cordial. Alfie's crushing the last of the potato into his gravy, and then scraping it up to his mouth with the side of his fork, his jaw and throat working like a gannet's.

Because maybe, by the theory of custard, the bikes will be fine. You might even find you develop a taste for them. They will be, at least, better than no bikes at all.

He leans back, tilting the chair onto its hind legs and looks idly down the length of table behind him, watching for the arrival of pudding. All along the line of chairs, men mop their plates with folded bread, chew on chop bones, or lean in and talk. But then he notices, sitting on the table top, three-four seats down from him, an untouched plateful of food. There are little beads of white fat on the surface of the cold gravy. The potatoes are crumbling and greyed. Billy looks up from the plate, and sees the lad sitting there. It's the same young fellow he saw yesterday, on deck; the one who'd bit a strip of skin off his finger, who'd stared at Billy.

Billy watches as he shifts his cutlery, touches his cup. He doesn't eat or drink. His lips are working, but if he's talking he's not talking to anyone Billy can see.

He's in a bad way. Barely holding it together.

Billy turns back to his table, to his men, lands the front legs of his chair back on the ground. It's not Billy's problem. Let the lad's own corporal deal with it.

But Gossum's seen Billy looking; he's twisted round in his seat, noticed the full plate.

'Don't,' Billy says, just as Gossum leans over, taps the kid on the shoulder.

The kid swivels round. 'What?'

'Don't you want that?' Gossum asks.

The young man's jaw is clamped tight. A muscle twitches. He shakes his head, like he's shaking himself clear of cobwebs. 'What?'

''S good stuff that,' Gossum nods to the plate. 'Puts hairs on your teeth.'

'Leave him be,' Billy says, giving Gossum a warning look: you don't want to go poking around there.

'Word to the wise,' Gossum says to the stranger. 'Get it down you while you can.'

The frail men of the catering corps, with their limps and their thick glasses, their stoops, weak chests, flat feet and rickets, move between the tables, carrying bowls of something sweet.

'There's pudding coming now,' Billy says. 'We'll get a cup of tea after too, I reckon.'

Billy knows the importance of pudding. He knows the importance of a decent cup of tea. All too soon there will only be field rations and whatever you can filch, and tea and sugar in a tin all

190

together, and boiling up on a Tommy stove and
before long there will be bleeding gums and boils
and cracked skin and constipation or the runs. He
knows that what's coming will have its compen-
sations; that there is something about being shot
at that brings a new sharpness, a focus, a bright
precise awareness of being alive; of still, for this
one moment at least, being whole in your own
skin; and that's something you almost miss when
it is over. But there is plenty about what's coming
– the hunger, the fatigue, squatting in a ditch shitting black water – that is entirely without
redeeming features. So that when someone offers
you a decent meal, you eat it, every last scrap of
it, and then scrape the pattern off your plate.
Gossum knows it too. Gossum is, in all fairness,
trying to be kind. Considerably kinder than Billy,
since Billy would rather just leave it well alone.

'That's good lamb, that is,' Gossum insists.

The young man shunts the plate away.

Billy can feel the lad's gaze catch on him again.
He knows it's the same puzzled, frowning, I-can't-
quite-place-you stare. But he won't look round.

'That's good food going to waste,' Gossum says.

'It's none of your bloody business.'

Billy glares at Gossum, but Gossum's attention's
fixed. And Billy suddenly wonders: is this kid right
to turn his nose up here? The food is better, and
there's more of it, than usual – fresh meat, not
tinned; two kinds of veg, potatoes *and* bread.
They've really pushed the boat out here. This is,

191

he thinks, the condemned man's last meal. You have to feed a condemned man well: you have to feed him better than you feed the living. A bellyful of sacrificial lamb will keep him going all the way through death and out the other side. You can't have him running out of steam before that, or he'll drift back to haunt you.

Those of us who've eaten, Billy wonders, are we now obliged to die?

Despite himself, Billy glances round; the lad just stares, unblinking hazel eyes. Then his face breaks into a smile.

'It *is* you, isn't it?'

He stretches out a knuckly raw hand towards Billy, not to shake but as if to keep him there.

Billy blinks. 'Sorry?'

'Hastings? Billy Hastings?'

So it's this. He hasn't had this for a while.

'Yes. Billy Hastings! I thought it was you. I saw you yesterday. On the ship.'

Billy nods. He's conscious of his men, the way they're looking at him.

'I saw you ride at the Easter meet in 'thirty-five, Herne Hill, my dad took me,' the boy continues. 'Jesus Christ, you gave that wop a thorough hiding!'

'Thanks.' Billy wants to go. Anywhere. Be anywhere but here.

'Ha! You shook his hand. I remember that. I remember my dad saying, look, there's a sportsman for you. Shaking the ol' fella's hand.' He's glittery with it, raggedly excited.

'Thank you.'

'So what the hell you doing here?' He leans in, an elbow on the back of his chair.

'Well,' Billy says. 'There's this war on—'

'I know, I know, I know, but I mean, you were really something. You were—' He shakes his head, sucks his teeth. 'Brilliant.'

He starts on about other races now, races that Billy has half forgotten, and some that he has tried to forget. Races that came after the Olympic trials, when things had continued to go wrong, when maybe his heart just wasn't in it, or maybe it was broken. But the boy goes on and on. He elbows his neighbour and tries to bring him into the enthusiasm too, but then he has to explain who Billy Hastings is, and Billy nods to the blank, bemused newcomer, his skin crawling with embarrassment.

His own corner of the room has gone quiet. Billy knows Alfie, Gossum and Barker are exchanging glances, but he doesn't look at them. They don't know any of this. Apart from Alfie, who was there, and knew it all already, without being told.

'S'cuse me, Boss,' Gossum leans over to the stranger again. 'You eating that or not?'

Billy sinks out of the way, straightens the cutlery on his plate, glad of the interruption.

'Eh? What – no.'

'All right then.'

Gossum lifts the plate, spirits it across the gap between the tables and lands it down in front of himself. He flashes Billy a look: eyebrows up, a grin. He ducks down to eat.

At the table behind him, Billy can hear the boy go on, pointing him out to someone else, listing races.

They should be in France by now. They should be storming along the French lanes, racing off ahead of the shambling columns, finding their crossroads, clearing out snipers, setting up their positions. But instead here he is, feeling queasy, listening to an account of his cycling career and watching Gossum shovel down a second plate of Sunday lunch.

'S'cuse me, s'cuse me, Mr Hastings.'

Billy grits his teeth, turns back to him. There are sharp points of red on the boy's white cheeks now, like he's got a fever.

'I just wanted to tell you—'

'Yes?'

'You were great that day, back in 'thirty-five. You were really great.'

'Thanks,' Billy says.

'We used to say you were going to be someone.'

'Right.'

'Dad, God rest him, and my brothers – God rest them too—' The words start to gain momentum, stumble over themselves. Specks of spit fly out with them. 'Cause of course they're gone too now, John and Alan; just me and my mum now.'

'Sorry—'

He shakes his head like a bridling horse. 'Still! Billy Hastings here of all places. Who'd've thought it!' He sits back, eyes still fixed and wide. A big tight grin hurting his face. And at the sight of that, at his desperation to be distracted, all misery and shame just falls from Billy, and what he feels, more than anything, is sympathy.

'This your first time?' Billy asks.

The boy looks at him. Swallows. 'What?'

'Is this going to be the first time you see action?'

The lad brushes the question away, like it doesn't matter. 'Oh. Yes, but.' Shakes his head.

'It'll be okay,' Billy says. 'You'll be all right once it gets started.'

'I'm not scared.'

'Didn't say you were.'

'I'm not.'

'It's just the waiting,' Billy says. 'It's not easy, all this waiting.'

The young man hesitates, bites on the ragged skin beside a nail, where there are already snicks of bare red flesh. 'Still! Billy Hastings! Well I never.'

'Don't look beyond the next ten yards,' Billy says.

Alfie looks up, smiles.

''S what we used to say,' Billy says. 'Back in the day, when we were racing. Keep your focus tight. Don't look too far ahead. 'Cause it doesn't help to look too far ahead.'

The boy nods, blinks, as though determined to commit this to memory.

'Best advice *I* can give you,' Gossum speaks the

195

words over his shoulder, round a mouthful of meat and mangled beans. He swallows. 'Best advice you'll ever get for free: don't get between the enemy and the Yanks.'

But the boy just looks to Billy. 'So what happened? Why'd you stop?'

Billy can feel Alfie's watching him. He could make some excuse. Blame that shoulder injury. He could blame their poverty: he grew up small and hungry. He could make excuses for himself.

Billy lifts a shoulder: half a shrug. 'I wasn't good enough.'

Kensington, 4 June 1944, 3.00 p.m.

Ruby clips breathlessly along the pavement. The sky was blue when she clattered down the steps into the Tube; now it's covered by grey swollen clouds, which doesn't seem fair.

At Marlborough Gate, she pauses to listen to the fountains whisper in the Long Water, and just look at the green space opening out ahead of her. One gloved hand on the cool grainy stone gatepost, she hesitates like a diver on the brink. She can hear her own watch as it ticks on her wrist, and she knows it's late and the music will have started before she gets there, but she still lingers on the threshold; like the slow unwrap of chocolate, the soft gloss of it before you bite. Because moments like this are the best that you can hope for nowadays.

A truck thunders along the Bayswater Road at her back, and she flinches at the whoosh and grit as it passes. After that, it's quiet.

She steps down from the gateway, and into the gardens.

And it's lovely, the air just a shade cooler than her skin as she walks along the waterside, the sweet smell of roses and lilies. She leaves the pool and makes her way out across the open grass, through the trees. *Asking for trouble*, Mrs's voice nags in Ruby's head, *A woman on her own*. And there is something in that. But if she can go to work in the morning all by herself, in the pitch dark, winter and summer alike, what with double summer time, then she can cut across the grass on a Sunday afternoon, and save her poor old feet a few extra yards and the hardness of the path in these worn old shoes.

She's climbing the slope, following the narrow path alongside the allotments. The ground is dry; the dust kicks up onto the toes of her shoes. She stops and tugs off her gloves, brushes the shoes off gingerly, then rubs her hands together. Her feet throb inside the old slack leather. She could just slip her shoes off and run barefoot through the grass – it's not like she's got any stockings on anyway. And she's lifting a foot, reaching down to hook off her shoe, when something shifts just beside her, making her start. An old man steps out from between the bean rows. He's stooped over, like an umbrella handle, squirting away at his bean blossoms with a little brass sprayer just like Mrs does. He nods to her.

'Good evening,' she says, in her best voice.

Because these are the royal gardens, after all, and you'd get a better class of allotment holder here. She draws her jacket round her. She climbs up past the plots, shoes still on, still chafing her.

Past the Albert Memorial, she lights up a cigarette and catches the first notes of the music, cool, inviting: a gorgeous ripple of the violins up and up and then down. The bandstand appears from out between the trees like a gingerbread cottage, twisted candy-cane pillars and sugar-frosting paint. The thrill is the same as it was when, her hand squeezed tight inside her father's, they would climb the wide stone steps leading up into the concert hall. The swags and moulding and fairy-gold and tobacco smoke and crush of the lobby, and then the passages that lead up and up and the stairs that get narrower and steeper until they're so high that they are almost in the heavens, and you could almost touch the plaster cherubs. *In the gods*, her father would say, and it really felt like that, holy, and they'd thread their way towards their seats in almost darkness, the glowing space of the concert hall swelling giddily beneath them. You tiptoe, speak in whispers, don't touch anything, as if the spell could be broken as easily as a spider's web.

But it's all gone. Turned to dust, and the dust blown clean away. She's here now, alone, in the park, quite grown up, no-one here to hold her hand. And it wasn't meant to be like this. And for a moment, one of those fleeting moments that she allows herself, she feels like she's carrying the emptiness around with her like a bundle in her arms, where the child should be.

Behind the bandstand the trees are thick and full. Some of the deckchairs have been drawn into pairs, and people sit intimately islanded in pools of empty grass; others have been dragged into clusters under trees as, earlier, people sought relief from the heat of the day. The nearest seats, facing the bandstand and away from her, bulge with anonymous weight. She drops her cigarette, crushes it out with her toe, grinding it carefully into the dry soil. Squints at the faces that are turned her way.

Bold little madam, Mrs would say, if she knew.

But she won't say. Because she won't know.

Because there's nothing *to* know. She's not a fumbling in the park, grass stains on your petticoat kind of girl.

She turns to the right, moving round the outer edge of the seating. There are empty chairs here and there, their canvas rippling in the breeze. The first is in too much shadow, and looks chilly; the next is too close to a cosy-looking couple whose crossed knees are almost touching. A man notices her, tries to catch her eye; an odd-looking fellow in a ratty old brown suit. She's not seen him here before – she evades his look, keeps moving on, weaving through the chairs, the music coiling around her. Here and there are real solitary listeners, people here simply for the music: eyes shut like fairytale sleepers.

She's come back round the seats, back to almost where she'd started. Not a soul in uniform today. And then she thinks: is it happening? Has the second front been opened up? The idea is like cold water in her face. There've been rumours but there are always rumours, and she makes it a point of honour not to listen to them. Billy's last leave: there was a quarter bottle of whisky, a party, the mayfly life they have together. He'd been nice. She'd thought that at the time: he's being nice. Did he know something, or even just suspect?

And then she sees him. The handsome man. Her hand grasps the back of the nearest deckchair; one of two vacant seats together. She sinks down into its canvas sling.

That last night. Almost like things were in the early days. He'd been gentle with her. She'd thought, the war suits him. But maybe there was more to it than that.

The handsome man is about ten yards away, across the open grass. She straightens her skirt over her bare knees, looks up at the musicians.

Anyway.

In a minute she will let herself glance over, but right now it's best just to listen, and to be seen to be absorbed in the music, and let him look at her unhindered, if he wants to look. She's never seen him in uniform. She thinks maybe he was wounded at Dunkirk, and that he's something high up and hush-hush.

A hand grips the back of the other empty chair.

'May I?'

She nods permission without looking round. She gets a vague impression of bulk, brown suit, shabbiness. The old fellow. He sinks down in the chair next to hers. A pair of heavy legs cross themselves, and a big brown brogue, worn into holes, nudges into the space in front of her seat.

He's going to want to talk, she knows. They always want to talk.

The legs uncross, weathered hands come down to straighten the trouser creases, and then the legs recross in the other direction. Then the man leans forward. She keeps her eyes on the bandstand. He bounces a foot, hems. She presses her knees together, angles them away. Doesn't look at him.

The band is made up of very old and very young men, and women. A boy of maybe fourteen frowns at the violin tucked under his chin; a white-haired cellist plays with her eyes closed. The sound swells from the bandstand out into the park, flexible, transparent, vast and delicate.

Ruby lets out a long breath. It helps, just to be here, at the centre of this act of pointless beauty. Though the point is, of course, the beauty itself; the reassertion that beauty is a thing worth the effort of its making. Because it puts the dirt and dust and shabbiness at arm's length for a time; it holds them all together: musicians, listeners, passers-by; it connects them.

Shuffling and creaking, throat clearing from the seat next to hers. She keeps her gaze fixed on the cellist: how lost to everything she looks. And Ruby's just losing herself in the music again too, when the man heaves himself into her line of sight.

'G'd afternoon,' he says.

She gives him one of her looks. A nod and a tight smile. Then she turns her attention back to the bandstand. He just sits there, leaning forward, studying her. His face is a blur in the corner of her eye. She gets the impression that he's smiling. Then, after a long while, he sinks back into his seat.

She eases herself round slightly, making a little more distance between them. Up on the bandstand the girl on the viola takes over; the instrument is gloomy, gorgeous. Without thinking, Ruby clips open her bag and cigarette case and tucks a ciggie in between her lips. Inevitably, there's a heave and creak from the seat next to her; her heart sinks. He looms round to offer her a light. The flame is transparent in the daylight. He's so quick, she thinks he must have just been waiting for his moment.

And there's no alternative, not really; even though Ruby knows, with all the experience of fifteen years or thereabouts of men thinking her beautiful, that nothing, not even a light, is ever given without expectation of something in return.

She leans down to the leathery cup of his hand and sucks up the flame. The smell of him. Old carpets, sweated mattresses, cheap rooms, drink. He watches her, closely; she can feel him studying her – his eyes running up the side of her cheek and over her hair and down her throat towards the top button of her blouse, which she wishes she'd done up now.

'Thank you,' she says.

He smiles. Stained teeth, side ones gone, and his face pulling itself into wrinkles. And then she notices. His left ear is just a twirl of sheared-off flesh, like fungus ripped off a tree.

It's not the worst she's seen, not by a long shot, so if he thinks he can play on her with that he's mistaken. There was a man who'd pass the shop, when she was little, who wore a painted tin mask. His forehead and the bridge of his nose were ordinary dull flesh, and his eyes where his own, but they looked out over rosy, shiny, painted cheeks, like the face of a clockwork toy. What it covered, that mask, she couldn't help but wonder. A great gaping hole, it'd have to be: the rubbery pink inner flesh that you wouldn't normally see. Her mother would drag her back from the window, scold her for staring. As a child, she couldn't understand that – isn't it better to look, to meet his eyes, to acknowledge the suffering, to sympathise with the damage done, rather than flinch and look away and pretend that there is nothing wrong, nothing worth noticing at all?

She glances over at the handsome man. He's watching the band, not her. Hat tipped forward on his head now. Smoking. There aren't many men left, nowadays. The rate they're getting through them, they'll soon be issuing coupons. You'd have to save up long and hard if you want a decent one. They'll have to lend them around, like party dresses and stepladders. Or just not bother at all. Like all those women left over from the last war, chumming up together and sharing flats and doing good works and some of them never had a man in their lives. Or like Mrs: still in mourning for someone she hasn't laid eyes on in thirty years. She's loving this war, though, with her garden and her volunteering at the WVS canteen and her important little office job. Happy as a sandboy she is, now. For all she's *tormented* with worry about Billy.

Ruby closes her eyes, draws deep on her cigarette. The old fellow is leaving her alone – so maybe a good long look was all he wanted. A bit of attention, bit of a leer.

She lets the music and the smoke wind all around her. Lets her deep-seated fatigue claim her. The air breathes cool on her face, and her eyes sting behind her eyelids. The cigarette hangs forgotten between her gloved fingertips, drips its ash onto the grass. Her closed eyes still register the stir of branches, the paleness of the sky, and she still feels the breeze on her skin. On the cusp of sleep, she steps into a certainty – she knows that she's been dreaming, everyone has – a collective, epic, confusing dream, in which hours and weeks and years seem to have passed, and the world changed irrevocably in blood and dust and broken stone and fire. When they wake, disoriented and blinking and desperate for a cup of tea, it will be to the sound of lost sons playing toss-ha'penny in the alley, and uncracked parlour walls, and a pat of yellow butter softening in the dish, and they'll be dazed by the normality of it all. Ruby will surface to find Billy sleek in the deckchair next to her. Summer suit and glacé shoes and the malty smell of success. A pink little boy sitting on his knee, plump in a turquoise jumper that Ruby's knitted out of smooth new wool.

The music closes sweetly like a box.

Her eyes feel wet. She blinks a little, runs her hands up her arms, fuddled. Her flesh is cool. The musicians are rifling through their sheet music. She can't quite clear her head of the images. Billy as he should have been. Their little boy.

But then the branches buck and toss. The leaves are dragged back, showing pale undersides. For a moment Ruby can't work out what's going on, then there's a clatter like a handful of gravel, and *Oh*, a woman exclaims, and the first drops hit Ruby's powdered skin, and then it's hammering down. The musicians stuff away their flapping scores; the audience scatters, clutching umbrellas, clamping hats to heads. Ruby dashes for the shelter of a tree, shaking out her headscarf. The rain crashes down through the leaves; already they hang limp and defeated from their scarlet stems. Drops thump right through her clothes to touch her skin like fingertips.

She flips the headscarf on, knots it under her chin. In an instant the rain has become a grey curtain, cutting her off from the world. What's her best way out of here? High Street Kensington: that would be her nearest Tube. If she runs for it, she'll get soaked before she gets halfway there. If she stays here, she'll get soaked anyway and still have to make it to the Tube. So, she'll run for it. She tucks her bag under her arm, wraps her jacket round herself in preparation. But then she hears something – a call, though she doesn't make out the words. She looks round and sees a man coming towards her, the odd fellow from earlier, hunched into the downpour, with no umbrella. He calls out something again. Hard to make out.

'What's that?'

He comes closer, ducking in under the ragged canopy of the tree. She rubs at her arms.

'I said, there you are. I thought, now that's a piece of luck.'

'Sorry? What?'

'It's you,' he says. 'And here we are.'

She wipes the rain off one cheek, then the other. 'I'm sorry, you're mistaken. I don't know you.'

'But I know you.' He taps the side of his head. 'Never forget a face.'

She looks at him in total blankness. Either he's lying, or he's got a screw loose, but either way it isn't good and she's not going to hang around to find out which. She gathers herself to duck out into the rain.

'Billy away?' he asks.

She turns back. 'What?'

'Off fighting is he, your Billy?'

'Of course he is.' So that's the connection. She's met him with Billy.

'Good man. Good chap. Off doing his bit.'

'Well, he's not a conchie if that's what you mean.'

'Oh no,' the man says. 'Always liked a scrap, did Billy.'

The way he says this, it's like there's some private joke. He smiles a leathery smile, tips his hat brim back, and just looks at her. There's a deep and bitter anger here. She's got no idea what it has got to do with her. She's scared. He leans in closer.

'He owes me.' His breath smells of decay.

She looks at him, really looks at him. His narrow angry eyes, his weather-ravaged skin. She just can't place him. She wishes she could. She keeps her voice steady.

'I'll certainly tell him you were asking after him. Mr—?'

'I did give him the chance. He could've made it up to me himself.'

A hand wraps itself around her wrist. Underneath the fear, she feels a kind of abstract outrage: this man is actually *touching* her. She pulls against his grip. It tightens.

'Whatever it is with Billy,' she says, 'it's got nothing to do with me.'

He jerks her close, twists her arm up behind her. 'So don't take it personal.'

She pushes at him with her free hand, but he's too strong; he crushes her arm up against her body, her back against the bole of the tree. The rain pounds down on them. The smell of him is terrible. His eyes, close up, are strangely pale and dry. This can't be happening.

'Just let me go,' she says. 'If you let me go now, I won't tell anyone—'

'No you see,' he says. 'That's the point, I want you to tell.'

He reaches down, pulls his coat open.

Never tell.

She remembers. What her mother said. *Whatever you do, don't tell him anything about the birth. He hears what it's really like, he'll never want to come near you again.* And so when the baby came, there was the pain, and the blood and mess, and then there was just the absence, where the baby should have been, and there were no words to fill it.

She pushes at him again, but it's useless. His body pins her against the trunk. He fumbles with his belt. The rain runs down her face, stings her eyes.

'I had a baby,' Ruby says.

The look on the nurse's face. Blood on the woman's hands and down her apron. She remembers the doctor still rumpled from his bed, rubbing his hands with a towel and frowning up between her legs.

Her head is fixed by his, pushed aside, her cheek pressed against his mottled cheek. Her mouth is by his good ear.

'He was blue,' Ruby says into the dark curl of his ear, the flakes of dead skin and bristling white hair. A droplet gathers on the tip of his earlobe, catching green from the trees. 'He was born blue. He never took a breath.'

Six years since the baby. It must have damaged her inside; they said it might. There's been nothing since.

He eases the pressure off. She blinks the wet from her eyes. For a moment she thinks he's going to let her go, that this has done what her mother promised it would do, but it's something else. It happens quicker than she can make sense of it. He stretches back an arm and then her head flings back, cracking into the wood. He hits her. The back of her head and her chin flare with pain. He presses hard against her again, pinning her into place. He hitches up her skirt, exposes bare legs – nothing but a pair of washed-thin French knickers between him and her. Hands on her thighs.

Her chest is a knot of fury: he's bigger and stronger than her, and so he can do this, and she can't stop him. She wants Billy here, now, to save her; it's his job to save her. She wants the baby, the boy who never breathed; she wants to be racing for shelter with her son. She wants her mother desperately. Nothing is as it should be. Nothing.

His cheek feels greasy with rain, stubbly against hers. His good ear is just there. A pendulous lobe of yellowish flesh, bristling hair, the glistening drop of water.

And then there's a shift and click, like finding the solution to a crossword clue. She sinks her teeth into his ear.

He roars. A great angry bellow and yanks away; but her teeth press through old skin and into rubbery cartilage. He shoves at her, but she just bites harder. It's thrilling. Disgusting, but thrilling. She's hanging, like some kind of bizarre circus act, from an old man's ear.

'Get off!' He paws at her. She's too close for him to get a decent swing. 'Get off.'

He tries to grab her throat, but she twists away, bites harder.

He scrabbles at her. 'Jesus Christ, get off me!'

Her teeth meet in the warm flesh. It's oddly satisfying.

'Fuck!'

He lunges away, stumbling, bent over, hand to the side of his head. He leaves his earlobe between her teeth, blood pooling behind her lips. The earlobe feels warm and faintly bristly on her tongue, like a strange fruit. She rips off a glove, spits the thing out into her hand. Blood spools from her mouth. She clamps her hand shut round the scrap of flesh and wipes the blood away with the back of her hand.

'Bitch!'

He hunches under the rain, hand cupped over his ear, blood dripping.

She wipes her mouth again with the heel of her hand. With her other hand she hooks off her shoes, one and then the other.

'Fucking bitch!' He looks smaller now.

'You didn't leave me with much choice,' she says.

'That was my fucking *ear*.'

He comes for her.

She darts away, runs. Barefoot through the long grass; it clings round her ankles and the earth feels cool and sound. She dodges under low branches, hair streaming, jacket flapping open. She has cleared fifty yards when she realises she can't hear any sound of him following. She glances back through the rain and tossing branches: she can just make him out – a dark shape, standing looking after her, hand clamped to the side of his head. Then he turns and walks away.

She turns too, and walks now through the pelting rain, out through the trees, putting as much distance between him and her as possible. She feels strangely alert, alive to the water hitting her skin, warming with her flesh, trickling down her. She can taste the freshness of the air, and feel the wet grass beneath her feet. Her headscarf is lost: her scalp tickles with raindrops. She slips her shoes back on, and her feet feel lovely, cool inside them. She fishes for her compact. The mauve lining of her bag darkens with raindrops. She peers into the small circular mirror; not as bad as might be expected: wet, makeup smudged, but fresh-cheeked and bright. She licks a corner of her handkerchief and rubs at her lips, wiping away the smear of blood, along with rain and streaked powder. She can still feel the give and crunch of flesh between her teeth. She rubs at her teeth with her handkerchief, wipes the inside of her lips, her tongue. The movement makes her more conscious of the thing still in her palm: she opens her hand and looks at the scrap of flesh nestling there. It is small, tacky with blood; it sticks to her skin. She's just going to shake it off like a slug, when:

'Oh hello there.'

Ruby looks round. Clamps her hand shut. Rain clatters off a big sturdy umbrella. The handsome man smiles. He looks comfortable and dry. He lifts the umbrella, tilts it. 'Can I offer you a lift?'

She clasps the handkerchief back onto her palm, bundles the earlobe up inside its folds, and drops the lot inside her bag.

'Thank you, yes,' she says. 'That would be divine.'

Portsmouth Docks, 4 June 1944, 5.47 p.m.

Alfie pisses over the side of the boat. The hot, musky hiss of it as it fountains out of the man and through the air and down into the water. Gossum is snoozing in the sun. The man seems to have an infinite capacity for sleep.

Billy blinks up at the clearing sky. A pale blue, but a blue you can believe in, scudding with clouds, making him narrow his eyes. He tries at the mental arithmetic of tides and daylight and crossing times, but he's too tired to make head or tail of it by now.

Barker's asleep too, his head nodding forward on his chest, and Alfie slides down beside Billy, buttoning up, then rubbing at his eyes. Of course sleep. Sleep is what you do. Once you have eaten and shat, then you do your best to sleep. Billy takes in a deep slow breath and closes his eyes. His thoughts swoop up to the threshold of sleep, and he dips out of consciousness. His head lolls. Dark corridors, water. And

214

then he blinks awake. Straightens, eases out the crick in his neck.

'What did you make of that fella?' Alfie speaks low, so as not to disturb the others' sleep.

'Mmm?'

'In the canteen? Your greatest admirer?'

Billy shrugs.

'Dull is it? A dreadful bore, being adored like that?'

There's a beat. Alfie's gazing up at the pale sky, hands folded on his chest, looking perfectly innocent.

'Don't take this the wrong way,' Alfie says. 'But do you think he was quite right in the head?'

Billy laughs softly.

'No, I'm serious. He seemed, you know, a bit off.'

'We're all a bit off.'

Alfie nods, 'Yeah.' There's silence, and then, 'He was right, though.'

Billy squints round at him. 'What?'

'You were something special.'

Billy rolls his head back round, eyes closed, the light making his eyelids scarlet. 'You weren't there, at the trials.'

'The Olympics weren't everything.'

They were. The trials showed him the truth: that he might be a sharp little cross-breed whippet, and do well against other whippets, but the university boys, they were a different species. Beautiful, glossy with health and generations of good feeding. He couldn't compete. And he couldn't live – at least, couldn't go on racing against the other whippets – with that knowledge.

'I ever tell you,' Billy says, 'my dad died at Gallipoli?'

'No.'

'That was one of Churchill's little adventures too. Fucking insane gamble, that was.'

Alfie looks sidelong at him. 'My dad died at home. Coughing up his lungs.' His face twists up.

'D'you ever think how it might have been, if it hadn't been for that war?' Billy asks. 'If all those men who died were alive instead? All the little brothers and sisters that never got born.'

'Place'd be getting crowded.'

'We'd have twice the army, though.'

'So would the Germans.' Alfie tilts his head. 'Course, your dad and mine, they might have just gone and died of something else.'

Billy considers the possible intersections between him, his dad, Churchill and death. Barker stirs, mutters. Billy and Alfie watch him for a moment.

'Even if you weren't going to race, you could have still stayed on at Butler's,' Alfie says.

'Oh, fuck off.'

'Well, you could have. You could still have done good work. Coaching, like old Rudd, or even design. You always had a way with that kind of thing. That whole one less ball bearing in the cranks thing: less weight, less friction. Made a difference.'

'Give over.' But for a moment Billy can smell the workshop: bamboo, rubber, solder. The low light through the windows, catching on the dust.

'Cut off your nose to spite your face.'

'It wasn't like that.'

'I stayed on.'

'I know that.'

'Building bikes. Working. Till all this kicked off – till we signed up.'

'Yes, but—'

'It was easier for me. That's what you think, isn't it? I was never going to be anybody anyway, so it was easier for me to just, you know. Fail.'

'Yeah. I had to work really hard at it.'

Alfie huffs a quiet laugh. They sit in silence a moment, the two of them aware of the bristling fleet around them, the breathing, sweating men.

Then Alfie says, 'You know Ruby?'

Billy rolls his head round to look at him. His broad brown face, the desert lines. 'My wife?'

Alfie nods.

Billy shifts on his backside, sitting up, stiff, uneasy. 'Yeah, I know her.'

'They have this thing, don't they?'

'They?'

'The Jews. They have this thing where they kill a lamb.'

Billy presses his eyes with thumb and forefinger. 'Not in Mitcham they don't.'

'But they do, don't they? The Yids. They kill a lamb, for the blood, to paint on their doors.'

Passover; that's what he's getting at. Not that Ruby does anything like that; she hasn't practised for years. His ma wouldn't stand for it anyway. He doesn't know, now he thinks of it, what Ruby believes, or if she believes anything. If she had a faith, and lost it. What with one thing and another. The disappointments. The baby. And everything.

'I don't think they do that any more. With actual blood,' Billy says.

'But they used to, didn't they? Slaughter a lamb.'

And serve it up with mint sauce and new potatoes. Is that where this is going?

'Lambs are always getting slaughtered,' Billy says. 'It's in the nature of lambs. They bring it on themselves, the little woolly bastards.'

'Yeah, but so that – what? So the people, they get left alone? The lamb dies so they don't have to?'

'I think it's the first-born sons they're protecting,' Billy says, struggling for details from Sunday school. 'I think that was the idea.'

'You're a first-born son,' Alfie says.

'First and only. Thanks to Winston.'

'Me too.'

The baby. He never saw the baby. Remembers Ruby's white and devastated face. Didn't know how even to begin to comfort her.

'So what I'm thinking is, we should do that.'

Billy blinks. 'What?'

'We should have a sacrifice.'

He leans forward. 'Kill a *lamb*?'

'Don't be daft.'

Billy sinks back.

'Where'd you think we'd get a lamb round here?' Alfie says. 'I was thinking, though, we could catch a gull, one of them big fuckers. Creep up on one from behind, Bob's your uncle. Burn it up on a Tommy stove.'

Alfie's expression is entirely serious.

'You're mad.'

'No, no, all we need is a couple of handfuls of sand for the stove, and a drop of petrol; burn it up nicely.'

'Seriously?'

'Yeah, why not? Them gulls, cocky wee shites. Got it coming. Snap its greasy neck.'

Billy leans back, laughs quietly.

'What?' Alfie asks. 'What's funny?'

'You are. You're mad. Mad as a brush.'

'Mad? Why? What's mad about that? Just want to even out the odds, get a little traction—'

Billy sputters, shakes his head.

'What?'

Then the air explodes. A hole ripped into the day. Billy flinches; Alfie ducks. The sleepers jerk awake. It was a gunshot. Billy's ears ring. There's no second shot.

Billy knows.

He heaves himself up and heads across the deck, pushing past the men who stumble to their feet and look around.

When he reaches the boy, the skin-chewer, the

greatest admirer, there's a smell of meat and scorching and hot metal and the tang of gunfire is bitter and strong. The boy slumps, his back against the rail. He is dazed: the noise, the shock, the pain. He's holding his left wrist with his right hand. There is a bullet hole through his left hand, between the base of his thumb and the rest of his palm. Billy sees the white of bone or cartilage; a cable of pink tendon. Either by good luck or design, he's done a decent enough job: he's missed the delicate bones, and, by the looks of it, the major blood vessels. He'll probably have some use of it again.

'Looks like your piano-playing days are over, son.' Billy is down on his knees in front of him. 'Hold it up high.'

Blood wells from the red of the hole and runs over the supporting hand, and drips onto the deck. The boy doesn't move, does nothing. Billy grabs the wrist of the undamaged hand, and drags it upward, bringing the broken hand with it. Blood drips down in front of the boy's white face. Someone else kneels in to help.

'Hold it there. Lifted. Above his heart.' He registers the stripes on the man's shoulder. 'Sir,' Billy adds.

The wounded man's helmet is lying by him; Billy reaches for it, fumbles inside for a field dressing. His jaw is tight. His eyes are unaccountably wet. It's just the unfairness of it all. It's this waiting. If it wasn't for this waiting. No wonder the kid lost his nerve. This is an accident of war, Billy thinks, as much as if the boy had been shot on the beach, as much as if he'd stepped on a mine. But that's not how it will be seen.

There are officers yelling, whistles blowing, footfalls thundering on the steel deck, making it vibrate beneath them. He speaks clearly, loud, so that people have to hear.

'Nasty accident, me old mucker, but we'll patch you up, don't you worry.'

The boy blinks, but doesn't answer. It must hurt like all hell. Billy tears the field dressing open with his teeth.

'Look out,' the lieutenant says. 'He's going.'

The boy slumps sideways into a faint. The two of them support him, lay him down on his side.

Billy speaks the words over his shoulder. To the lieutenant, the men gathering, to the other officers looking on.

'Accidental discharge of his weapon. Lucky no-one else was hurt.'

The lieutenant keeps the hand elevated above the slumped body. Billy wads the wound with lint. Between them they strap the hand back together.

Kensington Gardens, 4 June 1944, 6.15 p.m.

She's walking through the park, under an umbrella. She's conscious of her whole body as it moves – the brush of bare thigh against bare thigh, the cool weight of damp blouse against her collarbone, the press and release of skirt hem around her knees. Her body feels her own again, properly hers, for the first time in years.

The two of them walk on, down through the trees. He presses her arm, squeezing it with his. He smells of good leather and shaving soap. They wade through the long grass; it brushes Ruby's legs coldly, darkens his trouser cuffs. Her shoes are too wet to get any wetter now. He talks about the weather, about the importance of a decent umbrella, concerns for her comfort – normal things – and she chatters back, giddy with the evening, with a sense of freedom, with having effected her own escape. He offers her his coat, but she won't accept it – she's fine, really, she's fine. Anyway, she'd soak it through from the inside out.

The only thing she wants right now is the hush of a ladies' room, a mirror, water, towels.

She has her handbag clamped under an arm, and the thing is bundled inside it. She'll deal with it later. The rain is cleansing. They're heading for Kensington High Street. They reach a path, and turn to follow it. Water rolls down it in shallow terraces. She touches the tender spot on her jaw.

'What were you doing?' she asks him. 'When you found me?'

'Nothing much. Bit of a stroll.' The start of a smile. 'Might have been keeping half an eye out for you.'

'Oh.' She follows the course of a raindrop through the skin of the umbrella, watches it drop from the rim. A smile breaks across her face, and she covers it with a hand. She laughs.

'Is that funny?'

She shakes her head. 'It's just, the day I've had.'

'Really?'

'Mm-hmm. Terrible.'

'Sorry to hear that.'

'I lost my lipstick this morning.'

He pulls a sympathetic face.

'It's tragic. I'm serious. They're like hen's teeth nowadays.'

'I'm very sorry for your loss.'

'I'm bearing up, though. You can see I'm bearing up.'

'You are really quite inspiring.'

She smiles. She notices the sweet smell of wet earth. And she can hear the city sounds now – the sticky sound of wet tyres peeling down Kensington High Street, and from somewhere, God knows where, a whiff of coffee. And then, walking out between the trees, there is a couple under an umbrella, and another, hurrying along under their own private canopies, veiled by the rain. Her arm tucked under his, they emerge from the woods, like something from a fairy tale, and join the flow of people, like the raindrops racing down the umbrella and dripping to the streaming ground.

'So,' he says, 'maybe we could get a drink, or are you hungry? Fancy a bite?'

She just nods; if she tries to speak, she'll only laugh again.

It's just a neat little awning like a pram hood; underneath it, a glass door with a blackout panel fixed in place behind. No name or anything like that. The handsome man, whose name is Edmund Harrison, dips the umbrella to collapse it then shakes it out behind them, grinning at her.

'I love a good cloudburst, don't you?'

The rain falls like a bead curtain behind them. The glass door reflects it all: his clipping the umbrella into its band, tucking it underneath an arm. Everything is different. She has stepped through the looking glass – or, rather, that punch sent her flying, spinning through it, into a different world. She steps sideways to get a glimpse of her reflection, to check what state she's in. All she can see is a pale thin shape, herself, devoid of detail.

'Nice little place,' he says.

His reflection leans in towards him as he goes to open the door, then swings away as he pushes it open. He ushers her courteously, an arm just hovering behind her waist, not touching. And they're into a dim-lit entranceway, and then stairs descend, and she steps down into the hum of voices and the smell of seafood and cigarette smoke and drink, and a dim low room, all glossy surfaces and dark corners, like an underground pool.

It *is* nice. It's the kind of place she should be used to.

She must look a wreck. She reaches up to touch her hair; it's a tangled soaking mess.

'Half a tick—' he says.

He heads off towards the bar, into the bustle and hum. She looks around. The walls are teal blue, patched with the glow of table lamps. The table-tops are glossy in their pools of light; cut glass glints. And the people are lovely. Lovely clothes, lovely talk: high, clipped voices like at the flicks. This is how things should be: elegant, ordered; this is the difference money makes. An elderly white-coated waiter goes up to meet Mr Harrison. She watches as they talk. He's known here, and he knows how these things are done. A handshake, a gesture across the room, a nod – *satisfactory*, his expression says.

Mr Harrison comes back across the room towards her, smiling, at his ease, in the company of the waiter, looking as though pleasure is a business and must be taken seriously. The feeling is like a first gin and ginger-beer on an empty stomach. Giddy. Lovely. Making her smile foolishly. Which makes her chin hurt where the old man hit her.

'If I could just – wash my hands,' she says, and feels herself blushing like a girl, as though only she, and no-one else, ever uses the lavatory.

The ladies' room is an underground palace of white and green tiles. A bowl of pink roses and a pile of small, square-folded hand towels stand by the basin. She takes off her gloves, checking her reflection in the cool mirror. Smudges, smears, but nothing out of the ordinary for a soaking: her cheeks are rosy, her eyes bright. She lifts up her chin: there is already a faint blue bloom of a bruise, but it is mostly concealed underneath her jawline. There's a slight bulge on the back of her head too, which hurts when she explores it with her fingertips. She opens her handbag, gets out her comb.

Her movement causes a displacement of the air, a fall of petals. They land softly on the marble counter, like scraps of washed silk. The roses smell of childhood, of summers visiting relatives in Salzburg.

Inside the bag lies the bloodied, crumpled

handkerchief. She just looks at it a moment. Then she peels apart the folds. The thing inside is surprisingly small, about the size of an almond. The blood and flesh has congealed dark along the edge. Three wiry white hairs grow out of it. A wave of nausea, and a kind of delayed surprise at what she can do, if pushed to it.

Flush it?

But it's the ear she told her secrets to. She told it about the baby. The blue boy.

She bundles up the handkerchief, the cleanest fabric on the outside. She presses it into the bottom of her bag, scoops out her compact and mascara and sets them on the marble counter.

Another petal falls from the roses, lands noiselessly, cupping one inside the other. She dips one of the small hand towels into the hot water, and soaks it, and wrings it out. She washes her face, wiping away the final smears of mascara, the smudged and clotted powder. The city seems to stretch out from here, from the steaming basin, from the soft drop of rose petals, from the dark tangle of her curls. The rain falling over London, on the grey streets, dampening the nearby Kensington stucco, and further off streaking mustard-yellow brick and soaking the parched ground of parks and making the trees soften and breathe. Here and there are pockets of light, points of connection – Mrs sitting by the empty grate in Mitcham, the empty boarded socket where the old shop with their flat above had stood, the factory lying quiet and still, Billy out there somewhere in the dark countryside, wherever his camp is, listening to the rain hammering on the tin roof; and the old man walking on through the downpour, muttering curses, handkerchief pressed to his ear. The baby is out there too. They'll have buried him quietly in the hospital grounds, or in some municipal plot, in the company of other babies who were born but never breathed: a tiny throng of blue humanity, unknowable as angels.

She rinses out the wet hand towel. The room is still quiet and empty: no sound of anyone on the stairs, so she reaches down and lifts up her hem, and rubs the damp cloth over her thighs, scrubbing away at the ghost of the old man's hands. The soap smells good and expensive; she's not sure if the pawn-shop, brownish smell lingers on her, or just in her mind. She rinses out and wrings the cloth again, then drops it into the linen basket. She lets the water go; she watches as it spirals down the plughole, and away.

Outside, the rain falls on and on, cool and benign and drenching.

A place like this, she'd want a month to plan an outfit, an afternoon to get ready. But instead she presses powder to her nose, her chin, her forehead and cheekbones, and touches it across the sore patch underneath her chin. She clicks open her mascara, spits on the blacking, rubs the brush into it, runs it through her lashes. Her hair is drying into its ragged curls. She rubs Vaseline

228

between her hands and then runs her fingers through it, softening the curls out into waves. She combs it out and pins it up at the back.

She smears Vaseline onto her lips, and tries a smile.

Her wedding ring rolls slippery and loose round her finger. She eases it off to wipe away the Vaseline. She notices the empty space at the base of her left ring finger, where there is perhaps the slightest, faintest of indentations. The handsome man – Mr Harrison – has only seen her wearing gloves.

Billy owes her. Life owes her. Tonight is hers.

She picks up her glove, drops the ring inside, then rolls up the cuff. She tucks the glove into the inside pocket of her bag.

When the ancient waiter shows her to the table, it is empty; she slides along the banquette; the sleek coolness of the leather brushes the bare skin at the back of her knees. The waiter hands her a menu. The card is good quality, silky to the touch. She holds it out of the way as he polishes imaginary marks from the tabletop, then lays it down unread.

A smile keeps pushing at her cheeks, making them bunch up, making her eyes crinkle at the edges, making her chin hurt. He comes back towards her through the blue mist of cigarette smoke. An easy, comfortable stride. And his suit is so good. The fabric with that silky matte finish that shows that money has been spent. He looks like Robert Donat, she thinks. Robert Donat in *The Thirty-Nine Steps*. Poised, unrufflable, unsmudged.

He slides in beside her. 'Drink?'

She runs her fingers together casually. 'Please.'

'What'll you have?'

She doesn't know what to order, in a place like this. 'You choose.'

He orders, conferring with the waiter in hushed tones. Wine, and food too. The wine is a revelation: it makes the inside of her mouth expand. She's conscious of the line where her lips meet, the flesh of them tingling faintly.

He talks comfortably, used to being listened to.

The liquid sits above and below her tongue, behind her lips. She doesn't want to swallow it. Doesn't want it to be gone. Even though there's a glassful still in front of her, a gorgeous purply red. She watches his mouth as he talks – his lips are narrow but nicely shaped, the upper lip a seagull's wings – and she wants to kiss him. Just because the sensation needs sharing. A kiss that would tease at lips and tongue and feel the snag of teeth, a kiss to say *This is marvellous, have you noticed how marvellous this is?*

The waiter returns, carrying a broad silver platter, his upturned fingers like spreading branches. He slides the dish down onto the table.

'Your lobster.'

The coral beast lies on a bed of shredded green. A whole butterhead lettuce has been sacrificed to make its bed. There are nutcrackers, and two small dishes of glistening mayonnaise.

She smiles, just at the utter extreme incongruity of this. Food comes in tins and packets and small papery bundles. It's divided into careful portions – equal shares that once gone are gone. But a lobster, a whole lobster, to share? So very far from rationing, so very far from kosher, that it seems so incongruous that it seems almost a joke. Mayonnaise – what is that made with? Is that made with milk? She doesn't even know.

'Fantastic,' Ruby says.

She lifts a pair of nutcrackers. She has no idea where to start. She watches his tactics for a moment, then manages herself to dislocate a claw and crack it open on her plate. The flesh falls into strands between her tongue and the roof of her mouth, firm and sweet and melting and intensely savoury. She has missed so much, she realises. What else has she missed?

'So where's home?' he asks.

She swallows reluctantly.

'Hard to say, nowadays.'

He makes a sympathetic face. She lets him imagine the bomb damage, the flames, her beautiful imagined house in Kensington in ruins.

'You staying with friends?'

That works as an explanation. She nods. 'Little place,' she says. 'Out at Mitcham.'

231

Was that wrong? Does that mark her out? But he seems unconcerned.

'Drop you off there later, if you like.'

She looks up at him, leaving her fork wedged into the pink carapace. 'You have a car?'

'It's Ministry.'

The prospect is like sinking into velvet. A car ride home.

'But the petrol?'

He purses his lips, wafts her concerns away. 'Not even out of the way.'

She traces the route out from her house, beyond. 'So that's, what, you're heading south? Kent?'

His face buttons itself up. 'Maybe, maybe not.'

'Ah,' she says.

'Yes.'

'Walls have ears?'

'They certainly could.'

The engine throbs like a happy cat. Her head feels soft and fuzzy with wine. The leather seat creaks as she reaches out to touch the lustre of the walnut panelling. The windscreen wiper swooshes rhythmically. The rain is softer now; it seems almost not to fall any more, as if the air itself were saturated to stillness. She is torn between this new vision of the city at speed – spinning by white terraced townhouses, through the lush shadowy green of the park, shooting suddenly out across the river and under the grey wide sky, all veiled with rain – and the internal stillness of the car, the scents of oil and leather and the warm, well-dressed, breathing length of the man next to her. She'd like to ease off her shoes, but she daren't risk the smell.

South of the river, and he begins to need directions. The streets narrow and close in. She finds she doesn't know the way and is forced to guess. There are moments of clarity when they hit a patch around a Tube station, or cross a bus route, and are back within her frame of knowledge. Further south, and the streets begin to widen a little more, as they move into the newer houses built after the First War. Houses fit for heroes: what heroes need is a plumbed-in bath and a gas cooker and hotwater geyser and an outdoor lav and a handkerchief of back garden.

It hits her then. Not that Mrs will see him, though that would itself be irredeemably bad, but that he will see Mrs, her hair done up in rollers, and the pokey little front garden, and the path that's poured concrete, and the cheap brick house-front with its single bay and its two narrow upstairs windows, and the milk-bottle holder that Billy made, with the red enamel chipped at the base where it's hit the concrete path too many times.

They spin out across the Common, the road lined with dripping trees. The car is still a car, the handsome man still drives, the wet road still peels away underneath the wheels, but it is over.

'Can you—?' she says.

He glances across at her.

233

'Can you stop the car here?'

He pulls in. The car settles into silence; the windscreen wiper hangs still. The Common is deserted, wet, the light dim. Ruby watches the water land, bead, run down the slope of the windscreen.

'I want you to know, I don't normally do this kind of thing.'

'What kind of thing?'

'Get into cars, with strange men.'

'Am I strange?'

'You are to me.'

He shrugs. 'What's normal anyway, nowadays?'

'I wanted to say. I had a good time.'

'I'm glad.'

She is glad, too. Even though it is now over, things had been, for just a little while, how they should be.

She reaches out across the cool dim air between them. She puts her hand to his cheek, and turns the handsome man towards her, and kisses him.

She clicks the front door open, steps in, and just stands for a moment, on the threshold, listening up the dark stairs. Mrs has gone to bed, but it doesn't necessarily mean that she'll be sleeping. She could still be lying there, eyes wide open, hair all twisted up in rollers. But the house is silent, stuffy and dark. She steps in fully, and eases the door shut behind her, then toes off her sodden shoes.

Hung over the rack in the back kitchen, her

jacket will dry by the morning. The crocks are lying out on the drainer and the pig bucket stinks unemptied. At the back door she stuffs her feet into the old communal slippers, grabs the ragged umbrella and slip-slops her way down the garden path under its shelter. A hedgehog trundles along between the cabbages, stops to snuffle up a slug.

In the spidery cool of the outhouse, she hoiks up her skirt, lets her knickers slide down around her ankles and sits down on the old wooden toilet seat. Rain clatters on the bare slates above. The outhouse smells of damp plaster, urine, bicarb.

His skin too good to be real. A bloom like on a plum. The smell of him – piny, leathery, soft. His warm hands on her cool flesh.

She doesn't fret about trouble that might come of it: the events of the evening seem like a dream, proceeding according to their own inevitable logic. Repercussion-free. And it's not like she's going to do that kind of thing again.

She pees, and tugs a square of newspaper from the copper loop: an advertisement for Robinson's rhubarb cordial. The paper is thin and soft; it gets thinner and softer year by year, as the war continues, which, on the bright side, is better for the lav. She dabs herself dry.

It's only later, when she's lying in bed in her winter-weight pyjamas, smelling lanolin and wool and feeling the welcome weight of extra blankets, that she remembers, with a lurch, her wedding ring. She eases herself back out of bed, creeps down the stairs, heart thumping, and lifts her handbag off the hall floor, where it would have annoyed Mrs when she saw it there in the morning. *Fell right over it; nearly broke my neck.*

Back in her room, she fishes out the bundled glove; her ring's still there; she slips it on. And there, at the bottom of the bag, almost forgotten, is the bundled, bloodied handkerchief. The earlobe still inside.

Is it pride, she wonders, this sense of warmth, this satisfaction? The knowledge that for once, for just one evening, she bent the world to her will?

She rummages for the old tobacco tin in her bedside drawer. A few threads of tobacco still linger in the metal seams; it gives off a faint scent of her father, of childhood. The contents are all useless, unrelinquishable things: two odd earrings, a broken tin brooch of her mother's. She presses the bundle into the tin, squeezes the lid back on. She drops the tin into the drawer, pushes the drawer shut.

Lying back again, she heaves the heavy blankets over her. Her hand brushes over her hipbone and comes to rest in the warm declivity of her belly.

Denham Crescent, Mitcham, 5
June 1944, 6.45 a.m.

Amelia lifts the blackout cardboard from the window. The sunshine makes her blink and frown. Today is another day without Billy. Today is another day in which something terrible might happen to him. Today is another day to get through in the hopes of better days to come.

She rubs at her eyes. Below, the small front garden soaks in the morning sunshine. She unclips her rollers, pulls them out of her fine pale hair.

They let her have the big room because it's all she has now. Her whole life is in one room: an armchair, a wardrobe, a bed and a suitcase. The room is hers, but the house is Billy's and Ruby's. She hopes that they will stay here, for a while at least.

The blue suitcase still stands at the end of the bed. That's where she keeps the picture book. She's discovered, over these past few years,

237

that she can stand to lose almost everything but that.

The suitcase is solid, with its beech struts and its strong blue lacquered cardboard. It will keep her picture book safe. It will last.

In her quilted dressing gown and bare feet, carrying her brass water-spray, she goes out along the grass path, between the strawberry bed and the potato patch. The twisting runner beans offer their leaves up to the sun, like outstretched palms. The first fronds of new beans are pushing their way out of their green caps. The vines are dotted here and there with scarlet flowers. She huffs a cool mist softly on the remaining blossoms. Even this early in the day, bees are already busy all over the plot. Industrious and content. She makes her way down to the glazed lean-to, and pours her mix of liquid compost on the tomato plants. They are coming on well, swelling, blushing here and there with red.

Keep busy, that's what you have to do. That's what makes you happy.

Indoors, she boils the kettle and makes tea. She scrapes dripping over a slice of toast. There are bits of meat in the dripping, which flake satisfyingly across the gritty staleness of the bread.

First she will drop into church. Check that it's still standing. A quiet prayer and say hello to the Reverend. Then work. Late tonight to deal with the overtime slips, so she can't do a stint at the WVS canteen, but she'll make up for it tomorrow.

Her work there, looking after other women's boys, is done in the hope and expectation that another woman somewhere else is looking after hers. Then in the evening she'll get that golliwog finished off while she listens to the radio. It does her good to see the finished parcel, ready to go off for those poor children. A dolly, a few vests, a warm jumper. There is a lot to be thankful for, when you think about it. Sometimes, as she sits at her knitting, she's so deep in counting her way through the niceties of the pattern that she loses all sense of herself, and time passes very easily indeed.

Amelia is the first one in at work, as usual. She's got a little while before anyone else arrives. The only sound is the creak of the timbers as the roof warms up in the sun.

She slides open her desk drawer; it smells of India rubber and ink and sharpened pencils. She lifts out a small rectangle of mirror. A brisk turn of the head from side to side, a pat at her curled hair. The mirror is spotted, like some kind of mould is growing between the glass and the backing. She smiles – an artificial monkey grin – and turns her head to examine more closely the crow's feet and the lines that run from her nose to the corners of her mouth. She raises her eyebrows to watch her forehead corrugate. A good man can look beyond these things. A good man would see her finer qualities. A good man already does, she thinks: she's almost certain of that.

Her handbag lies in her lap. She puts down the mirror to twist open the metal clip.

She lifts out the lipstick, a gold-coloured cylinder about the length of her thumb. She's never owned one of these; she didn't used to hold with paint. But things change, so why shouldn't she? She'll put it back, of course she will: leave it for Ruby to find down the back of an armchair, or under the bath. She just wanted to try. The case is cool in her hand. She pulls off the cap, twists up the stick of coloured grease. There's just a stump left: hardly worth making such a fuss over. It's dark red. The red of veinous blood, of the deepest folds of damask roses. Amelia holds the tiny mirror in her left palm. She paints her lips. The lipstick smells how Ruby smells: oily, perfumed, sharp. She tilts her head to one side. Lips together, a red smile. She tries a pout. She's not sure about the paint. It seems to make her face uneven, as if her eyes have faded away. But nothing ventured.

She lays the mirror back down in the drawer, places the lipstick beside it, and eases the drawer shut.

She flaps the newspaper open; her eyes flicker over the headlines and down into the text. Rome has fallen – in the space of a day, it seems. She skims on through the columns: a neat, clean victory, the major monuments undamaged, the Vatican spared. He'll have read the paper on the Tube, and will arrive here pleased, and she can be pleased too, ready to share his pleasure.

She scans on through the columns. Sifting.

There's a clatter of a key in the door downstairs. It echoes through the empty building and makes her straighten, makes her face fall sober. She folds the paper briskly, opens a lower drawer and places it in and lifts out a duster – a scrap of old stripy towel from home. She slips through the glass door into the inner office, his office, and dusts down his desk and chair, straightens his blotter and pen. She likes to be surprised in here; caught in the act of caring for him.

It's clean work, and that's something she likes about the place, the bright cleanness, though the dust in the air can give her a bit of a catch in her chest sometimes. They make medical supplies: field dressings, bandages, lint and wadding. Thousands and thousands of surgical dressings, and it makes her dizzy and upset if she lets herself think about the wounds that they are needed for. The girls' gloved fingers work like spiders, shaping and stitching and wrapping and packing into boxes and the boxes into crates. The drivers fill their trucks with crates and they grind away out of the yard, and she doesn't like to think of it, where the wadding ends up, the amount of cotton lint that they process here, the sea of blood that there must be out there, to need all that cotton to sop it up.

Down below, in the workshop, his footsteps echo across the concrete floor. She recognises them immediately. And then there's the clatter of the women's shoes as they follow him in, and the busy, noisy bustle of their voices as they head for the cloakroom. She can hear his footsteps even through the noise of the other women; their different weight, their purpose.

She drops the duster onto the filing cabinet top, checks her hands: they're clean. Nail polish, would that be the next thing? Shine her nails up like berries. His footsteps tap their way up the wooden stairs. Like Fred Astaire. His twirling tails, his neat combed hair, his polished shoes clicking as he dances up the steps.

He's there, a dark ghost against the milky glass. The jacket shoulder crushing against the pane. The handle turning on this side too.

And that little familiar kick of surprise. The thrill of him. And his eyebrows flick up and he gives her one of his quick, foxy smiles from under his clipped moustache, turning to the hatstand as he shrugs off his duster coat. But he has that poise, that polishedness, of someone like Astaire, or Max Linder. And you don't often see that, not in real life. He hooks up his coat, then takes off his trilby and sets it on the curved antlers of the hatstand above. Tugging each jacket cuff into place, he makes his cufflinks flash gold. He's not really that much younger than her. He's in his mid-forties, she'd say. Hard to tell, really – he keeps himself so nice, so neat. Groomed like a horse. Curry combs and brisk rub-downs.

'Have we started?' he asks. 'Did you hear?'

242

She can hear the voices still, in the cloakrooms: the girls getting sorted, getting out of their coats and hats, and washing hands and scrubbing nails and soaping arms up to the elbow, and into their protective clothing, gloves and masks and turbans over the hair.

'Not yet, Mr Jack. The girls are just in.'

He turns round and smiles at her. And it makes her heart swell. Because it's a warm look, a kind look, direct.

'Haven't you heard?'

'Sorry?'

'France,' Mr Jack says.

She'd been going to say Italy. Rome, yes; Rome, the victory in Rome. She can't get into step with him.

'France?'

'They're on their way. They may even be over. That's what I heard.'

'There's nothing in the papers. Nothing on the news.'

He taps the side of his nose. 'Little bird.'

If it's France, if they're crossing to France, does that mean Billy?

'Your friend, the one in the RAF?' she asks.

He shakes his head. He's not prepared to say. But she can see that he's excited. All she can think of is the camp that Billy's written from the last few times. The rain hard on the corrugated roof. Is he still there? Is he in transit somewhere? Or is he now, already, out at sea? Mr Jack is talking about the fine brave boys. Her own fine brave boy, and how proud, and oh poor thing, how worried she must be. But she can't listen, her skin is creeping all over, and her head is light like a balloon and she wants to sit down. Did Billy know this was coming and not tell her? How could he not tell her a thing like that?

'I've so many good friends in the services, I know something of what you feel.'

He takes hold of her hand, squeezes it. She holds onto it, almost swaying.

'If it wasn't for my trouble, I'd be there myself. I'd be doing my bit.'

'You are,' she says, almost automatically. 'You are doing your bit. You know you are. Where would we all be without you?'

She has said this so many times.

His expression changes. His gaze drops, lingers on her lips.

He's noticed. The lipstick.

But Billy. Her head swims. What about Billy? How can she find out where he is, what is happening to him?

'Good news, though,' he says. 'Great news. A second front opened up and just at the right time. Stick it to 'em just as they're reeling after Rome.'

'Good news,' she agrees.

'But keep it to yourself, eh?' he says. 'Keep mum.'

She nods, blinking. He squeezes her hand again, and lets it go. It falls to her side. He grins his swift little toothy grin, and she has lost completely what he was saying, apart from *Keep mum*. Motherhood and silence: why the same word?

'Well,' he says. 'Well well. Tea?'

'Tea.'

'Good show.'

He turns away, rubbing his hands together, surveying his desk – blotter, inkpot, pen – all neatly laid out and clean. He draws out his chair, sits down. She goes to the little pantry to make tea on the gas ring, and stands there as the kettle boils, and thinks of Billy, out there on the water, out there on the sea.

He will be afraid. This is what she cannot bear. Her little boy will be scared, and there is nothing she can do to make it any better. She wants to sink down onto the lino, and press her face into her hands, and just sob and sob and sob at the unfairness of it all.

She just touches the damp away from her lower lids.

She makes tea. She gets through the moment, and will get through every moment that follows, through all the days to come, until she hears from Billy. Until she knows he's safe.

The English Channel, 5 June 1944, 4.30 p.m.

The sun is out, at least; not warm, but making the sea sparkle. It's choppy, but it's blue and clean; you could dive right in. They lean over the side of the craft, watching England shrink. Green downs, chalk cliffs, the fungal growth of seaside towns. Little craft beetle along behind them. Up ahead, the big ships power on. A brownish haze of diesel fumes hangs over the waves.

They're underway. It's now too late to even blow a hole in your hand: you'd have to take the hole all the way to France and back with you.

'You know what the Mad Bastard said,' Alfie says, looking back towards the shore. 'About if we got killed?'

'Yes.'

'Not to worry because there would be plenty more men coming along behind?'

'Yes.'

'I loved that. I thought that was the dog's bollocks.'

Billy snorts.

Alfie kicks idly at the base of the rail. His jaw is blurred with stubble; his eyes are shadowed and there are deep lines at the corners, like the creases in a slept-on sheet. He has three kids, Alfie. He's looking back towards the country and his kids.

The wake churns blue and glassy and crested white. There is a kind of calmness now, from fatigue, and from being underway and stuck with it.

'You ever think about what if Hitler wins?' Alfie asks.

'Ten yards and all that,' Billy says. 'Tight focus.'

'Yeah.' Alfie still looks back across the water, to the land. 'Point. But.'

'What?'

'The stuff they'd get up to, the Nazis. Stuff they'd do. We'd get special treatment. We'd be punished for all the trouble we've been to them. For not just rolling over and playing dead.'

'True.'

'And your missus, being Jewish and all that. You hear stories.'

'Don't like to think about it.'

'I do. I mean, I don't like to, but I think it helps.'

Billy squints at him.

'The missus, the kids, I mean,' Alfie continues. 'I can't live with it, the idea of them suffering. And it helps to think that: if you can't live with something, you might as well die trying to stop it.'

Alfie just gazes back towards the land. This is

love, Billy sees. This is what love looks like. The deep lines at the eyes. The frown, the anxious gaze.

'I'm not saying you *have* to die,' Alfie adds.

Billy feels his throat tighten. 'Good.'

'Look, I'm not being all bollocksy about this. It's just the trade-off, the price you're prepared to pay. I just think, if you can think like that, it helps you stop yourself from blowing your own hand off.'

Billy bites at his lower lip. What's the asking price, he wonders, for a second chance?

They both stare back at the receding coast. The colour leaches from the land.

Ruby. Always Ruby. Whatever else, always her.

If he gets his second chance, things will be different. If he can do this for her, then surely he can do the smaller things? He can be kind. He can be cheerful. He can make the world a better place for her every day. He can forget about what he can't have, and think of what he's already got.

'You know what,' Billy says. 'I'm thinking of getting a tattoo.'

Ravensbury Works, Tooting,
5 June 1944, 4.45 p.m.

Ruby takes the cigarette and bends to light it at Evelyn's match. Evelyn's nails are coral pink and she half wonders where she got hold of nail polish nowadays – some Yank, no doubt.

The first drag of smoke tastes strange, and makes her shudder. Evelyn lights up her own cigarette, blows smoke, talks.

They lean back against the brick factory wall, in the one remaining slab of sunshine in the whole dark yard. Ruby lets the smoke spool up into the air. She can feel the ghost of his touch still. His hands on her hips. His lips on her breasts. Him inside her. Her cheeks flush up, but it's okay because that could just be the sun. She squints into it.

Anyway: she got away with it. Mrs has no idea.

Evelyn's talking. Ruby turns her attention to her friend, trying to pick up the thread, like twisting the dial on a radio, the voices pulling themselves together out of static. She watches Evelyn's thick lips, blurred with crying, the lipstick worn to a thin stain. Ruby wonders if she could borrow a dab of it herself. Evelyn is a generous sort. That's what gets her into such a pickle with men.

Evelyn is upset not because one of her fellas has let her down, but because she and Joan have had a blow-up. Evelyn lodges with Joan and, Ruby's gathered lately, might have a bit of a crush on her too: it seems she just can't bear Joan's disapproval. But this morning they collided on the stairs, Evelyn on her way down to work, and Joan on her way back, tired from her stint at the ARP station. And Joan gave her hell, Evelyn tells Ruby, because she'd come home after Joan was asleep on Sunday night, but it wasn't that late, not really, but she had been with a fella. And Joan called Evelyn a tart, asked her who she'd been up to no good with this time, if she even knew his name, and made her cry.

'Was it Reggie?'

Evelyn blows a plume of smoke up into the air. 'Reggie?' She shakes her head. 'No. This was . . .' She squints, thoughtful.

'Someone else.'

Evelyn nods. 'Haven't seen Reggie in months. He wrote to say all leave had been cancelled. But I 'spect he's just visiting his missus instead.'

'Really?'

Evelyn rolls her head round against the wall, crushing her hair into the brick, and fixes Ruby with her pale grey stare. 'They can get away with anything nowadays, the men can. Say what they like and who's to know?'

'Just haven't seen many men in uniform around.'

Evelyn's mouth falls agape. Her voice drops to an awed whisper: 'Do you think it's happening?'

'The second front? Maybe.'

It makes sense. The emptiness of the town, the quiet. There have been rumours, but you don't listen to rumours, do you?

Billy's gone, she thinks. In the night. Without her even knowing, he's crossed the water, and is gone. While she was – with the handsome man.

Evelyn's rubbing at her arm, trying to be comforting, but her strong red hands are hurting. Ruby realises she must have gone white. Must be having a bit of a turn.

'I'm all right.'

Evelyn frowns, and reaches her arms around her friend, and holds her. Her bosom presses in underneath Ruby's, soft and strange. Ruby smells setting lotion and dirty hair. Evelyn lets her go.

'It'll be all right. You'll see.'

What does Evelyn know? What the bloody hell does anybody know any more?

'Yes,' Ruby says, and tries a smile. 'Of course.'

'Pecker up now. Doesn't do to upset yourself.'

'You're right,' Ruby says. 'Course you are.'

And she smiles, but all she feels is irritation: with Evelyn, with herself, with all of it. That life

251

just keeps dishing this stuff out and they're expected to keep on spooning it up and swallowing. She blinks away the film of wet from her eyes, takes a final sip from her cigarette, and pulls herself together. Because you have to; because there is, after all, no choice: you can't be permanently hysterical, so you might as well not bother getting started. She wonders, just for a second, *What if I'm pregnant?* Because there was Billy, on the last night of his leave, and there was the handsome man last night; and what a pretty pickle that would be. But she dismisses the idea: not now, not after all these years. After the blue baby, she expects childlessness.

She drops the cigarette butt onto the cobbles and presses it in between two stones with her toe. No wonder her shoes are so wrecked, she thinks: the blasted cobbles at this place.

'Come on,' she says. 'Let's get back to it. They'll put the radio on. We'll catch the news.'

Evelyn nods. She heaves herself away from the wall. Ruby leads the way back into the clattering workshop.

Surgical Supplies, Morden,
5 June 1944, 6.38 p.m.

Amelia sits at her narrow desk, under the dim light from the internal window. Her blunt fingertips sort and arrange the thin yellow overtime slips. She listens to the noises from the workshop below, the way they change as the working day ends. The clack and rattle of manufacture lessen and then cease, and voices take up the space instead, at first a thread, then another, a tangle of voices, a matted clot of noise.

At lunchtime he waved the early edition at her, and called out, 'No news!' quite cheerfully, as if that somehow confirmed things, or was reassuring. He had the radio on in there all day – the mutter of it, the faint music.

When William died, the world folded up on itself, turned to dust, and blew away. There should be exemptions for widows of the last war. They should let their boys off from fighting in the next.

She should just get home to Ruby. If Ruby's heard the rumours, she'll be worried too.

She has the overtime slips in order. She lifts out the payment sheet, with details of staff seniority, specialisms, rates of pay. She sets to working out who's owed what.

It's quiet now below. She hears Mr Sanderson draw the bolt across on the inside of the door, and then the shuff and tap of the long-headed broom as he starts to sweep up the cotton dust through the shafts of end-of-day dusty sunshine.

She tots up the last of the columns. The figure doesn't look quite right. She scans back through the records and can't see where she's gone wrong.

She goes through the numbers again, from scratch, writing them out on a slip of scrap paper and totting them up again, and spots her mistake – a machinist's overtime she'd missed – the kind of mistake you make when you're tired and preoccupied. She completes the task just as she hears Mr Jack getting up from his desk.

She fishes her mirror out of the drawer. Checks her face. During the day, though reapplied carefully, the lipstick has bled into the fine lines around her lips. She colours in her lips again. Rolls them together as she's seen Madam do. She lets out a long breath. It is important to maintain composure. She drops her mirror and the lipstick into her bag, snaps it shut.

Amelia takes a deep breath and lets it go, ruffles the yellow slips into a pile, traps them in a bulldog clip. She twists round in her seat to look back into the inner office. Beyond the rippled glass, Mr Jack puts on his coat.

She gets up and straightens her clothes. She moves towards the main office door.

'Ah, Mrs Hastings,' he says, and taps his hat onto his head. 'I'm meeting friends at the club, and I've left things rather late. Can you just sort out a few invoices for me?'

She folds her hands together. Her lips feel greasy and uncomfortable. 'Of course.'

'They're just on my desk,' he says. 'You are a pet.'

And he is gone, leaving a whiff of lavender hair oil.

Amelia is left there, in the dusty, quiet office, with Mr Sanderson sweeping below, and bumping into the workbench legs, leaving little bruises on the wood.

Denham Crescent, Mitcham,
5 June 1944, 7.07 p.m.

Ruby puts the kettle on. There are four crackers left in the bottom   of the biscuit barrel and she lifts them out and lays them on a plate. She scans the shelves for tins – sardines perhaps, ham; something she can just serve. She's starving. But there's nothing you could just lever out of a tin onto a plate. Which leaves the garden.

She plunges outside, into the cool air. A black-bird's singing, and Mr and Mrs Graves are talking next door, low voices, soft and companionable, as he trims the privet hedge. Little clips of leaf and sprays of twig fly across the top of the hedge as he works, like green confetti for a summer wedding.

She makes her way along the rows of vegetables – grassy leeks, the purple blooms of broccoli, twining beanstalks dotted with red flowers. At the end of the garden, behind glass, where they'll catch most of the day's sun, are the tomatoes, the fruit hanging hard and orange and the smell of them dusky and rich and sharp. She leans down to cup one in her hand; it's firm and warm from the sun. It's not really ripe; it's not really the right moment to pick it, but sometimes you just can't wait for the right moment to come along. There's a dull ache at the back of the mouth. She nips the stem with her fingernails, and hopes the sap won't stain.

Amelia closes the door carefully, letting the latch drop gently into place.

Her throat aches as if she's coming down with something. She peels off her gloves and folds them into her handbag, hangs it up, then slips off her old summer jacket and hangs it behind the door. As she eases off her shoes, she listens to Madam clattering about in the kitchen. What is she up to, what will she spoil, what will she break, what will she chip?

But it is not Amelia's kitchen. Not her things. She climbs the treads up to the bathroom and scrubs at her red-stained lips with a soapy flannel. She sets the lipstick down on the floor and gives it a nudge, so that it rolls a little way into the dusty under-shadow of the bath, where Ruby can find it later.

In her room, she kneels down at the suitcase, lays it flat, and clicks it open. She lifts the picture book out onto the rug. She opens it, and looks through the cards. The picture of a camel, a fishing boat, a mountain. She turns to the end and unhooks the last postcard from its moorings.

Beyond it are blank pages, with empty slots for cards that he never got the chance to send.

She holds the postcard, looking at the view that he had gazed at, thinking of her. She turns the card over. It is getting softened with wear. She doesn't need to read the words. She touches the slight smudge of William's name.

I am a fool.

I am a stupid fool.

I am a stupid old fool.

And there's no worse fool than an old fool.

Ruby clatters on the lid and stretches across the table to place the teapot on its trivet. Amelia comes in. She looks a little flushed, a little puffy around the eyes and her mouth is raw looking. Ruby wipes her hands on a cloth.

Amelia takes in the arrangement of tea plates, teapot, cups and saucers on the tabletop. A fan of those crackers Madam's so fond of, a small jug of blue watery milk. Their two unmatched saucers – hers blue, Ruby's cream with a green stripe – that contain their butter rations. And two under-ripe tomatoes, sliced in half and grilled. They would have been better left to ripen fully on the vine. Amelia glances up at her daughter-in-law. The girl's face is pale and tired; there are real hollows under her eyes. She's heard the rumours then. There has been no official news.

'I thought you'd be tired,' Ruby says, 'after work.'

'Thank you,' Amelia says. She sits down. The

tomatoes leach juice out onto the plate, translucent, faintly granular, like water poured from a rusty can. They give off a green-smelling musk. They will have sweetened with cooking, at least.

'How was the concert?' Amelia asks.

Last night seems weeks ago; a lifetime, another world. Ruby draws out the other chair, sits down. 'I'm not sure I'd bother going again.'

Amelia scans the table again; frowning. 'But you love your concerts.'

'Such a trouble though, getting there and back.'

'You must have been late in.'

Then she realises what's missing: Amelia shunts back her chair, gets up and darts over to the counter, lifts the tea cosy where Ruby had left it lying like a shed skin, still retaining something of the shape of the pot. Amelia slides it into place, stretching the crocheted wool over handle and spout to cover the hot round belly of the pot.

'Now,' she says, satisfied. She smiles at Ruby. Ruby pulls her lips back in a smile too. She watches Amelia's pale spoon-fingers lift a cracker from the plate, watches a knife dip into the tiny square of butter.

'This is nice,' Amelia says.

'You don't mind me picking the tomatoes?'

'Not at all. This is all very good of you. Very kind.'

Amelia bites her cracker.

'Did you hear the news?' Ruby asks. 'I mean, the gossip? Nothing certain.'

259

Amelia nods, swallows.

'I heard this morning,' Amelia says. 'I mean, as you say, just gossip.'

A whole day knowing, or not knowing – suspecting, worrying, working. The both of them.

Ruby's lips fold inward in a kind of smile. She reaches out across the table, between the saucers and plates and knives, and rests her hand on Amelia's. The back of the older woman's hand feels cool and fragile and bony.

Amelia looks up at Ruby. The younger woman's face is white, almost innocent of makeup. Amelia blinks. Her eyes are betraying her, welling now. And the girl too – Ruby presses her eyes – one and then the other – with the flank of her left hand.

'Shall I put the radio on?' Ruby asks.

'Why don't you?' Amelia says.

Ruby gets up, takes her hand off Amelia's. She goes through into the sitting room.

I can't be you, Ruby thinks. *I can't become you.*

The English Channel, 6 June 1944, 1.30 a.m.

Billy lies on his back. The deck tilts and shifts beneath him. The tarp ripples and flaps, low over his face. He can't sleep. The footfalls of the watch approach. He can feel his own heartbeat, thudding in the cavity of his chest, the thrum of the diesel engine in his ribcage.

This is the last night.

The footfalls pass, and are gone.

Billy flips onto his front, crawls backwards on his elbows. Standing up, he swings the ground-sheet round his body as a cape, grabs his helmet. The wind buffets him, fresh and damp on his face. He staggers with the ship's pitch, heading for the prow. The clouds chase each other across the moon; it's almost bright as day – too bright. All around the ships putter along, peak and dip over the waves. Any minute he expects it: a burst of flame, the shock of impact, the thrum of a distant German plane. But there has been nothing yet; and every moment that passes is another lived through, a moment closer to getting out the other side.

He makes his way to the prow. The wind snatches at the groundsheet. The deck pitches underfoot. He climbs the rigid metal steps to stand inside the gun turret. He stares out into the distance, towards France.

There is what you can live with, and what you can't. There's the price you're prepared to pay for something. It all becomes quite simple, when you think of it like that.

He can see land now. The darker streak ahead of them – the whole dark continent stretching out from there, thousands and thousands of miles, the sky-reflecting rivers, the fields and forests, the cities, the mudbanks and the ditches. Every inch of it.

H-Hour is fixed for 7.25. He knows that he is scared. He just doesn't really feel it any more.

Back to the turret wall, he slides down, feeling the cold steel through his greatcoat and ground-sheet. He lifts off his helmet, unpicks the picture from inside. He tips the helmet back onto his head. Unwraps her, holds her in his left hand. He can see her in the moonlight: the curves of her face, the dark blots of her eyes and lips. Her beauty. It conjures the scent of her; of cigarettes and perfume and skin. Silky white legs cool around his. Last leave. In their narrow bed. Oh God, she's good to him. He unbuttons his trousers; his cock nudges out into the cool rain.

He holds Ruby in his left hand, grips his cock in the right.

Afterwards, he stands up with his waistband bunched in his right hand, the spill of semen cupped in his left. He lets it drip off over the side, down into the water as it churns away from the prow. He watches it drift for a moment, and then sink away, like an offering to the Fates. He wipes his hand down the cold wet outside of the gun tower, wiping off the sticky drying film of it, anointing the boat. Though the gunner and the gunner's mate might not look on it like that, if they notice it in the morning.

But, he tells himself, they won't notice. They'll have other things on their minds.

Another swell hits the landing craft and flings spray over the side. The diesel engines throb. Billy wipes the water off his cold, salt-raw face. His right hand, gripped round the handlebar of his bike, is numb and white at the knuckles. HMS *Roberts* fires again, a colossal boom from behind them. A second later and the shell screams overhead, tearing a wound in the air. Everyone ducks. The vacuum of the shell's flight sucks the water up into a blunt wall for a moment, then it drops back into the roiling waves.

Smoke billows past them. Billy can't see the shore.

'It's like they're firing fucking jeeps—' Gossum shouts over the noise.

Barker crouches by the side of the craft, heaving up fried eggs and rum.

'I don't want to do this,' Alfie yells to Billy.

'Funnily enough,' Billy yells back, 'me neither.'

And then *Roberts* lets loose another shell, and as one they flinch down, hands still gripped onto their bikes, and the shell screams right over them, sucking the air from their lungs, sucking the hair up from their heads, making their eardrums pop.

They straighten up again, tentatively, still half-hunched. Now he can see the shore – the beach – a stretch of tan sand, darting figures, moving vehicles, smoke and fog. Billy swallows down the acid in the back of his mouth. Okay. If he can just get through this.

Then Alfie laughs.

'What?'

Alfie just gives him a look, shakes his head, then turns his gaze back to the shore.

'No, tell me, what?'

Alfie turns back to him, shouts: 'You owe me a quid.'

'What?'

'I bet you, remember?'

'What?'

'One day you'd ride for Britain?'

'Shithead,' Billy says.

'Yes sir.'

Billy looks at him. The two-day stubble and the raw eyes, and the water droplets glistening.

The tender skin at his temple, creased across with lines as he squints into the spray. He wants to say something, but he can't find the words.

He turns back to the beach. They are close to landing now. Billy can pick out their route across the beach. The sappers have pegged it out across the churned sand; little flags and ropes marking the way through the minefield. It looks oddly like the start of a road race. He's never rated road-racing: bunch of meatheads, road-racers; all muscle and dumb suffering.

Off to the right one of the minesweeper tanks, the Hobart's Funnies, flails for mines, and then one goes off and boom, sand flying up into the sky, and the tank lurches back like it's startled. Then there's a boom boom boom from up high, behind the beach, and Billy realises with a cold ripple of fear that an enemy gun emplacement is still active. All those shells from the *Roberts* and they still haven't smashed it up. The Germans tend to dig in good and deep: they should have learned this from the last war. They dig in deep and they make themselves comfortable and they wait you out and when you think you've wiped 'em out they pop up and massacre you. He holds the sweaty handgrip in his palm. The craft lurches up onto a sandbank, halts. They stagger. Billy shifts his grip on the bike. His palm is sweaty despite the cold. The ramp creaks open, dropping down towards the shallow water.

'See you on the other side,' Alfie says.

Billy nods.

Don't look beyond the next ten yards, he thinks.
Don't look beyond the next ten yards.

Normandy, 6 June 1944, 8.25 a.m.

He is cycling between flat fields dotted with cows, a wide expanse of green and a pale blue open sky. There's a farmhouse in the distance, but soon it's not so far off, and then it's just a few yards, and cushioned round with apple trees, and there are hens scratching in the gravel, and there's a woman who comes out to the gate, dipped over to one side with the weight of a milk pail. She stops, and stares at him a moment, then sets her pail down on the path and waves, both arms up, crossing above her head, flagging him down.

'M'sieur! M'sieur!'

He slows off, pulls over towards her, comes to a halt. Her cheeks are rosy with broken veins.

'Les Anglais! V'là les Anglais qui débarquent, dis donc!'

He slips off the saddle to stand astride the crossbar. His hands are shaking. There is blood across the back of the right one.

'J'me trompe pas! Z'êtes ben Anglais?'

He knows she's asking if he's English. There's a phrasebook. He remembers bits.

'We,' he says.

'Merci,' and she reaches out and clasps his hand. Her eyes are blue and prominent. 'Merci, mon p'tit!'

She smells of grain, of hen feed. He doesn't quite know what to do.

'Mais il a peut-être soif, ce jeunot?' she says. 'Un peu de lait, mon p'tit?'

She bends and dips a cup into the milk, and hands it to him. He takes the cup and drains the milk; it is still warm from the cow. He hands the cup back to her.

'Mercy.'

'A mon Dieu, mais il est blessé!' she says, and reaches up to his face, but he doesn't understand. 'Y a du sang là, sur vot' visage!'

He doesn't understand.

'Mercy.'

He takes her hand and squeezes it, and lets it go. He makes to shift back onto the saddle. He gestures down the road, into the distance.

'I've got to go.'

'Et ben allez, allez donc. Et encore merci, mon p'tit, merci!'

'Mercy, madam, mercy.'

He pushes on, bumping back up onto the road, and then heaving the bike back up to speed, past hedges and past fences and open fields. He is cycling through an orchard.

Branches overhang the road, and their shadows skim across him as he passes underneath. The boughs are dotted with bright green fruit. The same fruit lie on the road, hard and small as ball bearings, and look no different from the fruit still on the trees. It makes no sense why some just drop, and others stay and swell upon the branch. He looks at the spattering of blood across the back of his hand. The beach. The ramps thumping down onto the sand. Alfie's cheek glistening with spray, and the shells screaming overhead. And then—

His front wheel hits a fallen apple, and sends it skittering out towards the verge, and he nearly loses his balance. He rights the bike.

From far off he hears the thud of a detonation, and then nothing.

For the first time, he glances back. The road is straight and empty behind him, then there is a curve at the farmhouse, and you can't see past it. That's why none of his squad is in sight.

But they'll catch up. He'll wait for them at the outskirts of the village. They'll regroup, follow orders, secure the crossroads.

He belts out of the orchard, and is racing along between high hedges; through the branches he glimpses a clutch of brown shaggy cows that stand motionless and stare at him. And a slope up, and he just kicks up the effort, shoving hard on the pedals, not even getting out of his seat; he'd forgotten this, the pleasure of it; or rather his head had forgotten it, because his body knows, and is simply, easily capable, and it soothes him, to just be living in his body and no longer in his head, to just live in the mechanical perfection of it all. There's mortar fire behind him, and the faint clatter of a machine gun, but it seems so distant, unconnected.

There was noise. There was blood. And. He shoves the memory down.

At the gentle crest of the hill, he slows, and on the left side there is a horse nosing over the top bar of a gate, swishing her tail against the flies, and when he passes – he must make a strange bulky figure, field green, backpack, sweat and wheels – she shakes her mane, and whinnies, and turns to trot along her field beside him.

'Race you?' he says.

The horse is French and probably won't understand English, but she gets the idea, tosses her head, breaks into a canter. He grins, and ducks down and pedals harder, but the gearing is too low and he can get no more out of the bike, and has to cruise downhill, his feet circling uselessly, as the horse canters off beyond and reaches the end of her field before him, and skitters round, and turns her head to watch him reach her, and pass, and be gone.

And there's the village.

A roadside graveyard, and then an empty field, and then a waggoner's yard, and then the first few houses of the settlement, church spire further off, right in the centre, at the crossroads, which they have to secure.

He glances back again, over his shoulder. The road is still completely clear. And the horse, now trotting back up the field, just dips her head to snatch at the grass; so there's no-one within eyesight for her either.

He's almost at the graveyard now; there's cover there. He'll wait for them.

A low wall encloses the site, topped with the linked spears of iron railings. He cruises in to the side of the road, bumping off the tarmac and onto the gravel overspill, and slows to a halt. He grabs the railing, sits on his bike to wait. His jerkin is drenched in sweat. It was nice of her to bring him milk. It was good milk. He can't remember the last time he had milk that good.

He wipes his hand over his sweaty face. He looks at his palm. It has come away streaked with dark blood. He looks at it.

Then the first bullet zings past. He dives. The bike still between his legs, he crashes onto the gravel. Stones bang up into his leg and shoulder and arm. The crossbar of the bike whacks against his lower leg, and then the upper leg crunches into the crossbar. It hurts. His old shoulder injury crackles with pain. It doesn't matter. What matters is not getting shot. What matters is where the shot came from.

He snakes out from under the bike, crawls round so that he's half lying, propped on an elbow, his back against the low wall. On the far side of the wall is the graveyard. That's where the sniper is; must be; the road is clear, the field beyond it is empty but for a pair of crows that flap into the air, startled. There's nowhere else that shot could have come from.

He lifts himself up a fraction, to peer out over the wall. Another zing and crunch, and a spume of dust lifts from the capstone just by his chin. He ducks back down. On the gravel the bike's front wheel still spins slowly.

Perfect spot for a sniper: good cover, clear view of the road. Should have expected it. Should have seen it coming a fucking mile off.

The sniper'll have a, what? A Mauser, Karabiner? Five rounds and then he'll have to reload. And he's had two already.

But Billy can't work out why he's still alive. Did he take him for a local, even with the kit? Does the bike work as some kind of distraction, a disguise, a kind of hiding in plain sight? Maybe they just don't expect the enemy to arrive on a bike.

Lying low still, he twists himself out of his backpack. The movement tears at his shoulder, makes him wince. He unclips his revolver from its holster, breaks open the barrel, spins it, checking, even though he knows it's fully loaded. Then he clicks it back together and darts up and fires one shot off across the graveyard. He flinches back down, but not quite low enough: he has to see. And he gets lucky; a second before the sniper returns fire, Billy spots him. Just a flicker of movement from behind a headstone, enough to locate him. Billy ducks back down and the shot whizzes overhead like a hornet. Three shots gone: two left. Billy makes a brisk assessment of the angles, the distances, how far he has to crawl, how long he's got before the sniper susses him out. He drags the pack up against the wall, shunting it up so that a small hump of canvas shows over the top. From a distance, it could be taken for a bit of protruding uniform: a shoulder, bit of helmet, a foraging cap. At least, that's what he's hoping.

His revolver in his hand, his elbows in the grit, Billy snakes his way along, keeping to the cover of the wall, leaving his pack to take the shots.

A sharp twang as a bullet hits one of the railings behind him and sets the whole fence humming like a tuning fork. Four shots. And he's fallen for the decoy; but soon enough he'll hit it, or start to wonder why it's not returning fire. Billy has to be quick.

He drags himself round the corner, and up the side of the graveyard. By his reckoning, twenty yards should do it, get him to a spot where he can get a clear sightline on the enemy. Just as far as the shrub up ahead, lolling with pink flowers. There are flowers in the gravel too, tiny, flat-faced, soft red blooms that grow low and close to the ground, with delicate, neat leaves. He wonders if they are pimpernels. He hears a bird singing, and thinks it might be a blackbird, but he doesn't know if they have blackbirds in France. Billy reaches the bush, its lower stems are reddish, flaking with bark. The bare soil underneath is clayey and hard. Then another shot rings out, yards away across the graveyard, aimed at the pack. And that's it. Done. He'll have to reload now.

Billy heaves himself up to squint over the wall. He sees, about thirty yards away, a dark figure crouched behind a headstone, rifle laid across his knees, ramming in a clip. Billy lifts his revolver, aims, and fires.

The revolver jumps in Billy's hand, and the noise stuns his ears. The figure jolts back against the headstone, and then just stays there. It slumps slightly.

The day is muffled; there's a high-pitched hum in Billy's ears. Nothing happens. The body slips a little further over to one side. Grass, and headstones, and the blistered paint on the railings. Nothing happens. The bird starts to sing again. Billy straightens up, steps up onto the low wall and swings his leg over the iron railings. He jumps down onto the grass beyond, and makes his way between the headstones.

The sniper is quite small. His coat looks too big for him. His face is turned away. Billy comes up to the foot of the grave and looks the body over.

He can't see where he hit him. He moves round the kerbed edge of the grave, and crouches down, and reaches out and takes hold of the jaw to turn the face towards him. The skin is particularly smooth. It is still warm. It is a child. His greenish eyes are vague and dead.

Billy steps back. He shoves his hands in his pockets. He glances up and round, up at the empty road. He looks back down at the boy. He's fourteen, maybe fifteen. His face is round and he has freckles across his nose. Blood spreads slowly through his coat.

He takes the boy under the arms, and shifts him, laying him down on the grave.

'Sorry,' he says.

He tucks the boy's coat up round him.

'Sorry.'

Billy closes the boy's eyes for him. His hands are shaking. He glances up at the road again, but the road is clear.

He straightens up, shoves his hands into his pockets again. He looks back at the boy, at the way his boots point at odd angles to the sky. Then Billy turns, and picks his way out through the graves, towards the path, back to the road. The gravel crunches under his boots. He swings the gate open, and goes out, and picks up his bike, and tips it up so that it stands on its seat and handlebars. He checks that the chain's in place, then the wheels for buckling, then the alignment of the brakepads. Never liked brakes. He tips the bike over again, and sets it back on its wheels. Then he crouches down with his back to the wall, and waits for his squad.

He never tells anyone, ever. Not a soul.

Denham Crescent, Mitcham, 3 August 1947

H e liberated the pieces from the factory. Three short strips of light pine, tucked into a trouser pocket, then slipped into his bait box. Waste wood from the Houseproud frames. You have to go slowly, bit by bit. The screws too, and the glue – the glue scraped into an old fishpaste jar, glob after glob, every day for a fortnight, so they wouldn't notice the difference in the gluepot.

He cut and shaped the pieces and screwed and glued them into a rough triangle. You'd almost think it was one solid block. Then he set to with a chisel, and then sandpaper – a scrap of wadded sandpaper that had gone soft as leather and kept filling up with wood dust and had to be thwacked against the worktop edge to clear it. Now he holds the wooden shape in his palms: a perfectly proportioned saddle, scaled down for the small bottom of his two-year-old son, to fit onto the crossbar of Billy's bike.

He layers it with flannel, then gabardine, off-cuts

from Ruby's sewing box. He presses the wadded surface of the saddle. It has a little give in it. He holds it up to the light and turns it round. Sunlight catches on the surface of the gabardine, glints on the tacks. He runs his thumb over the nail-heads, checking for sharpnesses, snags. He thinks of what Alfie said, about a bike that looked like a bike but didn't taste like one. This isn't how you make saddles, not really, not with pine and glue and gabardine. But it looks like a saddle, at least: it'll work like one, and that's the best that you can hope for nowadays.

He's magpied a few bits of plumbers' fittings from a bomb site, uses them to fit the saddle to the crossbar of his Butler, judging the distance by eye. He tests it, twisting and leaning the small saddle in one direction, then another. He fits the screwdriver back into place and gives it another couple of turns, checks again, then leans the bike against the worktop and steps back.

The boy's little feet will rest on the top of the forks, his small hands grip the centre of the handlebars. Billy will hold the warm, breathing compactness of the boy safe between his arms.

He'd never expected this. The keenness of his love. The urgency of it.

Billy wheels the bike out of the garage, and through into the back garden. The light is softening. The garden smells of tomato plants. He can hear her in the kitchen, clinking something as she stirs, talking to the boy.

'Rube,' he calls. 'Ruby?'

She comes to the open back door, and the little boy pushes past her legs, and comes doddering down the path towards him, grinning wetly, dribble dripping from his chin. Billy smiles instinctively, immediately, then glances up and catches Ruby watching the child. He looks down at the boy, his delighted, staggering run. She worries too much. There is nothing wrong with him. Billy leans the bike against the fence and crouches down to pick up the little boy.

'Come on then, little man,' he says, and stands up with him. The boy sits on Billy's strong forearm. He sticks a finger in his mouth and stares fixedly at Billy's face. Ruby comes down the path towards them, wiping her hands on her apron, exposing the front of her washed-thin skirt.

'All done?' she asks.

'All done.'

She comes in close to the bike, crouches to see the fittings.

'It's safe,' Billy says.

'It's a lovely job,' she says. 'You won't be long?'

'Just round the block.'

With the boy sitting on his forearm, he takes the bike in his free hand and pushes it out into the back lane. The boy regards him thoughtfully, still sucking on a finger. Ruby follows, watches.

'Hold him a minute.'

Ruby lifts the child away, and Billy swings aside the crossbar, and then just looks at them both a moment, his wife holding his son, the pair of them with their dark curls, their eyes like black coffee; so alike, so beautiful. Billy takes the boy back. He lifts him high above the newly made saddle, lowering him gently so that the boy gets the idea and sticks out his two sandalled feet and sits astride it. Ruby winces, but Billy just leans forward and sets each foot in turn on the top of the front forks.

'All right, little man? Your feet go here, okay?'

Ruby twists the apron in her hands.

'He's all right,' Billy says. 'He's fine. You can't wrap him up in cotton wool.'

She nods. Tries a smile. He takes the boy's hands in his and reaches them forward, curling them round the handlebars.

'There,' he says. 'And there. Hold on tight.'

The dark head nods. Billy shifts himself back, into the saddle. The warm smallness of the child between his arms. The little concentratedness of him. He wraps an arm around the child and leans over to kiss Ruby. The warm press of her lips.

'Be careful.'

He knows she can't help herself from saying it. 'I will.'

'Be good for Daddy.'

'All right then,' Billy says. 'Here we go.'

Billy pushes down on the pedals, and they ease

forwards, finding their balance, leaving Ruby looking after them, a pinch between her brows.

They circle round into Bramcote Avenue. Just round the block, though there can be longer rides once the boy gets a taste for it. The boy's knuckles are dimpled and soft on the handlebars. He doesn't make a sound. They skim under the waxy green-red leaves of the flowering cherries, pass the boarded-up crater of a bomb site. He wheels round unfilled potholes. He can smell the scent of the boy's head. They bump up over the tarry join between one section of concrete and the next, and the boy crows with delight.

He's enjoying it, so Billy turns the bike, and they wheel round out and cross the empty road and turn onto the lane across the Common. The sun is low and the grass is long and dry. He can hear a game of cricket, the clack of the bat and the clap of spectators, but the cricket green is out of sight, and he can hear traffic, one car, then, after a while, another. He is alone with his boy. Billy's legs lift and sink and lift again, one after the other, on either side of the child. If he slips this way, I will catch him; if he slips that way, I will catch him too. The little head is heavy, it nods, and Billy puts an arm around the warm, slack body, and cycles one-handed. I will always catch you. I will always keep you safe.

He starts to look out for a turn, an easy shallow

281

loop that will take him round for home without disturbing the boy.

When they get back to the house, rooks are circling above the trees and Ruby is waiting in the twilight at the back door. He swings himself off the bike and scoops the child up onto his chest, and the boy nestles into his neck, making Billy's heart stir. Ruby stands, watching, smiling at the husband and the sleeping child. She opens her arms to take the boy.

'Sorry,' Billy says. It is later than he thought.

She shakes her head. It doesn't matter. He passes her the child, and she hefts him up in her arms, already too heavy for her to carry easily. She takes him upstairs. Billy sits down at the kitchen table, and flaps open the newspaper. His eye catches on news of the Darquier trial; stories are still emerging about what happened in Paris during the war. About the Vel d'Hiv round-up. He recalls the Vélodrome in broad sweeps: the interior curved like the inside of an egg, the way the crowd noise echoed like in a swimming bath. Ten years later, and they were holding the Parisian Jews there before shipping them off to die. And he reads now, here, this moment, that the Nazis asked for the men and women, but the French authorities handed over the children too. Imagine it. Huddling your kid close, knowing you can't do anything to protect it. Whispering lies. Trying not to show how terrified you are. Lying for as long as you possibly can.

He has blown his nose and got the kettle on and folded the paper away by the time she comes back down. He knows she likes this, his getting on with things – he doesn't wait, as some men wait, for his wife to make the tea. She reaches down the cups. She saved up her stamps for them. Aeroplanes on a creamy-coloured background. The boy loves to have his milk from an aeroplane cup, to run his fingers over their dark gloss.

'I'm going to get him a bike of his own,' Billy tells her.

'He's two,' Ruby says.

'When he's a bit older.'

'Right.'

He watches her. She's thinking, what will that cost? How can they afford it? But she says nothing.

'I'll ask around. Someone will have a kid's bike that's been outgrown.'

She nods, sets the teapot down. Her lips are pursed, she's frowning.

She's thinking, the boy will never ride a bike.

She's wrong, he knows she is, and she'll see it too, eventually. He'll prove it. The boy will turn out fine, better than fine. Billy insists on it. Anything less than this is unacceptable. This is his second chance. He's paid for it. That boy's death in Normandy was the down payment. The drip drip drip of guilt, that's just the interest.

The kettle's hum grows to a whistle: they both start towards it, fearful of disturbing the child. Billy plucks the whistle from the spout with quick fingertips. Ruby leans against the table, rubs at her forehead, at the tension between her brows. She has to take him to the doctor. She knows she does. The way he kicks out that left leg when he runs, like it's getting in the way. The way the creases in his chubby legs don't match. It's tiny, now; but the wrongness will grow with him, she knows it. It's her fault.

Billy turns off the gas, lifts the kettle, fills the teapot.

'I'll pick up something cheap, don't worry. I'll do it up,' Billy says.

He clinks the teapot lid into place, warm with the thought of cranks and chainwheels and candlewax. He comes round the side of the table and opens his arms; she steps into the space between them.

'He'll love it,' Billy says.

She nods, her face pressed into his neck, where the boy had rested his sleeping head before.

Denham Crescent, Mitcham, 5 June 1955

S orry,' he says, because Dad's already started, and Will had been   supposed to help. He'd been reading *Eagle*. He'd lost track of the time.

Dad grunts something; he's leaning out across the beetle top of the Ford Anglia, a soapy rag in hand, scrubbing off the dirt. Will heads into the garage for more rags. Sukie raises her head – her eyes catch the light but the rest of her is just a darker darkness in the garage, making Will come to a stuttering stop, almost overbalancing on his built-up boot. Sukie stands up so that Will can stroke her head. Her tail thumps against the workbench.

'Good girl,' Will says. 'Good girl.'

He bends on his good leg, calliper stretched out to the side, to rifle in one of the rag boxes underneath the workbench. There are three boxes, containing three different categories of rag. Four, if you include the ones in use, left twisted up and oily or dried crisp on the workbench and shelves. You have to be careful you get the right ones.

The shelves are stacked with old tobacco tins and biscuit tins and sweetie jars full of bike bits, bolts, washers, drawer handles, keys, and bits of tiny engineering that he can't name but could be sewing-machine parts, something like that. And hanging up on the ceiling, like an exhibit, is Dad's Claud Butler.

Equipped now with an appropriate rag, Will reaches up, and if he puts his weight on his callipered leg, on the built-up boot, and stretches as tall as he can, he can just touch his fingertips to the bottom of the wheel, and make it shift, make it move along three, four, five ticks. He loves the way it ticks.

He's just turning to go when he sees that there's a bit of wood in the vice; his dad's been working with a hacksaw. The outlines of a horse's head drawn on in pencil, part of the mane already cut out. There is one wide flaring nostril silvered in with graphite. She is getting a rocking horse. Or maybe just a hobby horse. Anyway.

It's not his kind of thing, he supposes.

He clumps back out into the back lane to help his dad.

The grass droops with gritty water. The gravel is wet and grey and leaves a film on his boots like plaster. Dad soaps across the bonnet and roof where Will can't reach. Will manages the doors, the side windows, the boot lid, wiping away the grey soapy streams of water. They work without speaking – just the little concentrating sounds his

dad makes, sucking his teeth. Will dips his rag
into the bucket, swishing it around; he slops it
back onto the car. You don't put your rag down
on the ground, not even for a moment. It'll pick
up grit and that would scratch the paint. And
then there'd be that slow explosion of him, like
the H-bomb going off. It goes from something
small, barely noticed, a tiny fracture in the material of things, and you just don't see it, you
blunder on oblivious, and then you're right in the
middle of it: a fury that plumes and boils a mile
up into the air. Will rubs at the silvery back
window rim, leans down to do the side panel. He
dips down further to attempt the running board,
but the calliper digs into his groin, and he yelps.
He didn't mean to. He looks up. His dad's eyes
are on him.

'All right?'

Will nods.

Billy juts his chin at the calliper. 'Need sorting?'

Will shakes his head, wants to avoid an uncomfortable limp down to Macklin's. Dad talking over
his head to Mr Macklin, and Will sitting on an
upturned box, bad leg dangling like a puppet's,
and the hot firework of sparks from the welding,
which he likes to watch; but he doesn't like the
way the men there fuss him, rub his hair, the way
he has to sit there like a broken toy, leg useless.
He doesn't like going to get fixed.

'It's fine,' he says. 'I just pulled a muscle.'

He hesitates, expecting to be detected in the lie,

since he doesn't really have much in the way of muscle to pull. But Dad just nods, and picks up the bucket, and shunts it so that a wave of gritty soapy water flings out down the back lane. He goes in through the gate, to the garden tap, rinses out the bucket, and returns carrying a dark pool of clean water in it, ringed round with a faint circle of old foam.

They are onto the dry rags by the time Mum comes to the back gate and calls them in to supper. Sukie gets up and ambles in after her.

'Be in in a minute,' Dad says.

Will follows him into the garage, into the oil scent and wood dust. Dad flips out the rags, shaking out the wet, and Will does too, until his dad takes them off him and hangs them up on the nails hammered in along the edge of a shelf.

'Go on in,' his dad tells him.

Will does what he is told. He goes down the back garden between the flat rectangles of lawn and the narrow flowerbeds, and swings himself through the porch, and up the step into the kitchen. Sukie is already there, settled underneath Janet's seat.

There is bread and butter and ham and tea and milk and sugar. There is Janet in the highchair Dad made for her, straining against the straps, reaching out for the bread which is just a quarter of an inch out of her reach, and yelling, 'My want it, my want it.' When Will comes in she turns and gives him one of her big wet smiles, and he grins instinctively back. 'My want it,' she says again, but this time asking him, and, as Mum's back is turned and she's doing something in one of the cupboards, Will picks up a piece of bread and butter and hands it to his little sister, who rewards him with a 'Dankoo' and buries her face in the bread. She makes him smile. He watches her eat.

'Wash your hands,' his mother says over her shoulder. Oh yes, that. He goes over to the sink, and stretches up, and scrubs his hands with the green soap, and dries them on the towel, and then Dad comes in. Will watches as his father ambles straight over to Janet and crouches at her side, big smile on his face. He talks nonsense to her, tickling her, making her sputter crumbs. Will rubs the slimy soapy wet off his hands.

Janet shrugs her dad off with a 'NO', and he leans away with a laugh. The baby shoves the bread and butter into her mouth; Dad watches her eat, his eyes tender and fascinated. Sukie licks up the crumbs as they fall, her broad tongue leaving shiny wet patches on the lino. Will watches, drying his hands.

Mum turns round from whatever it is she's doing and says, 'Wash your hands, Billy.' And then, clocking her daughter's food: 'How did she get hold of that?'

'Dunno. Didn't you give her it?' his dad asks.

'No.'

Will feels his cheeks burn. He can see his mum's not particularly bothered, just puzzled. His dad though, still crouching, swivels round on his toes and looks at him. Will swallows, tries to gauge this. Is this the moment before the explosion? His dad's face is changing – the smile fading.

'Was she not supposed to have it?' Will asks.

'That's not the question,' his dad says.

'Little monkey helped herself,' Will says.

His dad snorts. Mum's face breaks into a smile. 'Little monkey,' his dad agrees, and gets up to wash his hands.

His mum shifts the plate of bread and butter further across the table, out of the reach of little fingers. Will draws his chair out from the table, seats himself carefully, stretching out his leg and balancing his calliper on the lower rung of Janet's chair. Janet stuffs the bread into her face, and munches, and gags, and chews again on what she's just retched back up. Will waits, hands in his lap, for the bread to be offered him.

Brighton Beach, 6 June 1955

The air is so big – stretches miles and miles – a sweep of pebbles up along the coast; the air a woompfh and a slap, and the sea growling itself up onto the pebbles. Janet is shrieking in delight, leaning from her mother's arms as if to grab hold of the whole day, Mum complaining at the pull on her back. Dad is lugging Grandma's deckchair and bags and the new thermos. Grandma picks her way along in her black dress and tan coat, trailing blankets. And Sukie is just daft with excitement, skittering off across the pebbles, barking at seagulls.

Will swings himself along, all callipered up for the walk. He carries a football in a string bag. He and Dad will have a kickabout.

They follow the high-water mark, a trail of bobbled seaweed and worn shells. The pebbles are tan and gold and grey; he leans over, calliper stretched out, to pick one up. The stone fits his hand neat as anything, and is golden, and almost seems to glow from inside. He drops it into his shorts pocket, and it makes the fabric droop to one side, weighing him down like a diver, pulling at his snake-link belt. Sukie bounces round him, black as a scrap of left-over night, and he laughs at her happy jowly face and dips for another stone, and reels his arm back and flings the stone overarm, putting as much welly into it as he can, sending it towards the sea, staggering with the after swing, his boots scuffing unevenly through the pebbles. Sukie flings herself after it. He watches the nearest waves for a plop and splash, but the pebble falls short, clatters, and Sukie scrabbles to a halt, legs going all directions, scattering stones as she searches, making him laugh.

He glances round to catch the others' attention; Dad is spreading out the blanket. Grandma stands like a stooped bird, waiting, her skirts and coat stirring in the breeze. 'Awfully windy, Billy.'

Dad sets out her deckchair, unfolding it and grinding it down into the stones. Grandma huffs down into the seat. 'There.' She looks up and around her. Squints into the bright sun. 'Billy, can you pass my knitting bag?'

Will swings himself up towards the family. His big boot clumps and drags and is hard work uphill on the stones.

'Are you having a nice time, Grandma?'

Grandma peers up at him. 'Lovely, thank you.' She clicks her false teeth. 'Lovely to have a day out with the family.'

He's sure it is. It wouldn't be nice spending all that time alone in her flat. It's dark, and smells funny, and she makes him look at old pictures; that's all she seems to do. Knit, look at old pictures, and drink tea.

But he is having a nice time too.

Dad is unfolding the windbreak. Mum strips Janet, peeling off layers of cardigan and pinafore and blouse and vest and pants. The baby stands naked for a moment, all belly and goosepimples, before being hoisted into her swimming costume. It is yellow and knitted and elasticated round the legs so that it balloons out round her backside. The straps are already slipping from her narrow shoulders. Dad hammers the windbreak into place with a stone. The shopping bag is stuffed with sandwiches and bottled pop and biscuits, but that's all for later. Dad eases himself down onto the rug, lies back, lets out a sigh, though it can't really be that comfortable.

Will sets down the football, and the bag slumps over it like a fallen parachute. Grandma says something, and Dad says, 'Eh,' and leans up to her, but she's not talking to him, she shakes her head: she's counting stitches, or she's talking to herself. Sukie comes scrabbling up towards the blanket with a mouthful of leathery seaweed, slapping it around, growling happily.

'She'll knock the baby flying,' Mum says.

Dad lifts up a stone and flings it way off towards

the sea; Sukie goes bounding after it happily, dealt with.

'Fancy a kickabout, Dad?' Will grinds a foot into the pebbles.

Dad tweaks his cap down over his eyes. 'Not now. Later. Play with Jannie.'

He worked all week. He cleaned the car. He drove all the way down here. He put up the windbreak. He's not playing football now.

Mum sends Janet on her way with a pat on the bum. The baby waddles a few steps then squats down to examine a bubble of dried seaweed. She picks it up and starts to chew on it. It must be quite satisfying, popping the bubbles, but Will wouldn't fancy the salty cabbageyness of it himself.

Mum looks up at him from where she sits on the blue-green-red tartan rug. Her beautiful lipstick. Her eyes blacker than anybody's eyes. She reaches into her handbag and gets out her cigarette case. She lights up.

'You going down to the sea with her?' she asks.

Will nods.

'Right then, love.' She sets about unstrapping his calliper. 'Be careful.'

Janet's hand is cold and small. Her head, at waist height, is a ball of blonde fluff. She is like a little yellow chick with her fluffy hair and her yellow swimming costume. He'd like to scoop her up and kiss her big round tummy, but he's not strong enough. He's been told, and won't do it again.

Anyway, Janet's not keen on being kissed. She yells and struggles when you put your arms around her. Pushes your face away.

He feels light without his calliper and built-up boot. His limp is different because he can't put much weight at all on the bad left leg without the support of the metal frame. It hurts too much. So he skips along, using the good leg for weight-bearing and the bad leg for balance, tiptoe to the ground. His shorts flap around his thin leg like a skirt.

Janet, small but smart, has worked out that she can step from pebble to pebble, fitting her small feet to their smooth surfaces comfortably. Her cold little hand in his, her pink toes placed carefully among the stones, the fat dimpled knees bob in and out in front of her as she walks. He though, he can't control his body like that. He lurches along at her side, like her pet monster.

He tries not to pull on her as he limps, in case he makes her lose her balance. They come up towards the creeping water's edge.

Sukie rushes up; she brings a half-shredded bit of driftwood, white as an old bone, and dances up to Will's side with it, taunting him; he drops Janet's hand to grab the stick, and Sukie digs all four feet into the stones and tugs against his grip, shaking her head and play-growling. If she could laugh, she would be laughing now, and it makes him laugh too. He says, 'Leave it,' in a big deep voice, and she does, and he lifts the piece of driftwood and skims it out towards the sea.

Sukie races after it, bounding into the shallows, then swimming. Will leans down to catch Janet's hand again. The sea comes curling up towards them, washes over their toes. She laughs, a big laugh that makes her belly shake, and she looks up at him, her face all crumpled up with delight, and he laughs back down at her, out of happiness.

The water swoops up and over their feet, their ankles. They step out further – good leg bad leg – into the water. It slaps up Will's shins, up to Janet's knees. He steadies himself against the drag of the water, against Janet's pull. She's trying somehow to stretch herself up and out of the sea, shrieking at the cold, delighted. It makes his hip hurt, but she's so happy. Sukie's got her stick, and swims back towards them, head sleek and black, eyes big as a seal's, like she belongs to the water. Will is up to his knees, good leg firm, bad leg supported just on the ball of his foot. Janet is up to the roundest part of her round belly, and is shivering. Sukie stands dripping. She drops her stick and shakes, spraying them all over with ice-drops of water, making Will yell, making Janet squeal. The stick washes up towards him, and he drops Janet's hand to get it. He's just thinking how it's easier in the water than on dry land, the water wafting it towards him, suspending it at knee height so he doesn't have to stoop, when the wave peels back, pulling out to sea, and Janet goes down.

It happens so suddenly that he can't make sense of it – she is there, and then she's gone – landing on her backside completely under water and dragged away by the wave's pull. He looks down at her little pink and yellow form through the surface of the water, like he's looking at her through a glass lid. There is just a moment of blankness. She'll stand up, she'll get to her feet and reach up and grab his hand. But she doesn't.

He reaches for her. For a moment his balance has gone too, and he's going to land on her, in the water, but it's just a second, less than a second, and he's got his arms round her, got her up again, on her feet, and from there he lifts her up onto his good hip, and he can hold her, he can actually, after all, lift her. She is freezing cold. Sputtering. Big eyes wide and wet and red. Too shocked even to cry.

'It's okay, petal, it's okay.'

He is strong enough. He is strong. Her wet body clings to him, hard; she lets out a great wail; she's shaking and crying, salt in her eyes and one arm round his neck, her fingers digging in, and the other fist up to try and rub the salt away. She shivers, jolts with sobs.

'I've got you, it's okay.'

A wave rolls up and over his legs, cold. He feels such an ache of tenderness. He wants to crush her to him, pull her right into his body, make her safe; he edges himself round on his good leg. And there is Dad running towards them, and Sukie's skipping around his feet, and Grandma's standing up on the blanket at the top of the beach, crying, 'Oh my gracious, oh my gracious me,' and the pebbles are flying out from underneath his dad's feet, and he's cursing at Sukie and kicking her out of the way, and Mum is coming down behind him, a hand covering her mouth, the other flapping around for balance. But it's okay, because Will has got her. He takes an awkward step towards them all. Dad'll take the weight off him and carry her safely back; Mum can wrap her up and give her a cuddle and all will be well. A drink and wrapped up in a towel and they will soon have her warm and dry and happy again. Because he was strong enough.

His father crashes into the surf in his eight-shilling shoes, his trousers not even rolled up.

'It's okay—' Will says, shifts his hold on Janet, her cold, wet weight, her dampness. Dad grabs her, his fingers grazing Will's chest. He whisks the weight away. Janet wraps herself onto Dad's Sunday shirt like a baby monkey.

'She fell,' Will begins, 'But I—'

His dad smacks him round the head. Will's good leg skids out from underneath him, and he falls. He lands on his bad hip, in the water. The pain is sudden. The cold is sudden. He struggles to get up. A wave crashes into his face. He splutters, blinks, can't breathe. His dad grabs him by the wrist, hauls him to his feet.

'You stupid little bastard,' his dad says. He

doesn't shout. His voice is low. 'You stupid little bastard, what on earth were you thinking?'

His dad drags him up onto the shore. Will's toes scrape and stub on the stones. He stumbles, loses his footing, scrambles to catch it again. They are on the beach, wet pebbles, then dry. His dad heaves him upright; Will hops and staggers. He looks up at his dad. Will's cheek hurts, his ear burns, his eyes sting with salt. But the pain from his hip is bad. It feels very bad. His dad shifts Janet up higher, an arm wrapped round her little wet body, the darkness of sea-water leaching out across his chest.

'She fell,' Will begins. 'I got her—' If he could just explain. 'Dad—'

But his dad just turns and climbs back up the beach, arms wrapped around his daughter. His mother stumbles down to meet the two of them, her arms outstretched, a towel billowing between her hands. They pause in a huddle of arms and fabric and exclamations. Then his mother breaks away, and comes towards Will. She melts into a blur of red dress and dark hair against the cool blue sky.

His neck is tight from the drive; when he double declutches and changes down the gear for the turn, his shoulder hurts.

He wants to be home. He wants to take the deckchairs out into the back garden, and split a bottle of Guinness with Ruby, and watch the bats dart in the evening sky.

He feeds the steering wheel through his hands and straightens up after the bend. He should never have agreed to bring them to the sea. They could have gone somewhere else, out to Hampton Court or Epsom Downs. He'd thought today that he was going to lose her too – his little girl, the solid vital strength of her, sucked into the waves. Like he'd lost his little boy; the little boy Billy had imagined he would be. This was not the deal. Billy wants to bang his hand on the steering wheel. This was not what he signed up for.

The world is fucking treacherous. You can't trust it.

Ruby's quiet. Angry with him. She's turned away now, onto her left side on the seat, curled onto her hip and shoulder, and breathing deeply. Janet whimpers in her sleep from time to time; or that might be Sukie, curled up in the footwell, shivering with dreams. His ma sits in the middle of the back seat, her head lolling. She snores. He hears nothing from the boy, but he knows he is awake. He just knows it. Awake and stewing. That's what he does: stews.

It's not like he meant to hit him. Sometimes he just brings it out in him. The anger. The fear.

They rumble down Madeira Road, reach the edge of the cricket green.

'Rube,' Billy says, and then when she doesn't register, louder: 'Ruby.'

She stirs, turns, blinks at him. 'Mmm?'

'Drop you off first, with the kids.'

'Okay.'

He has to lift Will out of the back seat, and the boy puts his arms around his father's neck, and Billy feels the slight weight of him, all bones and air, and the dragging calliper and built-up boot hanging like lead weights from a balloon. The boy digs his face into the man's neck.

'Sorry,' the boy says.

'Shh.'

'Sorry, Dad, I'm really sorry.'

Billy pushes through the garden gate, sets him down on the cement path. The cement is crumbling, and needs patching.

'Sorry,' the boy says again, arms round his neck still.

'Don't keep on saying sorry,' Billy says. He detaches the arms from round his neck.

'But you keep on being cross,' the boy says.

'Just shush.' He feels the grey drip of guilt. He wants a drink.

Ruby nudges the gate open with a hip, carrying Janet. The baby sleeps, slumped forward onto Ruby's shoulder. Billy strokes her hair back from her face. Flushed cheeks and a salty crust trailing from the corner of her eye.

'I'll be back shortly,' he tells Ruby.

'Right.' She doesn't meet his eye.

A sudden flare of anger. 'What?'

'Nothing.'

'Don't start on this, Ruby.'

'I'm not starting anything.' She meets his eye for just a flash, then reaches out for Will's hand.

'C'mon, love,' she says.

He feels his anger flush through him, satisfying. She will ruin the boy: he doesn't understand, he doesn't listen, doesn't give a damn. He needs sorting out and it's Billy who has to do it, like he has to do everything. If he doesn't, who will? He's his father after all.

She shuts the door quietly behind them, and Billy turns back to the car, where his mother sleeps.

He'll get her home. Then he'll drive round to the Cricketers. Perfect for a summer evening pint. A view of the Green, and a canvas roof, and barrels set out in a row behind the rough timber bar, like a marquee for a fete. Sprung up on the foundations of the old pub, it had, which had been flattened in an air raid. Gives you hope.

Just as he's pulling onto the London Road, his mother says something from the back of the car. It makes him jump. He'd thought that she was sleeping. He doesn't catch the words.

'What is it, Ma?'

But she doesn't reply. He twists round; she's slid over to the right side of the car, where Will had been sitting, and is looking out the window.

'You all right, Ma?'

Nothing. Then, after a moment, 'Where are we going?'

'Home.'

He watches her in the rear-view mirror. She just looks out of the window. Frowns.

She's still not used to the flat. But there's no room for her in the house now there's Janet too.

'Have you there in a jiffy,' he says.

He notches the car down a gear for the bend.

They pull up outside the squat block of flats. The lawn slopes towards them. Pots of red geraniums stand beside the white-painted front steps. In the dim evening light the blooms look brilliant, like gouts of freshly spilt blood. It's the new couple in the other ground-floor flat; they are nice, and keep everything nice. They look out for her.

He gets out of the car, and helps her out of the back. She leans heavily on his arm. She is bulky now, solid with support garments.

He'll just get her in, get her settled, and be on his way. He has a few bob still, despite the expenses of the day. A couple of pints of cold wallop. Do him right.

She looks up at him as they go in through the front door into the narrow communal hall, as if she doesn't know where she is. Still half asleep. He takes her key off her and opens the door. She stands looking in, but doesn't move.

'C'mon, Ma, let's get you sorted.'

She looks up at him, her pale irises are clouded-looking, her whites lined with broken capillaries. He takes her elbow and steers her down the hall, past the cubby-hole kitchen and into the sitting room. She doesn't shake him off: she lets herself be steered. He stops at her sagging chair, the one from the parlour in Knox Road. She sinks down into it. He crosses briskly back to the door and flicks on the light.

'There we go.'

She blinks round at the room.

'Too bright?' he dodges to switch on the lamp on the card table, then switches off the main light again. The little lamp casts a cool glow through its blue satin shade, and a cone of light like a UFO hits the ceiling.

She blinks up at him. She doesn't look quite right.

'Cup of tea, Ma?' he asks.

'Mmm.'

He makes the tea. The kettle is slow to boil on the gas. He drops the tea canister and it clangs against the counter: he hears her suck in her breath from the next room. He brings through a laden tray: the teapot with the cosy hastily bundled on, a bottle with an inch of milk in it, a cup and saucer. She looks disapprovingly at the assortment of tea things, as he knew she would, but does not complain, as he also knew.

'I wonder sometimes.'

'What, Ma?'

She reaches across and turns the cup around on the saucer, so that its handle faces towards her.

'I don't know. Just.'

'What?' He feels a flare of irritation, a wash of guilt. 'Go on.'

She shakes her head. She tugs the tea cosy down, like she's straightening a child's jumper.

'You'd better go,' she says. 'You'd better get back home to them.'

'I'd better.'

She nods. Purses her mouth, making her lips fold up into deep creases.

'I'll call by tomorrow,' he says. 'After work. I'll bring you something. A bun.'

'Good boy,' she says, and he dips down to let her kiss him. The faint press of her skin is cool as glove leather.

'Right then,' he says.

'Right.'

He turns to go. 'Good night, Ma.'

She sucks in a rusty breath, and says at last: 'Be careful with that boy.'

Billy blows out a sharp breath, irritated. 'Ma. Don't.'

She reaches for his hand, squeezes it, and smiles at him. Her teeth are perfect now, a row of even white plastic, and candy-pink gums.

'Are you sure you're all right now,' he asks her. 'You've got everything you need?'

She nods. 'I'm happy,' she says.

'Good,' he says. She really does look happy. He glances at his watch.

'I'll drop by tomorrow, then,' he says. 'Bring you a cream bun.'

'I'd like a cherry bakewell.'

'Cherry bakewell it is then.'

He kisses her. And he leaves her there, sitting in her chair, in a solitary pool of light. He'll get something for the boy. Make him something. Billy can't quite think what.

Amelia pours her tea. She lifts the milk bottle and trickles some in.

'I suppose it's just too much trouble to fill a jug?'

She glances up at the shadows in the other chair; there is nothing there.

She takes up her knitting, and tries to pick up where she left off, but something has gone wrong: she's lost count shaping the sleeve, and she has to ravel back. The wool bumps along, unhooking itself from the loops before, rolling back onto the ball in tight waves.

When she doesn't look directly, she can almost see him. A dark shape, a shadow of him in the chair. If she doesn't look too closely, if she doesn't stare.

'He's older than you now,' Amelia says.

Her hands, as they twist and tug the wool, are dark and knotted like driftwood.

'I used to think he looked like you,' she says. 'I'm not so certain any more.'

Because there are no photographs, there's nothing to compare, and despite herself, despite her determination to remember, she can't be sure.

She glances up, looks directly at the armchair. There is just dark space there, emptiness. He was never the kind of man to sit around in armchairs, anyway. Always off and up and doing, fixing something, pulling something apart and putting it back together again. But sometimes, in the stillest room, she catches the scent of the sea, the roar of waves, and an unexplained joy floods through her like sunshine, and it feels, for a moment, like he is coming home.

This is her secret. She can't tell. This is her happiness.

Sister Kathleen whisks past, gives him a smile. Sister *Kathleen*. Even in his thoughts, her name seems to come out with a sigh. Will glances round at Cosimo, who raises a bald eyebrow in appreciation. Sister Kathleen is a peach: they have agreed it, though they're not sure what it means. She goes to open the French windows and sunlight catches in the curls that escape from underneath her cap.

He is having a break from traction today. Traction as in extraction and as in tractor and as in intractable. The pulleys and weights dangle from the end of the bed, and even though he's released from them he's still unable to walk, because he's in plaster from ball of foot to just above his hip, his toe pointed like a dancer's and his hip joint held immobile. He's leaning up against a stack of pillows.

He has Perthes disease. They are trying to fix it. They are trying to stop his hip bone from grinding his hip socket into bits. He imagines it like the mortar and pestle in the chemist's shop: his hip bone is the pestle, his hip socket is the crumbling mineral that is being ground up, and not the solid white bowl it should be.

Sister Kathleen heaves open the French windows. The net curtains billow in the breath of sweet damp air. She comes back to fetch the first of the patients.

Today, while they are out on the veranda, getting their dose of fresh air and sunshine, the nurses are having a Big Clean.

Which gives him, what? An hour? There's the dusting, the sweeping, the mopping, the polishing. And then there's the fetching and carrying and the sit-down feet-up cup-of-tea afterwards. Hour and a half? If the boys keep quiet – not too quiet, not suspiciously quiet – they'll be left alone. And by the time the nurses come back to fetch them in again, he and Cosimo will be long gone.

'You ready, Cos?' Will asks.

Cosimo gives him his lopsided, scarred smile. It makes his whole left cheek and forehead dent up like moon craters. 'I ready.'

Cos reaches his good hand down and lifts his backgammon set onto his knee. He clicks open the box and displays, inside, the squashed-flat collection of sandwiches from the week's teas. Some of the older ones look a bit crisp around the edges.

'Good,' Will says.

Cosimo nods and clicks his backgammon set shut.

Will glances up and down the ward – Sister Kathleen's back is turned, Sister Joyce is rummaging around in one of the silent boys' beds. All clear. He leans round to reach into his locker. Toffee tin, penknife, box of matches with a wad of paper stuck inside to stop them rattling, then the hank of string and his bow and arrows. He's taken the suckers off the arrows and sharpened the tips with a pencil sharpener: they look pretty serious and deadly now.

He shoves the supplies beneath his blanket, then lifts his stack of comics from the locker. *Eagle*, *Tiger*, and *The Beano*: he lays them out over the bulging blanket as legitimate veranda reading and quite effective camouflage. He surveys the landscape of his bed.

Good.

The broom handle is stowed between the mattress and the bedframe. His fingers curl round the reassuring strong beech. No-one has noticed it's missing yet. Who's really going to miss a stray broom handle anyway? They'll just think that someone has taken it away to fix a head to it. Last night Cosimo had moved like a cat – a three-pawed cat – to fetch it from the broom cupboard while Sister Brenda dozed at the nurses' station.

Down the far end of the ward Sister Kathleen and Sister Joyce begin to shift the beds and the boys. They get in behind the tubular steel bedheads and shove at the frames until the castors swivel into line and start to roll. The little wheels can be tricky – they creak and stick and there are halts while the nurses mutter and dart around to kick them into line with the hard black toes of their lace-ups. He and Cos will have to watch out for that.

Will and Cosimo's beds are a third of the way down the ward. Cosimo, being ambulant, doesn't need to be rolled out into the sun. He slides out of his bed with his backgammon set clutched under his arm, and gives Will a nod as he passes. Will nods back. He watches Sister Kathleen, her shoulder to a bedhead, her backside bulging against the starched sheet of her skirt.

'Pppssst.'

It comes from Mickey, on the other side.

Will turns towards him. His stomach grazes against the rough edge of the plaster.

Mickey has something wrong with his muscles. All of them. In the summer he beat Will at croquet. Will is pretty sure he cheated. Mickey's eyes seem to have got too big for his head now, and his head seems to have got too heavy for his body, and he's not playing croquet any more.

'I'm coming too,' Mickey says. The words are difficult for him. They come out loose and wet.

'No you're not.'

'Yes I am,' Mickey says, 'or I'll tell on you.'

Croquet is a game for toffs, for girls and vicars. Football; that's a game that's worth winning at.

And even with a calliper on, Will is pretty handy: he may not be fast, but with his built-up boot, he's got a right foot that no-one can argue with. Granted, he doesn't know of any professional footballers that use a calliper. But he won't need a calliper for ever. He's getting better. Everyone says. He'll be fine, if he's just given the chance.

But if they pin his hip, that's it, over. No-one can have their hip pinned and play football.

Mickey is serious. Mickey is a complication. And Mickey is also a toe-rag, and will stiff you given half a chance.

'Look,' Will says. 'You're all right here.'

Mickey just stares at him from his pillow; wet pebble eyes.

'Me and Cosimo, you know. We have to go. We've got no choice.'

A slow blink.

'But you, they take care of you, you're best off here. They're not going to . . .' The word is like a blister in his throat. 'Operate. Not on you.'

Mickey swallows. It looks like hard work. 'Please.'

Mickey has been getting sicker now for years. When his parents visit it's clear his mother has been crying all the way here, and is going to start up again as soon as they are off the ward. Mickey is going to die. Everybody knows, including Mickey.

And this is his last request.

Which is fair enough.

'Okay,' Will says. 'So. How?'

Mickey licks his lips. His tongue is pale as chicken paste.

'Cosimo and me,' Will explains, 'we've got it worked out. You need a system.'

'Pete's coming,' Mickey says. 'He'll push.'

Will leans forward as far as his cast will allow, and looks beyond Mickey at Spastic Pete who's in the bed beyond. Pete grins back at him; Will nods. Pete's all right, though Will only plays cards with him for matchsticks nowadays. And with his callipers on, he's not bad on his pins, once he gets going: he'll have the bedhead to hold onto for balance.

He should have thought of Pete before, truth be told – Pete's legitimate – he's been operated on, and they'll do it again, it's just a matter of time. Will's heard that Mr Smyth discussing possibilities with the students. All of them crowding round Pete's bed and jabbering away about what they might do to his tendons to help him walk, what they could do to his throat to clear his voice. Like for some reason they've decided that Pete is deaf, or stupid or something. It sounds bloody awful.

So Pete's in, and Mickey too.

'Got any food saved up, any supplies?' Will asks.

With massive effort, Mickey pulls back the sheet to reveal a newspaper-wrapped parcel.

'Arrived today.'

Mickey's parents send him tins of sardines, peaches, handfuls of Kit Kats. Will is quite partial to all three, and Mickey hasn't previously been inclined to share.

'All right,' Will says. 'You're in.'

Mum and Dad and Janet are supposed to be coming next Thursday, like it's prize day. Mum has promised to bring ice cream, a block each, one for him and one for Cosimo too. Cosimo's parents are in Rome. Mum does the things they'd do if they could.

On Thursday they're going to pin his hip. He doesn't know what the operation will involve because no-one's told him. But he imagines the pin itself – a great iron pin, the kind you see on breakwaters and jetties, sticking out of the white skin of his hip. Grinding along for ever on a rusty lump of iron. He's not having that. He's seen people with pinned hips, the way they move. As if ice cream would make up for that.

And Cosimo. Blimey. Cosimo.

They are going to actually open Cosimo up. They are going to make – he heard Mr Smyth telling the crowd of student doctors – an incision in his abdomen. In his *belly*. And when they have sliced him open they are going to slip his bad hand in under the skin there and stitch it up. Then they will strap his arm down, bandage his whole body to stop him from tearing at the wound. The procedure, Mr Smyth told the crowding student doctors, will help the damaged hand heal.

Will doesn't know how much of this Cosimo understood. He hopes not much.

From what Will's gathered from Cosimo's attempts to explain in his patchy, ragged English, there was waste ground – an old bombsite – back in Rome where Cos is from, and there was a hand grenade. And Cos, who was out playing on the waste ground with his pals, picked up the hand grenade to throw it, and wasn't quite fast enough. Will reckons he's lucky that there are no hand grenades left lying around London, because chances are that if he found one he'd pick it up and throw it too.

The way Will sees it, Cosimo's fingers are never going to grow back, no matter where you stick his hand.

So they are going. They are off and away. Him and Cosimo against the world. Though now it's him and Cosimo and Mickey and Spastic Pete against the world.

And if he ever sees his dad again, when he's grown up and strong and is playing for Carshalton Athletic, if he sees his dad in the crowd at a match he'll jog over to him at half-time and say, See, I can do it. You did it your way, and I can do it too.

And then the whistle'll go and he'll run off to the game, and he'll score a goal, the goalie'll never even see it coming, his boot's got so much power behind it. Shoots like he's firing rockets, that's what they'll say of him; and, you'd never even know he used to be a cripple.

And maybe someone will see him in the street and want to shake his hand.

Spastic Pete slides out of bed and onto the chunky arm of Sister Joyce. They stagger across the lino towards the French windows and the sun. Sister Kathleen slides in behind Mickey's bed; her head turned away from Will, she pushes.

Mickey gives him an uneven smile as he's wheeled away. He mumbles back towards Will, 'I can snare rabbits. My uncle taught me.'

Will doesn't believe him. And it was stupid, to say that in front of Sister Kathleen. But she doesn't hear, or doesn't catch on anyway – thinks it's the kind of thing boys just say.

Though if it's true, it could come in handy; with his bow and arrows, and Mickey teaching them all to snare rabbits, they'll be well off for dinner. He's got matches and they can roast rabbits and ducks and whatever there is, build a fire in the woods. They'll be like outlaws.

They'll *be* outlaws. Fugitives from the law. Or from the hospital, which is much the same thing if you're in it.

Sister Joyce wedges herself in behind Will's bed.

'All right then, my lovely,' she says, and shoves, and he jolts forward, rolling out across the lino towards the sun.

He lies blinking. The air is cool. Sister Kathleen comes to tuck his blankets straight.

These few moments are filled with terror and

delight. Terror that she will notice the supplies. Delight at her proximity: breathing her lemony scent and gazing at the downy skin on the back of her neck. The way that through the blankets her chest brushes against his legs, the starched bulge of it shifting against the hard cast on his left leg, where he can kind of feel it, and on the right leg, where he can really feel it.

No more tuck-ins from Sister Kathleen; no more lifting and shifting and holding as they put him into traction; no more bed baths.

He'll live with it. Because a woman like Sister Kathleen wouldn't want a man with a pinned hip.

She straightens up and smiles at him again. He wants to say something grown up and manly, a John Wayne kind of thing. But she doesn't wait around for him to speak. She turns away and draws up a chair for Cosimo, whose pyjamas are buttoned up to the chin and whose dressing gown is pulled tight around the middle. He looks like Tom Kitten. Tom Kitten if he'd found a hand grenade to play with instead of a ball of wool.

'There you go,' Sister Kathleen says.

'Thank you, sister,' Cosimo says, which is one of his good phrases.

She smiles at him, her cheeks bunching up into apples, looking at Cosimo's messy face, and she gives him a little pat on that ragged cheek of his. Will loves her, he realises. And he will never love anyone else, not the way he loves Sister Kathleen. With her hands and her smell and her curls, and her bosom like a pillow in a cool, starched case.

But. There will be snaring rabbits, shooting ducks, building fires, eating Mickey's Kit Kats. And no-one pinning his hip.

The veranda stretches the length of the back of the hospital. Back in the First War it used to be for soldiers to get sunshine and fresh air and peace and quiet after everything. The theatre is where they used to try to put them back together again, or at least tidy up the ragged edges. That's where Mr Smyth got his idea that doctors can just try stuff out to see what happens, and patients will just say, Oh, thank you, Mr Smyth, and stump off home, because if you're half mangled in a war then you're glad to get whatever help you can, and if what's wrong with you is completely different and completely new then they'll have to experiment then, won't they? But back before the wars, this place used to be posh. You can tell by the space. The marble in the front hall. The grounds. Back then, people had old-fashioned diseases, and men like Mr Smyth did what they were told to do by the people who paid them. The doctors didn't get to do any of their experiments, because people won't pay to be experimented on.

They drug you up before you go. They wheel you in while you can't do anything to stop it. Then they strap you to a table and do whatever they like to you.

The back lawns are bounded by a lane and then a stone wall. The lane is lined with great spreading trees, a lane for grocery vans and the coal man and the gardener. Their vans pass from time to time, half-hidden by the bank, flicking between the grey trunks of the trees. Beyond that the Hampshire fields rise and fall; woods grow in the nooks and dips between them. He has his eye on one particular spot. A patch of trees growing up the side of the hill, bigger than the rest; he can see the leaves ripple in the breeze. It's like home in a game of tig: he knows that if he can just get there, he'll be safe. He'll cut off this bloody plaster cast. His penknife is good and sharp. He will smash the plaster into dust. He will throw it in a stream. Or, maybe, he'll leave it somewhere out along the road, drop it by the verge for someone to find. Like a shed snakeskin, a thrown-off disguise. They won't find him, because he will be transformed. This is not who he is, the boy who lies on the bed weighted down while people do things to him, while Mr Smyth decides what experiment to try next. Get this plaster off, and given half a chance his leg will grow strong, he knows it.

From back in the ward, pails clank in the empty long room, voices pealing out with 'Whistle While You Work'. Will scans the line of beds, checking the route. There is a low rail along the length of the veranda, to keep beds and wheelchairs from rolling off, but at the far end, to the left, a ramp slopes down to join the gravel path below. That's their way out. All clear.

'Next song,' Will says to Cosimo. 'Soon as they start up on the next song, we'll be off. Should cover any noise.'

Cosimo nods, grins, making the bald scar on his head wrinkle up.

Pete ambles down along the veranda in his callipers and crutches like a dizzy giraffe, and clanks down onto the chair next to Mickey's bed. Cosimo lays the backgammon set down on Will's lap, doesn't open it. Spastic Pete nods to Will: *Ready when you are.*

The lawns are smooth and green and tempting: an invitation to run like a mad thing, shouting, waving your arms in the air.

But there's quiet from the ward. Just the swoosh and clank of mopping. Will's skin prickles. Perhaps they won't sing again. Perhaps Matron has forbidden it. Perhaps they've got to work in silence now. But he has to go anyway, cover or no cover. He has no choice. He's just steeling himself to give Cosimo the order, and there's a crackle from inside, they're tuning in the radio – then it's the Light Programme, and it's the Wilfred Pickles show *Have A Go*. He can't hear what's said. A cackle of laughter, and then the women laugh too. Good dense sound. Great cover.

He smiles to Cosimo, jerks his head: *We're off!*

Cosimo scrambles to his feet. Will swivels round to catch Mickey's eye, and Spastic Pete's. He gives them a look. A Lone Ranger kind of look. Then he drags the broom handle out from underneath the blankets.

And this is it. D-Day. H-Hour. Go go go!

He punts down against the concrete – Cosimo shoves the bedhead, and they're rolling along the veranda, past the row of stationary beds and bent-wood chairs, where the other boys cheer them on in silence, throwing pillows, waving comics over their heads, scattering clouds of playing cards up into the air.

They career down the ramp – only a two-foot drop, but the sudden swoop of the descent makes Will's stomach lurch. He can hear the rattle of Mickey's bed coming along behind, the hard clank of Pete's boots and callipers on the concrete. It feels good, the punt of the pole against the ground, the beechwood sliding easily through his palms, the unexpected strength of his arms. Will they notice they've gone, back indoors? His bed spins out onto the compacted gravel, and then lurches up onto the grass; they soar out across the lawns. It is smooth as plain sailing. The light and distance before them, the cool air on Will's face, stirring his hair: it makes him laugh. He leans into the work, paddling like an Indian in his canoe, racing across the green lake of the lawns.

Will hears the crump behind him as the second bed hits the edge of the grass, and then rattles on across the lawn. They'll make it: he and Cosimo will make it – he knows this. He's not so sure about the others.

'Going great guns—' he calls back to Cosimo, and Cosimo, being a boy of few words, and out of puff to boot, just smiles red-facedly at him.

They come up to the trees. A glance round and Mickey and Pete are doing okay, a hundred yards or so behind. Ahead, the ground is dotted with small whitish flowers. Then Will hears the first shout. A cry really, more than a shout. Sister Kathleen. In his mind's eye she is standing there with her sleeves rolled and hair loose and a hand to her heaving bosom, looking out across the lawn after him, realising she will never see him again.

The second shout is a bark from Matron – and then after that a series of blunt, angry orders. They're after them.

The tree roots make the ground lumpy, and they bounce and jolt and for a moment he thinks they're completely stuck, but he shoves hard with his broom handle, and they lurch onwards and up and then they are teetering on the brink of the bank down to the lane, and they are no sooner at it than they are over it, crashing down onto the chalky white surface, careering round, Cosimo hammering away behind, and the pain from Will's leg searing up his back and down all the way to his big toe like a shock of red electric. He blows out a breath.

'Good fun, no?' Cosimo calls over the clattering and the speed and the yells from beyond, and Will, clenched against the pain, nods.

They hammer down the gravel track, the

branches whisking overhead, patches of dappled sun, tree trunks slipping past like the legs of giant elephants. A green smell, and the mossy banks twisted with roots, and Cosimo chuckling to himself even as he runs, and Will, despite the pain, feels a thrill of delight. They are on the track now. They are heading for the gate. No-one's ever got this far before.

They're going to make it.

Which makes him think again of Pete and Mickey. He leans round to look for them, and, glimpsed between the lantern-show flicker of the tree trunks, it's exactly as he imagined it. The bed is stalled, its wheels jammed in the lumpy ground. Mickey is too far away, too flat against the pillows for Will to see him. But he sees Pete staggering on alone across the grass without the support of the bed or his crutches. His arms flail. Sister Joyce steams up behind him, her cap hanging by a pin, her dark hair tumbling loose, and then she flings herself forward and tackles Pete, sending him sprawling to the ground like a dropped bundle of sticks. Will flinches for him. Then Sister Kathleen staggers up to Mickey's bed, one hand to its frame, the other pressed to a stitch in her side. She looks down at Mickey, says something, shakes her head. She reaches round him, fussing, tucking, checking he hasn't come to any harm. And then she looks up, straightens up, and looks out after Will.

Will's heart flips. The trees thicken; the view is

gone. He turns to look ahead. The driveway dips away, and he can see the gate.

It stands wide open: beyond, there is a curve of tarmac – the road. His heart lifts like a lark, soars. Almost there. They rattle down the final slope towards the gateway.

He hears men's voices, but they are far off: they won't catch him and Cos. Once they're out of the gate and heading downhill along the road, Cosimo can step up onto the bedframe to coast, getting his breath back, while Will steers their trusty ship with his pole. They will put distance between them and this place. Later, when they've made their camp in the woods, they will build a fire and eat egg sandwiches. Kit Kats would have been nice, but he doesn't mind. He's glad that it is just him and Cosimo, after all. They can teach themselves to snare rabbits. He'll shoot a duck.

From a way off, he recognises the accent of the groundsman, Jackson; the posh voices are the student doctors', pitched high with panic like the bunch of girls they are.

But the two of them are almost at the gate now. The main gate stands back, sunk on its hinges, as if it's not often used. There's a little side gate too, Will notices. Painted white with black hinges, latched shut. They rattle on towards the open gateway. He wonders vaguely why you'd leave the big gate wide open and latch the little one shut.

Then he sees why, but it's too late. Too late to stop, too late to do anything but to drop his broomhandle, spin himself round to clutch at the bedhead and meet Cosimo's startled eyes.

'Cattle grid!'

Cosimo can't get the sense, but he gets the panic. He tries to pull back, but it's no help now. The front wheels drop down into the pit. The front legs jolt against the rung. The bed tips forward and in an instant, Will is flying, his stomach spinning and his only thought, this is going to be bad. Toffee tin and penknife and triangles of white dry bread and fragments of egg and sharp-tipped arrows and comics and string fly through the air. Sheets crumple into a heap. The mattress slumps, flops forward and exposes the supporting wire mesh underneath. Will lands half on the angled foot of the bed, half on the rails of the cattle grid. The bed jolts again as Cosimo slams into the wire mesh of the base.

Everything stops.

Will is looking down into the pit. It is deep with last year's leaves. He can lift his head, but he can't move his fingers. His arm is an explosion of pain. He knows that he has broken it. He lifts himself up on his good arm.

The bed looks like it has hit a mine. He rolls onto his back, his broken arm across his chest, heaving himself up on his good elbow. It hurts. Cosimo retrieves himself from under the bed, a dazed bundle. He has a cut on his forehead; another scar to add to the collection. For a moment they just look at each other. Cosimo touches his sore head. He looks very grave.

'You okay?' Will asks.

'I okay.'

He nods at Will's limp arm. Will grimaces, shakes his head. The toffee tin and penknife are lying on the gravel at his feet. He shoves at them with his good foot: 'You go on.'

Cosimo looks at him, doesn't seem to understand.

'You take them,' Will says. He feels faint.

The men are close now. He can hear them calling breathlessly, their heavy running tread.

'Go on, get out of here,' Will says. The world has narrowed to a tunnel; it fizzes. He is done for; but Cosimo still has a chance. 'Go on!'

Cosimo obligingly ducks down, picks up the toffee tin.

'Now run,' Will says.

Cosimo looks at the tin, then back at his friend.

'Please.' The pain is really bad. He's going to black out. 'Please, go.'

But Cosimo just squats down beside Will. He sets the tin aside, and reaches into the pocket of his flannel dressing gown. He takes out his cigarettes. He shakes them so that a couple of them stick out, nips one between his teeth, angles the packet towards Will.

Will looks at him for a moment. Then reaches for one unsteadily. His eyes blur.

They light up. Cosimo grabs a pillow and shoves it in under Will. Will lies back. 'Thanks.'

They blow spools of smoke up towards the blue September sky. Will's head gets clearer. His arm hurts a lot. He feels sick. But he's not going to black out now. He wishes he could. He thinks he might cry. The men come into view. Jackson a column of blue trousers and brown coat, and then the flapping white coats of two of the younger doctors.

'Sorry, Cos,' he says. 'Sorry, sorry, sorry.'

On Thursday, when they wheel Cosimo back in after his operation, he looks like he is dead and half mummified already. The doctors – Mr Smyth and the students with their pathetic moustaches and shaved-over spots – they all look so proud of themselves. Will just wants to be sick.

Will's left arm is angled, set solid and hammocked in a sling. The cast is newish still, and clean. It smells of the workshop, of canvas and plaster. He got a new cast for his leg too. They're treating him, he thinks, like an important prisoner, like a captured officer. Distant, respectful, occasionally cruel. When she cut the old cast off him, Matron left a beaded line of blood up his leg; he gritted his teeth and bore it. Given what Cosimo was going through, it didn't seem right to make a fuss.

There was a shower of dead grey skin in there. Grey as Cosimo's face.

He'd thought he was going to be brave, but in the end he'd been very far from brave. His arm had hurt so much; moving him had hurt so much. He'd gone into a total funk, wailing, streaming tears. He doesn't like to think back to that, to see himself in that state. But, somehow, it had done the trick. Sister Kathleen promised she'd talk to Mr Smyth. And then Mum and Dad drove down, and Mum looked huddled and anxious in her new jacket and lipstick, and Janet scribbled in her colouring book and sniffed, and Dad kept calling Mr Smyth 'Doctor' until Mr Smyth corrected him.

There was a hissed scolding about the fuss and bother, and the nurses and the doctors who knew best, and were doing their jobs, looking after him and making him better and him thinking *he* knew best? Will watched his dad's hands clench and unclench. There was oil beneath the nails – the car had broken down on the way – but he couldn't hit Will, not there in the public ward, with the nurses stalking up and down and Mr Smyth actually listening to Sister Kathleen and Matron, heads together at the nurses' station. And with Will up to his waist and shoulder in plaster of Paris.

So he got away with it. They won't pin his hip. But they won't give him any ice cream either.

Cosimo, though, hadn't cried and wailed and got into a state. He'd been in not that much more pain than usual. He'd followed Will as Jackson carried him back, walking between the two doctors, stumpy bandaged hand swinging, calmly finishing his cigarette. On Thursday he was wheeled off to theatre while Will was still sleeping.

Will thinks it was a nasty trick to do that, to sneak off with him in the night. But it was also a relief to wake and find the bed next to his empty. It had already happened, so he didn't have to try and stop it.

At first, the curtains are kept drawn round Cosimo's bed. Will can imagine every detail of it – the bloody cut, the flap of skin stretched over the stump, the skin stitched back onto the scarred wrist, everything scabbing up; all of it swaddled, strapped down tight. Because you would tear it straight out otherwise; you wouldn't be able to help yourself. Waking up to find they'd turned you into a freak.

When Cosimo is awake again, and the curtains are drawn back, Will tries to be as he always was. They play backgammon, both one-handed, on the ridges of Will's knees. They crunch Will's Maltesers from the box. Later, Will passes him a fresh comic. Cosimo can read the pictures, and gets the sense of words like Aargh and Achtung and Phew. And it goes on like this for a while, for days, even a week. But Will can't really look at him any more. Can't think about him even. That hand tucked and sewn inside himself. Though he unwraps him sweets and passes comics and slides his backgammon chips around the board for him, he keeps his mind averted, from what he thinks and feels and what it must be like to be Cosimo now. An experiment.

Mickey is worse too. His speech has somehow

slumped, and Will finds it embarrassing trying to pick apart the words.

The nurses keep a close eye on Will. They've confiscated his arrows and his penknife. Bed rest, and a set of exercises, supervised by Mr Smyth. This is a new kind of experiment for Mr Smyth, rather different from his usual hack-and-slash approach: physiotherapy, they call it. Will rather likes it.

They start off with a football, in the lobby. He has to kick it with his good foot, which means balancing on the bad. Then the other way. He grits his teeth and tries and wobbles and clutches Sister Kathleen and tries again. Mr Smyth looks on, frowns, takes notes. Will kicks the ball. Sister Kathleen laughs and claps and runs to fetch it, her footfalls echoing off the marble floor.

The old isolation ward upstairs is being cleared of beds. Will can hear it going on from where he lies playing cards with Cosimo – the rumbling of the wheels on the boards, the shuffling as new equipment is moved in. When Sister Brenda takes him up there, along with another three boys from off the ward – Spastic Pete is one of them, one's a new boy with a compound fracture that isn't healing right, the other is Humpy Hoggarth, who has scoliosis – there are parallel bars and mats and balls and ropes and it looks like great fun, but it turns out that it is exhausting too. Nights are just black oblivion, he sleeps so deeply. He doesn't mind the hard work, or the pain, because it's for a reason.

Make the muscles strong and they'll support the joint; keep the joint supported and the damaged bone won't fail. This is what Mr Smyth says. He says it directly to Will now, rather than over his head, involving him in his treatment, making him take responsibility for it. The problem is that the joint is so damaged and unsupported at this point that it just wobbles around – it's these minor dislocations that've been causing Will the pain. That's what the pin was supposed to do – stop the wobbling. But if Will works hard, and builds up that muscle to hold his joint in place, then his pain will be reduced, can be made perhaps to just go entirely away. No need for that pin. He can be like other boys. He can even play football. This, Will wants to say, is what he's been saying all along. But he doesn't say it now, in case that makes them decide to take all of this away.

'We could take them swimming,' Sister Kathleen suggests.

Mr Smyth gives her a look. 'Do they look like they need a dose of polio, sister?'

And she blushes and no more is said, which seems a shame as it would be nice to go swimming with Sister Kathleen.

Soon, he has read all his comics to rags. Mum has stopped sending them, as a punishment. When the library cart comes round, he asks to have a closer look. He borrows a book. It is Robert Louis Stevenson's *Treasure Island*. It's smashing.

Cosimo has new friends, Clive and Trev and Tiny Brian, from down the far end of the ward. They play darts together, the four of them. It works out quite well for Cosimo; he's got better balance than the other boys, a steadier hand, even if it is only the one of them.

Will finishes *Treasure Island*. He picks a paperback next, with a cowboy on the cover, and that's quite exciting. He ploughs through the *Just So Stories*, but finds them silly and a bit boring. Then he finds *Kidnapped*, which is by the same old fellow as *Treasure Island*, and he just romps through it. When he has read his way through the library trolley, Sister Kathleen starts to fetch books in from the library in town. He likes westerns, and adventures, and war stories. One day she comes in with a book as fat as a loaf; she hands it over to him and it drops in his hands, heavier than he'd expected.

'I asked the librarian. You've got through all their Junior Readers.'

He turns the book over. No exciting cover picture, just blank maroon cloth plastered onto cardboard. He can't hold it comfortably.

'It's very heavy.'

She smiles at him. 'It'll build up your strength.'

He turns it over, reads the spine. *Great Expectations*.

Denham Crescent, Mitcham, 12 October 1965

She can't make sense of it. The room is smaller than it should be, and the bed is in the wrong place. She has to get ready, get herself sorted out. She can't get the blankets off her. She struggles up and sits, their weight across her knees. She heaves the blankets back and drags her legs round, her nightie all rucked up, and there are her slippers on the rug. She feels her toes into them.

She has to get herself tidied up and dressed and make some breakfast. He is coming home. It has been such a long voyage.

She goes over to the window and drags back the curtains. It's dark, which seems strange, but it doesn't put her off. What seems stranger is the shape of the sky. It should be a narrow strip above the houses opposite – and Knox Road itself a ribbed band of cobbles below – but here it is an open plane; a bald flat moon stands on the sky, and makes everything blue-silver – the gardens, the sheds, the back lane with chalky runnels and the backs of houses beyond.

For a moment she is intensely troubled by this, where she is and how she got here, and what she's going to do, and how he's going to find her here, and then something shifts in her thoughts, and she knows it will be fine. The arrangements are made. They have agreed it. She will be safe. That's why she's here.

She stands on the bedside mat, her flesh goosepimpling. She is going to wear that suit. The new suit in the longer line, and her new hat. He'll be so proud when he sees how their boy has looked after her. She moves towards the wardrobe, but then remembers, the album, her picture book; she has to find it. Show him how she kept the postcards that he sent. She casts around the room – and it is tiny, narrow, pokey – how they will fit his sea-chest and him in here as well she doesn't know. She stumbles back across the bedside mat in her slippers, and flicks on the light. She can't see it. There is a blue suitcase lying flat by the end of the bed, and there is the wardrobe with its knobs like petrified lace, and there is a dressing table pushed up next to it, and a chair with her cardie over the back of it, and a bed and beside the bed a nightstand with a glass with her teeth in it. She catches sight of her reflection, and sits down at the dressing table.

She turns her face from side to side. A good man doesn't mind. She picks up her powderpuff and pads it against her cheeks and nose. A thick dust of lavender-white sticks there. She opens drawers and peers inside and tips a toilet bag out onto the glass top of the dresser. She finds a lipstick and draws it on.

She shivers. She picks up her cardigan and holds it for a moment, and then hooks it over the back of the chair carefully so that it will keep its shape and will not crease. She opens the door and goes out onto the landing. She knows this place but can't work out how. There is one window on the landing, casting a pale rectangle on the patterned carpet. The stair treads are silvered with light from below. She climbs carefully down. He will be coming up the garden path. He will be about to step onto the doorstep, raise his hand to knock. A wooden sun rises across the door; its rays fan out across the frame, holding the glass segments in place. The light through the panes is muted blue, but then it flares into astonishing brightness. It's a blessing, she realises: a promise. Any minute, his shadow will move across the light, and he will be there. He will be home. But the brightness grows, and then explodes. And it hurts.

It is Ruby who finds Amelia there, lying half on the hall carpet, half on the bottom two steps, her nightdress trailing round her calves, her mouth open. In that instant Ruby realises that she has been dreading this for months – this very moment, this very image. Amelia hurt. She might have been lying there all night, caught a chill. Ruby stumbles down to her, clutching the handrail, her own nightie and dressing gown bundled up in one hand to stop herself from tripping. She should have had Billy fit a gate across the stairs. They knew she was wandering: that's why they moved her back in with them, to the room vacated by Will's departure. They should have thought it through.

'Amelia?'

Ruby's first concern is to get her up, get her into the sitting room, get the gas on and get her warmed up, get a hot cup of tea into her, call the doctor. But Amelia doesn't stir.

Ruby crouches down beside her. 'Mum?'

The woman's mouth is open and dry and pale. Her eyes are open too. Ruby reaches out a hand and takes her wrist, and the skin is cold, and feels already different; the skin hardening, the flesh underneath gone somehow spongy.

It feels strange, but Ruby doesn't let go. She takes Amelia's hand between hers, and chafes it. The bulging knots of her fingers. The worn-in strip of gold. Like where a tree has grown around the wire of a fence, coming to some kind of accommodation with it, an acceptance.

Janet will sleep for another hour or so. Billy will sleep until Ruby wakes him. She leans down over the body and flicks the skirts of the nightgown straight. She holds the hand, rubs at it again. She should wake Billy, even though it is an hour and a half or so before his usual time. He should be told. But she doesn't know what will happen then. His mother is dead. What is he going to be like, once he knows?

She lays the cold hand down on the thin fabric of the nightgown. She turns and climbs back up the stairs.

At first he seems to be handling it well. Between them they move the body up the stairs and back into Amelia's bed. Then he calls the surgery and Dr Bennett comes round even though it's still so early. It is evident that this was not unexpected, at least as far as Dr Bennett is concerned.

'She had a fall,' Ruby says, hushedly, standing over the narrow bed. Amelia lies there, pale and solid and waxy. Billy flashes Ruby a glare, like she's mentioned something shameful. 'We found her at the foot of the stairs. We didn't like to leave her there.'

Dr Bennett tilts his head. 'I don't think that was it. Any headaches, strange behaviour in recent weeks?'

Billy stands silent, dwarfed by the tall professionalism of Dr Bennett.

'I don't know. Maybe,' Ruby says. 'Yes. I mean, she'd started to wander a bit.'

Billy turns stiffly away.

'Maybe we're looking at a stroke,' the doctor continues. 'She might have had them before, little ones. I'll ring the coroner. We'll have to be certain.'

'What for?' Billy asks.

'For the certificate. There'll have to be an autopsy.'

'Oh.' Billy doesn't look at his mother.

'Is that really necessary?' Ruby asks. 'She was an old lady.'

The doctor nods sympathetically. 'I do understand, believe me. I'm very sorry for your loss.'

Billy goes out of the room. He leaves the door open behind him. She watches him cross the landing and go into Janet's room. There's a moment's quiet, and then a sleepy mumbling from the girl, and then Billy's lower voice, and then the girl's exclamation, *Oh Daddy*, and the rustling of bedding as the girl reaches up to hug him. It doesn't seem fair, that – to go and tell her, insist that she wakes and knows. To claim her like that; to claim her sympathies.

Billy pushes his wide-headed broom around the gymnasium, collecting clots of shed hair and the fibres from coconut matting and the stuffing of vaulting horses and medicine balls and the threads that fall from the climbing ropes. He moves through the white grids of light from the high windows, scattering dust motes. He can hear one of the classes down the corridor – the massed voices chanting out their seven times tables. He knows his times tables better now than he ever did as a boy.

She has money saved with the Co-op for a funeral, he knows that. He's known for years.

At lunchtime the children queue at the hatch and take their plates with slopped-on mince and mash and swede, and he could get his too, if he wanted to, but he doesn't. Instead, he goes out into the October sunshine and crosses the grey, gritty cement and goes out the school gates and keeps on going until he's standing at the corner of Denham Crescent even though he hadn't meant to go home at all.

Ruby is at work. Janet is at school. Will is away at college. His mother is in the hospital mortuary. The house looks down at him with its blank glass. It is a good house. A clean and comfortable house. It's his; he pays for it. That's something. He kept her comfortable in her last years. That's something too.

He goes down to the end of the street, and back up the lane behind the houses. He goes into the garage. For a moment he just looks up at his old track bike, its hanging wheels, its dust-filmed frame. If he had been stronger, fitter, faster, better – but he can't even imagine it, because then the world would have to be such a different place, and he a different man entirely.

He lifts the bike down. He wipes the frame and forks with a clean rag. He drips oil onto another cloth and rubs at the joints. He lifts the back wheel, pulls the pedal round with a hand. It ticks round perfectly, the greased links of the chain meeting the gear teeth with easy precision. He'd forgotten this, the clarity of it, the perfection.

When he first gets on and tries to pedal, the bike doesn't shift; the gearing is too high, and he's too unfit, too old to make it move. It's a track bike; it's meant for athletes.

He needs Rudd – the shove from behind sending him flying out into the drum of the racetrack. But there is no Rudd. Rudd is thirty years ago, a world away. Billy stands on the pedals, one hand on the back fence, in his duster coat and cap, and uses his whole weight on one pedal, pushing down, and the wheels begin to inch forward, and he lets go of the fence, and begins to roll, and heaves down on the other pedal, and he's moving, reaching the end of the back lane and out onto the street, and for a moment the struggle to get moving is like the first morning at Cheeseman's, the bulk of that Alldays & Onions, the way he'd had to drag it into motion, and then the discovery of speed.

He turns into Bramcote Avenue, and then Cranmer Road by the cricket green, and then joins the traffic on the London Road.

He just rides. He slips through traffic and out of the press of buildings and alongside ribbon strips of semis, then villas. He's in perfect synchrony with the bike as its gears are with the chain. He'd forgotten this, the feeling of the body fitting itself into the mechanism, the way space concertinas, the way time folds in upon itself. The way you disappear.

Soon the road opens out straight and long, letting him pick up speed. He cuts through plain countryside – past wide, dull fields, hedges, through woods and villages; fewer and fewer cars.

He stops in a market town and, still astride the bike, dips his head to drink from a municipal drinking fountain. He doesn't feel tired, or hungry, or the burn of muscle use. He doesn't even feel sad, not while the road is empty and open in front of him, and he can just ride.

But as darkness falls he finds himself approaching a fork in the road, in exposed, open countryside. To his left, an expanse of muddy, ploughed field; to his right, a field of broken stubble and a copse. No signposts. He slows off, comes to a halt. Tilts the bike, one foot to the rough gravel.

He wipes his face. Checks his watch. It's getting on for six. Ruby will have expected him home hours ago. He thinks of that wintry street when he was little, standing at his mother's side, the protecting squeeze of her arm. He was right, Billy was, to get rid of Sully. Whatever her regrets might have been, they'd have hurt her less than that poison. True or not true, it doesn't matter now. Her peace of mind, at least, was left untainted. His father died a hero. Everyone knows that.

Her lumpen knuckles, wrapped round with knitting wool. Her loneliness.

But the children. She'd had that. The children were an uncomplicated blessing; she could take them for who they were and not wish them different. When the boy was first in callipers, three years old, clanking around like a wind-up toy, she'd lift him up onto her hip, carry him out to the garden, show him the berries swelling on the fruit canes, or the birds' nest in the hedge.

The fields stretch out and away and a faint rain begins to fall. The world is empty. Nothing stands between him and eternity.

He has to try harder with Will, before it's too late. If he could just explain. About that day in Normandy; the price he paid for this.

Because already the boy is pulling further and further away; first A-levels and now off to college; he's almost out of earshot. He's doing well. He's got pluck; he's not daunted by anything. Soon as he was out of that calliper he was kicking a ball around all day long. From cripple to captain of the football team in three years. Making Billy feel, though he'd never say it in case it just made matters worse, that if the boy had only had two decent legs, they could have made a genuine athlete of him. He's had choices though, the boy has. He's had his books. His college grant.

I must try, Billy thinks. Next time I see him, I will really try.

Billy walks the bike round where he stands, and slips back onto the saddle, and wobbles off, slowly, back the way he'd come.

When he gets home, it is three in the morning or thereabouts. His legs are uncertain and his backside sore. Ruby is dozing in the chair. He sits down in the other seat. He doesn't want to wake her, but doesn't want to leave her either. Her face is soft in sleep. There is loose skin under her jaw.

She's beautiful. After a while, she blinks, and stirs, and looks at him.

'Billy,' she says.

'Sorry.'

'Oh God, love, Billy.'

Ruby pushes her way out of the chair. A rug falls off her knees and she steps over it. She wraps her arms round him.

'I'm sorry,' he says. 'I'm sorry.'

Magdalen College, Oxford, 14 October 1965

Frost still lingers in the corners of the quad. Will makes his way down the path, past Grammar Hall, heading for Fellows' Garden. He can feel the capital letters. Everything seems to be worth a capital here, and not to need an article. Not the grammar hall, but Grammar Hall. Not the fellows' garden, but Fellows' Garden. As if everything were the original, the only, the ur-thing.

The air is still as a pond. It brushes his skin, teases up the hairs on his legs, makes his breath puff.

He glances down at his leather football boots. They're pretty good. Heavy, but that doesn't bother him. Cost a week's wages. His bad leg is lean still; it doesn't match the good one in terms of bulk, but it's muscular. He's worked hard to make it so. He needs to keep it that way. And even then he still has to be careful; it doesn't do to twist or tear anything.

They have gathered in a loose huddle, puffing,

jumping, keeping warm. A miscellany of football shirts. A big bloke with dark hair carries a net of balls, like onions in a bag; another has a cluster of sashes in his hand, hanging like a bunch of limp flowers. Will skips into a run to join them.

Bare trees stand against the pale sky, and birds rise like flakes of burnt paper. He can feel the openness of this place, as if the cold emptiness of the countryside was slipping into the centre of the city.

It's only when he gets close to the crowd that it becomes obvious. These young men are built on a different scale from him. He slows to a jog, joins the edge of the group, and he feels like he has come up on the edge of a wood. They're oblivious to him, talk in familiar loud tones, like they all know each other already. Will stands on his right leg, drops his hip and hooks his booted left toe back into the earth, tries to keep the wasted limb out of sight. He's finding it hard to make out what's being said. Even just on the basic level of the words: vowels seem somehow high up in the mouth. *Eh dint neh,* someone says, and that's *I don't know,* he thinks, but it's a strange and ugly way of talking, and everyone seems to do it. He thought the students would have come from all over, but they sound like they've all come from the same place.

'When are we starting?' Will asks the guy next to him, and the guy glances down at him.

345

'When are we starting, Michael?' the guy asks.

Michael is the big dark bloke with the bag of footballs. 'We ready then? Everyone here?'

There is a chorus of cheerful assent. Michael opens the bag and lets the footballs spill and bounce and scatter. Will scoops for a passing ball, but it's gone, caught up by someone else's booted foot. The boot is beautiful, lightly crafted, clean, barely worn. He catches the back view of a sandy-haired giant who thunders off down the pitch dribbling the football as if he owns it.

They divide into teams. Will is handed a red sash. Michael tells him he's playing fullback. Will hates defence; it does him no favours at all. But he takes his place, marks his man, because this is just try-outs, and he'll get a chance to show off what he can do later, and show off his goodwill and sportsmanship now.

He bounces on the spot to keep warm, watching the action down the far end of the pitch, bloody miles away, and the tall spreading fat trees at the end of it, and beyond that the river, and a pair of scholars walking along the riverbank, gowns flapping. The rooks settle in the high branches.

He glances across to the other defender. Indian lad. Smaller than many of them, about his height. Skinny legs coffee brown against his white shorts. Must be feeling out of place.

'Bloody cold, isn't it?' Will grins.

The Indian lad glances at him with his big clear eyes, then looks back to the action. 'It is October.'

The way he speaks is butter smooth. It makes Will see his own words, as if they're buzzing around him like bluebottles; he says *cowld* not *cold*, he realises, and here that's wrong. He jogs carefully on the spot again, looking back towards the game.

'Which school did you go to?' the boy asks.

Will looks back round at him. His school smelt of boys and boiled meat. The corridors were a greasy shade of yellow. The classrooms swam with dust and when you passed the staff-room door it reeked of tobacco and coffee and soup. Why would anyone want to know about his school?

'Glastonbury Road,' Will says. 'I was in the grammar stream.'

The Indian boy's eyes are really beautiful. Big and brown and glossy as conkers, and the whites as clear as milk. He blinks, and then nods, and then turns away, looking back up the pitch towards the game. Will's eyes follow his. The scrabble and surge of play.

'And you?' Will asks, to be polite.

'Eton.'

'Right,' Will says. Then, after a while, 'Wish they'd let us have a go with the flippin ball.'

The moments tick by, and he glances round at the Indian boy, whose name he didn't even think to ask, who is watching the play, and Will feels stupid, and that he has somehow already failed.

* * *

347

When he lies full length his feet don't touch the end of the bath, because it has been built for the giants.

The sky is dark through the high window. From somewhere far off he can hear a girl's laugh, and music. He strains to catch it, but it's a distant ghost. He gets a trickle here and there of piano, and it's Mozart. And the girl will be someone over from St Hilda's, or down from Somerville. The graze hurts, but he's not soft enough to let a graze put him off, not even the ancillary discomfort – the red burn in his hip from getting jolted. The yell and the break for it and Michael steaming down the pitch towards him, followed by an undisciplined brawl, sashes flapping, faces taut, thundering to catch him. Michael coming at him, and Will gathering himself up into a dodging obstructive run. Michael's eyes wet and hard. Will nipping in to scoop the ball off him and away – to show off the skills that made him captain of Glastonbury Road Seniors soccer team.

His right foot made contact with the ball, he's pretty sure of that. He thinks he felt it. Before he felt himself land on his backside on the hard ground. He got to his feet. His hip hurt. His shin bled through the mud. Standing, he tried his weight on his bad leg, and the whole leg sang out in dismay. Michael came over, and put a hand to his back, and said something, and Will shook his head, no, okay, okay, I'm okay, old injury, and Michael said something more. Will shook his head again, and straightened up, and dragged in a big breath, and let it go. On the way back through Fellows' Garden, he watched the birds rise in the sky. It hurt too much to feel embarrassed at the time. He feels embarrassed now.

He feels slight. Not just in size. He had been captain, but here he won't even make the team. He is just *tiny*.

Even the steam can't take the chill off the bathroom. The vast claw-footed bath sucks the heat from the water. He shifts himself up, wincing against the pain, and reaches over the edge for his trousers. He dabs his fingers on the cloth to dry them, then lifts his cigarettes out of his pocket. He lies back in the tepid water, looking at his toes – the wiry structure of tendon and bone – and lights up. He turns his Ronson lighter round in his hands, looks at his initials scored into it: *WAH*. Like a baby's cry. It was a gift from the boys he'd taught, that year after A-levels, when Mr Tate was coaching him for the Oxford exams. It had been something, to teach at his old school, to even sit the Oxford entrance papers; his mum had gone all tight-lipped with pride.

There is a fire in his sitting room. There is Sweet's *Anglo-Saxon Reader* to get to grips with. He is not in the mood to be sociable, let alone face up to the football squad toasting the newcomers in the JCR. But he had promised Ollie, and Ollie had promised there would be girls. Literary Society girls, as if that itself is some kind of inducement. As if that makes them all liberated Lawrentian females. Ursulas and Gudruns and Lady Chatterleys, all brightly coloured stockings and heavy limbs and easy morals, keen on cocks and swoony sex in the outdoors. They will just be girls. Girls from Somerville and St Hilda's. The red-brick, buttoned-up colleges out on the edge of things.

Top of the Pops is on tonight. Janet will be sitting on the pouffe, chin in hands, elbows on knees, staring at the screen, shushing everyone who dares walk in. Dad will be out in the garage, tinkering. Mum will be confined to the kitchen by Janet, who can't stand her comments on pop music. Anne Graves will be holed up there with Mum, taking a breather from Mrs Graves who's something of a trial now Mr Graves has died. She calls it a breather but they'll smoke so many fags that the ashtray fills and overflows and looks like something out of Pompeii.

What he really wants is to find a telly, and settle down in front of it and watch *Top of the Pops*, even though he doesn't know who'll be on. Wilson Pickett, Dusty Springfield, maybe; 'Some of Your Lovin', The Yardbirds. He misses Janet, who doesn't sulk at him: they'd watch it together, know when it was okay to speak in a way his mum can never quite work out. But he hasn't seen a telly since he got here. There probably isn't one in the whole of Oxford.

And he did say to Ollie. And Ollie shares these

rooms. It wouldn't do to annoy him. Fag tucked between his lips, he presses his hands down on the cold enamel edges of the bath, and lifts himself cautiously out.

They are playing jazz.

He bloody hates jazz.

Ollie is barking into someone's ear, almost directly above Will's head. The room is noisy and hot and smells of damp wool and cigarettes. Will has a bottle of Watney's ale in his hand. His suit is sharp. He likes this suit. Nice narrow tie. Ollie wears a cream cable-knit jumper, cords; doesn't seem to think anything of it. Will glances round, trying to spot girls, but he can't see any. He tries to pick up on the conversation, to grab a thread he can drag himself in on, but it is all about people that he doesn't know but with whom Ollie and Geoff both seem to be easily familiar: Geoff's cousin who's standing for the Union presidency, and someone else who's thinking about one of the minor posts coming up, worth standing for, because you can build on that, build on that profile. People get to know who you are, you see, and that's the name of the game, isn't it? Getting known. Geoff swigs his beer.

'So how do you know each other?' Will tries.

'Young Geoff here,' Ollie says, 'was house captain year before me.'

Will nods. He doesn't know what this literally means, but it has a clear associative sense to it:

351

they know each other because they all know each other because they just do. They've got the shared code, the friends of friends, a web of association.

He doesn't know the code. He doesn't know his way around. He doesn't know anybody. And it seems like he can't even work out how to get to know anybody here.

The music swings up overhead, then dips into a fiddly scrambling fall like a sparrow shot with an air rifle. Then a drum solo. Bloody *drum* solo. Jesus.

'Sounds like a drum kit falling off a cliff.'

Ollie barks a laugh. Geoff looks at him. Smiles thinly. Then turns back to Ollie. 'So, I was thinking, treasurer this year—'

And Ollie clicks back in, nods along.

Will looks around the room. It is packed tight with cords and slacks, with saggy knitwear, floppy hair, duffel coats. And the footie team over in the corner all laugh at something Michael says.

He swallows a mouthful of beer over the lump in his throat.

It's better than shunting a broom and unblocking toilets and fixing leaky gutters at the infants' school, he tells himself. This is Oxford, and that's worth something. It's like cauliflower, he decides. He doesn't have to like it; he just has to get it down him. Find a way of making it tolerable.

Sport is out, clearly. Social life: not so far. Study. He can study. He can always study. He is good at studying. He has a capacity for nine-hour reading stints, for essays that fly across the page. Mr Tate used to rest his hand on Will's shoulder when he gave the essays back. Will tips his bottle to his lips. His chest feels hollow and grey. Finish this, then back to his set, back to the unfamiliar Anglo-Saxon script, attempt translating those first sentences.

He sets his bottle down on the bar.

Anglo-Saxon, then.

The music stops. There's a click and swoop as the needle is lifted, and there is a sudden space in which voices crisscross like wires overhead, supported by nothing. Some drop away, others bray louder as if in protest at the silence. He cranes his neck to look over towards the record player. He can't see what's going on: too many people.

Then the record player starts up again. The soft fumpfh of the needle set into place. He loves this moment. The moment before the thing happens, when there's a possibility of something great. Even if it's only going to be deadened in an instant by more loopy bloody jazz. The soft hssk, hssk, hssk as the needle traverses the smooth tuneless rim of the disk. Then his heart is lifted by the great raw yelp of Lennon's voice. *Help.*

'Scuse me.'

He steps round, past Ollie. Elbows his way through the crowd. Above him, the music powers out like a train, uninterruptible, into the stone vaults of the JCR.

The crowd thins a little, further from the bar.

The coffee table, the record player. A girl slipping the previous record back into its sleeve.

A girl with amazing legs. Her hair catches auburn under the nasty electric light.

She turns to hand the jazz LP to her friend, who's cross, and trying to pretend she's not. The girl with the nice legs is trying to be friendly, *You'll like it, Claudia*, but the other girl won't listen, turns to rifle through her box of records to slot the rejected one back into place. She shakes her back-combed head dismissively, it doesn't matter, of course Madeline should play her record if she wants to, it's no trouble to her, but is she sure that pop music – the way she pronounces *pop* is so careful, strange, like she's puzzled to find a marble dropping from her lips – is appropriate to the time and place, well, that is fine. The girl with the nice legs folds up her lips, turns away, and catches Will's eye. She folds her lips in tighter, strangling a smile. But her eyes sparkle. Will's stomach dips. Christ. She is amazing. Holy Christ.

The confidence of it. The sheer bloody confidence of it. Will hadn't even realised Ollie was there until a large hand clapped onto his shoulder. Conversation was dropped into so smoothly: the girls like pop music? Ollie has a cousin in the record business. Scandal of the family. Uncle had wanted him to go into banking. Cousin has met – has had nights out with – the boys at the Ad Lib club, the Bag O' Nails. He means The Beatles, of course.

And then he twists the conversation sideways, before any detail can be gone into, and they're hearing about a place out at Boar's Hill that Ollie would just love to show them. Will has got a car. And they are out of the warmth and smoke of the college bar, and in the chill of Will's little old Singer Gazelle (six months' wages), Ollie weighing down the back left-hand suspension, next to the slim girl in green. Madeline.

'Thought Singer just made sewing machines,' says Claudia, buttoned up to her chin in a yellow coat.

'They do,' says Ollie, and lets out a great guffaw.

Madeline, in the back, says nothing. They pull out of the town. The car hums along the pale road between the fields. Will's hands are cold on the steering wheel, but his cheeks burn.

'Take a right,' Ollie says. 'Keep on this road.'

Moonlight. Faint trails of fog here and there, but mostly it's clear stubble fields, dark and bristly; skimming hedges; a tree slowly traversing the corner of Will's sight. Claudia wriggly on the other side. Picking off lint, settling skirt and hair and hands into place. And Madeline in the back, curled into a corner by Ollie's bulk, and him talking away to her and laughing. Will notices the quiet from her. Asks, over his shoulder, whether she's comfortable.

'Yes,' she says faintly, and then, 'thank you.'

And he warms with the words. He likes her.

✳ ✳ ✳

The road is direct – up ahead there's a sudden steepness and then woodland.

'Boar's Hill,' Ollie pronounces, as if he's produced it from a hat.

They climb into the woods, the little engine struggling. With every gear change, Will's uneasy that his knuckles will brush against the mustard wool of Claudia's flank.

'What now?' Will asks.

'I'll tell you when,' Ollie says.

'If you could just give me some indication—'

'I'll know it when we get there. It's been a while.'

Will bites back a sigh. The tunnel of trees whisks along through the headlights. Claudia's gone still. The headlights skim a gateway.

'Ah . . .' says Ollie from the back.

'Was that it?' Will glances up at Ollie's blank face in the rear-view mirror. Ollie's eyes skip along the road. His mouth hangs open.

'Ah – no. There!'

And Will turns his eyes back to the road, just in time to spot the gateway, and a house sign. He slams on the brakes, crunches down a gear. Spins into the drive with a rattle of gravel.

'But this is someone's house . . .' Will says.

In the mirror, Ollie nods him onward.

'But won't they . . .?'

In the mirror he catches the side of Madeline's face, a curve of pale cheek, the drift of her hair. The car bounces on along the chalk track, white in the moonlight.

'S'all right. My aunt's place,' Ollie says. 'Used to come here when I was a nipper.' Ollie glances at Madeline to include her in his pleasure. 'Lovely grounds here. Acres. Won't disturb the old dear.'

There's a bend, and Will's caught off guard, his attention on the mirror. He brakes, jerks the car round. Eyes on the road from now on. Eyes on the road.

They have reached the far side of the hill. To the left, there are woods: tall, slender trunks grey in the moonlight, deep shadow in between. To the right, the countryside opens wide in a sweep of grey-blue fields. Here and there stand broad, spreading trees. Far off, there is a speckling of lights. A village or a town; Will doesn't know. He doesn't know where he is, where anything is.

'Anywhere here,' Ollie says. Meaning, park the car.

'Right,' Will says. He can feel his neck, the bare back of his neck, tight as twisted rope. He wonders if it's obvious.

A hundred yards more, and there is a field gate. He slows the car and bumps up alongside the gate. Jerks up the handbrake, switches off the engine. For a moment, there is silence. Then the creak of the suspension as Ollie opens the back door and levers himself out. Packed in there like Spam in a tin. Then Will is out of the car too, and the night air brushes him like silk. His leg has frozen up with the drive, and he half hops, half skips round the car to open the back door, while Ollie stands, looking speculatively up the steep bank into the woods.

The space is massive. The sky and the emptiness and the cool, and the moon standing bare and bright.

Ollie heads up the bank.

Will opens the car door and Madeline lays her hand on his arm, stretches a leg out of the car. He doesn't let himself look at it. She stands up. The length of her unfolding. She's an inch or so shorter than him. He can smell her hair, the faint scent of lemon like a memory. And then she smiles at him, and he smiles back. But then Claudia's getting out. He has to offer her his hand.

'Gentleman,' Claudia says, smiling up at him. She closes the door, doesn't let go of his hand.

'Come on, you sluggards!' Ollie stands at the top of the bank. In the moonlight he is just a big fawn rectangle of tweedy coat, a tangle of silvery-blonde hair. His arm waves them over. Claudia maintains her grip on Will's hand. Squeezes it even. He looks to Madeline, who gives him what looks like a smile, but it's hard to tell in this light. She heads off across the road, and up the bank, towards Ollie.

Claudia talks. He helps her up the bank. His hip hurts. He must have trapped a nerve: it spins pain up his back and down to his knee. As they move through the woods, Claudia keeps reaching up to touch her hair, and exclaiming over her shoes, her stockings. She's excited, he realises. About the dark, about the isolation, about him. It's a weirdly disappointing thought. They stumble on, Will straining after the paler shape of Ollie's overcoat and hair; the dark flitting figure of Madeline is harder to keep tabs on. And then through the branches Will glimpses quicksilver, and smells mint and mud and damp. He comes up beside Madeline. Her coat makes her a deeper darkness in the dark. Just her face glowing, catching moonlight.

'There it is,' Ollie says. 'Auntie's lake.'

Ollie's auntie has a *lake*. Will's mum has a bit of garden. His dad has talked about digging her a pond. He hasn't got round to it yet.

'Fancy a swim?' Ollie says.

Claudia's hand flexes in Will's. Clammy-damp. Anxious. Eager.

'It's October,' Madeline says.

'And if it were August?' Ollie turns his attention to her so completely that Will wants to punch him.

'Well, that would be different,' she says, and there is a rich insolence in her tone, making Will remember that passage in Lawrence, can't remember which book now, or even which of the Brangwen girls it was, stripping off her clothes and stepping into a moonlight pool, followed by her soldier lover who can't quite keep up with her, can't quite be what she needs him to be.

But Ollie has taken Madeline's hand, and they are moving off through the trees.

Damn.

Claudia tugs on his hand. She talks. Will looks round after Ollie and Madeline, but Claudia draws him on, into the dark. He can hear their voices still; low, moving further off.

Claudia's telling him something. About taking the bus up to London, about going to the Flamingo Club to see The Ronnie Ross Quartet. He realises with a flash of horror that she's talking about the two of them, that they might do these things together. Does he have people they could stay with in London? All her people are in Gloucestershire. His parents? Would they mind a girl staying in their guest room overnight? Would they be scandalised? She's only half joking. He'd be mortified if he wasn't at that moment deciding that he would never see her again, that if he ever bumped into her in the street he would turn and run away. Literally, spin on his heel and sprint for it.

'Shall we go and look for them?' he asks.

'They'll meet us back at the car.'

How does she know that?

They continue along the path, his hand in hers. But he's thinking of Madeline and the slender contours of her legs. The weight of her hand on his arm. The bulk of Ollie, and what he will want to do to her, what he'll try to do to her, what she might let him do. He doesn't know what she might let him do, because he doesn't know her. She seems nice, but Ollie is confident, convincing, overpowering. Maybe she even likes him. She went with him, after all, not Will. Does she like Ollie? He realises now, himself, how intensely he does not.

Somewhere a bird cries in its sleep, and far off a dog barks.

Claudia, fortunately, doesn't need him to talk. She tells him about the family home near Gloucester, the horses, the brothers. He follows the path without thinking. The trees thin; moon-light blots through. They step out, look down on the metal shell of the little car, and beyond across the grey counterpane of fields. They stand at the top of the bank. She squeezes his hand again. She waits breathily.

'It's a beautiful night,' she says. She wants him to kiss her, he realises.

'We should go looking for them,' he says.

'She'll be fine.'

He looks round at Claudia. Her pale face looking up at him. A blink.

'She'll be fine,' she says again.

How does Claudia know she'll be fine? Has this kind of thing happened before? Is this what Madeline does? Go off into the woods with men?

'How do you two know each other?'

'We're next door. In halls.' But now she doesn't want to talk. Her eyes have gone all hooded.

He is not going to bloody kiss her.

He drops her hand, slithers down the first yard

of the muddy bank, then reaches back up to her. 'C'mon.'

They scramble down the bank together. Will's hip hurts badly, but he got out of kissing her. Back at the car, and he opens the door for her, so she has to get in straightaway. She drops herself down into the seat, hooks in her legs, and he slaps the door shut and goes round to his side, and stands there for a moment, looking out over the moonlit woods, the faint ghosts of tree trunks and the heavy mounded canopy. No sign of their return. He can't delay it for ever: he'll have to get in. And then they'll be in the car together, alone, her sliding up to him across the front bench seat.

He gets out his cigarettes, ducks down to offer her one. She shakes her head. He was banking on that – gives him another few minutes safety, standing smoking outside the car.

'I'll just—' he says, and she nods for him to go on ahead.

He stands and smokes. He scans the woods. Time ticks by. The cigarette flares in the darkness, and he sucks it down to a sharp red coal. He crushes out the stump.

'There she is!'

Madeline steps out of the woods, hands extended as if feeling her way blind. Her face, from this distance, is just a blur. The relief is extraordinary. She makes her way down the bank, crosses the track to them. She has a look of someone who's tidied herself up without a mirror. Head high, alert for how people look at her, for signs of something being amiss. Instinctively he starts towards her. Then Ollie's there too, ploughing out of the woods, taking the bank with one sliding stride. Madeline goes straight past Will. He twists round after her, and opens the rear door for her. She gives him a tight little smile. She doesn't get in.

'Claudia,' she says.

Claudia looks up through the window. Madeline gives a rap on the glass: 'Claude.'

Madeline gestures her out. Claudia winds down the window. 'What is it?'

'I'm in the front,' Madeline says.

Claudia looks to Will. Will looks away. She tuts, swings her legs out of the car. He doesn't think to offer his hand till it's a fraction too late. She ignores it, slides into the back seat.

He closes the door on her. Ollie drops himself on the other side of the back seat and claps the door shut.

Madeline and Will stand eye to eye on the track. Actually he can't look her in the eye; his gaze dips away to her hands, which are white and beautiful. She has a big oval-stoned ring on one finger.

'You all right?' he asks.

'Yes.'

'Shall we?' he gestures to the car.

'We'd better.'

He offers her his hand.

'Gentleman,' Madeline says. It's almost a question.

'I try,' Will says.

She considers this a moment. She takes his hand. Her fingers are as cold as silk. 'That'll do then.'

It's as if something's agreed between them. He doesn't know what the agreement is, but he knows that he can never ask what happened: not Ollie, not her. She slides into the seat. He lets go of her hand, tries not to look as she slips those legs into the footwell.

Cricket Green Road, Mitcham, 6 June 1966

Will pulls the car into the side of the road, yanks up the handbrake. Madeline peers up the street, then glances across her shoulder: a parade of shops down one side, a cricket green on the other, cars motoring past. She can't see why they would be stopping here.

'Is this it?'

Will just sits. He just looks out the windscreen, hands on the wheel. She looks at him a moment, the clear line of his features, and underneath, that shadow. She is reminded again why him, why not anybody else. He doesn't glance round at her, so she looks ahead, where he is looking – the suburban high street, the cricket green, a junction where a street peels off to the right.

'Will? Why are we stopping here?'

He looks tired. There's a line between his eyes.

'Are you in pain?

'I'm okay.'

'It's not good for you, sitting in one position

like that for so long. You should have let me drive.'

He turns then, and fixes his dark eyes on her. Smiles. 'We'd still be doing rings round Abingdon.'

'Cheeky sod.' She wallops him on his shoulder.

He shrugs. 'It's the simple truth.'

'You're simple. It's your directions.'

'There's nothing wrong with my directions.'

'There's nothing wrong with my driving.'

Will lets a breath go, seems to slump.

'Do you think they won't like me?'

'They'll love you. That's half the problem.'

'I don't understand.' She lets her hand slide down the muscle of his upper arm and rest in the dip of his elbow. 'What is it?'

His face bunches up oddly. She can't work out what's bothering him: it's just dinner, it's just a visit, it's nothing. He was fine at her mum and dad's.

'I'm not them,' he says.

'Okay,' she says. 'I know that.'

'Good,' he says. 'Right then.'

He lifts his arm to put the car back into gear, and her hand falls away. He looks up into the rear-view mirror, finding his place in the traffic. 'So long as we're clear.'

The house takes up so little space it seems to be standing on one foot. There's a small bow window on the ground floor, and on the first floor the two windows have a raised brick ridge above them, so that the house looks like it is grinning at her, eyebrows raised.

She follows him through the hall, straight into the sitting room, and a skinny girl, Janet presumably, stares at her from a leatherette pouffe. The air is warm and dry and smoky. The girl stands up and seems almost to back away.

'All right, Jan,' Will says. Janet nods back.

His accent has changed: the *l*'s sound like a *w* and there's a glottal stop now too. Madeline looks at him, but he doesn't meet her eye.

There is an archway through to the dining room. A sliding door opens onto the kitchen beyond, and there is daylight from the garden. A woman is coming up the step from the kitchen. She has Will's dark colouring, his clarity of feature: that's where he gets his good looks from. She must have been beautiful once, but her skin is deeply lined now – a smoker's face.

'Mads, this is Mum.'

'Mrs Hastings.' Madeline moves towards the woman, hand extended. She half anticipates a foreign accent, even though she knows, South London, Jewish.

'Ruby,' the woman says, shakes Madeline's hand.

'Where's Dad?' Will asks.

'Be down in a minute,' Ruby says, and ducks to pick a smouldering cigarette from an ashtray. There is pink lipstick round the butt of it. She draws on the cigarette; she's very precise in all her movements, carefully elegant. She speaks to Madeline over the smoke: 'Won't you sit down?'

But then there are footsteps on the stairs, and the hall door opens. The man there has the same light build as Will, but an entirely different presence. Will is measured, considered – but there's a muscular acuity here, a pent-up fierceness.

He nods.

She smiles. 'Hi.'

Then he comes over towards her. He offers his hand to be shaken, and she takes it. She glances to Will, but Will has taken himself over to the windowsill, and is leaning there, a dark shape against the white nets, unreadable. It's easier for him, leaning like that; it's less strain on the damaged joint than if he were to sink into a soft chair. And he's sore already, after so long stuck in the driver's seat. But it feels somehow unfair, as though he's taken a step back from everything, and left her to get on with it.

'I'm Madeline,' she says to Will's dad. 'Madeline Hurst.'

He nods, lets go of her hand. 'Billy Hastings.'

So Will's named after him, she realises.

He speaks to his son without looking at him. 'Aren't you going to fetch your guest a seat?'

'We're going out, aren't we?' Will says.

'Fetch her a seat.'

A moment. Madeline looks from Billy to Will. 'Really, I—'

Will pushes away from the windowsill, but Ruby bats him back.

'You sit here, Madeline.'

She gestures to her own seat, and goes over to the dining area to bring back a chair. Janet hunches on the pouffe.

Madeline would love to go over to the window, to lean in beside Will and have him reach his arm around her waist and hold her. But he doesn't beckon her over, doesn't even catch her eye. So she sits down in Ruby's chair. The springs creak. She smiles at Janet, who blinks back at her.

'I like your shoes,' Janet says.

Madeline looks down at her blue shoes, with their neat strap and button. 'Thank you.'

Will's dad settles into the opposite armchair. He smiles; he has bridgework there, gold loops on his side teeth.

'He's told us nothing, you know,' he says.

Will gives an exasperated huff. She glances up at him. He shakes his head, looking down at the dizzying Axminster. She doesn't understand.

'So what are you studying?' Ruby asks.

'I'm training to be a teacher,' Madeline says.

'Isn't that marvellous?' Ruby says. 'Now, Janet's thinking of teaching.'

Janet just rolls her eyes.

'I work in a school,' Billy says.

'Dad,' Will snaps.

Madeline looks up at Will. What's got into him?

'What? I do,' Billy says.

369

'Yeah, but.'

Billy leans back in his chair. 'You can't say anything round here nowadays without being told you're wrong.'

'What does your father do, Madeline?' Ruby asks.

'Dad's a GP.'

'Gracious me!'

'Well I never.'

'Mum works for the practice too. She does all the office stuff.'

'Isn't that nice.'

It is nice. And it's secure and comfortable and warm. And it means she could ask her dad offhandedly, over a family dinner, about Will's condition. He'd sucked his teeth and shaken his head, sympathetic. If Perthes disease didn't resolve itself in childhood, then there was nothing, really, that could be done, other than analgesia as necessary, and exercise to keep the supporting muscles strong around the joint. There was some work going on with joint replacement but that was a long way off. Will would have bad times, and better times, but all in all the lad is stuck with it. She'd asked what the cause was, and he confessed he didn't know: no-one did. Maternal malnutrition perhaps, lack of calcium or vitamin D. But at least it didn't seem to be heritable.

'I'd like a drink,' Will says. 'Mads?'

'Please.'

'Sherry?' Billy asks, getting up. 'Or whisky, or rum?'

'Sherry'd be lovely.'

She watches as Billy goes to the sideboard in the dining room and lifts out bottles of Lamb's and Bell's and QC. He fills a tiny schooner, and when Will reaches to take it off him Billy just sweeps past him. He brings the glass to her himself.

'There you go. Don't want it spilt.'

She smiles. Sips. The liquid is extraordinarily sweet. She wonders, did he mean spilt because of Will's limp? She looks to Will; he pours whisky, takes his glass back to the windowsill and drinks it in three quick swallows. Doesn't say a word. He seems to be sulking. She has never seen him sulk before.

'So where's this place we're having dinner?' Ruby asks.

'Yes, what delights have you got lined up for us?' Billy adds.

'It's called Vesuvius,' Will says. 'It's Italian.'

'Bellissimo,' Billy says, and Madeline laughs.

Billy watches the slim twist of her figure against the faded pattern of the armchair as she turns to look at Will, to include him in the laughter. Her hair catches the light and glints red. He'd promised himself he'd try, but now the opportunity is here, he can't do it. The boy is steaming away without a backward glance, with nothing standing in his way, with no idea of just how lucky he is, no idea of what this has cost. It's all been handed to him on a plate. An education. A chance to make

371

something of himself. And a girl like her, gazing after him, thinking he's the bee's knees. And, so far at least, there's been no war to come along and knock it out of his hands.

Billy swallows a bolt of rum. There never was any talking to him anyway. Collecting words like other kids collected insects. Baffling you with them. He's all right; he's doing all right for himself. Getting on in the world. Which is better than they could have hoped for, in the circumstances.

The streetlights sweep orange across Will's face as they pass. Hands clamped to the steering wheel, he looks tired, the shadows deep beneath his eyes. He must have had at least a bottle of wine at dinner. And the whisky before that. He reaches up and digs his fingertips into his neck, trying to ease out stiffness.

'You okay?'

'Yeah.'

'I wish you'd let me drive.'

'It's fine.'

Then silence. She watches the light flickering across his face. He frowns out at the road ahead. She wants to tell him to stop being so moody, but can't quite bring herself to do it. She wants to tell him to take himself off for a swim tomorrow, get some exercise for that leg.

'You never told me you were named after him.'

'It's no big deal.'

'Family tradition, though. I like that.' She slips off her shoes, curls sideways, knees crooked over towards him.

'Not so much a tradition as a paucity of imagination.'

'That's pretty harsh.'

Will shrugs, loosens his fingers then regrips the steering wheel. 'Or maybe it was rationing. We only got the one name and had to make do. He was named after his dad, you see. The father he never had. The guy who died at Gallipoli. So we're both named after this great gaping hole in existence, this dead guy nobody knew.'

'It's special.'

'It's boring. I was considering changing my name, actually.'

'What to?'

'Arthur. It's my middle name. Art.'

She snorts. 'I am not calling you Art.'

Will shifts in the seat, lifting himself on the knuckles of his left hand, then settling himself again. His face creases with the pain. It marks him out, his pain, makes him different from other people. It's like a kind of faith, or talent, a strange gift: he has a whole other side to himself you don't see, not immediately.

'I love you,' she says.

He glances round at her. The creases soften and shift. A smile spreads across his face. It's lovely.

St Giles, Oxford, 11 December 1967

When he comes out of his tutorial at St John's, the street is bustling with end-of-day shopgirls in their short skirts and rib-knit tights and office-boys in trilbies, their overcoat collars turned up against the damp. He tucks in his scarf and buttons up his coat. In a fuzz of satisfaction and sherry, he moves out into the chill of the city, amongst the ordinary people.

His hand in his pocket, pressing against his thigh, he makes his way down towards College. The pressure of his palm against his leg mitigates the pain, which is firing down his thigh like a shock of red electric. Long hours in the library, long hours just sitting still. The muscle's wasting, he knows it is. It hurts. He'll take himself for a swim tomorrow, though that will hurt too, after so long. He's been careless of his exercise, of his physical self.

But the upside – the payoff – is worth it.

In solitude, in silence, his thoughts grow and proliferate, and in silence and in solitude he tends to them. When required to, he picks them carefully, one or two, and brings them out into the light. He watches to see what is made of them. Today, his tutor didn't just nod, and frown, and pinch his upper lip. He didn't just come back with shades, with nuances, with suggested further reading. Today, along with sherry and cigarettes, he offered Will a fellowship. If he gets the First he seems destined for, Will can stay on, with a stipend, a set of rooms, and pursue his research. Which is why Will now moves through the humdrum, everyday bustle, cushioned with light.

He's almost back at College when he sees the tramp, sitting on a doorstep, his feet stick out onto the pavement. Passers-by stream along and he just sits there, still, in the edge of the light cast by a streetlamp, like he's just dabbling his toes into the world. Will has his hand in his pocket anyway: he feels expansive, can afford to share in his good fortune. He starts to rake the coins up in his pocket, slows his pace.

The tramp clocks Will. He pushes back his hat, watches him approach. His beard is dirty-white, streaked with yellow. He's wearing an ancient overcoat, buckled at the waist with a leather belt. These past two years in Oxford, Will's seen more vagrants than he ever did in London. It's like this city is some kind of crossroads, a way-station on their unmarked routes around the country: they all seem to pass through here. Will comes up to him, picks through the change in his palm. Even from a couple of yards away he can smell the old man's stink.

'Evening,' Will says.

'Evening.' The tramp watches Will's hands.

'Cold night.' He'll give him five bob: he's feeling generous.

'Certainly is.'

The tramp holds out a hand and it is filthy, thin as a monkey's.

Sod it. He can afford it now. Will scoops all his coins together, drops them into the thin palm.

'Get yourself a hot meal,' Will says.

The old man glances at the heap of coins, then it's gone, tucked away inside his coat. He struggles to his feet, pushing up against the doorframe. He reaches out for Will with his dirty monkey paw. Will doesn't want to shake it, doesn't want to touch it.

'It's fine,' Will says, backing off. 'Really, it's nothing.'

But then the tramp grabs his arm, catches Will mid-step, jolts him. It hurts. He looks at the hand, then at the tramp.

'What?' Will asks.

The tramp's face is ancient, tanned and dirty. His eyes are stark. He narrows them.

'I know you,' he says.

Will recoils from the poison of his breath. He's mad. Clearly he is mad. But for a moment Will almost believes him.

'No,' Will says. 'You don't.'

He grabs the tramp's wrist – a bundle of bones – and twists. The old man's hand turns and the fingers peel off his coat.

Will drops the filthy wrist and drags his handkerchief out of a pocket and wipes his hand as he walks away. He brushes at his coat-sleeve where the tramp had gripped it. He should have kept his head down, kept his money to himself. He shouldn't have got involved.

The old man's still stumbling after him. 'Hey! *Hey!*'

'Look, just leave it, will you?' Will calls back at him.

People are staring. He grits his teeth against the pain flaring down his thigh; he pushes his handkerchief back into his pocket and presses his hand against his leg. But it's just a few yards now to the College gates and he can duck in there and that's that. The tramp won't be allowed in there. He'll lose interest and wander off. Fixate on someone else.

Will ducks through the gate, into the entrance archway, into the cool quiet of the College. The door into the porter's lodge is just to the right. The flagstones are worn from centuries of feet. He glances back round the edge of the gate, and sees the old man skittering up the street towards him, one bootsole flapping loose, coat fluttering around him like ragged wings. Will's very conscious that passers-by are slowing to watch, that at any moment one of his tutors, one of his fellow students, could come sauntering up the street, or across the quad. The tramp bundles up to the doorway, his chest heaving, eyes wide and bulging.

'You can't come in here,' Will hisses. He bars the way with an outstretched arm.

The tramp's hand flaps in the air, spit spindles from his top to bottom lip.

'But I know you. I do know you. You shouldn't be here.'

Will feels it in his core: *He's right.* All this time he's been pretending, play-acting. He'd thought he was doing a pretty convincing job; the fellowship was evidence of that. But this mad old man sees through him. Lunatics and fools; they see the truth; at least, they always do in Shakespeare. He's not an Oxford man, not really; he never will be. He does not *belong.*

Will looks more closely at the tramp: does he know him? He tries to see through the dirt and hair. Might it be someone from back home, from years ago, who's fallen off the bottom of the ladder? But he can't connect this man's features with any memory.

'I earned my place,' Will says.

He glances to the porter's lodge. Any minute and they'll be out here to clear him off, and it's going to be embarrassing.

'I *know* you.'

'Look,' he says, hands out, trying to be conciliatory.

'You're thinking of someone else. We've never met. I've never seen you before in my life.'

The old tramp looks at Will's soft white hands, looks up at his face. He frowns.

'I remember . . .' he says. He's struggling now, losing his certainty. 'I . . .'

His eyes cloud.

He's not coping with the world, Will thinks. He needs to be looked after. He should be in a home.

Anyway, he shouldn't be here.

'Go on,' Will says. 'You should get out of here. Before they sling you out.'

Will puts a hand on his chest, and pushes gently, and the tramp steps backwards, out into the street, and Will follows after, propelling him.

But then there are voices from behind, and Will glances round to see Ollie and Geoff bundling across the quad towards them in full evening gear. Coats and silk scarves and everything, heads back, hooting over a shared joke. And then Ollie spots Will, and the tramp; and his lips turn up at the corners. And Will's fellowship, Madeline, all the pretence, everything that he's struggled for, puffs out of existence. Ollie steps out through the open gate, saunters up to Will, Geoff following in his wake. Ollie knocks his knuckles into Will's arm, nods to the tramp.

'Aren't you going to introduce us?'

Geoff snorts. The tramp's eyes flicker from one to the other. He looks actually afraid now.

'Oliver Harrison,' Ollie says. 'My father's the MP for Beaconsfield.'

And Will recoils inwardly at this: *Know me by what my father does, by who my father is.* The tramp is looking away, shaking his head, cowed. It makes Will wonder what treatment he's had before, from the college boys. Sleeping rough in this town: late at night, a shop doorway, a bunch of tossers like Ollie and Geoff on their way back from a drinking club. Not nice.

'And you are—?'

'Sully,' the old man says. He straightens himself, drawing himself together. 'Leading Stoker George Sully.'

He looks to Will as he says this, as though it's expected to mean something.

'Old friend of the family?' Ollie asks, all innocence.

'He's ill,' Will tries to explain, but it's hardly worth it. This is meat and drink to them. From now on, every time he sees Ollie or Geoff they'll have some jape, some jibe about his family, his acquaintances. They'll be chuckling over this.

The tramp looks from one of them to the other, timid. Any minute now and he'll have dragged enough confidence together to start on again about knowing him, about Will not belonging there. He pushes the tramp again, lightly, in the chest, and he staggers backwards, and gives Will a wounded look. Will feels for him. But he can't stay here, babbling, humiliating him.

'Go on, go and get yourself some dinner.'

'Oh you didn't give him money, did you?' Ollie asks. He nudges Geoff, jerks a thumb towards the porter's lodge. Geoff nods in reply. 'You shouldn't give them money. It just encourages them.'

Geoff ducks through the College gate, into the lodge.

Will thinks, you make it sound like money is a little thing, not a necessity. That it isn't, for some people, a pressing need, a matter of life and death.

In an instant Geoff is back, the porter following.

'Sorry, sir, I thought it was just you gentlemen.' He taps his bowler onto his head, sidesteps Will. 'Excuse me, sir.'

The porter takes the tramp by the shoulder and the wrist, and then has his arm twisted up his back. The tramp struggles, flapping, in his grip. The porter winces at the smell.

'Place is getting lousy with 'em.'

Geoff slips up beside Ollie and says, 'Are we for the off?'

'Ah yes. Well then, Will, old fellow. Cheerio.'

Ollie and Geoff head on up the street into town, a flutter of scarves and coat tails. Ollie says something to Geoff and the two of them burst into laughter.

Will steps back inside the College gates. He lingers in the archway, looking out at the dark bowler-hatted figure of the porter, the ragged bundle of the tramp, all fight gone out of him.

The porter looks up the street, lets go of the tramp's shoulder for a second to put his fingers in his mouth – Will flinches at the thought of the grimy coat they'd just been touching – and whistles.

A whistle in reply: a bobby's footfalls clatter down the street.

Will watches as the old man is handed over.

'Making a nuisance of himself. Been giving him money, the young gentleman has.'

Will feels hot. Ashamed.

'He's not well,' he calls out. 'He should be in a home.'

The bobby and the porter both glance round at him, an are-you-still-here kind of look. The tramp doesn't look round.

'Oh, we'll look after him, sir,' the bobby says.

The old tramp is steered off across the street, looks tiny in the policeman's steadying grip. He'll have somewhere warm to sleep tonight, at least. A police cell is better than the street, surely. He'll be fed. Maybe they'll find him somewhere permanent.

Will brushes down his coat. He straightens his lapels. He should forget all about this. It has nothing really to do with him.

He could put a trunk call in to London, tell his parents the good news about the fellowship, then explain to them why it's good news, try and make them understand the honour to be even considered, the hard work that underpins it, the triumph he feels at being put forward. And feel all the fizz go out of it as he does so.

He could ring up Madeline at her digs, tell her about the crazy tramp mistaking him for someone that he knew. Make her laugh at his good deed gone wrong. Keep the news of the fellowship to himself, at least for the time being. Because as soon as he hung up she'd be straight on the phone to her mum and dad, who would understand the significance of it all without needing an explanation, and be delighted for them both because he'd proved himself. Because he was, after all, good enough for her.

He could go back to his rooms and catch up on some reading.

He gets out his wallet. He still has a ten-shilling note. He stuffs it back into his pocket, swings himself out through the gateway. Hand pressed to the tearing muscle of his thigh, he heads back up the hill.

He goes into the Mitre, where Joanie works. He orders a pint. He offers her a drink. She accepts coyly, seems flattered to be asked: he's a university man, an Oxford undergraduate, that simple fact lends him substance here. Joanie is pretty, in a soft and pink and friendly kind of way. He's heard how friendly she can be.

It's a quiet night. He talks to her, asks her questions. She leans in, sips her gin and orange. He catches her eye and smiles and she smiles back. There are dimples in her cheeks. And then he shifts on his barstool and winces, and he sees her smile collapse. She asks what's wrong, and he says, Nothing, nothing, and then just hints at his pain – an old injury. And her eyes soften, and she reaches out to touch his arm. This is easy, he thinks. This is something I can do. By the time her shift is over he's had four pints, she's had two gins, and his leg doesn't hurt that much any more. He walks her back to a damp-looking lodging house up Cowley Road, and slips into the dim hallway, and she hushes him up to her room, where he screws her on her little creaking bed.

Rose Lane, Oxford, 6 March 1975

He is as nervous as one of the rabbits that have come loping out across the gravel, finding their way up from the meadows to pick the green shoots of the primroses. Ears up, prickling – scattering when a light comes on in one of the upstairs windows. And this place, more than any other, makes him feel calm and focused. He often writes here. If he feels this jittery here, then he's in a bad way indeed.

The room is tucked away towards the back of the building. The tall Georgian windows look out across the leafy twigs of the rose gardens. The green and red leaves have been unfolding themselves this week, in the first mild days of the year. Later, there will be buds twisted tight as fists, then there will be the great lush lolling heads of the roses, silky pinks and velvety reds. They come into their full gorgeousness only as the students leave, while the city sleeps through summer.

His desk faces back into the room, towards the

bookcases and the faint stripes of the wallpaper. The bust of Milton looks outward though, towards the roses. *Through the Sweet-Briar, or the Vine, or the twisted Eglantine.* No gardener, the young Milton: sweet-briar and eglantine are just different names for wild roses. Which just goes to show that you can get your verse perfect, you can get it correct and satisfying as a crossword puzzle solved – you can get the scansion and the lineation and the meter and the rhythm absolutely undeniably right and true, and then life just comes along and trips you up with inconvenient facts. Though Milton probably wouldn't have minded, if he'd known. For all he was a formal stylist, you can tell he loved the messiness, the irresolvabilty of stuff. All that heaven lets slip. Satan, in other words. Form, for Milton, is the tongs you use to pluck the hot coals from the fire.

This is a formal place. There is order here. Even nature is kept tidy: the clipped roses contained within their neat gravel walks. He likes to take a stroll through the Botanic Gardens with a post-graduate and a cigarette. Over time he's got to know his hellebores from his heliotropes, almost by osmosis. A heliotrope, he thinks: a device of the sun.

He glances at his watch. She is uniformly punc-tual. And she is due in a minute. He has arranged the tutorial for six thirty, which is the latest time it is reasonable to schedule a tutorial. The corri-dors are quiet. The old fellows have sloped away to pre-dinner drinks in the SCR, or are flapping off home on their bikes.

If he just moves to the corner of the window, he can see out onto the street. The wall, and the railings. She'll be along in a minute.

Beneath the window the bushes stir, and a blackbird hops into view. It bounces across the gravel, flutters up to a perch amongst the thorns, opens its throat wide, and pours out song.

And there she is.

She flings her leg back over the saddle – she never steps over the frame even though it's a lady's bike, an old blue Puch – then she locks it carefully to the railings. She comes swinging breathlessly through the gate and up the path, almost at a run. In through the front door of the building, up the corridor, to his door.

And then she stops. Every time. The headlong rush, and then the pause. It's what started him thinking about her. Really thinking about her, in a way he's never thought about a student before. You worry about the odd one, the smellier ones, the glittery-eyed, the ones who show up and then can't talk. But you don't *think* about them, don't find yourself wondering about their motives, their inner lives, the pulsing of their youthful hearts. It's just that pause before knocking. That moment when she stands, breathing, dewy with sweat, in the corridor, and he stands, alert, listening, reaching for his cigarettes, inside.

He tugs his jacket straight, smoothes over his

hair, then, rethinking, ruffles it again. Drags thumb and forefinger across his moustache. He goes to light his cigarette, thinks better of it, slips it back into the pack. He can offer her one when she comes in. He looks at the smooth white panels of the door. His heart is hammering. He hears a shuffle as she does something – arranges herself in some way, does whatever it is she does. Catches her breath after the bike. He can almost believe that he can hear her breathing.

Then she knocks.

'Hello,' he calls.

He turns to his desk, slides her essay across the leather surface. Her looping inky blue. His pencil scribbles. It is careful, thorough, balanced. And the plan for this tutorial, in so far as he has got a plan, is to elicit a bit more wildness, a bit of daring.

She knocks again.

'Hello, come in,' he calls louder.

She eases the door open, sneaks round the edge of it. She blinks at him. 'I wasn't sure if you said hello, or no.'

'Hello,' he says. 'Why would I say no?'

She smiles. 'I don't know.'

'Have a seat.'

He gestures to the old chintz settee. He still gets a kick from the fact that he has a sofa in his room. She slips off her jacket, perches on the edge of the seat and roots in her bag for a pen. He helps himself to a cigarette, offers her one. She stops rooting to accept, then has to dig around again with one hand, the cigarette clamped unlit in the other. He shifts his ashtray – a carved wooden font of a thing – into her reach. He feels her watching him move. Those big liquid eyes.

First few weeks, he'd find himself just thinking about her. Wondering how she was getting on with the reading. He'd imagine a room for her up at Somerville: he didn't actually need to imagine – they can't have changed that much in ten years. A narrow bed, a bookcase, a desk. Across the hall, a long room of wooden stalls each with a porcelain sink to wash in. Where she would strip wash. Rivulets of water rolling down her naked back, down to the tilt of her hips. He'd shake the thought away. Try to. Turn the pages without taking in the words, nod along in meetings. He started daydreaming about how it might happen. A chance encounter in the Radcliffe Camera, late, empty: hands touching over Lydgate. Chaste, really: a kiss between the bookcases that no-one but they would ever know about. Now, by the last week of Hilary Term, things have progressed considerably, in his daydreams at least. In his daydreams things are far from chaste. Drives out into the Cotswolds in his Austin Allegro; sex in the dappled shade. But his imagination scuppers itself: there are always walkers, birdwatchers, balloonists. He imagines her here, in his study, last tutorial of the day, and she will stand up to leave, but instead of going she'll come towards him, unbuttoning her blouse. But someone always blunders in, wanting to clean or to borrow a book, and he is snapped back to reality, to the faculty meeting, item eight on an agenda fourteen points long, with an uncomfortable stiffness in his underpants, and Catherine Aldridge looking at him quizzically over her new glasses.

Catherine's at Somerville. She must know Sarah.

He has to stop thinking like this. It is not appropriate. It is not good.

He moves in to light her cigarette with his Ronson. Her eyes go slightly squinty, focused on the conjunction of flame and cigarette tip. As she leans towards him, her small breasts dip forward into the shadow of her blouse. He lifts his gaze to the business of his own cigarette. She blows out a cloud of smoke. She's not very good at smoking, but she's working hard at it.

'Before we start,' she says.

Which is not like her. It could be the beginning of a fantasy itself.

'Mmm,' he says.

He turns away and limps to his desk, sliding in behind it to be confronted by the white blind eyes of the statue. He creaks it slightly to the right, so Milton's eyes are angled to the far corner of the room.

'I just wanted to say—'

'Mmm.'

She's flicking the ash off her cigarette unnecessarily. She looks up at him. He's never been that bothered by brown eyes before. Madeline's eyes are blue. Her irises are blue as irises. Blue as the dashboard light that says your headlights are on full beam.

'I wanted to say,' the girl says, 'just really, thank you. For the term. For your help. For everything.'

Madeline has the fire lit. It glows red through the boxy grille of the fireguard. She meets him in the narrow hallway, feet in grey socks on the tiled floor, drying her hands on her apron.

'Oh, hello.'

He kisses her. He hangs his coat up on the peg.

'I didn't expect you for a while,' she says.

'Finished earlier than I thought.'

He grimaces inwardly at the truth of this. Her attention is half back in the living room, over her shoulder. The door is open. The child babbling in there. He's been at work all day; he should be allowed some peace and quiet now. He's earned it. A drink, the paper, dinner. That's what he needs. But Madeline is already turning away into the sitting room.

'Come and see,' she calls.

She kneels down beside the baby, who is sitting in a washing-up bowl in front of the fire. She's not a baby, not really, not any more. She's eighteen months, a toddler. But until there is another baby, she will be the baby. And there is not going to be another baby.

'Dadda!'

The little girl splashes her hands down in the water, sending up spray, looking up at her father, grinning with her new teeth. Madeline folds her skirts in under her knees, kneels down. He's always astonished by the child's enthusiasm for him. He doesn't really get it. He's tired and busy and he keeps shunting her away to get on with work. He rubs the chill out of his hands, creaks down onto the fireside rug. She's lovely. He smiles at her.

'Dadda!' the baby says again.

She has other words now, but this one was her first. She seems particularly proud of it.

'The bathroom's arctic,' Madeline apologises.

He dips his hand into the baby's bath, trickles water down her round smooth alien body.

'Just the one kettle,' Madeline explains, 'let down with cold water from the tap.'

He smiles up at her. 'Good thinking.'

He occupies his study. He can be here quite legitimately until she calls him down for dinner. The baby sleeps in the room below. Her sleep fills the room like cushion stuffing, muffling, impenetrable. Downstairs, in the kitchen, Madeline cooks, sorts laundry, that kind of thing.

It is not a big house. His parents were astonished, really, at how little he could afford, at how little he was paid, after all those years training. They called it training, like a fellowship was an apprenticeship and not an accolade. Admittedly, the house is small, but there is air here, and space

392

– vertical space, if not lateral. There are flights of stairs between its rooms, their occupants.

He can play a record here without disturbing anyone; in fact, he can do pretty much anything up here, because it's his, the trade-off for everything else, for all that family obliges you to give up. This is what he gets out of the arrangement: one room. He traces a finger over the narrow spines of his albums. Not much money for luxuries any more; there won't be till the child's in school and Madeline can start back teaching. He tugs out the Beatles records – their greatest hits, his most recent purchases, now already two years old. He looks for a moment at the cover photos side by side. The same photographer, the same shot, the only difference being the passage of six years, which writes lines upon the faces, grows hair, changes clothes, spirals people off in disparate directions, darkens everything. He slips the red album back in – not those early years, not *Help*. He can't face that. He slides the blue one out of its sleeve, lays it down on the platter. He switches on the turntable, and sets the arm down with its careful click and hiss.

He should work. But as the familiar music scrolls out, he turns to the window, looks out across the back gardens. They form a reservoir of green between the houses. His tree – he owns a tree – sends its keys spiralling down into the garden every autumn, causing tiny ash trees to sprout within its shade. He mows over them when required to do so, beheading all the tiny hopeful shoots.

It was Madeline's idea, the baby. It was her idea too, the name. Before the child was even born. Good for either boy or girl, she said, modern, androgynous, and yet with family tradition behind it. And then there's the great Billie precedents: Whitelaw, Holiday. He went along with it, just like he went along with the whole thing because it was what she thought she wanted. The naming never felt quite right to him, though, never felt fair. It's like she'd been born to affect some kind of reconciliation. You can't burden a child with that: you can't make a person then decide on what she's going to be. She thinks people should just get along, Madeline does. Of course they should. It doesn't mean they can.

Little Billie Hastings, with her belly like a boiled egg and her narrow little shoulders. Too much for her to carry.

Paper lolls from his typewriter. Grey typescript, carbon paper, then a grey smudgy copy underneath. He is supposed to be tapping away, typing up the manuscript. But Madeline can't hear from all the way down there, as she clanks nappy pails and rattles the grill out of the cooker to look at the lamb chops. She'd type it up for him, with her fifty-seven words a minute, and her knack of deciphering his scrawl. But the typing up, finger after plonking finger, is as much a part of the process as the first long-hand draft.

Perhaps he should let her, though. Perhaps it would help. Them, if not the book. A shared project.

He sits down on the edge of his desk. A big Victorian desk, bought at auction, nudged and strained and scraped up the stairs. It's like the tree. Like the bust of Milton. Like the settee in his office, its chintzy cover left crumpled and marked and smelling of sex. It proves him.

He will have to take a cloth, a handful of soapflakes. He'll have to be careful. He feels a shudder of disgust. At himself, at the notion of dabbing away stains from the College chintz.

Then, with a start, he sees Madeline come out from under the angle of the house, a laundry basket balanced on her hip. She makes her way down the garden, towards the washing line, which hangs with the fluttering white flags of nappies. She unhooks the prop, and the washing line droops down into her reach. He watches as she takes the corner of a nappy, and lifts it and holds the terry cloth to her face. He knows she's testing its dryness. But. But. He feels his eyes filling. He watches as she touches the baby's clouts, so recently wet and filthy and stinking, to her cheek. The tenderness of it.

The cloth is dry, it seems, because she folds it into a fat square, and lets it fall into the basket, and reaches for the next one in the row. He watches her as she empties the line. The way her sweater lifts and reveals pale skin, the gentle inward curve from hip to waist. His nose prickles; he rubs at it with his palm. When she lifts the laundry basket, and turns back to the house, he ducks away from the window. He sits down at his desk, and rereads the last line that he typed, and glances back at the manuscript's inky scrawl. He reads back through his own handwritten words, but he can't find his way through them, back into the argument.

He gets up, and picks his way downstairs, sideways, good leg bad leg. He stands in the kitchen doorway, and watches her fold the nappies, and says, 'Can I help?'

That night, they eat lamb chops and pot barley and mashed potatoes in front of the fire. He tears the final bits of flesh off the bones with his teeth, observes her doing the same. When she takes his plate, he takes her wrist, and draws her down for a kiss. Then he puts the plates aside, and tugs her sweater up over her head, revealing her softened belly and her breasts, traced with silvery stretch marks, in their functional white bra.

She kisses him, tasting of lamb and mint. Her body is beautiful in the firelight. She is not a girl any more, he realises; she is a woman. It's somehow daunting, the way that she's grown up on him. He never knew that this would happen.

Howard Street, Oxford, 6 May 1985

Billie takes her building society book from the bureau drawer. She has twenty-five pounds in her Junior Saver account. She takes knickers and socks and a clean T-shirt and a spare pair of jeans and by the time she's rolled it all up together her Smurf bag is so full the seams are pulling themselves apart. There are little holes where the stitching drags against the fabric.

She works her smallest sketchpad in between the bundled clothes, thinking can she manage to bring her other things – her damaged, secret things. Her hare's skull, staved in at the back like an eggshell. A leaf-skeleton hung with a thread from a twist of driftwood, turning slightly with her displacement of the air. Her dried-out newt, tiny as an insect, coiled like a dragon, its eyes dimpled and parched.

She looks down at her bag. There isn't space. They'd get crushed. And her mum would notice, in an instant. Walk in the door, see Billie's

397

bleached-out collection of oddments gone, and know that she'd gone too.

Instead, Billie slips in a 4B pencil and a sharpener. Their shapes are visible through the side of the bag.

She read somewhere – she thinks it might have been C.S. Lewis – that the best way to escape is not to climb out the window in the dead of night, but to saunter, in broad daylight, out of the front door. That way, if someone sees you going they'll not suspect a thing. If you're spotted halfway out of a window at three in the morning, chances are it's going to look suspicious.

Billie has told her mum she's going to meet up with Jenny and Claire, go shopping, and then see a film. It gives her a good four hours before anybody will even notice that she's gone.

She knots the cords and slings her Smurf bag over her shoulder and clatters down the stairs and heads for the front door. No-one stops her. But her mum hears her, and leans out round the side of the kitchen door.

Madeline is drying her hands with a tea towel. Her hair is bundled up into a ragged ponytail. She wears a long skirt and flat canvas shoes. She tries to look like it's all normal, but she's not fooling anyone.

'Have a nice time.'

'Thanks.'

'Don't forget your key,' she says.

'I've got it.'

'Good girl.' Her mum gives her a smile, which makes her skin crumple up like tissue beneath her eyes. You can see that she's been crying; she's been crying for weeks. She just won't admit it.

And this is what's driving Billie mad. The floorboards are about to crumble, the roof to fly away. The walls will fall out flat like water-lily petals, and they will, all three of them, be entirely exposed to view. And they keep on pretending that everything is normal.

'See you,' she decides on, and clunks the door shut behind her.

She goes to the building society branch on the High Street, where no-one knows her.

'All of it, please,' Billie asks.

The woman has a flicky fringe sprayed into place with lots of hairspray – Billie can see the dried droplets of it hanging off the individual hairs like paint. The woman doesn't make any comment on Billie's withdrawal. She just slides a paper slip across the counter, asks Billie to sign.

Billie walks to the station, out at the back of Oxford. Crossing the river on Hythe Bridge Street she is caught there for a moment, watching the drip of weeping willows towards the water, watching upstream the men and women in big sweaters and jeans going about the business of living in their narrow boats. Big black buckets and knotted ropes and strapped-down jerry cans. A mottled hairy dog keeps a grave eye on things. It seems the best way to be here, if you have to be here – to be always ready to be gone.

The train ticket costs her three pounds and seventy-five pence, which is quite a lot, and she has to wait half an hour for the next train to London, which she does, sitting on her hands, bag resting on the seat beside her, arm still through the cord loops so that no-one can nick it.

A man sits down near her, and lights up a cigarette, and looks at her, and offers her one, but she looks away and pretends not to notice. He says something, and she gets up from her seat, and walks up to the steps, and up and over the footbridge, and down back into the ticket hall, and waits the rest of the half an hour there, keeping quiet on a bench, avoiding catching anybody's eye in case it's somebody that she knows, or somebody whom she doesn't know but who knows her parents and would recognise her. She jumps every time the tannoy bings into life, expecting her train to be announced. Five trains are announced before hers, and on each occasion she feels a faint flicker of relief: it is not too late yet; she could just go back, and be home, and no-one will ever know that she was leaving, and maybe everything will be all right. But then her train is called, and when that happens there's suddenly no question. She hares off over the footbridge and skitters down the steps and bolts through the nearest door before the platform guard slams it just behind her.

She makes her way down the carriages until she finds an empty seat. The train shunts into movement. There is no getting off now. The city peels away like a curtain, and they gather speed, pass the backs of terraced houses, suburbs, trading parks, and out into the fields. The woman opposite unpacks corned-beef-and-onion sandwiches, then carefully peels a hard-boiled egg, dropping fragments of shell into her clingfilm sandwich wrapping. She takes a bite from the egg, a bite from the sandwich, chews them together. It's pretty disgusting, what with the smell and the sound of her chewing.

Billie weaves her way to the buffet car to get away from the woman's lunch. She buys coffee and a four-finger Kit Kat. When she gets back to her seat the woman has finished her meal, and is reading a fat creased paperback. Billie slips the paper sheath off the chocolate bar, runs her thumbnail down the foil.

Granddad has always been on her side. He was when she was little, and he will be still. He made her that green aeroplane with the pedals. And it never mattered to him what she'd done, how cheeky she'd been, whether it was well past bedtime. She could always go to Granddad, and he'd lift her up onto his knee and defend her from all comers.

In London, she finds her way by the blurred recollection that comes from tagging along at her dad's heels, hand clamped in his hand, an awareness of crowds and crush and the warm pelt of his moleskin or elephant-cord trousers, and the colourful abstractions of the Tube map, and the black line being the only one that's needed, and the litany of names, Clapham, Balham, Tooting Bec. Her hands get dirty from nothing in particular.

She sits, swaying on the orange-mottled Tube upholstery, and nods with tiredness. She doesn't know how she can be so exhausted – it's as though just being moved from place to place causes wear upon the body – the drag away from home, like sucking your feet out of sticky mud. The gravity of where you're from that doesn't want to let you go.

Follow the black line right to the end. Climb up into the daylight and head – she blinks round, looking for a landmark, spots the green corner of the park – that way.

It turns out right. The park, with its tiny straggling river, and then businesses, and then playing fields. She turns up the London Road, and spots the cricket green, and is nearly there. She has flashes of memory: the place where pineapple weed grew between the paving stones, the corner with the scary dog. Like pebbles dropped thoughtlessly and years ago, for her to make her way back now. The pram shop with its yellow translucent blinds and the sweetie shop where they sell the best ice cream, and down Bramcote Avenue, and the cherry blossom is in bloom, and into Denham Crescent, and she's there.

The house is as it always was. The green square of lawn neatly mown, fat-looking grape hyacinths and fleshy tulips in the borders. The single bow window curtained in swags of net and lace. It is all actually really and truly normal. So normal and unchanging that she reaches out to touch the front gate out of a simple need to connect with it, and it creaks. In the front window the net curtains lift in a sudden dark swoop, and she can't see whoever's looking out, just the pink hook of their hand around the bunched lace.

Granddad. Grandma.

She pushes open the gate and runs up the path.

The nets in the front bay window fall back into place. She can hear her granddad's voice, calling out: 'Ruby!'

And he's there, she doesn't even have to knock, she can see him through the glass panes of the door, trapped between the rays of the wooden sunrise.

He opens the door. She steps up and into the house and into his arms.

He smells familiar, of Old Spice, and sweetened coffee, and mints.

The hall is as it always was. Wallpaper dizzy with roses. Warm and stuffy. His cream nylon cap; Grandma's navy coat.

'Billie,' Granddad says. He breathes against her. Her cheek lies on his chest.

'Granddad.'

'Thank God.'

He rubs her hair. Grandma appears in the doorway to the sitting room. She has a duster twisted up in her hand. She has a headscarf on over her grey curls. Billie smiles at her, but her grandma blinks away tears.

'Sweetheart.'

Billie steps away from Granddad and goes to hug her. 'What's wrong, Grandma?'

'You've given us all a proper scare.'

She's looking over Billie's shoulder at Granddad; Billie can feel it. Some kind of look they're giving each other.

Then she lets go. Billie ducks down and fusses the wriggling dog. It's a skinny black and tan mongrel, got from Battersea Dogs Home. It's the second Sukie since Billie was born, but she knows there were other Sukies before.

'Are you hungry?' Grandma asks.

'I am a bit.'

'I've got crispy pancakes,' Grandma says. 'I've got fondant fancies, and I've got these little frozen mousses. Chocolate and raspberry.'

Billie smiles. She rubs at the dog's head. 'Thank you.'

'Come on through,' Grandma says.

In the front room, the chairs sag on either side of the gas fire. Grandma heads on through the arch into the dining room, and then into the kitchen. She makes a rattle with the kettle and the cups. Billie pauses just before the sliding door into the kitchen, glances back for Granddad, but he has stayed in the hall.

'Coffee,' Grandma calls, 'Or tea?'

There's a framed photograph on top of the cabinet just by the kitchen door. It's of the three of them on a boat. Mum is in a cream tunic dress with yellow and brown flowers embroidered round the neckline; her hair is all loose and shiny. Dad has a moustache and an open-necked cheesecloth shirt. The little girl's wearing dungarees and has her hair cut in a blunt fringe. She's three years old, maybe. It's Cornwall, she remembers: she ate too much fudge, and was sick. In the picture they are all smiling.

'Tea,' Billie says. 'Thank you.'

Billie hears the click of a lighter. She moves away from the photograph, and steps down into the kitchen. A cigarette spools blue smoke from her grandma's hand.

'Or milk or water? Or I can send Granddad out for cordial.'

'Tea would be lovely, please, Grandma.'

She can hear him in the hallway – the tock-tock-tock-tock-tock and whizz of a phone number being dialled. She glances back round for him.

'Who's he calling?'

'Sit down, honey.'

'Is he calling them?' Billie asks.

'You look shattered.'

Billie pulls out one of the chairs, sits down on the creaky vinyl, but tilts herself to look through the open kitchen door and back into the dining room and sitting room and the open hall door. Granddad is standing there – she can even see a strip of him, the fawn back of his trousers – talking on the phone.

'But who's he on the phone to?'

'Your mum and dad, of course. They're frantic.'

'But it doesn't work like that any more.'

'What do you mean?'

'It's not mum-and-dad any more. Not like that. Not as a pair.'

Grandma slides open the frosted glass door of the kitchen cupboard, lifts down the cut-glass sugar bowl. She taps her cigarette into a red plastic ashtray.

'We'll see.'

But she doesn't know, not really. She gets out a small mug and puts it down in front of Billie. Inside it's glossy dark brown glaze, outside matte and creamy, decorated with brown-glaze aeroplanes.

They can hear the conversation; Granddad's end of it. It starts out quiet, urgent – not to worry, yes, yes, she's turned up here. No, no, she's fine, yes, he will tell her. Billie knows it's her mum on the other end. And then it changes, and there's a big silence, which means her dad has taken over. The call ends abruptly – a brisk signing off from

406

Granddad, then the clatter and ping as the handset is set down.

Granddad comes back in. He and Grandma exchange a glance. They don't say anything. She thinks she might cry. He's supposed to be on her side.

'Don't make me go back there.'

'One thing at a time, honey,' Grandma says.

Billie feels hot. She holds her hands to her cheeks. Grandma pours her a cup of tea, gives her an awkward little smile.

'It's all right, love. It'll be all right.'

And Billie shifts her hands across her eyes and cries.

They eat ham-and-cheese Findus Crispy Pancakes and tinned peas, and new potatoes from a tin. Billie helps in the kitchen, opening the tins, pouring contents into aluminium pans. Her eyes are sore but she is keen to show how calm and reasonable and cheerful she really is. The potatoes emerge from the tin white and faintly porous, like deep-sea creatures used to living in the dark.

As they eat, Grandma watches Granddad, Granddad frowns. When he does that, he looks just like her dad. Something serious is going to happen. They are going to want to talk. If she lets them talk, they will tell her that she has to go back.

Grandma gets out the mousses. Billie asks for chocolate. It is still a little frozen in the middle.

She digs it out with a spoon. It is frosty on the tongue.

'It was before the war, wasn't it, Granddad, when you were cycling?'

He looks up at her, blinks. After a moment he smiles. And he starts to tell her again about his racing days. Grandma smiles at his smile, chips in eagerly. Familiar phrases. People would stop him in the street. People would want to shake his hand. Billy Hastings.

Just like her. It's her name too. Give or take a couple of vowels.

He looks up at her then, blinks his soft blue eyes, and another silence falls.

'And then there was the war,' Billie says.

'Did I tell you about D-Day, about how we were going to sacrifice a gull?'

'Forty years ago now,' Grandma says.

'Forty-one. Nearly.'

He goes quiet. Taps at the side of his mug.

'Go on, Granddad.'

Billie's heard the story a dozen times already. It doesn't matter because she's listening only enough to nod and smile in the right places. Her mind's searching for the next thing, a new question, a question that will keep this freewheeling on along through warm familiar memories for a while longer. They drink tea. A little later the box is got out. The campaign medals, the war medal stamped with an eagle and a dragon, and the cycling medals. Amateur Pursuit Cycling Champion

1935, one in French from 1935, then a Veteran's Medal, 1946.

'Veteran as in war veteran?'

'Veteran as in old man.'

'You were an old man in 1946?'

Grandma and Granddad both laugh. 'In a manner of speaking,' he says.

She turns its weight round in her hands. *William Arthur Hastings* engraved on the back.

'We could go out later, Granddad. I could borrow a bike from next door.'

'Roads are so busy these days,' Grandma says briskly, setting a plate of Mr Kipling's Fondant Fancies down in the middle of the table. Billie picks up the pink one. The icing sticks to the roof of her mouth. She teases at it with the tip of her tongue.

'What about this one?' She picks out the French medal, turns it over to peer at the inscription.

Grandma looks at him. An unfathomable look.

'Won that in Paris. At the Vélodrome d'Hiver,' he says.

'The winter—?'

'Cycle track, that's right. Famous, it is. Infamous—'

'Billy.' Grandma's voice is warning.

'Why shouldn't she know? Jesus, if things were not so very different, she wouldn't be here—'

'Please.'

Granddad gets up. He opens a kitchen cabinet, rattles around. Billie sneaks her hand into

Grandma's. Grandma gives her a wobbly smile. Billie doesn't understand. He returns with a quarter bottle of something. Rum, Billie supposes, because Granddad is known to be partial to a drop of rum. He doesn't look at either of them. He slops the liquid into his tea, screws the cap back on, sets the bottle down too hard, making Billie jump. The smell of it is sweet and peppery. No-one says anything. Grandma's face has fallen into a deep-lined frown; Granddad's flushed and defiant.

Then the doorbell goes. Granddad looks at Grandma, and Grandma gets up stiffly from her seat. 'I'll get it.'

'Oh,' Billie says. 'Oh no.' She knows it's him.

She hears the briskness of the greeting at the door, a kiss, and then the two of them – her dad and Grandma – coming in through the sitting room and back to the kitchen. Granddad wipes a drip of tea from the side of his mug.

She doesn't dare look at Dad. He's there on the edge of her vision, blue jeans and pale top and a loose navy jacket. He's slumped slightly, favouring that bad leg, sore from the drive. So she has to feel guilty about that now.

'Right, Billie,' Dad says. 'Come on. We can talk in the car.'

Granddad looks up. Billie doesn't shift.

'Don't mess around, Billie. Get your stuff.'

'I'm not coming.'

'I don't have time for this.' He grabs her arm, tugs her out of her chair. It hurts.

'Dad—'

'We're going.'

Grandma turns away – does something busy on the counter. Granddad's chair scrapes back, and he grabs Dad's arm, and stops him dead. Dad looks at the old hand on his arm, and then looks at his hand on Billie's.

'Don't,' Dad says.

There's a moment, then Granddad's hand drops away. And Dad lets her go.

'Sorry, petal,' her dad says to her.

It's worse, his apology: it's more upsetting than him pulling her out of the chair. 'S'all right.'

'I was worried,' he says. 'Terrified. Jesus. Anything could have happened.'

But it didn't, Billie wants to say. I'm here and nothing happened and everything was fine until you came. She sits back down. Dad shifts uneasily, takes hold of the back of Grandma's chair. His leg is hurting him.

'And why d'you think she'd go and do a thing like that?' Granddad says.

'Jesus. Do we have to?'

'But why do you think? Smart girl like that, doing something so daft.'

'Her mother and I are sorting things out.'

'Sorting things out? Ha! How exactly? Maybe to your convenience, but bugger everyone else, hey?'

411

Billie's head drops down onto folded arms. For a while there are just voices, and Grandma's arm around her shoulders. Billie nods to the soothing noises that she makes, dabs her eyes with her sleeve. Sniffs.

'The thing about you, son,' her granddad says. 'The thing I don't understand—'

'Billy,' Grandma warns.

Billie glances up at her. She looks trapped, somehow, alert and anxious. Billie's dad stands back from things – back against the counter, as if he's restrained, held in place by something. The room is full of unseen cables, linking, pulling, tense.

'Your mother and me – we thought we'd brought you up better than that.'

'Jesus Christ—'

Her granddad just talks over him: 'A good home, a stable home, all these years. And this is what you do.'

'Keep it vague, why don't you? You're not going to want to go into too much detail.'

'You know your problem, boy?'

'I'd be fascinated to hear.'

'You never had a war to go to. That's your problem.'

'You reckon? You reckon that's it, do you—?'

'When is the baby due?' Billie asks.

Attention spins and fixes on her. They didn't know she knew.

'I mean, it'll be my half-brother or sister. I think I should be told.'

Her dad lets out a slow thin breath. 'It's early days yet. We don't know – Carole has to . . .'

Billie nods, looks down at her hands. Moves her fingers so the glitter in her nail varnish catches the light. This is what the family will be now, this is what it will be shuffled out and sorted into: a new neat unit. Dad, Carole, new baby. If it's a boy, will they call it William too, as though she'd never been? And all the mess will be sorted out and cleared off and got rid of. Billie has an image of herself, on a lilo drifting out to sea, and everyone she's ever known is crowded on the beach, all talking and far too busy and preoccupied to look out after her, and watch her disappear.

The museum's dome is off to their right. The air is dirty with fumes: it tastes like pennies. They cross at the lights, walk along beside the railings.

They have agreed that she can have this: these few days here in London before she has to go back. She needed to calm down, her dad told her, to have a break from home and all that disruption: he knew things were difficult right now. And Granddad and Grandma were glad to have her there, he'd said. And she'd wanted to say she knew that, and that was why she'd come. But instead she'd just said thank you.

Granddad's hand swings along beside her. She catches it. He squeezes her hand, and that makes her smile. The railings flicker by, her reaching slightly up, him reaching slightly down, and it feels at once strange and awkward and really nice. She remembers the green gloss of the pedal-aeroplane he made for her, the bulls-eye markings on the wings.

'There we are,' he says.

They head through the gates. The vast naval guns rear up overhead, silvery, cold, incongruous.

'They're from the *Roberts*,' he says. 'At least, one of them is, I think.'

'Go over,' she says. 'I'll take your photo.'

He walks away from her. His trousers hang loose around his legs. His backside is flat underneath the polyester. He stands between the guns for a moment. His right hand almost lifts away from his side, as if he's going to reach out and try and touch the gun's flank. But instead he dips it into his pocket. He turns round and squints at her. Smiles. Jerks his head towards the doors: *Come on then*.

She lifts her camera from her pocket, snaps his photograph. Winds it on.

She sits on the spare bed, making a dent in the powder-blue candlewick, and waits for him to finish in the bathroom. The walls are thin. She can hear the slow, strained dribble of his pee onto ceramic, the volcanic toilet flush, the scrub and spit into the sink. He comes out onto the landing, passes her door. She catches a glimpse of striped pyjama bottoms, vest, the softened skin of his chest and arm, the fuzz of white chest hair, and the vague smudge of his tattoo. *Ruby*.

She steps out onto the landing. Bare feet on patterned carpet. Through the half-open door, she can see her grandparents' twin beds. Grandma is already in hers, a hump under the purple nylon counterpane. Her breathing is loud and ragged.

'Granddad,' Billie breathes, not wanting them to hear. 'Grandma.'

It feels like she's sticking a pin into a map, saying these words. Then she can twist a thread around it, and wherever she goes and however far away, she can reel the thread off behind her; then, whenever she needs to, she can follow it back again to where she started from.

She gets into bed. The bed is soft; it creaks when she turns. She is going to come back. She can follow the thread back here whenever she wants. Whenever her mum and school can spare her.

She can hear the city noises. Layers of traffic, a dog's straining hysterical bark.

Dad slept here as a boy. Ran down those stairs, good leg bad leg, out that front door and off into the streets, and then off to Oxford.

She rolls round onto her side, eyes level with the bedside cabinet. In the next room her grandma wheezes uneasily. Granddad softly snores. The sounds weave together into waves, spilling onto sand.

Tomorrow is the train home. Walkman on. Trying to look like she knows how to be in the world, how to fill up the ticking minutes. Mum at the station, with her too-bright smile and her hair needing a cut. They are going to see the new house again. The paved back yard. The damp patch under the back bedroom window. The neighbours two doors down shout at each other in the middle of the day. She and her mum are going to measure up her new room for curtains.

Later, there will be Mum's work piled on the dining table, her glass of wine, her elbow on the tabletop and her hand raked into her hair. Billie will go to bed and listen to the emptiness upstairs and down. This, at least, will go with the move: the noticeable absence, the sense of too much space.

She blinks at the bedside cabinet. Her sketchpad lies askew on top of it. She'd better pack it.

She shuffles upright in bed, flicks on the bedside light and lifts the spiral-bound pad from the top of the cabinet. She flicks through. A sketch of Grandma catches her attention. She's not quite got the line of the nose right – it needs to be a bit more . . . She reaches for her pencil, fumbles it; it goes skittering off the surface, down between the cabinet and the wall. Damn it. She twists round, drags the cabinet away from the wall: there it is. She lies flat again to stretch down for it, reaching blindly, her cheek against the edge of the bed. The dust is thick like mouse fur: her finger-tips brush the pencil, she goes to grab it, but her knuckles knock against something hard and hollow. Metal. She closes her hand round it, lifts it out – a sweetie tin, she thinks at first.

A tobacco tin in fact, all white and blue and gold. It's old. It's been there a while. It's thick with dust. Maybe it's Granddad's. Or Grandma's, rather, since she's the smoker. But Granddad's always got tins of screws and hinges and bits of bike: maybe he's lost it. She shakes it. It's light, doesn't rattle.

Probably empty then. Billie has a go at opening it, but it's stuck, rusted hard. She tries again, pulling and then twisting. Can't shift it. She casts around for something to wrap it in for a better grip, something that won't stain. A sock. A black one. She scrambles out of bed, scrabbles one out from the bottom of her bag. Wraps it round the tin and twists.

This time it grates open. Lid in one hand, tin in the other. There's a handkerchief stuffed inside the tin: that's why it didn't make a noise when she shook it. She sets the handkerchief aside; there are a few things in the tin after all. Grandma things. She lifts out a crystal drop earring and it catches the light and scatters it with gorgeous softness; a single pearl stud is creamy between the fingertips, cool and waxy on the lips. Then there's a brooch set with glittering metallic black stones, but the catch is broken.

She'll give the tin to Grandma tomorrow. She's lost it, maybe even forgotten she ever had it. These are all broken things; easily forgotten. But when

Grandma has them in her hands again, she will remember. She'll tell her where they've come from, what they mean. Things have this power: one look, one touch; memories come back like that.

She goes to put the handkerchief back, but it unfolds itself in sharp creases, reveals a dark patch, a stain, which sticks the cloth together. Is it blood? Inside, there's something loose. A bit of leather – she places it in her palm. It's the colour of a penny. She holds it up to the light and there are three white hairs bristling out of it. They glisten in the light, entirely human.

It's an earlobe. Someone's earlobe. She's certain of it. Though whose, and how it came to be here, with these lost treasures, she can't imagine. Something nasty happened, that's clear. The blood on the handkerchief, and this thing wrapped up for safekeeping. A messy accident. Something to do with the war.

And then it's been kept hidden here, for years, long enough for it to turn to leather.

A shiver gathers in the back of her neck. This is a secret. She can't ask her grandma about any of this.

And she wants it. With the same certainty that she wanted the hare's skull, the newt, the flesh-less leaf. But this, for all it's tiny, this is more than all of that put together. This is *human*.

If she just puts everything else back as she found it – she sets the scrap of leather down on the bedside table, then tucks the handkerchief back into a bundle and grinds the lid back into place; leaning right over the side of the bed, she tips the tin in and lets it roll back underneath, minus that one little thing – no-one will ever know.

She picks up the little scrap of flesh again and presses it. It gives slightly between her fingernails, making her shiver delightfully. It's hers. She'll have to keep it hidden. Billie tweaks a tissue from the box on the bedside cabinet. She wraps up the ancient severed earlobe, pushes it into her bag.

Billy's taking their granddaughter to the train station. Ruby's tidying up. She strips Billie's bed, flings back the blanket and grabs the bottom sheet, and the bed creaks out from the wall, but the sheet doesn't come untucked.

'Bother.'

She moves round the far side of the bed and pushes up the sleeves of her caramel-coloured sweater and leans in down between the bedhead and the wall to tackle the problem. And then, in the dusty gap between the bedhead and the wall, she sees the tin.

For a second she's caught between the moment and the memory and just stands there, her dry hands full of crumpled pink polycotton. Then she tugs the bed further out, gets down carefully on creaking knees, and reaches into the dusty shadows.

She sits down on the half-unmade bed. The house is empty. The tin is in her hands, gritty with rust. She can't even put it down in case the rust marks something.

Ruby tries at the lid. It grinds uneasily. She doesn't open it.

She feels the sense of it in her mouth. The bite of it. The blood behind her teeth.

The inside of the car and the smell of leather and the creak and sweep of the windscreen wipers. The rich smell of him.

Her belly pushes out against her waistband as she breathes. She saw him, at Will's graduation, feet planted on that lovely lawn like he owned the place, and her tiptoeing, hushed, like she was in a church. And for the briefest of moments, before she'd even registered the shock of it, or the back-wash of worry about Billy noticing something, she'd wanted to go up to him and say, well fancy that, you and I meeting again, after all these years. But then she felt it – the crackling nylon of her C&A suit round her calves, and the pinch of her hat, and Billy there beside her, stiff in his black suit, and instead she'd lit a cigarette and looked the other way, and asked Will which one of the men in their flappy black gowns was his tutor. So they didn't meet again, not really. As far as she knows, the handsome man hadn't noticed her at all, he'd been so busy talking with other, substantial men. Anyway, he wasn't so handsome any more: he'd gone to seed. And his boy was a great blond fleshy lump, and nothing like her Will.

And if Billy suspects, if he thinks, if he even for

a moment imagines that there'd been a cuckoo in the nest, then it's clear as day now that he's wrong. He's so like his dad, Will is. He might look a bit like her, but his ongoing bloody-minded battle through the pain, that's pure Billy.

She pushes down onto the bed with her free hand, and gets to her feet. A strange tingling sensation prickles out from her chest and down her arm.

She goes into the bathroom, sets the tin down between the taps. She stands at the mirror. Her bones are good. Her eyes are good. She tries a smile. Her skin folds into creases at her eyes; there are deep lines etched from nose to lips, and her lipstick feathers round the edges. Mrs had always said the cigarettes'd give her wrinkles.

It was gradual, the fade-out from beauty. It wasn't any particular thing, no hard line, no threshold from one state to the next. But gradually the men stopped staring; and they stopped being angry at her, because they'd stopped wanting her. And she finds that she prefers it like this. To go unnoticed, unremarked upon. She's enjoying her anonymity.

She makes her way down the stairs and through the house. In the back porch she lifts a trowel from the shelf. Her heart feels fluttery, uneasy. She pads along the garden path in her house slippers.

She goes right to the end of the path, just before the garage, where Amelia used to grow tomatoes.

She kneels carefully at the border, easing herself onto her knees. She thwacks the trowel into the soil, lifts out a clump of sweet william, and digs out the earth underneath. The flower garden is hers. He's not going to be digging here.

She digs a hole a foot deep, eight inches wide.

She never did find out where he was buried, the blue baby. If he'd lived, then everything would have been different. That Sunday before D-Day would have been different, she'd have been chasing after her little boy. But if he had lived, there would have been no Will, no Janet. Other children perhaps, but not them. There would have been no Billie, no Madeline; and Ruby can't conceive of a life without these threads, the tug of them.

She lays the tin down in the dark soil. Pain licks out across her chest. She tries to catch her breath. She scrapes the soil over the box: lay it all to rest. She tucks the plant's roots back into place. The flower stands to attention, its petals rimmed and blotched with purple.

St George's Hospital, Tooting, 15 May 1995

'There you go, love.'

The nurse sticks on the wad of lint, pressing lightly along the adhesive strips. Then she tugs his pyjama top down and lifts him up against the pillows. The wound twists and pulls and he winces. She bobs down to empty the bags. He watches the white seam down the centre of her head, where her mousey roots are parted. Brisk, she is, this young woman. Already she's back on her feet, peeling off her gloves, whisking back the curtains. Doesn't stop to chat.

Billy peers down the ward, between the beds. Will is supposed to be coming today. He said that he'd bring the children. That means Billie, which is sunshine and spring air; but it also means Matthew. Billy will be nice to him. He always is. It's not the lad's fault, how he came to be.

There will be tea in half an hour. A mug of milky tea and two digestives, because that's what the doctor says he should have, because they are good for the digestion, and a chat with the nice lady who brings the trolley. And then dinner at five. Cold cuts and salad. Which he likes too. It's not bad in here. He feels looked after.

And then he spots her, hair shining, coming down the ward towards him bright and smiling. She ducks down and gives him a kiss. Slides into the chair, takes his hand.

'How you feeling, Granddad?'

Where did she get those green eyes? Is that from Madeline's side, or his own?

'Not too bad, love.' Even to him his voice sounds weak. 'Where's your dad?'

She jerks her head, gesturing down the ward, towards the corridor beyond. 'Talking to the doctor.'

He peers, eyes rheumy. 'Is Matthew there?'

'He's just waiting for Dad.'

'He'll be bored.'

She shrugs. 'He'll live.'

'What are they saying?'

'Who?'

'The doctors.'

'Don't worry.'

She knows something. He can tell by her tone. He looks at her with sudden clarity. She's grown up: she's included in grown-up information and discussion and decisions. And he isn't. Not any more.

'Dad'll sort it out,' Billie says. 'Really, don't you worry. We'll have you home in no time.'

★　★　★

She's making such a fucking hash of it. Her cheeks burn. She glances back round at her father – who's just disappearing through the door that the registrar, Dr Nurbhai, holds open for him – leaving her nine-year-old half-brother, Matthew, slumped on a plastic chair in the corridor for her to keep an eye on.

Her granddad's hand feels weirdly soft. She can't look down, because if she looks down she'll see the snaking tubes and the bags suspended underneath the bed, filling up with yellow fluids. So she looks him in the face, even though it's difficult nowadays, even though it makes her chest ache. He's been dwindling away all these years, ever since Grandma died, really. His cheeks are hollow. The skin beneath his eyes droops into translucent swags. She'd need watercolours to try and catch that kind of transparency, that softness over hard structural bone. She hasn't used watercolours in a while.

She shouldn't be thinking like that. This is Granddad. She shouldn't be looking at him in that way, as a thing with shades and angles and bones. He taught her to ride a bike. Hand hooked under the back of the seat, his breath on her ear. Pedals white and rubbery underneath her trainers. In Port Meadow, weaving along the worn paths, bumping across the hummocky grass.

'He'll sort it all out,' she says. He has to.

'Sort what out?'

'Whatever needs to be done. Dad's good at this

kind of thing. Good with professional people. They've just got to work out what you need.'

He nods, acquiescent. She bites at the inside of her cheek. She sounds so posh, so pompous, so bloody fucking articulate. *Come on, Dad. Hurry up, you bastard.*

Then a cloud shifts somewhere high above, and the sun floods in through the window, pooling this far corner of the ward with light. And in the sunshine, the old man is blue. His cheeks, his nose and his fingertips are all turning a beautiful shade of lavender, as if he's freezing slowly, from inside.

'Are you cold, Granddad?'

He rolls his head against the pillows. No.

'Can I get you anything? Cup of tea?'

'Tea's at half three.'

'There's the machine.'

He considers this a moment. 'That'd be nice. You fancy one, sweetheart?'

The gold glints at the side of his teeth. He leans round towards his locker to scoop up change, but the movement makes him wince, makes the leashes of tubing snake.

'S'all right, Granddad, I've got money.'

Out in the corridor, Matty scrapes one trainered toe back and forth under the chair. He glances at her sullenly. He looks powerfully bored. Like he's the centre of everything. Like making sure he's happy is all that anyone should bother with.

'You want a hot chocolate?' she tries.

He looks up at her. He smiles, seems grateful for the distraction. She shouldn't be so hard on him; he's only nine. Who knows what goes on inside their heads?

He has Carole's fairness, but his hair spirals into curls just like Grandma Ruby's used to do.

'Gimme a hand then.'

She holds out a palmful of coins, and he picks through them, looks up at the machine. His fingernails are rimmed with little-boy dirt.

The room has been portioned out of some bigger space in ersatz wood and ceiling tiles and plasterboard walls. A rubber plant droops on the desk. The registrar, who is about fifteen, stands by the illuminated light box. Will stands beside him, his hand to the back of a chair, taking some of the weight off his hip. He has good days and bad days. This is a bad day. He is on a waiting list now. He'll be having his own X-rays to look at soon.

When the light clicks on behind the images, Will's stomach swoops. The two men look on in silence. Dr Nurbhai draws in a breath, but then doesn't speak.

'So what do we do?' Will asks.

He looks round at Dr Nurbhai. The registrar does a thoughtful, professional face: inclination to one side, slight frown, twist of the lips. Will has an expression of his own just like it, used mostly when pretending to consider predictable comments from undergraduates. He grits his teeth, turns back to the light box, to the X-ray of his father's lungs. The glow escaping round the sides gives the image a kind of square halo. He tells himself that he's misinterpreting what he's seeing. It's some different, new technique; this is not a standard X-ray. This is something else. How else could the two sides come out so differently, in such stark contrast?

'First thing to say is, the X-rays are just confirming my initial diagnosis. The treatment your father has already undergone will have dealt with some of this. This is a snapshot, really, from when he was admitted. Of the untreated condition.'

Will shifts, uncomfortable. He should have brought his stick. He doesn't like to use his stick. He thinks people will think it is an affectation, and therefore that he's the kind of man who would affect a stick. He tangles himself up in other peoples' imagined imaginings of him, feels cross at what he thinks they might be thinking.

'Do you want to sit down?' the doctor asks.

'I'm fine,' Will says. He clears his throat. 'So, what now?'

The professional face again – a more extreme version this time. Mouth pulled down at the corners, chin pulled in a touch, head tilted to one side, eyes half shut. Oh he'd just love to punch him. Nice neat little jab to the nose. Make him bleed onto his lovely white collar. Will notices his free hand is clenched tight into a fist. He looks down at it, the tendons standing proud, the veins snaking across. Just like his father's hand, his father's fist. He loosens it, flexes his fingers: all men turn into their fathers, eventually.

So what's his father turning into then? A drowned man?

'Well the point is really,' Dr Nurbhai says, 'what we've got here is a symptom.'

'Right,' Will says. Because of course there's nothing different or new about the X-ray technique here, he knows that. He's not a fool. You don't need a medical degree to interpret this image: one lung is black and therefore clear, the rays passing cleanly through it. The other lung is entirely white, X-rays bouncing back off something denser than tissue. That's what they're draining out of him at the moment, the liquid that's been filling up his lung.

This is it. It is coming. He is going to have to deal with it.

'What it comes down to really is his heart.'

Will nods.

Dr Nurbhai talks about the condition and its treatment. Monitoring. Drug regimes – ongoing care. Will just nods, says yes. He finds himself looking at the spider plant on top of a filing cabinet. It is drying up from the tips – they've gone brown and papery, crumpling up on themselves. He should have watered his, back in his college room, he thinks. It was dying too.

'Do you mind,' Will asks, 'if I sit down?'

Dr Nurbhai takes his arm. Will feels old. He sinks down into the chair.

'Are you all right?' the doctor asks. 'Can I get you a glass of water?'

Will shakes his head. 'It's just, it's quite—'

'Of course. Just take your time.'

She hands the flexing plastic up to Matty.

'Careful.'

'Thanks.'

'It's scalding,' she says. 'Leave it a minute.'

He winces, adjusts his grip. They walk back down the corridor to the row of empty chairs. He sets his drink down on a spare seat, shunts himself back up onto his. His feet dangle. He watches the steam rise from his cup.

'Don't you want to come and see Granddad?' she says.

He looks at her. His wide hazel eyes, his soft face. He has a sprinkling of freckles across his nose.

'Dad said to wait here,' he says. He sounds apprehensive.

'It's just up there,' she nods sidelong up the ward. 'We won't even be out of sight.'

He follows her gaze, between the rows of beds, towards their granddad. She sees it, for a second, through his nine-year-old's eyes: the starkness and the sickness and the hush, and in the middle of it all the inexplicably difficult old man. Matty's afraid. Not prepared to admit it, but he is afraid.

And this is how he will remember their granddad:

sickness, fear, and boredom. Her memories from his age are all fresh air, safety, uncomplicated love.

'Okay,' she says. She wants to say something to reassure him, wants to ruffle his hair or hug him or something.

'Wait here,' she says. 'He won't be long.'

Halfway along the ward, one of the occupied beds has been left uncurtained. The woman's arms lie over the white fold of the sheet. They look like the kind of sticks you find on a woodland floor, blotched and dark, that would fall away into fragments if touched. Billie looks away, but when she blinks she can still see the white sheet, the lines of dark flesh, the crumbling frailty.

Her Converse make creaky sounds on the lino; her jeans brush together at the rolled turnup. When she gets back to the bed, her granddad is sleeping. His eyes are shut, his mouth has fallen open. She can see the neat gold hooks of his bridgework.

She glances back down the length of the ward; in the corridor at the far end, Matty is hunched like a comma round his drink, still waiting. He is too young for this.

She puts the tea down on the tray table, and sits down on the black vinyl-cushioned chair. She lays her hand over her granddad's hand again. She waits. Because it is, after all, only a matter of time.

★   ★   ★

They sit side by side on the Tube. Dad's leg in washed-out denim; her shoulder creaking into his leather blouson jacket whenever the train sways them; Matty on the far side of their dad. She can see his reflection – all their reflections – duplicated in the double panes of the window opposite, underneath which sits a tiny Chinese woman wearing a belted mac and beautiful gold earrings.

The train swings again, and pushes her into her dad's side, and their reflections sway closer to each other. Seen at an angle like this, there is a striking asymmetry to what is still, even at his age, a handsome face. His reflection, for just this moment, looks like it has had a stroke: the lips dipping at one side, the left eye at a different angle to the right. As if his face too has a limp, one side dragged along by the other.

He looks old, in his reflection.

His father is dying.

She glances round at the real him. He catches her eye, then peels off his specs, presses his thumb and fingers to the bridge of his nose, where the flesh is bruised by their weight. The glasses – a metallic stick insect – rest on his knee.

She rubs his arm. The leather sleeve is smooth and cool. 'Okay?'

He puts his glasses back on. Nods.

He thinks of the conference he won't be able to attend. There would have been sun and wine and late-night bars and talk till the small hours and Pavla was going to be arriving on the second day, a paper on Italo Calvino, her lunatic black hair bouncing round her as she made her points. He thinks of six thirty when all the department lights were out, and he'd chewed gum to cover his coffee breath, and his spider plant was looking parched, and Samantha had come up from the college bar, smelling of cider and Anais Anais, and had buried her face in his neck and made a sound like a puppy. He thinks of Carole who, he's pretty sure, has been going through his pockets; who has never really trusted him, because she knew all too well that he couldn't really be trusted.

'How's Mum?' he asks.

Billie, caught off guard, says, 'Okay.'

The smell of diesel making him gag. The smell of vomit might be his. There's the churning rumble of the craft and its lurch and dip beneath him. And the smell of men. Body-stink. Billy's stomach twists and heaves. He grips onto the bike, onto the side of the craft. Every instinct is to pull away. His body tears against itself, away from the cold shore, away from what's coming, away from what it's being pushed into. Glimpsed through smoke. Shells scream overhead. The landing craft hits an underwater obstacle, judders, grinds on. Lurches free. The shake rises up through his feet and legs and the bike and he is rattling like a skeleton. He must make a decent show, for the sake of the squad. He tries to look round at Alfie, but for some reason he can't turn his head. He's worried about Alfie. The landing craft bumps up onto a sandbank; they stagger at the jolt, and the ramp swings down. And Billy, unable to turn his head and take a last look at his friend before they leap out into the surf and race towards the guns with the shells screaming towards them, rolls his whole body round in bed, and Alfie, fifty years ago, white with terror, looks back at him.

Which is when the shell hits.

And Alfie's head is gone. The body hits the deck, splashes into the wash of vomit and bilge. Blood stings Billy's eyes, is spattered across his hands. Blood heaves out of the body. Billy searches round desperately for Alfie's head. As though finding it would help. As if he could slap it back into place, set the body back on its feet, set it going again. But there is no head. No head rolling around the deck. It is gone. Atomized.

Alfie. Alfie. *Alfie.*

'Dad—'

Billy's cold. His vest is drenched against him. The bed is wet. He struggles up against the pillows.

'It's all right—'

The movement makes him cough. The coughing hurts. His wound tears and puckers, his chest feels tight and raw. Underwater light: cool and blue and grey through the thick nets. Street light outside. Chest a heaving pain.

'Dream—' he manages.

'It's okay, it's okay, it's over now.'

434

He tries to heave in a breath. Tries again. Can't get it, not enough air.

The son says something, and he nods. Then the son goes; over the rasp and rattle of Billy's breath, the painful thud of his heart, he hears the boy's uneven skip down the stairs. The phone lifted. The rattle of the dial. Billy coughs hard, hard, and brings fluid up into his mouth. He spits it out into his hand, rubs it onto the sheet. A nasty brownish smear. The wet tangle of his sheets. Oh God, no. He's pissed the bed. He scrabbles at the covers, pulling them off. He swings his legs out of the wet bed. His heart is pounding; he hasn't got enough breath. He heaves at the air, desperate to gulp it down. From downstairs he hears 'Ambulance, yes, please, quick as you can.'

Little sips. Little sips. He can feel the rattle deep in his chest, threatening. He tries to breathe shallowly, over it.

'It's on its way.'

The son is back. He takes his hand. Billy looks up at him. The boy's face is lined. His hair is thin. He is important. People listen to him. He is good with professional people, that's what she said. He will sort it out. He'll fix this.

'Son,' Billy says to him.

The bed crumples as Will sits down on the edge; he takes the old man's hand. Billy wants to tell him about Alfie. About the landing craft and the ramp thumping down and the guns and the shell that turned Alfie's head to a spray of blood and bone and matter. How Billy'd raced away from that and pushed the memory down into a box and locked it tight. How the box has started leaking now, and he is terrified. I killed a child, he wants to say. I didn't have to kill the child. I could have found another way. I could have died. His life paid for mine – it paid for all of this.

'Son . . .'

And the bed is wet. He wants to tell him about the piss.

'Don't talk,' Will tells him. 'I mean, breathe, just breathe.'

Billy nods, and it hurts to nod. He should get up, get clean, get changed before the ambulance comes. He can't talk. He's not allowed to talk. He hasn't got the breath.

'Hold on, it won't be long. Hold on, Dad.'

The old man grasps his son's hand, and breathes, tries to breathe, tries to breathe. Blue lights flash through the nets, fling around the room. Underwater light.

Billy is swimming through dark water. The hulk lies beneath him dark and creaking. He kicks out towards it.

He has to get back to the surface. He has to get a breath.

The hatchway is dark. He pulls down through it, and down a ladder, into the body of the ship.

His chest hurts. He needs air. He pulls himself

through a flooded corridor. A door stands open into a cavern.

He must go back. He must get back to the surface, to the people. The girl with the green eyes. The limping man. The blond boy.

There is no air.

The cavern is a boiler room. He swims into the dark. There is no breath. There is no air. He must go back.

But then he understands, and everything clicks beautifully into place: he was wrong, he has always been wrong – he doesn't need air; he can breathe the water. He breathes it deep, fills his lungs: his head fizzes, sparkles. It is wonderful to breathe.

He doesn't need to go back now: he never did. There was never anything to fear. Just breathe the water, and go on. He can swim down here for ever. He can find his father now. He can go as far as he needs to go, now that he accepts the water into him, and belongs here.

And then, up ahead, a darker shape in the darkness. He pulls himself towards it, as he always did in his dream; but this time, the figure does not just hang still, it turns, and comes towards him too; it strides through the water as though it were air. His eyes are clear and familiar. They look like the girl's.

The young man smiles at Billy. He holds out a hand. Billy breathes deep, and smiles back, and takes his hand.

Denham Crescent, Mitcham, 17 June 1995

They are clearing the house. It just needs doing.

He opens his dad's side of the wardrobe. It creaks on its cheap hinges. Downstairs he can hear Billie and her aunt Janet moving around in the kitchen, emptying the cupboards. They're talking. He can't hear the words, just the shape the words make in the air below him.

The clothes inside are all shades of cream and fawn and dusty blue, apart from the old man's one good black suit, bought in 1965 for his mother's funeral, which also did for Will's graduation and wedding, and then Ruby's funeral too. The wardrobe smells sour. He must have started to put worn clothes away unwashed. The charity shop can deal with it.

Will hooks out an armful of clothes, dumps them down on the bed. He takes out another armful, and that's it. Two pairs of comfy grey-beige shoes, a pair of unworn slippers that Will gave him one Christmas, still with their connecting tag intact, and a pair of black dress shoes to go with the suit.

Vintage, they will be, by now.

He lays them out along his mother's empty bed. Still made up, after all this time. Still with the same old purple nylon counterpane. Outside, a car passes; and there are voices – kids circling the crescent on their BMXs.

He goes back to fish out the blue suitcase from the top shelf.

He swings it down and jolts his arm with the weight of it. It's an old suitcase, cardboard, bound with strips of dark, close-grained wood. Used to be his grandma's, he thinks.

He hoists the suitcase up onto the bed. It bounces; the springs jingle. He flips the catches.

It is full of photograph albums. Three, four, five stocky A4 books, and smaller, A5 size ones here and there, and heaps, drifts of slithering loose photographs. He lifts one of the albums out. It is vinyl-covered, stripes of aquamarine, purple, blue. Madeline bought it for his mum, a birthday, he remembers. There are still, after all these years, these ambushes. Underneath, a black papery one that used to be his, hospital photos. And for some reason he thinks he can smell lemons, but that might just be the soap his mother hoarded and which still lingered in its paper wrappings until he and Janet and Billie divided it between them. Coal Tar and Imperial Leather and Lux and Zest. He shifts things aside to look down at the earlier, older things at the bottom of the case. Loose photos: his dad on a bike, his mum lipsticked and smooth-skinned in black and white. The blue postcard album that had been his grandmother's. The picture book, she called it. From before cameras were a common thing.

Footsteps on the stairs. The brisk thumpy tread of his daughter's feet. He flips the suitcase shut. Wipes the wet from his eyes.

Billie has that worn, parched look about her that she's had ever since the old man died. She holds up a mug for him to take. It's powdered coffee, clots of whitener swimming on the surface. It's all the old man ever kept in the house.

'Thanks,' he says, taking it off her.

She takes in the room, the heaped clothes, the open suitcase.

'You okay?' she asks, and stuffs her hands in her pockets. Her voice sounds sore.

He nods, scans round for somewhere to put the coffee, considers ducking down to put it on the floor, but that would hurt.

'Here,' she says, realising his predicament. She takes the mug back off him, and sets it down on the bedside cabinet. 'What's in the suitcase?'

He looks at it. Back at her. 'Photos.'

She nods.

'We'll go through them together if you like,' he says.

'Not today.'

'No. Not today.'

'I'll come up to Oxford sometime.'

He nods.

She turns to go, then stops, and speaks back over her shoulder. 'I think I want something. I mean. You know. Something permanent, not just the soap.'

'That's all right,' he says. 'Plenty of time.'

She nods, still looking away.

He listens to her go down the stairs. She goes slowly. He sits down on the end of his father's bed, crumpling the hem of the laid-out beige trousers, dimpling the fabric of a blue nylon jacket. He can hear her back in the kitchen now, the dialogue starting up again – Janet, Billie, Janet, Billie, Janet, Janet, Janet, silence. He puts his face in his hands. One palm hot from the coffee mug, the other cold from the chill of an empty house. He sobs. Hard. Silent. So that downstairs they don't hear.

Billie clears photographs from the sideboard. Places them in the box. Grandma's Spanish dancing dolls and china figurines. The photograph of the three of them in the boat. Mum with her long hair and her clear skin, and Dad so young, not much older than she is now. And she, a little girl with a blunt fringe and a belly. She opens the drawer and lifts out her granddad's cardboard box, where he keeps – kept – his medals. She doesn't open it.

'Billie?' Janet calls from the kitchen.

'Mmm.'

From in the kitchen comes the clockwork tinkling of 'The Blue Danube'.

'Shall we do this?'

'Yes.'

Billie leaves her box on the dresser and steps down into the kitchen. The jewellery box lid is thrown back, and the dancer twirls in her faded skirt, arm stretched up in the air above her. Billie sits at the table. Auntie Janet picks through the jewellery. The room smells of Vim and bleach. She has the whole kitchen, bar tea-and-coffee-making things, packed up and put away; the cooker and sink and work surfaces are shiny-clean.

'This place hasn't been this clean since Grandma died,' Billie says.

'You want to leave things nice.'

Outside, the garden softens into evening. A black cat springs into existence on the lip of the fence, gathers itself, spills down. Billie watches it cross the grass and climb into the flowerbed between the splodgy purple flowers. Janet works at the muddle of jewellery, unhooking wires, pairing earrings.

'Just bits and bobs,' Janet says. 'She didn't have that much.'

Janet's raspberry-pink sweater is spotless. Billie feels grubby. She rubs her arms, remembering the odd earrings, the broken brooch, the folded bloody handkerchief. She still has the earlobe; even if she'd dared to, there was never a chance

442

to ask Grandma about it. And that in itself, its unknowability, is part of its charge. She keeps it, wrapped in tissue paper, in an old toffee tin. Along with a desiccated starfish, extracted molars, and the cartilaginous picked-clean skeleton of a fish found on the meadow after floods. She gets them out, again and again, to draw them. There is a fascination to their alien, interrupted structures.

'Did you find a tobacco tin when you were cleaning up?'

'The workshop's full of them, if you want one.'

Billie nods. Janet's boys have got the bike. She can have a tobacco tin.

'So,' Janet puts together a pair of gold-plate studs with a click of satisfaction. 'What's the plan?'

Janet means, now you've got your Fine Art degree, now you're out in the big bad world, now that you are overqualified and underexperienced and without a single practical, sellable skill.

Janet's boys are doing well. Steven's just finished his Business degree. Andy's studying Medicine.

'I've got a job. You know that.'

'Mmm,' Janet says, unconvinced. 'The bookshop.'

'It's fine. I like it. I do okay. I've got time to paint.'

Janet looks up at her, suddenly smiles, the skin fanning at her eyes. 'You might want to think about a Plan B. Keep your options open.'

Billie sits back. Chews her lip. There is no Plan B. There are no options. This isn't even really a choice. It's not what she does, it's what she is. She has to paint.

443

'Boyfriend at the moment?' Janet asks.

Billie leans back in her seat. God, this now.

'There was that, who was it, Tom? That not work out?'

'Auntie Janet. Leave it.'

Janet tilts her head, accepting. She pulls at a knot of chain with her pink pearlescent nails. She's doing this – picking away at Billie, and at the jewellery – to distract herself, Billie realises. The chain frees, and she lifts it up with a smile. 'There!' She lets it pool down onto the red Formica, smiling with the satisfaction of this small achievement.

'Course, they'll rip everything out,' Janet says, after a while. 'The new people.'

'That's what new people do,' Billie says.

Something catches Janet's eye: 'Oh.'

'What is it?'

Janet lifts a slender gold ring out of the box.

'Grandma's?' Billie asks.

'Yes.'

There's a silence.

'It's so fine,' Billie says. 'Wartime wedding, I suppose.'

'They were married before the war. They just didn't have much money.'

They both consider the ring a moment. It catches the light, glints. It's buckled, oval, scraped. A soft coppery colour.

'Looks big enough to have been Granddad's.'

'She had it enlarged, I remember. Because of

her arthritis. Couldn't see Granddad Billy wearing a ring.'

Billie smiles. No.

'Get in the way, wouldn't it? When he was tinkering, making things. D'you know he even made my highchair when I was a baby? Out of off-cuts. People just don't do that kind of thing any more. It lasted for donkey's years. Did both the boys.'

That is who Billie's granddad was; not the failing bundle of bones and desperate eyes. He was the man who could make anything out of nothing. The aeroplane that she flew off the garden steps: that was her granddad. Between the teeter on the brink, and the crash into the paving slab, she was, for just a moment, she is still and always certain of it, really flying. She reaches up and slides her fingertips back and forth across the scar on her forehead. There's a line in the bone there, not just the skin.

'Go on,' Janet juts the ring closer. 'You take it.'

Billie looks at it a long moment, then looks at Janet, wondering what is implied. Her aunt's expression is innocent, but if she takes the ring, Billie wonders, does she somehow take on the future Janet sees for her: failure, loneliness? Plan B? But the ring was Grandma's, and she loved Grandma, and Granddad gave it to her, and she loved him too: now that he is gone, there's a hole left in the world.

She takes the ring. It is too loose for her middle finger, so she slips it onto her thumb.

'Thank you.'

Will carries the suitcase. Billie carries the cardboard box of figurines and medals. She has tucked the old man's dress shoes in her bag – his feet were tiny for a man, the same size as hers – and it dangles bulky from her back. There is no room to turn round in the hallway: she steps out over the threshold, to give her father space to move.

He follows, locks up. Pockets the key.

'He . . .' Will says. He pauses, tries again. 'When I was growing up . . .'

He looks past her at the overgrown laburnum, the privet hedge. He's very conscious of himself – the grey bristle of his chest hair against his shirt, his toenails pressing out against his shoes, his left leg still hooked back, still thinner than the other. The still shameful weakness of it. He puts the suitcase down, flexes his hand. The palm is red from the grip.

'You and him, though,' he says. 'That was different.'

'He was always kind to me.'

'He liked you. I mean, he loved you but he liked you too. He never liked me.'

'No, Dad.'

He picks up the suitcase. 'I don't blame him. The calliper, the disability. It must've been worse for him than it was for me.'

She steps forward, hugs him, lets him go.

'What'll you do with it all?' she asks.

They both know Carole won't stand for china figurines, for Spanish dancers, for photographs of people who are not to do with her.

'I'd take it to mine,' Billie says, 'But, you know.'

Billie shares a small flat in Deptford with her friend Norah, who is half-Iranian and beautiful and generous. But Billie's shelves are already stacked two books deep, and dotted with driftwood, photographs, animal skulls, paper-thin fragments of found wild birds' eggshells. She has to pick her way round piles of books and cardboard boxes and stacked canvases to get from the door to her bed.

Will wants to ask her about her life, the life lived there in the flat and in the city, about what it is like to be twenty-one nowadays. Her college friends; Norah, and that Irish boy she knocks around with, the photographer Ciaran. He feels an uneasy kind of admiration. He'd have liked a life like that, he thinks. Arty friends, of both sexes, the freedom of it: a job she isn't particularly invested in, a passion that doesn't earn her a living; perfect, really, in its possibilities, its openness.

He'd like to have something of her in the house. He'd like to have one of her pictures. Even a tiny sketch. He could get it framed. One of those inked life studies. A fat, wrinkled nude. Carole might even like it, so long as it didn't clash with anything.

He's never mentioned it to Billie, but her work sometimes reminds him of Blake. Her pen-and-ink stuff does. She'd love Blake's work, he thinks. This is something they could have in common.

'I'll put them in the attic,' Will says. 'Till we get the chance.'

Brown's Café, the Covered Market, Oxford, 24 December 1999

It's bright inside the café, loud with conversation and the hiss of the espresso machine. The room is shabby and ramshackle, papered-over plywood and mismatched chairs. She sips her tea, which is getting cold. She glances at her watch. She'll give it three more minutes and then she's leaving.

Outside, the crowds thin for a moment and she catches sight again of the butcher's stall across the way. Three deer and half a dozen hares hang by their back legs, tendons stretched as if running at full tilt. Their heads have been cut off; white plastic bags have been tied round the stumps to catch the dripping blood. It keeps catching her eye: the row of carcasses, the translucent whiteness of the butchers' bags, the blood darkening and stretching them with its weight. That's what's obscene about it, she thinks. Not the bloodshed, but those bags.

She's wasting her time, really. Dad phoned last night; he can't make it this time, has to pick up

Carole's parents in Reading. She'd wanted to say, actually, Dad, I do mind. But instead, she'd been nice, been accommodating, and now she's here, waiting for Matty, and Matty's late, and he probably won't turn up at all, not without Dad to drag him along, and it's for the best, really, because if she does find something to say to him he'll only answer in grunts and refuse to make eye contact.

She digs her fist into the small of her back. Double shift at the bookshop: Christmas rush. Her feet throb in her boots. And her arms are sore too, the muscles rigid from lugging books: ferrying deliveries out of the stock room, shunting stacks of paperbacks into display bins and onto tables, slipping purchases into black plastic bags. She should just give up on this. Go back to Mum's, have a bath, try and ease some of the aches out of her body. She watches her second hand tick round. He'll be coming down from home; if she dodges out the other side of the market, chances are she'll miss him. Put the parcels in the post.

She lifts her cup to drain it.

Over the thick ceramic edge, she notices him. He stands at the counter profiled, sifting through the change in his palm. Matty. With his curls all cut off. He looks so different.

She chinks the teacup down into the saucer.

He speaks to the stout woman behind the counter, and she smiles and nods, arranges things on his tray: the little metal teapot, strainer, milk jug. Billie watches as he turns towards the room

450

and scans it, looking for her. When he spots her, his expression shifts into a grin of recognition. It's unexpected and sweet. He nudges past a pair of teenage girls, all nail polish and hair, who stop talking and watch him as he passes. He's got that knack, it seems, like his dad, of making women interested, though he doesn't seem to have noticed it yet.

He's at her table now, and sets down the tray.

'Hey,' he says.

Last time she saw him he was a surly thirteen-year-old. Six months on and he's smiling, looking her right in the eye.

'Hey.'

'Sorry it's just me.'

'That's all right.'

She pushes the seat opposite out for him with a foot, watches as he drops his bag in under the table, sits down, then shuffles the bag around so that it lies between his feet. He straightens up and sits back in his chair. His jaw has strengthened and squared off: his face has planes and angles now. She watches his hand, the broad back of it, as it lifts the teapot lid, picks up a spoon, stirs his tea. She can't get used to him.

'I like this place,' he says.

'I've always liked it too. It's got a kind of cobbled-together feel.'

'Like little kids playing at cafés.'

'Like an allotment shed.'

He stabs his teaspoon into the crusted sugar

bowl. It makes a sound like snow. He shovels two, three spoonfuls of sugar into his tea, stirs. She wants to say, You'll rot your teeth, but stops herself in time. He sets his spoon down in the saucer. Even these tiny moves are confident, poised: he's hit his stride, somehow.

'How is he then?' she says, after a moment.

'Dad? You know. Working hard. Spends a lot of time up at College.'

Will's in one of those phases then, when you lose track of him for months. It must have been hard on her mum, Billie realises, because she'd never really know. Could be work, could be women; she'd only find out afterwards.

'And your mum? How is she?'

He tucks his lips in, shakes his head. 'Mental.'

'You've got a houseful for Christmas, then?'

'She loves it really. But she always does her nut.'

This is fine, Billie thinks. This is actually really nice. If there hadn't been all those years between them, if there hadn't been all that mess, perhaps it would always have been like this.

'Hang on a tick.'

She ducks down and lifts up the silvery gift bag from where she'd stowed it underneath the table. She passes it across the tabletop.

Matty peers into the gift bag. 'You get me a CD?'

'Dad said you were into your tunes now, so I . . .'

He fishes out the silver-wrapped square, looks up. 'Can I open it?'

'Go on then.'

He rips off the paper. It's a Gram Parsons album. *Grievous Angel.* He turns the CD round to look at the back, frowns at the tiny print.

'I took a punt,' she says. 'You can always change it, if you want.'

He shakes his head, still reading.

'I mean, you'd be mad to. There are songs on there, the duets with Emmylou Harris, they're just amazing. 'Hickory Wind'. God, that song'll haunt you.'

He glances up, grins. 'You're a total muso. I didn't know that.'

She smiles. Shrugs. 'Well, there you go.'

She watches Matty as he opens the case and scuffs out the covernotes. She drinks her tea. The noise of the café is dense and white. He's completely absorbed in his reading. She feels a new tenderness for him: his unfurrowed forehead, the clear lines of his features, the silky fuzz of his hair over an eggshell skull. She feels a flush of warmth for the little boy he was, now that he's leaving it behind.

'Thanks,' he says, after a while.

'No problem. Seriously. You tell me if you like it and I'll have a think about other stuff you might get into.'

'Thanks, sis.' He lifts his bag back onto his lap and goes to stash the album away. She smiles.

And then, for no reason in particular, she asks, 'What's with the hair?'

'Eh?'

'You've gone all, you know, minimalist.'

'Oh. Yeah.' He rubs at his shorn skull. 'It's been a while now. I don't notice it really any more. It's for cadets.'

'Cadets?'

'Officer cadets.'

'You mean like scouts?'

'More like junior army.'

'Woah. And what does Dad make of that?'

He drinks, sets down his cup, pinches the wet away from his lips. 'He hates it.'

She laughs.

'What?'

'I dunno. I used to just let him catch me smoking.'

'I'm not doing it to piss him off.'

'Why, then?'

'I'm serious. I'm joining up. When I'm old enough.'

'What? The army?'

He nods.

All the laughter's gone. 'God.'

The clink of china, the hiss of the espresso machine, the blur of voices. A woman at the next table is talking about perfume. Billie wants to say, you can't do this. This isn't fair. Not now. Don't turn out lovely and then go and join the army.

'I was banking on you,' he says. Clears his throat.

'What?'

'I thought you'd understand. You must know what it's like.'

'I have no idea.'

'But it's the same thing. Your painting, it's the same as this. It's what you have to do with your life.'

She sits back, baffled. Is this how he sees her? She's never even considered it till now. All these years, locked up in her own preoccupations. How distant has she seemed, how disconnected?

'Art's your thing,' he says. 'This is mine.'

'Matty,' she says. And then, 'Matty, it's not the same thing at all.'

'I want it, though, the same way you want yours.' He gives her a small smile.

'The worst I'm going to get is a paper cut.'

'It happens. I know. People get hurt. I'm not stupid. But I'm not going into the infantry. I'm thinking engineers, maybe gunners. And it's not like there's even a war on.'

But there will be. Give it time and there will be. There always is. She remembers what he is too young to remember: the grey southern islands and the men in fatigues going up the hill, and the men on stretchers coming back down, and her mum getting up to change the channel, and her dad saying, *No, leave it on, she should see this*. She doubts he was even aware of the wars of his lifetime. When Yugoslavia exploded into flame he was still a kid. And his parents would have kept it from him, the way Granddad had suffered, the way he'd carried the war around with him for a lifetime. Not just his sunny stories, his medals in a box. At the end, the truth of it had come leaching back. Those nightmares. All the darkness. All the things he'd left out, never said.

'It matters to you then,' she says. 'That much?'

Matty nods, solemn. Matty is fourteen years old, and therefore still immortal. And there's no arguing with that.

'Okay, then,' she says. 'Do you want me to, I don't know, talk to them – to Dad, I mean, sometime?'

He smiles. A big smile that makes his face brighten. 'I was hoping you'd say that. Thanks.' Then he remembers: 'Oh, yeah. Right.' He reaches into his bag, drags a giftwrapped parcel out and heaves it up onto the tabletop. 'This is for you.'

It's a book. She can tell by the weight and shape of it that it's one of the recently published art books she's been selling in bucketloads in the run-up to Christmas. It's wrapped in plain red wrapping paper. It's been nicely done by whoever was on that day at the Oxford branch.

'Thanks,' she says.

'Dad usually says that it's from both of us,' Matty says. 'But that's just because I'm usually so crap. It's just from him.'

'Don't worry about it, Matty. I don't expect anything.'

'Well, anyway.' He scrambles out a roughly bundled package. 'Here.'

It's last year's paper, creased and white where the print is worn away. It's clearly a mug.

'Mum broke one of them,' he says. 'So I thought you should have this.'

He's waiting for her to open it. But she knows already, by the heft of the package, what's inside. She covers her mouth. Not sad. And not because of the thing itself. Simply, that he understands. He knows the weight of this.

'Thank you.'

'You haven't opened it.'

'Okay.' She peels off the Sellotape, unfurls the paper. Glossy brown aeroplanes skim across a cream sky. She nods, can't speak.

'Is that okay?'

'Yes. Thank you. That's – thank you.'

'No worries.' He grins, then shunts his chair back, makes to stand up.

'Are we off?' she's wrong-footed. Overwhelmed.

'I said I'd meet up with Josh and Sam.'

'Okay,' Billie says. 'Well.' She clears her throat.

She slips the aeroplane mug into her bag, slides out from behind the table. She wants to say, Come down to London sometime soon, come and stay at the flat: Norah will make a pet of you. She wants to ask if their dad taught him to ride a bike. She wants to say sorry for not being ready for him all these years. She wants to tell him that when their father had put him in her arms, a raw and purblind baby, she'd been too furious to love him. Her world had peeled apart, fallen away, because of him. And that now she's not furious, not any more. She wants to tell him that she loves him, and that she's terrified.

For a moment he's just standing there, waiting as she gathers up her things. He's so young, and, for that moment, sublimely unselfconscious, with his big coat hanging loose around him, his hands in his pockets, half a smile. She opens her arms. Without a thought he steps in closer, leans against her, and wraps his arms around her, bumping his bag against her back. They're almost of a height. He gives her a bit of a squeeze. Then he lets her go. She manages not to say how much he's grown.

'You got to head on straightaway?' he asks.

'No,' she says, and brushes her hair back from her face. 'No rush.'

He gives her a sideways, cheeky look. 'Do me a favour then?'

'Of course, yes. Whatever you need.'

'Come down the offie with me; buy me some beers?'

Cardigan Street, Oxford, 25 December 1999

The old crowd and the hangers-on. Ciaran's bringing this girl Petra, and Norah's still seeing Daniel, and then Luke of course.'

'Sounds nice.'

'We're cooking dinner at ours, then the fireworks – that whole river-of-fire thing, then Luke and I are going on to his friends' party.'

'Petra. Wasn't that one of the Blue Peter dogs?'

'Dunno. Maybe.' Billie watches her mum's hands as she lifts a Brussels sprout, slices off its base, peels the ragged outer leaves from off the shiny inner globe. 'She's posh, though. So. That kind of thing's okay if you're posh. He met her on an assignment.'

Petra: the girl in an oyster-coloured gown, who did some modelling for pocket money; who'd taken his camera off him and fired off some shots and, when she handed it back, asked for his phone number. Billie wishes that she had that kind of nerve.

Billie shifts on her seat. 'He just looks kind of stunned.'

'Well, you know, maybe she's stunning.'

'Yeah. Maybe. Yeah. I've just never seen it before.'

The window is filmed with condensation. The oven glows and hums. The kitchen is warm and close and tiny, so that Billie perches in the doorway, on the solitary kitchen stool, at a slight forward tilt: its back legs sit on the carpet in the dining area.

'How are things going then, with work?' her mum asks.

Billie shifts her weight. The stool wobbles. She grabs the counter to steady herself.

'Oh, you know how it is.'

'I mean the painting.'

'I know you mean the painting.'

'Sending your slides out?'

'Yes, Mum,' Billie laughs. 'I even entered a couple of competitions last month.'

'And the pictures, the ones you had up in the restaurant?'

'I sold one.'

Her mother turns to her, her face brilliant. 'That's wonderful.'

Billie nods. It is. Of course it is. And it helps with things like Christmas presents, and she even had a new coat this year. She should be thrilled, and in some kind of abstracted way she is. But it wasn't much of a thing – a pen-and-ink study of a nude – and she wasn't satisfied with it. When she was a kid, when the millennium had first appeared on the horizon, she'd worked out that by then she'd be twenty-six. She'd be a grown-up, she'd thought. She'd be an artist. The two had seemed to mean almost the same thing, and be the answer to everything.

'And Luke?'

Billie laughs. 'Oh God, Mum, what is this? Twenty questions?'

'You're my little girl.' Her mother shrugs. 'I can't help it.'

Billie pulls her bottom lip in between her teeth. 'Well . . .'

He makes her stomach swoop. He picks her up from work and takes her out for what he calls supper but she still thinks of as dinner. His skin is perfect. His cologne, all woody notes and cinnamon, just does her head in: she notices it not so much when he embraces her, but once he's turned and walked away.

He's thirty-five; she's twenty-six. Sometimes she really notices.

She feels shabby. Grubby. Workstained. That she smells of coins from working at the tills.

She's pretty sure that Norah doesn't like him, but then Norah never likes any of her boyfriends. Ciaran has been away, and hasn't met him yet.

'It's good. I think. It's okay, yeah. Anyway, it's early days.'

She notices a patch of blue acrylic paint, dried

into cracks on her right forefinger. She scrapes at it with her stubby thumbnail.

'D'you have an emery board, Mum?'

'In the mug.'

Her mum nods to the chipped mug on top of the microwave. Billie pulls out a grey emery board from amongst the pens and pencils and stray screwdrivers. She starts to smooth the ragged edges of a nail.

'He's in Italy actually,' she says. 'Skiing.'

'Isn't that nice.'

'It's a family thing. They do it every year.'

'Ooh.'

'I know.'

Her mother's expression shifts: she raises her eyebrows, purses her lips, doesn't look up from the sink – paring knife in one hand, Brussels sprout in the other, heap of shed leaves growing on the counter.

'And so, let me get this straight,' her mum says, 'he's currently in Italy, but he's coming all the way back from there to spend the millennium night in a pokey little flat in Deptford?'

'Norah's flat is not pokey,' Billie says. 'It's compact and bijou.'

'It is in Deptford, though.'

Billie gives her mum a look. A smile. 'He'd be coming back anyway.'

'Yes, but still.' Her mother's eyebrows go higher. 'He's spending the millennium with you.'

'Mum,' Billie laughs. 'Seriously.'

Her mum waves a dripping hand in the air. 'Okay, okay.'

462

'It's a bunch of us. Not just me and him. It's not this great romantic thing.'

'Okay, okay.' She rinses the peeled sprouts under the tap. 'You be careful, though, love, while you're out.'

'Because of the planes falling out of the sky, and the nuclear missiles going off, and the Terminators stalking the streets?'

'I was thinking more muggers, rapists, pickpockets. That kind of thing.'

'You are *so* this century.'

Her mother laughs.

'Don't worry,' Billie says. 'I won't be alone.'

'Good.'

There's a silence. Billie feels her cheeks go hot. She recrosses her knees; her left leg presses against the cool fridge door. She watches as her mother lifts the colander from the sink and turns to set it down on the far countertop. Billie searches for something to say, some kind of explanation or apology, but she can't quite put a sentence together. She thinks of the semi up in Summertown, stuffed full of people: Carole and her parents and her sister and the cousins, and Matty, and their dad, the heating on full blast and Carole grumpy and flustered and Dad opinionated with drink. Here, there is just the burr of the fan oven and Mum's careful peeling of vegetables. Billie notices a swirl worn into one of the floor tiles from the press and spin of her Mum's foot as she turns from one kitchen counter to the other, day after day.

'Actually,' Billie says, 'I'm hoping the cashpoints will go bananas and start spewing out twenty-pound notes.'

'Wouldn't that be nice?'

Her mother turns the heat up under a saucepan, setting it to boil, then crouches to open the oven door. There's a billow of steam: rosemary, garlic, olive oil. She shakes the potatoes round in the roasting tin; the oil spits and pops.

'Look, can I do something?'

'There's not much more to do.' Her mum closes the oven, straightens up. Winces at the creak in her knees.

'What are your plans then?' Billie asks, meaning for New Year's Eve.

'I was going to do a lemon glaze for the carrots. That sound okay?'

'Lovely.'

'Tell you what, open the bubbly, would you? It's in the fridge.'

Billie slips off the stool, sets it out of the way, and hunkers down to fish out the bottle of Cava. She stands the bottle on the counter and reaches into a cupboard for two of the green-stemmed hock glasses that serve for this kind of thing. They are older than she can remember; they've always been in cupboards, standing at the back, gathering dust. She rinses them, fills them with crackling wine.

'What are you going to do, though, for the millennium?'

'I've never really liked New Year.' Her mum lifts her glass. 'Cheers.'

'Cheers.'

'All that pressure to have fun.'

'I know.'

'And this year it's in spades.'

'Do you remember when I was a kid? We'd just settle down on the sofa with cups of tea and chocolates, and watch stupid telly?'

'We'd always say we'd stay up, but usually we'd be in bed by ten.'

'But still, Mum. It's the millennium.'

'It's just a number. There's some people say it falls next year, really, mathematically speaking.'

'Yeah but in all fairness, they're tossers.'

Her mother laughs.

'You've got to do *something*,' Billie says.

'I will. Tea, sofa, box of Thornton's Continentals, early night.'

Billie slides back up onto her stool, wine glass in her hand. She feels an urgent anxiety on her mother's behalf, the need to make things right.

'Come to the flat, come and see the fireworks.' Norah would be lovely and welcoming, she always is. But then there's Luke, he has to be taken into account. His expectations. He's not expecting someone's mum to come along.

Her mum wafts an oven glove, dismissing the notion. 'With all you young people? Playing gooseberry? I don't think so.'

'I'll come back up here, then.'

'Really, love, there's no need. I do have friends; I could have arranged something if I'd wanted to.'

'But, Mum—'

Her mum raises her hand, shakes her head, brooking no argument: 'Go. Have fun. Be happy.'

Later, Billie lies in bed, looking up into the grey dark of her old bedroom. The bedside clock reads 01.47.

She thinks of her room in Norah's flat. The makeshift stop-gap of it; a bed, a wardrobe, sheaf upon sheaf of sketches, her clutter on someone else's shelves.

She thinks of her thin web of connections – friends, colleagues, and now Luke – a fragile crystalline structure built out into the dark. She is sure of none of it. If Billie put pressure on any part of this, it'd just fall away in a shower of salt.

Norah won't always be wanting a housemate, won't always have a room to spare. Ciaran's there and then gone, like a breeze. There's no point wishing he were different, because then he wouldn't be him.

She had thought she'd be grown-up. She'd be an artist. It would mean something. The imagined and the real shift and slide across each other like layers of tracing paper, and can't be made to fit together.

She sits up, reaches for the bedside light. The room springs awake. The chimney breast is a soft slate colour. Bookshelves fill the alcoves on either side. Her mother's blue ceramic cormorant sits on top of the cast-iron fireplace, its wings permanently outstretched between the photographs of godchildren, friends in fleeces on country paths, Billie's graduation picture, and a snap of her suntanned mum on a Mediterranean summer's evening with a dark-haired bearded man who has his arm around her shoulder. Terry; just a friend, her mother says.

Billie gets up, crosses the room and pulls open the curtains, looks out on the back walls of other houses, at the narrow yard below. It's dotted with planters. In the diffuse orange street light she can pick out the bare twigs of dwarf fruit trees.

There used to be a damp patch on the wall here. She reaches down, lays a hand on the surface beneath the windowsill. The paper feels sound and dry.

It's too late to sleep now. She wraps her cardigan over her nightshirt, pulls on a pair of socks. She goes downstairs, through the quiet living room, with its slumped sofa and pale throw and tartan rug, and its potplants and its bookshelves and its unlit Christmas tree, past the bare dining table and into the kitchen. The clean dishes are stacked on the drainer. She clicks on the kettle, reaches down a mug. The tiles suck the warmth from her feet.

Billie takes her tea, and sinks into the sofa, and draws the rug up over her. Baubles glint on the tree. She picks up the book her dad gave her. It's an illustrated edition of Blake's *Songs of Innocence and Experience*; she'd underestimated him; this is thoughtful, not what she'd expected; at a tangent to his usual gifts. She opens the book, starts to study the prints. The fluid, dynamic shapes, the way the text seems to emerge organically, growing from the images. A car crawls past the end of the street, cautious in the fog. She's aware of the house around her, its small, contained spaces. Her mother sleeping upstairs. Her distant, quiet breathing seems to fill the house like the hush and drift of waves.

Go. Have fun. Be happy.

Deptford, 1 January 2000

The traffic lights phase on and off, casting pools of red, gold and green, making nothing happen, because there are no cars, not this late, not tonight. Stragglers wander along the pavement, stumble off and back up the kerb. Billie, though, walks the custardy bulge of the white line down the middle of the street. Luke paces along the pavement, glancing her way from time to time, keeping pace.

The city spreads out away from here, from the slight give of the paint beneath her feet. She wants to call out to him, how wonderful is this that you can walk down the middle of the street? Never mind the millennium, a whole new century, a whole new thousand years; how wonderful is this, the night, the people; a city, for a moment at least, without cars? But then she looks round at Luke and thinks better of it. She feels responsible. He and Ciaran were like sandpaper: whatever one of them said it seemed to grate at the other.

She steps off the white line, and crosses the tarmac to him, and slips her gloved hand into his. He glances at her, smiles.

They pass the derelict pub, the windows patched with cardboard, and the Londis, shut but still spilling out a pool of white neon light. A girl in a pale puffa jacket with scraped-back hair leans slack against her boyfriend, her arms looped around his waist, her cheek pressed into his chest. He watches Billie and Luke as they pass; his face is thin.

They left Norah and Daniel after the fireworks. Norah with her too-high heels hooked over her fingers, her foot soles black with dirt, her arm looped through Daniel's, the two of them chattering away and watching out for broken glass. Ciaran and Petra they'd lost hours before, in the crowds near the river. Or maybe, Billie thinks, Ciaran and Petra lost themselves. Ciaran had his camera and wanted to get some shots in. But he was just being tactful. She'll see him before he leaves for Mexico, she hopes. Wonders how long he'll be gone this time.

Dinner hadn't been easy.

Then the party at Luke's friends' house: a whole house, stairs and everything, for just the two of them. They had matte-black clothes and perfect skin. Billie trod their white carpet uneasily, spent most of the evening in the glass-and-timber extension, the garden beyond winking with fairy lights, trying to get a fingernail into the conversation: it was all so concrete, so full of things. Things that one might buy or had bought. A friend's disappointment with his new car. Another's satisfaction with exactly the same model. There must, she thought, be something I'm not getting here. Something I just haven't grasped, that makes it all mean something.

The tug of Luke's hand makes her look up: they're near the turn for Norah's. She follows his pull. The flat's the top floor of a subdivided terrace down the end of the street. She's conscious of the length of his expensive coat, the brush of his sleeve against hers. Above them the sky is a dirty orange, full of smoke and cloud and street light. He could be anywhere, she thinks, he could be with anyone, but he's here with me.

'A nice night, wasn't it?'

'Mmm?'

'Lovely party.'

'Mmm.'

'Did you have a good time?'

'Yes.'

They pass through the glow of a streetlamp, alongside the loose stitch of a chainlink fence. Someone cordoned off this patch of weeds and grit two years ago. They haven't done anything with it since.

Norah will have gone back to Daniel's. Ciaran will be at Petra's by now. Which leaves them the flat to themselves, thankfully. The table, pulled out into the middle of the sitting room, will still be thick with the debris of the evening: dishes, smeared glasses, empty bottles, an ashtray, the coloured gossamer of streamers. She'd thought the party poppers were fun.

'God,' Billie says, after a moment. 'What about that Petra?'

'What about her?'

'Well, she didn't really . . . gel, did she?'

She'd spoken only to Ciaran, and then so quietly that no-one else could hear. Refused everything but the wine she'd brought. She'd clearly been missing something rather better to be there.

They walk on. Their breath plumes in front of them in the cold air. But then Luke hadn't gelled either. He'd really gone for Ciaran. It had started out sounding friendly, but soon the questions about his work became questions about how badly paid it was, its precariousness. Ciaran had taken it pretty well, considering. He'd laughed it off, made a joke of it. But she can't figure out what it was that had made Luke so angry. What did it matter, Ciaran's hand-to-mouth existence? What difference did it make?

'I just thought she was a bit, you know, difficult,' she says. 'Bit high-maintenance.'

'Well,' he says. 'She's beautiful. She can get away with it.'

Billie laughs.

He smiles back at her, faintly puzzled. She realizes that it's not a joke. He means it. And he is, of course, right. Petra is beautiful. Sullenly, smokily beautiful. And she did get away with it. They kept on being nice – she and Norah and Daniel did anyway – and Petra kept on being sulky, and Luke kept on not looking at Petra, and grilling Ciaran in that high-handed way, and at the first chance he got Ciaran steered Petra off into the crowds to save everyone the effort of keeping up the niceness and the sulking and the looking-the-other-way.

And the point is, of course – why didn't she see it before? – Luke could be with Petra. Or at least, someone like Petra. Someone with that gloss, that patina, that self-containment. This is why Luke is annoyed: Ciaran, with his scruffy coat and his Timex watch, doesn't deserve to have that kind of beauty at his disposal.

So why is Luke with her? Billie wonders: because she's easy-going, no trouble to him? She makes an effort, tries hard with his friends, is *grateful*?

She bites her inner lip. 'So.'

'So what?'

'So what's this then?'

'What?'

'This?' She squeezes his hand, raises the pair of them up in front of them – the joinedness of them.

'You and me?'

'Yeah,' she says. This is it, she thinks; this is the collapse.

He stops dead and draws her round to face him. The tarmac glints. A cat crosses the street behind him, right to left, its tail held low. He takes up both her hands. She looks down at the smooth wool of his coat, his neatly tucked scarf. A burglar alarm starts screeching a few streets off, is silenced. She wonders what he sees when he looks at her. An ordinary kind of asymmetry.

The crystals crumble away into darkness. Norah and Daniel, Ciaran and Petra, they've already drifted off in pairs into the night. And now Luke, any moment, peeling off from her, to go and find someone beautiful, leaving her to float away.

'You're jealous,' he says.

'No.'

'Well it sounds like it.'

She shrugs. She can't frame her anger in any way that makes it reasonable. It's fine that he thinks Petra is beautiful. It's fine that he said it. It's fine that beauty brings privileges. It should be fine. It's true.

'Don't be.'

She glances up. He's still looking at her. She sets her jaw. She catches a ghost of his scent, of cinnamon and woody notes. She thinks, this is it; this is what I'll remember of him. The scent of him will linger as he walks away.

His eyes are shadowed; his cheekbones catch the light. He says, 'I love you.'

She smiles, despite herself.

'I was saving this,' he says. 'I thought, maybe tonight, but there was never the right moment.'

'What? Saving what?'

He shrugs. 'Marry me?'

She blinks up at him, eyes cool and wet in the night. She nods, her chin dimpling. It is, more than anything, a relief.

Magdalen College, Oxford, 11 March 2003

The rain plummets down outside, soaks the earth. He can hear it falling from the guttering, streaming down into the flowerbeds. He can hear the Cherwell too, usually such a slug of a river – rushing now, churning, hammering past the College.

Knock at the door. He clicks 'save', closes the document. 'Come in.'

Hannah Moriarty is all kinky yellow hair that frizzes out around her head like a blonde Afro. She has the button nose and blinky blue eyes of a doll. And if it hadn't been for her catching his eye and holding it while she gave him a slow smile in that first tutorial, he wouldn't have looked at her twice, so to speak – not in any out of the ordinary way. But he'd looked at her every week for eight weeks now, and has to admit that there is something about her. He can't quite put his finger on it. Those slobby jeans that hang half off her backside. That accent that's so affectedly rough. When she leaves at the end of the tutorial, she leaves in a strange lingering way, jabbering away with her tutorial partner, that meaty boy, about some mutual acquaintance, as if Professor Hastings weren't there. But somehow still alert to him, as though her awareness stretches back and includes him, obliges him to notice that he is being excluded.

Got on his nerves. Got on his wick. Got on his mind, and he couldn't shake her. So when she emailed to make the appointment, and suggested six thirty, it loosened up his thoughts. Made them slippery. Lubricious.

She slips into her usual tutorial seat – the deep leather armchair. She shifts the cushions around and settles herself in with a wriggle that makes her jumper slip, exposing a curve of creamy shoulder. She doesn't tug it back.

'I love this chair,' she says.

'Family heirloom,' he says, as he always says, though he bought it at auction in Banbury.

He knows it's a cliché, but he offers her a sherry anyway.

'Mmm.'

When he leans closer to give it to her, he detects a whiff of marijuana. Her eyes have that big glassy look too. Interesting.

'I'm going to miss all this,' Hannah says.

He limps over to his own seat – an upright bent-wood chair. He's forbidden the deep floral recesses of the sofa nowadays. Since the hip replacement. Not worth the risk of dislocation. Not that he has been tempted, not recently, by the pleasures of the office sofa. Not until Hannah Moriarty shoved and elbowed her way into his thoughts.

'So,' he says, neutrally. 'What can I do for you?'

Outside, on the rose garden, the rain batters the leaves, the first buds, soaks into the earth.

'Well, I've been thinking.' She pulls out a cushion, squeezes it, stuffs it down beside her. 'About the future.'

'Good idea.'

'And you know, final year and everything. I mean—' She nods out at the rain. 'I mean, just starting out in life.'

'Yes,' he says. 'An exciting time.'

She smiles, pleased with herself, and with the adventure of it all. She sips her sherry. Leans over the arm of the chair to put her glass down. And he remembers the girl, the one with the brown eyes and the blue bike, who used to hesitate outside his study door. She had left him, and Oxford, in September nearly thirty years ago, and it had been both a heartbreak and a liberation. She went off to do an MA in Birmingham, for which he'd written her a glowing reference; then a PhD, and then, after a few years' silence, she wrote to tell him she was getting married, to that Early Modernist from Sheffield, and he'd written back, wishing her happiness and good luck. He'd heard she'd moved to Belfast, taught at Queen's. He saw her, years later, at that conference in

478

Stirling. Her hair badly dyed; she'd put on weight. Her paper – Aphra Behn read through a Foucauldian lens. God, what was her name?

'I've always thought I'd like to work in TV.'

When she was a girl, though. With her brown eyes, and her blue bike. She'd been so lovely.

'Mmm.' He gets up from his chair, goes to refill his glass.

'And this internship has come up, no money of course, but I can live at home, and Dad knows the execs, he'll put a good word in for me, but you know, you have to go through the process.'

'Of course.'

'So, that means references. And I was wondering . . .'

He drinks his sherry still looking at the wall. The soft green stripe. Edwardian, he's often thought. The girl with the brown eyes, who turned into the heavy-looking woman, who spoke so briskly, who seemed somehow cross.

'So would that be okay? I can put you down as a referee?

'No problem.'

'Cool.'

He turns back, to be polite. She gets up from the sofa, her jeans half hanging off, her jumper slumped down over her shoulder. She comes up to him, brings the waft of marijuana and perfume. Then she leans in and kisses him on the cheek.

'You're a poppet.'

Oblivious, she turns away, hitching her jeans up

onto her hips. 'There's a few of us over in the bar,' she says. 'If you fancy it?'

'I'm, I've got to work.'

He leans on the desk, moves himself round the edge, back to the computer. It traces a pattern idly across its screen.

She leaves. He sits down, clicks open his document. His paper appears, unfinished. He reads back over his final paragraph. This had been going somewhere, but now, he's not so sure. His chest hurts.

Jericho, Oxford, 20 March 2003

Billie helps her mother across the threshold. Luke lingers on the   doorstep, clutching mobile phone in one hand, a bunch of paper-wrapped daffodils in the other.

'Look,' he says, gesturing to the street with his mobile phone, 'I've got to . . .'

Make a call. Again. 'Right now?'

He nods, holds out the flowers: Billie has to set her mother's case down to take them off him.

She's going to say, *Please be quick*, but she swallows it. He's only away from the office because of her. He has to check in, keep an eye on things. He can't be held responsible for how long it takes.

'I'll come back for you when I'm finished,' he says.

Then they'll head back to London. He's got work tomorrow.

'Okay,' she says. Then, 'Sorry.'

She follows her mum through the sitting room, hears the front door click shut behind them. Madeline sits down on the sofa. She is pale, sweating.

'Put your feet up,' Billie says.

Her mother looks around her, remains still. 'It's so stuffy.'

'I'll let some air in.'

Billie drops the daffodils on the coffee table, goes into the bay window. Close up, she can see through the blinds: the houses opposite with their clean front steps and painted brickwork, above them a brisk spring sky, and off to the left Luke's retreating back as he walks away, staring down at his mobile, tapping at it.

It was good of him to come at all.

Billie shoves the window open and lets in the soft spring air, the street noise. She turns back to her mum. Her mother looks so fragile, so slight. Billie had been focused on this, on just getting her mum back home; she hadn't thought beyond it.

'Better?'

'Mmm.'

Billie sinks down on the end of the sofa, lifts her mum's feet into her lap, and slips off her shoes. Her mother's feet are smooth in nylon tights. Billie strokes them.

'That's nice,' her mother says. And after a while, 'I'm sorry, love.'

She means, for being ill. For making you race up from London again. For making things more difficult than they are already.

'Don't be silly.'

And anyway, it will be fine. Her mother will be

fine. They've caught it early, and have tackled it, it seems to Billie, with exhausting thoroughness: first surgery and then chemo have left her mum wiped out, looking sicker than she did before. What she needs now is rest, and good food, and the chance to build herself back up. That's what matters. How Billie feels is irrelevant. She just has to get her mother through it, and out the other side, to a point at which they can pause, and realise it's in the past, and say to each other, *God, that was awful, thank goodness it's over.*

Her mum swallows. Maybe she needs one of those tablets, the ones they gave her for the nausea. They're in her case. The nurse recommended ginger too. Billie sets her mother's feet down on the cushion, tugs the rug over her. She stands up, lifts the bunch of flowers from the tabletop.

'I'll get you a drink.'

Her mum nods.

Billie fetches the case from the hallway, and in the kitchen loads the dirty washing into the machine: pyjamas and nightshirts and underwear and a dressing gown; smelling sour, of hospital and sweat and sickness. She washes her hands, flinches at the soap. Her skin is cracked with weeks of scrubbing away the taint of outdoor germs, rubbing on disinfectant gel, soaping off clinging smell of hospital.

She fills the kettle, peels a chunk of ginger, crushes it beneath the blade of the knife, then lifts a lemon from the fruit bowl and cuts a slice. The knife is blunt and mangles the fruit, making juice spurt and spread. It stings her skin. She puts her hands down flat on the counter, either side of the board. She breathes in lemon, ginger, the first trails of steam. The kettle begins to rattle. The washing machine fills itself with water. Weekends with Luke, Christmas at Luke's parents, bank holidays with his friends: time has just trickled through her fingers; she hasn't been here enough. Once things are back to normal, she'll make a point of coming home every other weekend; birthdays and Christmases will be spent here. Luke will just have to get used to it.

She lifts a vase out from underneath the sink, fills it from the tap. She unwraps the daffodils.

The cup is white and rimmed with silver; one of the three still remaining from the good china set. A wedding present; but from whom, Madeline can't recall. Billie sets it down on a coaster, lays the blister pack of pills beside it.

'Thank you, love.'

'No problem.'

Billie puts her mug of coffee down too, then goes round to place the vase on the windowsill. The flowers seem almost to glow in the spring light. All these little things, these kindnesses that Billie does for her: it's an odd reversal, being looked after like this. Madeline catches the scent of ginger and lemon, and the flowers' sharp musk, and beneath that the warm oiliness of her daughter's coffee, and then under it all the rank whiff of wool from the rug over her knees, and it makes her stomach churn. She swallows, raises her face to the breeze from the window. She feels a wash of love and gratitude, and after it an undertow of grief. Deep in her flesh, she knows what's coming. What she's going to put Billie through.

'Are you okay?' Billie asks.

Madeline nods.

'Tablet?'

She shakes her head. She's afraid she'd just throw it up. She can feel the nausea build inside her. It's the smells. They don't even have to be bad – the slightest thing can have her running to the bathroom. And even then the smell of a used towel, or toothpaste, or even soap as she leans over to rinse her mouth at the washbasin can be enough to make her retch again.

'I'm okay. I just need a minute.'

Billie sits down, starts to sort through the clutter on the table. Madeline rests her head against the back of the sofa, allows her eyes to close. She's so tired. Her bones ache. She wants to talk. About anything at all. Just talk. But she can't summon up the energy to put one word in front of another.

The washing machine churns in the kitchen; a neighbour's dog, left for the day, is barking. Luke, pacing on the pavement outside, speaks into his mobile phone. Madeline can't hear what he's saying, just lets the abrupt, serious patter of his words fade out of her hearing. He belongs to another world, where people stream in and out of office blocks and wear suits and make money out of money; what he says counts somewhere, even if it doesn't quite make sense here. But she's glad of him. It doesn't matter now, that he seems so different from Billie; what matters is that he'll look after her through all this, and be there for her when it's all over. He is reliable, and she must be thankful for that.

Madeline opens her eyes, watches her daughter's dry hands as they work. She used to be so wildly untidy. Perhaps the bookshop has trained her into tidiness. Perhaps she's just grown up.

'How are you feeling?' Billie asks.

'Better,' Madeline says. 'How are you?'

'Happy we've sprung you from that place.' Billie grins. There are lines at the corners of her eyes.

'Me too.'

Billie lifts a handful of paperbacks, takes them over to the bookcase. She fits the volumes back into gaps.

'Sweetie, you don't have to do that,' Madeline says.

'S'okay.' Billie turns back from the shelves, brushes her hands. 'Can I get you anything to eat?'

Madeline shakes her head. 'Sit down, love.'

Billie sits. 'Not even a bit of toast?'

'No.' Her mouth is too wet. She fumbles for a tissue, presses it to her lips. 'No thanks.'

'God, sorry.'

Billie just sinks down into the armchair and looks at her, as if there's some solution to be found if she studies long and hard enough.

Madeline pockets her tissue, manages a smile. 'It's all right.'

All of this reminds her, uneasily, of when she was pregnant: the concern, the appointments, the indignities. That and the overwhelming queasiness, the fatigue, and the sense that your body is up to something. The clock ticking. Madeline wonders, suddenly, how Will is getting on. She should call him. He'll be tangling himself up in knots about all this until she does. She thinks of him now with a different, more informed kind of sympathy. His body has been failing him every day for a lifetime.

'Drink that though, Mum. Try. It'll do you good.'

Madeline sips. Just a little. The liquid is hot and sharp and faintly sweet, and with a pleasing after-burn of ginger. She swallows. It doesn't heave straight back up. That's something. She smiles to Billie, and Billie nods back.

Billie's hands return to their work; she gathers up scattered sections of newspaper. They're old, from the Sunday before Madeline went in for treatment. Billie heaps the papers together, shuffles them into a neat pile. And then she lifts the colour supplement. She stops. She just holds the magazine, looks at the cover. For a moment Madeline is puzzled, but then she remembers. The cover image is a photograph of a group of Afghan schoolgirls. Half a dozen young women, sitting on a dirt floor, schoolbooks on their laps, looking up towards the camera. The warm light comes from high windows off to the right. The composition is immaculate, the palette gorgeous blues and browns and creamy white. And the girls are beautiful; their faces are so bright and clear.

'Oh yes,' Madeline says.

Billie looks up, smiles at her. For a moment it seems like she's going to say something, but then doesn't. She just looks back down at the magazine cover. Then she flips through to the feature, presses the pages out flat on the tabletop.

Ciaran's photographs.

'They're wonderful, aren't they?' Madeline says. 'I can't believe I forgot they were there.'

Billie gives her a look. 'Mum, seriously, you've had plenty on your mind.'

'You tell him, when you see him next, tell him I thought they were stunning.'

Outside, in the street, Luke's voice is getting closer. *Yeah, yeah, no, still up in Oxford.* He passes the window, a brisk shadow, and continues on.

Billie nods, studies the photo spread, head bent; Madeline studies her daughter. Her hair catches the light and glints auburn. She turns a page, still looking at the photographs. Her expression is unreadable.

'I mean, if you think he'd like that.'

'Of course he would. You know Ciaran.'

She does, a bit. She's met him a few times. The Irish boy with the cheeky smile and the slate-blue eyes who was in Billie's class in their foundation year. In the years after college, when Billie and Norah were flatmates, he used to crash on their sofa. He'd stay a week, a month, and then he'd be off again, on assignment overseas. But Madeline always knew without being told when Ciaran was staying, because Billie'd suddenly be full of buzz, enthusing about his work, excited about her own. And then he'd be off, away, and she'd be low for weeks. Just a friend, Billie always said. But Madeline never quite understood it. You either love a man, or you don't. You don't mess yourself around like that. But then there was Luke, and that seemed to work well, and she's settled now, and that's good.

'Have you seen anything of him lately?'

'No.' A pause. And then, 'He's renting my old room off Norah. But he's in Iraq right now.'

'Oh my goodness,' Madeline says.

Billie looks up, shrugs. As if to say, I have no claim on him. I have no cause to be upset.

'He's actually with the troops, is he?'

'Embedded, I think they call it.'

'That's really brave of him.'

'No braver than the soldiers.'

'They have guns.'

Billie tilts her head. 'I suppose.'

She turns back to the pictures. Madeline watches Billie's eyes flicker across them, watches her attentive, assessing gaze.

'And Norah? How's she?'

Billie closes the magazine, places it on the top of the pile. 'I don't really know. We keep missing each other.'

'Right,' Madeline says. She rubs at her arms.

'Chilly?'

Madeline nods. That must be it.

Billie gets up, closes the window. 'Sorry.'

'Thanks.'

But the chill doesn't go. It's something else. Something's not right. Billie keeps missing Norah. She hasn't seen Ciaran. Is this a normal fading off; are these friendships that have simply been outgrown? It doesn't seem quite right.

Billie pushes her hair back, catches her mother's eye and tries a smile. It doesn't really work. She looks so pale and drawn. There are purple shadows underneath her eyes.

'Will you be seeing Matty later?' Madeline asks.

'There isn't time.'

'Why's that then?' She speaks lightly, careful.

'We've got to get back.'

'Oh yes?'

'Luke's got a lot of work on, it's just madness at the office, they're coming up to the end of the financial year, so it's difficult . . .'

'Of course.' Madeline lifts her tea. Another sip. She swallows.

'Is that still hot?' Billie asks.

Madeline nods. She can hear Luke's voice approaching in the street. She can hear her daughter breathe. The cup is warm in her hand. Steam rises to her face, softening her eyes. She watches as Luke passes again, hears the sharp sound of his leather-soled shoes. *No, no we're not doing that. No. I told him. Look, no, I'm driving back tonight. I'm in the office first thing tomorrow; I'll send the documents straight over—*

'Are you getting much work done yourself?' Madeline asks.

'Bit of sketching,' Billie says. 'In the park, the street, that kind of thing.'

'Can't you work in the flat?'

'The light's too poor.'

Billie was given the back room to paint in. It had seemed generous. But, Madeline thinks, what if it isn't? What if it just keeps her work, its mess and muddle, out of the rest of that immaculate flat? She recalls the pristine furnishings, the matte white walls, the shop-bought, obvious prints that Billie could not possibly have chosen.

She feels an uneasy shiver gather again in the back of her neck.

'Did you think any more about that residency?' she asks.

'I sent off for the forms.' Billie lifts her coffee. The cork coaster has stuck itself to the base of the mug. She plucks it off, twists it between her fingers.

'Good. That's exactly what you should be doing.' Madeline relaxes a fraction. 'I'm glad.'

'Mmm,' Billie says. She sets the coaster back down, sets the mug on top of it, without drinking. Then she screws her eyes shut, rubs at her forehead.

A wash of concern: 'What is it, love?'

'Nothing. Just—'

'What?' Madeline lowers her legs off the sofa. Her scar twists as she moves. It hurts. She clenches her jaw, leans forward. Billie opens her eyes, doesn't look up. It doesn't matter, Madeline wants to say. Whatever's wrong I'll sort it out for you. If you're not happy, you can just come home. Come home, and we'll muddle along together for a while. For however long we've got.

'Tell me?'

Billie takes a breath. Hesitates. 'This residency, Mum. I'm not sure about it. I just can't face it.'

'Why not?'

'Right now, even filling in the forms just seems like too much.'

'You can't keep putting things on hold, Billie love.'

Billie nods, her lips folded in together. Nothing is said. The moment stretches, and goes thin, transparent.

'It's next year, isn't it? Ages off . . .' Madeline says. It's beyond the horizon, and slipping further away moment by moment. She sets down her cup, says, as lightly as she can muster, 'I'll be back on my feet by then, you'll see.'

Billie just nods, and says, 'I know. I know. I know.'

'So,' Madeline clears her throat. 'What's stopping you?'

Billie's chin dimples. She scoops up the magazine again, flicks through to Ciaran's photographs. Madeline watches Billie's face, pained by the sight of her contorted, congested features. She waits for her to speak. When Billie was fourteen she'd been caught bunking off school. She'd been sneaking into anatomy lectures at the university. Her drawings were astonishing; the confidence, the energy of them. She'd have gone to the practical sessions too, she'd said, glowering defensively up at Madeline between curtains of hair, but they wouldn't let her in: they only had so many corpses to go round. Madeline had tried to tell her off, had managed not to laugh: she'd felt, more than anything, a delighted pride. Not just at the brilliance of the sketches, but at the sheer bloody-mindedness, the determination of her little girl. When she was a child, Billie used to know exactly who she was, exactly what she wanted. She wouldn't have hesitated a moment. She'd have grabbed an opportunity like this with both hands. Sucked the marrow out of it.

'Well,' Billie says.

'Mmm?'

'I've got to be realistic,' Billie says. 'I've got to be practical.'

'Realistic about what? In what way practical?'

Billie shrugs, doesn't reply.

'Billie?'

Finally she meets her mother's eye. Her face is settled now, as if this is the easy bit: 'Maybe I've got to accept that I'm just not good enough.'

Madeline feels a surge of bright, invigorating fury. That's not you, she wants to say. That is not my daughter speaking. And I am not standing for this.

Madeline leans forward. 'You do me a favour.'

Billie lets the magazine hang slack between her hands. Her expression is intent and serious as a child's. 'Of course.'

'You take it seriously,' Madeline says. 'Even if no-one else does. Because I know you and I know that if you're not painting, then nothing else will ever make you happy. Not long term.'

A slow flush reddens Billie's cheeks. Madeline doesn't know why. Guilt or embarrassment or pleasure; a mixture of the three.

'I've got to be *practical*—' Billie says again.

'Yes! Christ yes. *Be* practical. But that just means putting in the hours, working hard, making it happen. It doesn't mean giving up on all you've ever wanted just because it's—' she wafts a pale hand,'—inconvenient.'

Billie blinks. She nods.

'Fill in those forms,' Madeline says. 'You do that for me.'

'I will.'

'And love?' Madeline lifts her cup again. 'Do it for yourself too.'

The Churchill Hospital, Headington,
14 October 2003

Billie sits beside her mother's bed. She has one foot tucked back up onto the edge of the chair to support her sketchpad. Her jeans are worn through just above the hem.

The traffic outside sounds like the sea; the sky through the window is tumbling with clouds. There's a vase of Michaelmas daisies on the locker, and the smell of dinner being cooked somewhere, and the quiet blur of voices by other beds, and a nurse passes down the ward, striding softly in her trousers and tunic, and there is the glissade of graphite across the paper's grain, and there is the ache in her throat that spreads down her chest sometimes, and sometimes, when she is not careful, it tightens into a knot and tightens and she can't breathe, doesn't even want to, just wants to press her forehead into the wall and close her eyes and let the impossibility of it just choke her.

Her mother's head dents the pillow. She frowns in her sleep. The skin over her bones is so white now, translucent, like skimmed milk held up to the light. After the last bout of chemo, Madeline's hair grew back blonde. Silvery-blonde. It's like the treatment had somehow bleached her from the inside. Billie makes herself consider the angled rim of the eye socket. The bird-boned bridge of the nose. The junction of the jaw, the mauve-shaded dent above it and beneath. The dark hollow behind the ear. Her mother's bones are beautiful.

The ward door swings open, closes. More visitors pass the end of the bed. A dark cluster of jackets, jeans; a swinging bunch of chrysanthemums, a cool pool of outdoor air. Everyone seems to bring chrysanthemums now. Billie can't stand them. Funeral flowers.

Billie shifts the pad, straightens out her knee to ease out the stiffness, props it up on the other, tilts and turns it till she gets the angles right. She measures by eye the angle between jawbone and clavicle. Her pencil accounts for distances, spaces. Light catches on her wedding band, and on the thin scuffed gold ring round the base of her thumb. Her throat is tight. She works. She marks out the space her mother takes up in the world.

Terry brings anemones. It's the first she notices of him, the patch of colour in the edge of her vision; the blotchy blues and pinks of them, the blur of white wrapping. It makes her look up; makes her smile. He smiles back. His cheeks crease underneath his beard, showing old acne scars. He looks tired.

'You okay?' she asks. She lets her knee fall, so that her pad lies flat on her lap.

He nods. He puts the flowers down on the locker, draws a chair forwards, sits down.

'She's sleeping,' he says.

Billie nods. They both look at Madeline. The soft rise and fall of her breastbone. The fan of her fingers over the yellow cellular blanket. Her veined eyelids.

He leans forward, making his jacket crumple. His hand reaches out as if to take Madeline's. It stops short though, drops. Billie recognises this – the urge to touch, the fear of hurting. He meshes his fingers. Two fingertips are stained black with ink. From along the ward there are voices, the squeak of soles on non-slip floors, the clatter of a trolley, the swing and creak of the doors.

After a little while he looks round, and says, 'How are you?'

She smiles thinly. Shrugs. She closes her sketchpad and puts it away, tucking it down between her chair and bag. She tucks a foot up underneath her, swings the other leg slightly. She is vile. Brittle. Furious. She is difficult to live with. She is difficult – at the moment she is difficult, she knows that she is difficult, she has been told as much – to love.

Then he says, 'Billie.'

'Yeah.'

'Really?'

'What?'

'How are things? You know, at home?'

She nods without looking at him. 'I'm okay. It's all okay.' Because it doesn't matter. Nothing else matters now but this.

Then Madeline's eyelids move. Billie gestures to Terry, urging him to look. Madeline's eyelids flicker; beneath them her eyeballs slip and shift. They sit, together, watch her dreaming.

Above London, 6 October 2004

Billie looks down at the city in the rain. The damp square blocks of offices, houses, trading estates. The plane turns, rising into the grey hard haze.

If she could see it, as the city falls away beneath her, the pattern of her life trailing through the streets like a coloured ribbon – tracing the way alongside Luke's thread for a while, down the high street and in and out of neighbourhood cafés and the park and cinema, and spinning off from his to dip down into the Underground and back out again at Edgware Road for work, and then the snarled tangle of this last year, the kind of knot you just can't unpick but have to take a pair of scissors to, and the thread trampled into the oily London mud, and Luke's peeling off to coil itself round Sophie's, and Billie's own now drifting up and off into the air – if she could see that, it would help, because eventually she could trace it back to when the line ran clear and clean and silky; and wind things back to there.

The plane lifts into cloud. The thrum of the engines shifts and changes as they climb. She tucks her earphones into her ears, flips through her iPod, looking for something.

It's daunting to think of what's to come. Of what waits for her when she returns. Her things are still in boxes and bags in the spare room at Norah's new house. She'll have to talk to Luke. Talk properly. They'll have to get divorced. She'll go back to what there was before: Norah's spare room, shopping for one, finding things to do.

Granddad always used to say, *Don't look beyond the next ten yards.*

And the next ten yards are good. They are the best ten yards there've been for a long while. The next ten yards are the first bright patch in a dim, grey, unfixable year. The whole residency thing had slipped so far out of sight that she'd almost forgotten that she'd applied for it. The envelope had landed on the mat while she was packing up her books; it had seemed like a letter from another world.

She'd stood there, in the empty hallway, looking at the printed page, the letterhead, the signature, failing to take it in. Then she'd thought: my passport. I'll have to get my name changed back.

★ ★ ★

The island is red-gold. It swims up into detail: a cell structure of stony dusty fields. The towns are like patches of lichen growing on the water's edge.

When she steps off the aeroplane in boots and jeans and shirt and jumper and coat, she feels how much closer to the equator she has come. She's adrift between seasons: it's still like summer here, but her body's in the sleepy drift towards winter. She shrugs out of her jacket, peels off her jumper, slumps them over the top of her case. She will wake up.

She emerges into the arrivals hall blinking in the brightness, and she spots a name, written on a piece of card. *W. Hastings*. The man scans faces as they pass. For a moment, she thinks, Dad's here, and then she thinks, Granddad. She catches herself. Winter boots hard on the polished concourse floor, she crosses over to the man. She holds out a hand to be shaken.

'Hi,' she says. 'I think that's me.'

The short sleeves of his shirt flap in the still air as he lifts her hand up and down. He's John; he runs the Arts Centre.

'Ms Hastings? Wilhelmina?'

She laughs. 'Billie.'

'Billie. Welcome to Malta.' He commandeers her case and wheels it along, ushering her towards the car park.

'If you're not too tired, I'll show you round the studio first. While the light's at its best.'

★   ★   ★

They enter the building through a tiny sally port. The steps are wide and sweep up in an unbroken flight underneath an arch of golden stone. The steps go on and on and on, straight up into the heart of the building, into the deep weight of golden stone. The place is vast.

A door opens onto a long vaulted room, spare and beautiful. The windows are small but there are many of them, and the openings are flared to make the most of the light. The walls are painted white. Her footsteps chime off the floor. Here and there are echoes of previous tenants: paint-stained rags, jars of brushes, driftwood, worn seashells, fragments of torn masking tape still adhering to the walls. He sets about opening cupboards, heaving drawers out to show her materials, equipment; talking about the rest of the facilities, and who they've had there over the years. Names she recognises. Artists she respects. She feels herself expand within this space, as if some kind of pressure is released.

'But of course you've brought your own things. And if you need anything else there's a good little shop on the—'

'Yes,' she says, nodding, not really hearing. 'Yes.'

She crosses to a window, touches the chisel marks in the sill. This is hers, all this. For a while it is hers.

'So this is it,' he says.

'Yes.' She looks up at the ceiling, the layers of vaulted stone. The ancient work of it.

'Is it okay?'

From below come voices, faint with distance. She tries to pick out the languages. She catches a few words of Italian, then English, then what she thinks must be Maltese.

He clears his throat. She glances back at him.

'Sorry, sorry.' She shakes her head to clear it, grins. 'It's amazing. Thank you. Thanks.'

He drives her to the accommodation afterwards.

Valletta is a city in miniature. Narrow streets, high baroque buildings, the sky a strip of blue.

'It's quiet,' she says.

'Out of season.' He shrugs. 'And no-one lives here. They come here to shop, to work, but it's mostly old people live here nowadays.'

'Why's that? It's amazing.'

'People want space. They move to Sliema, St Julian's. No-one wants these tiny apartments.'

Her place is on the top floor, up four flights of ringing stone steps. John swings her case up like an inflatable toy, telling her about the best bars, the quietest beaches, the buses, the bad parts of town.

He unlocks the door on a high narrow room, tall windows. There are stairs up to a mezzanine floor where the bed and bathroom hang suspended. It's cool, quiet, calm.

'Thank you.'

★   ★   ★

504

When John has gone she showers, and the shower tastes of salt. Afterwards, she feels as though she's just out of the sea.

That night, window open on the dark space between this building and the golden stone of the one across the street, fly screen like a haze of smoke over the night, she can't sleep. She feels like she's adrift on dark waters. It's strangely comforting. When she finally does slip under, she dreams of the room in Norah's new house, her boxes stacked in the centre of the carpet, and Ciaran – whose room it had been until he finally bought his own flat a few months back – leaning on the tower of boxes, because in her dream it's still his room, and it's still got all his clothes and books and cameras and equipment and he's shaking his head, and saying, *I don't know where we're going to fit all your stuff.*

She gets up, picks her way downstairs in her nightshirt. She drinks water from the tap, and it leaves her thirsty.

Morning, but it's still dark out. She thumps down the stone steps in her running gear and pushes out of the door. It clumps shut behind her. The noise echoes up the stairwell. She thinks the other flats are empty, but doesn't know – hopes she hasn't disturbed anyone. Six fifteen and it's mild as a July morning, but October-dark. Votive candles glimmer from the open door of the church.

She tucks her earphones into her ears, puts her iPod on shuffle. It comes up with 'Seven Nation Army', which is perfect, just made for running to.

She tucks the iPod inside her vest-top, stretches out her calves, dips down into lunges, pulls each foot in turn up behind her. She sets off in an easy loping run down the hill. Footfalls drop into the rhythm of the song. Her route, sketched in from the map at the back of the *Rough Guide*, will take her out to the harbour, then up to the city walls; she'll follow them as far as that little park – the Barrakka – then cut back through the city streets to the apartment building. A wedge of city.

The great crunchy guitar riff makes her feet hit the pavement to its pace; but she hadn't reckoned on the flights of stone steps that make her skitter half sideways down, and it's difficult to find her rhythm on the steep descending streets which stretch out her step unnaturally, but when she's out on the harbour road she hits her stride, falls into the pattern of breath and footfalls, mindful of the juncture of sole and stone. She's just passing a messy queue of schoolkids waiting for their bus in the early dark. They bundle together, nudging, laughing, and one of them shouts something at her but she doesn't catch it; she tugs out an earphone, but then another kid lurches into her path, pushed by his mates.

'Sorry,' he says.

She grins, dodges him, not yet breathless.

He was beautiful. Sharp contrasts of clear skin, dark

eyes, in the early morning dusk. Bone structure. Something familiar.

What'd he be like to draw?

She slows, turns. The music motors on. She steps backward, along the empty street, looking at the jostling crowd of youngsters. They're handsome kids, the lot of them, but he stands out. He's laughing and jostling with the other boys, an easy physicality. Not too beautiful to be interesting. He's young; he looks like Matty, she realises, though his colouring is utterly different. Like a negative of Matty: dark against his fair.

Then the bus pulls up, and the kids surge towards it, and heave themselves on, and she stumbles, and catches her step, and runs on.

The light is growing, the sky brightening. The road is lined with trees, the leaves dull and dusty. Her trainers crunch over fallen olives. Climbing back up the steep streets and flights of steps here stretches at her hamstrings, makes her chest tight and her breath raw. Her body's not used to this; it's used to the gentler slopes of the streets and park back near the flat. She'll find a new circuit, round Norah's area. There's a park, Norah said. A lido.

She pushes through the ache, the burn, and climbs up towards the Barrakka, the public garden built right onto the city wall, that marks the point to turn for home. Up ahead, not far off now, there are trees, and she catches the honey scent of jasmine. Billie slows to a lope, hand to the stitch in her side. Beyond the fence a fountain flings itself up into the air, trees haze the morning. The place looks empty, cool with shadows. She takes her earphones out, pushes in through the gate. Beyond the trees is a wide blue distance. She heads along the gravel paths, past the pattering fountain and between the borders and under the olive trees and right up to the wall. She leans out, her breath still heaving.

The Grand Harbour opens out below her like a miracle. The water is a perfectly calm deep blue. Fishing boats lie still at their moorings, their painted eyes dark against white-painted keels. They paint them there for good luck, she knows; to ward off the evil eye: she read it in the *Rough Guide*.

Beyond the harbour lies the open sea, the sky meeting the water.

Matty is not too far away from here, out there in the desert. With his straight back and his cropped hair and his sweet sudden smile. When he gets back, he'll marry Gemma, she reckons. Far too young, but not actually too young because it'll be right and good, and they'll have married quarters, and before you know it they'll start having babies and she can be an auntie. And that will be good too.

She looks down at her hand on the golden stone. The two wedding rings. The sleek wedding band that Luke bought for her, still new; the thin, battered ring around the base of her thumb that her granddad bought for her grandma nearly seventy years before. Both glint in the sun. At first she'd thought they'd formed a set; one's battered fragile permanence somehow substantiated the new one. She glances back out again to sea. Is it too much of a cliché, she thinks? Is it something people really do? She twists the newer, fatter ring off her finger. Weighs it for a moment in her palm. Then she skims it out into the blue.

A gift to the deeps and distances. An offering to the Fates. For Matty's safe return.

It is still very early – the street is quiet. She has bought bread and ground coffee and bottled water from a corner shop. She makes coffee with bottled water, the drip and hiss of its percolation familiar and soothing. Sunlight shreds through the blinds. She tears off fragments of bread. The bread tastes of salt.

The first channel is Maltese, and is showing a news feature on a yacht race. She flicks over, and picks up an Italian channel.

Her Italian is basic, but she doesn't really need to understand the words. The pictures are enough because she knows what's been happening, just like everybody else already knows. An establishing shot: the desert, and the twisted carcass of a car, blood in the dust. Then there's an interior caught on a grainy digital camera. Each time it is slightly, horribly worse. The shot is framed so that the captors themselves seem headless – you can only see their torsos, the longbladed knives, like machetes, held diagonally across their chests. The man sits, hands tied behind his back. He speaks. They've overdubbed him into Italian. His lips move but she can't understand the words.

She fumbles for the remote. Her hand shakes. She switches the television off.

The sun has not yet penetrated the depths of the street. She climbs the cobbles in sandals, her arms bristling in the chill. It's still early. She's not sure when the Arts Centre opens. She turns a corner and she's facing the cathedral; a wide sweep of golden stone. The Caravaggios are housed here.

She presses up against the door, listens: silence. She pushes cautiously in.

The interior is dark and quiet. Candles flicker in raked banks. Death's heads grin from the arches. She follows the signs for the side chapel.

She is alone at first, and just stands dead centre of the dark floor, and looks up at the painting. As the room fills, she moves into the empty spaces, finds new lines of sight. Her toes grow numb. The small of her back aches. Her neck is stiff. It doesn't matter. From the left side of the room, she can study the expression of the handmaid, the glint of gold off the platter that she carries, the deep shadow of the folds in her skirt. From the right, Billie can better see the prisoners peering out through their cell window, straining to get a view

510

of the drama in the inner courtyard. From right up close against the security barrier, she can see the victim's pallid face, the wound, the blood.

She has been playing, she realises. Like a child she has been playing with her inks and her paint and her pencils and her paper and her pens. With her skulls and her bones and her shells and her scrap of human leather. You do learn through play. You try things out.

It is time to stop playing.

The picture is *The Beheading of St John the Baptist*. The beheading is performed in the Arabic fashion: a long-bladed knife is sliced back through the throat, severing artery and vein, trachea and oesophagus, splitting the links of the spine. The handmaid waits, platter ready, to carry the severed head away to Salome and Herod. We don't see them. We don't need to see them, with their veils and cushions and dishes of figs. The powerful are not what matters here. What matters is the blood and flesh and bone.

The victim is already dead. His wound gapes like a second mouth. The blood pools scarlet on the floor, and then trickles out to scrawl, as if by its own volition, *F. Michel.* Michelangelo da Caravaggio. It's the only piece he signed.

The gallery fills with Americans and English and Scots and Irish and Australians, becomes dense with noise and trainers and bodies and rucksacks. She's kept here, kept looking by the sense of something connective, expansive about this picture. She can see it in every figure, in all the absences, in the way that primary focus is given to neither the executioner nor the victim, so that the gaze shifts uneasily between the other prisoners, the guards, the handmaid with the platter who only stands and waits. That's what matters here: everybody shares the searching light; they share the act, the state of being. Everyone's complicit in this death.

You can't switch off. You can't walk away. You have to look.

Polstead Road, Oxford, 6 November 2004

I t has rained all day. It has rained for weeks. There are pools of water between the gravel. The lawn looks like a swamp. The lights are on upstairs, which means the Canadian couple are in. Will rattles his key into the door. He has a bottle of wine tucked under his arm. His mouth tastes of old sherry.

He dodges through the front door, then through the hall and into his flat. It is cold. He takes off his wet overcoat and hangs it up. He goes into the kitchen and opens his wine. He will drink half the bottle. Half a bottle is a reasonable amount. Up fresh tomorrow morning, because he's promised Billie he'll pick her up from the airport.

God knows she needed the break, as in time off, as in bit of luck. After the year that it was. Mads. That utter shit Luke. All surface gloss, no substance. Leaving her when he did, at the very worst time; but at least they didn't have kids. He shrugs the thought off. Doesn't do to pursue it.

In fact, he goes on to drink the whole bottle, finishing it off over *News at Ten*, stumbling through to his bedroom and climbing into bed in his pants and shirt. He wakes, stark awake, at three. He doesn't know what wakes him, but he gets up and limps to the toilet for a piss.

His right hip is hurting him now, which seems like a final bloody betrayal. But then with all the years of favouring the bad leg it's done far more than its fair share. He can tell it's not far off complete breakdown: the loose grind, the sudden shocks of pain. He'll go private this time. But what will he do about the convalescence? Could Billie be persuaded to camp out with him for a few weeks? They could go through those boxes properly then.

Outside the bathroom window the rain still hammers down. The guttering is blocked: water spilling from its edge in an uneven waterfall. He'll have to talk to the couple upstairs about getting that fixed.

He wanders through to the kitchen, fills a glass at the tap. Stands there in his pants and shirt and drinks.

He misses Madeline. Suddenly, viscerally. He clutches the edge of the sink, and sobs hard, until he's retching, and then brings up a flood of water, acid, and wine into the sink. When he can heave up nothing more, he turns on the tap, and rinses away the mess, and raises his hand to touch the wet away from his eyes.

He always knew that she was beautiful, he always knew that she was clever, but he never really noticed, when he was young, that Madeline was kind. Or, rather, he didn't see how necessary kindness was.

Outside, the water cascades down from the blocked guttering, pools under the gravel, oozes through the seam where the coalhole has been imperfectly sealed, and drips down into the dark. The remaining dusty coal, which has lingered there since 1957 when the gas fires were put in, softens into a treacly morass, and oozes out from its dark corner.

Water also soaks through the brickwork of the cellar walls, growing mould on the wooden shelves, easing into the concrete floor and making it bead with damp. From the brick itself grows a white crystalline material, delicate and beautiful and unseen in the dark. Unseen, because Will hasn't been down there since he carried down the unopened boxes of stuff that Carole had tumbled together on his behalf four years ago now. They're mostly old notes and manuscripts and outmoded office supplies, and bits of drafts of books long published and gone. And whilst he can't be bothered to check through them, he also can't be sure there isn't something worthwhile in one of them, and so leaves them down there, unopened, to rot. Though, in fairness, he doesn't know they're rotting.

The blue suitcase lies on the cellar floor. The cardboard wicks up the water from the concrete. It still looks solid enough, but it is weighed down by its own damp, and fragile. Inside, the vinyl album on the top hold some photos safe, though water seeps in and blots others, making the inks separate into the constituent colours, blurring the outlines of a young woman's face, a toddler's sundress, a graduation gown. The earlier albums – paper pages stuck with black and white photos – are drenched. A boy in his hospital bed. A rug on the beach. Different Sukies. A man on a bike.

Billie flicks on the light, heads down the stairs. Cobwebs droop from the light fitting. Will follows her down awkwardly, sideways.

'You okay?' she asks.

'Fine.'

'Is your hip hurting?'

'Is it a day?'

'You need to go and see a doctor. Get it checked.'

On the cement floor, a glistering of water.

'Shit.' He starts forward, past her, then stops. The walls are streaked with dark. They hear the drip of water coming from the disused coalhole cover. They see the boxes damp and softening, bulging out like bellies.

'What's in them?' Billie asks.

'Nothing. Just crap. Office stuff.'

He goes over to the wall and touches the white

bloom on the brick. The crystal crumples back on itself.

'So where's the suitcase?' Billie asks.

He scans round; spots it, lying on its side, on the floor. He gestures to it. Billie darts over, as if her swift action would make any difference now. It looks, for a moment, all right. But when she kneels down and touches it the cardboard dips away, leaving the impression of her fingertips.

'It's sodden.'

The wooden strips have bulged too, he sees now: they are bloated with water and splitting round the screws.

'Shall I lift it?' she asks.

'Go on.'

'It might just come apart.'

'Well, we can't really leave it.'

He leans his weight on the top of the nearest box, watches as she slips her hands in underneath, lifting the suitcase like a sleeping child.

'It's cold,' she says.

'Can you manage?' he asks.

'Yup.'

She eases it up, clutched in her arms, and makes her way between the boxes, back towards the stairs.

They sit on the living room floor, in the weak November light from the French windows. The case lies open on a folded throw, to keep its must and wet off the new green carpet. Billie lifts out the contents.

517

The stripy vinyl album is first. There are dewdrops inside the plastic sleeves. She slips the pictures out of their casings, and lays them out in the sunlight.

'Mum,' Billie says, of a girl in a green dress.

'Yes.'

Billie holds the photograph a moment longer, then lays it on the carpet. 'Can I keep it?'

'Yes.'

'Thanks.'

'S'okay.'

There's a moment when neither of them can speak.

'That'll be me,' Billie says, fingertip suspended over the pink bundle of a child in Grandma Ruby's arms.

'Yes,' he says. Her tininess. He remembers the washing-up bowl in front of the gas fire, her belly round and taut.

The older albums are buckled and softened and let their pictures loose. A boy in a hospital bed, holding a bow and arrow.

'That's me,' Will says.

She looks at it. 'You look like Matty. A fat Matty.'

'Fat! I was bedridden! I was in traction for a year.'

'Yep. Fatso.'

There are loose photographs too, and these she eases apart with minute care. A studio shot of Grandma Ruby, smooth-skinned, dark-lipped, beautiful and young. The photo is creased and battered and soft. And there's another studio pose of Granddad Billy, a young man on his bike – *To Mother, with love* washed into an inky blur.

At the bottom of the case, drenched, is the post-card album, his grandma's picture book. The wet has sealed its paperiness around itself. When Billie eases the pages apart, they peel into strips, fall into fragments like tinned fish. The postcards themselves are wet and soft, but more robust than the paper. One comes away in her hands.

'Shit. Sorry.'

'I think the album's done for, love; don't worry.'

She turns the postcard round to look at it. The picture is of the Grand Harbour in Malta. Her skin fizzes. 'Whose was this?'

'My grandma's. Granddad sent the pictures, during the war.'

'The one who died? Gallipoli? Granddad's dad?'

Her dad nods.

'I was just there. I mean, I was just looking at this view; like, yesterday. This is Malta. Fuck.'

She tilts the card, dips her head to read the underside, as though afraid of turning it over fully in case the picture might drip off onto the floor. The writing is in pencil; sloping, even, very careful.

Dear Amelia

'Amelia?'

'My grandma.'

Thank you for your letter, which came in today's bag. I am well, thank you, and longing

to see you, and the child. I am glad to hear
what you say of the offer of work. I thought
you would like this picture. I am sitting now,
looking out over this particular spot. I think
you would find it quite beautiful.
    Yours ever
    William

Billie lays the card down on the carpet, touches it again, straightens it, dazed by a new sense of privilege, of unaccountably good fortune.

'He was in Malta, and it was wartime,' she says.

'Yes. That's about as much as I know. He used to take Grandma to the cinema. She'd talk about that.'

Billie sits back on her heels. He is *well*, he is *longing*, he is *glad*. This is what you write if you're writing home from war. If you're writing on a postcard, that anyone could read. This is what is expected.

'What?' he asks.

There are things you can't say, of course there are. Things you wouldn't even consider saying. About fear, and its deferral. About what you'd do to stop yourself from looking too far ahead. She feels choked with it. With what must have been felt, and may have been done, and could not be said.

'It's sad,' she says.

She peels apart another page. He watches the care, the precision of her movements. She has become something, this past little while, while he wasn't looking. Out of all the misery, she has pulled herself into focus.

'How was it, Malta?' he asks.

'It was good,' she says. Then, 'Are there photographs of him?'

'Of my granddad? Don't think so.'

'She didn't have a single photograph of him, your grandma?'

'I never saw one. She always said my dad looked like him. He was named after him.'

Billie huffs a laugh, shakes her head.

'What?'

'The lot of you. Like a set of Russian dolls.'

'What?'

'All you men. Chips off the old block, the lot of you.'

He glances at her. 'You think so?'

He means, does she think he's just like his father. And there's such a sharpness, an unease to it. She feels a rush of love for him. The boy he was. The years of pain. The damage done.

'You're yourself. That's the thing. Same block maybe, different chips.'

He says nothing.

'Is it okay to do this?' she asks, reaching out, almost touching the album. 'You don't mind?'

He nods her on: 'I want to see.'

She sets the postcards down on the carpet like she is laying out a game of cards. She lifts one of a straw-roofed hut and places it next to another of some fishing boats. Turns them both over and reads the messages, the pencilled printing, the careful words. She turns them back. The colours are inked in on top of black-and-white prints. The shades are subtle, capturing the water's rippled surface, the textures of rock and cloud. The pictures are what matters here, she realises. He'd seen the world, and even in the depths of war he'd found it beautiful. Whatever he'd written or failed to write, he'd communicated that.

Lancaster Station, 12 December 2004

He's standing on the platform as her train cruises to a halt. She recognises him from his description on the phone. The black blouson leather jacket and jeans, the close-cut grey hair. As she makes her way through the alighting passengers, she watches him scan the crowds for her. His erect bearing, his stillness, give him away. Ex-serviceman.

He greets her with a nod. A brisk handshake. He says, 'There's something I want you to see.'

She buttons up her coat against the cold, slips her folder under her arm and stuffs her gloved hands into her pockets. She keeps pace with him up the narrow cobbled street towards the black hulk of the castle. He walks fast. Their breath plumes. Above them the sky is clear and bright.

She hadn't expected to go straight to the Centre – this is just a first meeting, after all, and she understands his reluctance to introduce her there. She'd thought maybe they'd go to a café, where she could spread out her slides to show him. But instead they head past blank Georgian terraces and around the flank of the castle. To the right, the ground falls away, and Billie looks down on the slate rooftops below, dusted white with frost.

The castle is a functioning prison, he tells her. Mediaeval, she says, looking up at its dark, high walls. He asks her if she knows the proportion of ex-servicemen in the prison population. She says no, even though she has some idea. He tells her, and she expresses the necessary shock and sympathy. And then the homelessness? Does she know how many former soldiers end up on the streets? She shakes her head. The support, he says. The support is just not there.

They walk under the bare trees. It is a still, quiet day. The trees and dark stone buildings are stark against the sky. The air is fresh and clean.

He's doing up a house – the other side of town – he gestures over to his right, and she glances round, and sees the terraces snaking up another hill, and beyond that woodland and the whale-back of moor. It's a nice town, he says. Quiet. He's been doing this a few years now, since he left the forces. Buying a place cheap, which you can round here, even now; doing it up, selling it, moving on. That, and the work at the Centre. Keeps himself busy. Her gaze catches on his hand, swinging by his side – the nails are scuffed and blunt and white with plaster dust. Like her granddad's hands, capable of making anything out of nothing. She used to hang around the work-shop when she was little. She'd get sawdust in her hair.

They turn the corner round the flank of the castle, through the priory gates; the old church squats dark and low along the line of the hill. They walk through the graveyard.

She asks about the men he works with. He gives her a sidelong look. She wonders if she has been too brisk, but then he nods. And he starts to talk. About their wounds, the nature of their injuries. The multiple amputations, the disfigurements, the scarring. He talks about how the charity he works for kicks in once medical treatment is over, and the men are sent home to get on with their lives. To adjust.

They pass headstones, and kerbed graves, and graves with iron railings round them, and an angel with her head knocked off.

'There are some things,' he says, 'you just can't adjust to.'

He is a good man. Decent. She likes him. She's pretty sure that he has killed people.

They come up to the graveyard wall, a gateway. He pauses here, one hand on the gate. He doesn't open it. This must be what he wants her to see. Below them a meadow slopes down to the woods below. Dry grasses and the dead heads of cow parsley stand rimed with frost. There are stands of hawthorn trees, scarlet berries and a rustling of birds. Further off, there's a sweep of silvery water, and then, blue with distance, a scalloped line of peaks and hills.

'That's Morecambe Bay,' he says. 'Beyond, those hills there, that's the Lake District.'

'It's really lovely.'

'Those hills there,' he says, gesturing to the distant peaks. 'That one's Helvellyn, that's Hawkshead Moor, and that's the Old Man of Coniston.'

'It's beautiful, really.'

He nods. She looks round at him. There's a muscle twitching in his cheek.

'Sometimes I go climbing,' he says, and then for a moment he says nothing more. She follows his thoughts down what is clearly a well-worn track. The life he has. That there is no particular reason that he should have it when others don't.

'I'm sorry,' she says.

He shakes his head. 'No. It's okay. My point is, you could paint that.'

He looks round at her. His eyes are startlingly blue.

'Seriously,' he says. 'Why not paint that, that kind of thing? That's breathtaking, that is.'

She nods. He's right. Of course he's right, it's beautiful, it's sublime. It's wonderful to look at, to be in, to climb, to breathe. She wants to tell him about the hare's skull, the dry newt with its dimpled eyes, the earlobe. These things, these damaged treasures, they need to be looked at, considered. They have their own beauty too.

'I know,' she says. 'I know what you're saying. You're absolutely right.'

'So?'

'So I'm not a landscape painter. I don't need to be. There are like a gazillion paintings of those mountains.'

She pulls a hand out of her pocket, tugs off the glove.

'Look,' she says. 'I'm – I want to paint what we, what people don't look at. I want to paint it and put it in a frame and make it something that people *really* look at. Deliberately. That they linger over.'

He studies her face, assessing her. She straightens herself up, brushes a strand of hair back from her cheek.

'You think it's going to get you noticed?'

She shrugs. 'I don't care either way. It doesn't matter.'

'Because, what, you think it's worthy?'

'It's necessary.'

She slips her folder up onto the flat surface of the wall; she goes to loop the black elastic.

'Can I show you?' she asks.

He nods.

She lifts out a polypocket of slides, hands it to him. Her fingers are pale. It leaves her raw, bringing these pictures into the light. But if she's not prepared to do it, to expose her inner self like this, she can't ask anybody else to open themselves up to her scrutiny. He takes the sheet of slides off her, and holds it up to the sky. She watches his eyes as they move from image to image, following the descent of her mother's illness. When his gaze lingers, she glances from him to the sheet, trying to work out what in particular has snagged him. Her cheeks burn. She feels ashamed of herself. Overeager.

'Who was this?' he says. He doesn't look at her. She swallows. 'Mum.'

He nods. He puts the page down. She slips it back into her folder.

'I'll ask for you,' he says. 'At the Centre. If they're up for it, I'll introduce you to some people.'

She paints other men, but these are the three that matter most.

She paints Corporal Simon Gregg in front of his patio door. You can just see a glimpse of foliage and the red metal cup of a barbecue in the back garden beyond. He lost his right arm to a sniper bullet on patrol outside his FOB in Afghanistan: his sleeve is pinned up to his shoulder. He is planning to do a degree; he's not quite sure what yet. He's still working on his one-handed typing. His girlfriend is blonde, pretty, harassed, straight in from work and glancing at the drinks tray on the sideboard. He never seemed drunk, not once, not all the time Billie was working on his portrait. But he was never without a drink. She paints his whisky glass in his left hand.

She paints Private Louis Hargreaves in his

bedroom. He sits on his single bed, his duvet cover a spread of stars, the wall behind him still stuck with posters. He's lost both legs at the knee. The stumps are shiny and livid. He keeps his guitar on his lap, between him and what isn't there. He keeps his face turned towards the guitar. He's civil, but he doesn't want to chat. He picks out tunes as she paints. He has a nasty scar up the side of his head: you can see it through his stubbly hair. He got that in a motorbike accident. Lost control on a bend and slammed into a tree: he was just a kid, still at school. She thought the army would sort him out, his mother did. She feeds Billie coffee and biscuits after the sittings. Custard creams and Bourbons and garibaldis. Billie sits in the immaculate, tired kitchen, trying to dislodge clumps of biscuit with her tongue, listening to Mrs Hargreaves talk, hearing, between the statements, the faint thrum of Louis's guitar from his room upstairs. Mrs Hargreaves talks about how good this is for Louis, Billie's taking an interest, Billie's being there, being company for him. He's not a talker, doesn't find it easy. And Billie, she's been a real help.

Captain Peter Reynolds she paints in the sitting room of his family home. His wife stands behind the armchair, her hand on his shoulder. She is a neat, faded woman with pale hair and an upright posture. She wears a lavender cardigan and fawn skirt, and says very little. Her husband is chatty though. The scar tissue wrinkles up the side of his

529

face as he speaks; it catches the light differently, makes it harder to paint him. She wonders if he always talks like this, on and on, asking questions, asking his wife to remember, telling Billie family stories: it's his attempt to fill up the empty space around him, to populate the darkness. Billie makes assenting noises, can't really listen, not while she works.

One of his eye sockets is a darkened pit. He still has the other eye, but it's not much use to him any more.

'Light, a kind of milky light. Bits of colour.'

Their son, Christopher, comes home from school. He sits nearby, and watches Billie paint. He watches first the way her eyes flick from canvas to subject, then back again, tireless, scrutinising both. He moves in and stands at her shoulder, small in his school uniform, and looks down at the sweep and dab of her brush, then back up at his mum and dad. His gaze falls into synch with hers. She glances round at him and smiles.

'Sorry,' he says, and is about to step away.

She reaches out a hand, stilling him. 'Not a problem. Do you do art at school?'

He nods.

They stare back at his parents, considering lines and shapes and distances. Then, quick as a cat, Mrs Reynolds pokes out her tongue. Billie laughs, the boy laughs.

'What?' Captain Reynolds turns his face up to his wife. 'What is it?'

His wife bends down to explain; her hand cups her husband's ruined cheek.

Her first instinct is to turn on her heel and walk right back out again, but Alexis is there, and grabs her by the elbow, and moves her into the cool white room, talking smoothly. Billie is ushered along and introduced, and her hand is shaken, and she makes some comment about the weather (clammy, threatening a storm) to a man in a grey suit, and thinks, *If this is the best I can come up with, I just shouldn't talk. I just shouldn't talk at all.*

She should have come with Norah. She could just be with Norah; she wouldn't have to make conversation; Norah would understand. But Norah's coming straight from work, and bringing unspecified people with her, which is in itself alarming: more strangers, more small talk. Or old friends, and that's alarming in its own way too.

Her paintings – there aren't many, but this is a good gallery, this is a game-changing gallery – hang along the end wall. She can't even look at

532

them. Ed's and Jake's pictures take up the sides, and three of Clare's ceramics stand glittering on pedestals down the centre of the room. Alexis and Gabrielle have done a good job: everything looks gorgeous, and the room is busy and loud, and she spots Ed himself standing chatting in good jeans and trainers and a sharp jacket, completely at his ease, and Captain Reynolds, Mrs Reynolds with her hand under his arm, and Christopher on his other side. The three of them are looking at one of Ed's abstracts; Mrs Reynolds is standing up on tiptoe to speak into Peter Reynolds' ear, describing the pictures for him. He nods. Christopher just stares. Billie goes over to them, says hello. Together they stand and look at the abstracts – a glory of complementary colour, of aquamarine blues and sunset shades of orange.

'Are you able to get any of that?' Billie asks.

Captain Reynolds turns his head towards her voice. He pulls a face, making his scars twist.

'Lorna likes them,' he says.

Mrs Reynolds leans round her husband to peer at Billie. 'How are you feeling?'

Billie laughs. 'God.' She shakes her head. Mrs Reynolds smiles sympathetically.

The guy in the grey suit reappears beside her, and he starts to ask her about her work, and it makes her palms sweat. She's looking round: there are little clusters of people she half knows, and her eyes bounce from one face to the next, catching an eye here or there, smiling a hard little smile, wishing Norah would get here, with or without whoever it is she's bringing.

And then there's Dad.

She watches as he limps up to the drinks table and stands, sloped, leaning on his cane, saying something probably slightly flirty to Chloë, who smiles compliantly and pours him a glass of white. Then he turns and looks around the room with that kind of assuredness that seems almost natural after all these years, but causes him, she can see now, a vast effort to summon up and project every time. She watches as he moves away from the table, and limps across the room, alone. It was a difficult invitation to send. She'd wanted him to be here. She hadn't wanted him to see this. All this time, she'd hoped something last minute would keep him away. The way it often did.

'Excuse me. I just have to—'

She ducks past the man in the grey suit, and heads over to her dad.

The closer she gets to him, the more she wants to turn and run away. She can see the pictures in her mind's eye, all the separate blobs and smears of paint and not what they add up to. This is going to hurt. But she keeps walking to him. He's studying one of Clare's vases, and so doesn't notice her till she's up close and touches him on his arm. He looks round at her, and smiles, and says, 'Petal.'

His worn, tired face, and that one word. She slips her arm in through his.

'Show your old man, then.'

They move together between the patches of people. Over the frisson of anxiety she wonders if Terry will make it, if Dad will manage to be polite to him. Norah's here now: Billie spots her blue-black twist of hair as she turns, but doesn't catch her eye. And there's Tim, and Gil and Kate and James from work, and that's all good and fine, and then there's a man in a creased jacket and jeans, and she just gets the back of him, and she thinks, who's that, and he leans in to give Norah a drink, and she sees, Ciaran, and her skin prickles with delight. Then Norah's gaze shifts and she spots Billie and comes bundling through to her, kisses Billie's cheek – a whiff of Jo Malone and smoke.

'This is fabulous, hon, fabulous.'

'Thanks.'

She dips in to kiss Billie's dad.

'Well, Professor,' Norah says, 'you must be very proud.'

'Always have been,' he says.

Her dad stands, holding himself almost military erect, and then takes a sip of wine. He glances at her, his lips twisted.

'You haven't seen them yet,' Billie says.

But then Norah squeezes her arm. 'I brought people!'

'I see that.'

'Aren't I good to you?'

'Norah, please.'

Norah holds up a hand, smiles. 'Okay, okay.'

'Show me the pictures, petal?' her dad says.

She nods. She has to face up to this at some point. It may as well be now. 'Come on.'

There are four pictures. She has painted dozens, but it is just four full-length portraits that have made it to this final selection. Her dad moves along the row, considering each of them carefully, pausing, leaning on his stick. Stepping close to examine the brushwork, stepping back to get the overall effect. Captain Peter Reynolds and his wife, Private Louis Hargreaves and his guitar, Corporal Simon Gregg and his whisky glass.

Billie's aware of the scuff and shuffle of other viewers, the hum of their voices, their murmurs of assessment. But somehow it feels as though the two of them are alone, that there is no-one else in the gallery at all.

They come to the last picture. Lieutenant Matthew Hastings. Her dad just looks at it a long time. He says nothing.

In the picture Matty stands, arms folded behind him, upright in his uniform, looking straight out of the frame. He's the only standing figure; the others are all seated. Matty's expression is sheepish. Billie knows what no-one else here knows – that just off to the left of him, out of frame, Gemma had fallen asleep in an armchair, exhausted with the early months of pregnancy: the baby will be born in September. She has captured her little brother perfectly; she knows she has: she has laid down in paint the thoughtless, undamaged beauty of the nineteen-year-old boy. Just as she has captured the wrinkling of a scar, the rawness of a wound, empty spaces.

She feels a kind of bullish, nauseous pride. But she knows that this will hurt her dad. It hurts her.

Her dad just stands. She watches as he sucks in his left cheek, bites down on it with his back teeth. She touches his sleeve, and he looks at her. His eyes are old and tired and the lower lids fall slack and show the pink inner rims.

She touches his arm. 'I'm sorry.'

'Oh, love.' He gestures to the painting, his wine glass sloshes.

'I know.'

'Seeing him up there like that. He just looks so . . . vulnerable.'

'I know.' It's their everyday, grinding, relentless fear, that some harm will come to Matty. She's looked at it every day for months now, stared right at it. It's harder for her dad, though, confronting it suddenly like this, having it dragged out into public view.

'It's like you're . . .' he shakes his head. 'I don't know, it's nonsense, but it makes me scared.'

'Like I'm tempting fate?'

He nods. His face looks pinched, his lips tight.

She looks away, back to the picture. 'For me, it's the opposite of that.'

'How?'

'I think, whatever it is, by not looking at it, not saying it, not admitting it to yourself, that's the temptation, that's the danger. You've got to look fate right in the eye. You've got to stare it down.'

'It's just . . .' he shakes his head, words failing.

'It's Matty.'

'Yes.'

She turns to look at the pictures again. 'Good.'

'I need some air.'

'Yes.'

She gestures him through the blur, the room, the press of people, till they're standing in the outdoor evening with the smokers, and she leans back against a low window ledge and he takes his handkerchief from his pocket and hands it to her, and she wipes her cheeks with it, presses at her eyes. She's crying.

'Fuck,' she says. 'Sorry. Sorry.'

He leans himself carefully beside her. He takes the handkerchief back, blows his nose.

'I don't know what difference it makes,' she says, 'but I didn't do it to upset you.'

'It's okay,' he says. 'I know.'

'Thanks.'

'I mean, it's not okay. But not because of you.'

People trickle in and out of the gallery. They gather in small groups to chat and smoke. Billie leans there and her dad fetches them both a drink, and while he's gone she checks her mascara in her compact, and when he comes back there's the fumbled management of his stick and the wine glasses.

'Well,' he says. His voice is cracked. He raises his glass. 'Here's to Matty.'

'Matty.'

'Here's to the work.'

'Thank you.'

'Here's to you.'

She blinks, tries to smile. They drink.

Her eyes sting. They talk. They pull themselves back together, back to normal. He asks about the way she works and about the men who sat for her. An enquiring, careful, interested approach. A tenderness. She can't quite process it. He's impressed.

And then Ciaran comes down the gallery steps into the street, and looks round. For her? He gets cigarettes from his inner jacket pocket, and tucks one between his lips, and then he spots her. He smiles. She smiles back to him. And her heart lifts. And he's heading over to her.

But then someone touches his arm, stops him. He turns away. A young woman. Billie watches him, the line of his shoulders, the way he has to bend a little to listen. She remembers the photographs of Gaza; the last ones of his she'd seen. A teenage boy on crutches; a girl sitting in the back of a burnt-out car with a chicken in her lap; the Lego layers of flat roofs in the rain.

Her dad's saying something. He finishes his drink, sets down his glass on the windowsill. Then he sets about gathering himself together, buttoning his jacket, mustering his stick and glasses.

'Are you off?'

'I'm going to have to get a move on if I'm going to catch this train.'

She glances at her watch. It's later than she thought. But she doesn't want this to be over.

'Do you have to? You could stay with us; Norah won't mind. I'll take the sofa.'

'I've got that appointment.'

She remembers. He's seeing the specialist tomorrow, up in Oxford. The second hip replacement now; the new pain. She smiles for him. 'No. Right. That's good. Phone me afterwards, will you? Let me know how you got on.'

'Will do.' Her dad pushes himself away from the wall, finds his balance, better leg, worse leg, stick. He hesitates. He speaks without looking at her, rifling in a pocket, checking his wallet, putting it away again.

'I was wondering, could I have a picture?'

She wants to laugh, it's such an unexpected delight. 'Oh yes, of course.' She very nearly says, 'Thank you.'

'If it hasn't sold already, I'd like the one of Matty.'

'It's yours.' She kisses his cheek.

'Well. Thank you. Cheerio then, petal.'

She watches him, his half-slumped, swinging walk through the patch of smokers and up the street, heading for the Tube. He will always be like this, she realises: he'll always be at arm's length, always moving away.

And now she's alone and she doesn't know what

to do with herself. She should go back in, be sociable. She should see if Louis or Simon have made it down; she should see if Terry's turned up. And Ciaran. She glances over and Ciaran's looking right back at her. He detaches himself from the crowd with a few words. And he's coming towards her.

'Hey,' he says.

'Hey.'

He leans against the window ledge beside her. For a moment they just stay there, side by side, then he takes her empty glass off her, and holds out his full one. She looks down at it. He touches the cool glass against the back of her hand.

'Go on. It's yours. I got it for you.'

She takes it. 'Thanks.' The glass is cold in her hands, but she feels hot.

'I like your work,' she says. 'I've been keeping up with it.'

He shakes his head, laughs.

'What?'

'Isn't this, tonight, isn't it about yours?'

'I suppose so, yes.'

She wants to ask him what he thinks, but doesn't dare. She wants to tell him that her mum said his photographs were stunning, but can't bring herself to. She's aware of the shape of his jaw near her temple, and the lines of his dark blue jacket, and his boots on the pavement. He scuffs a toe against the pavement, flicks a fragment of ash.

She wants to tell him about Luke and Sophie.

About the Caravaggio painting and the aeroplane her granddad built for her and the postcard album and the Lake District hills. She wants to ask about who he's come with and who he's met in Gaza and Afghanistan and Iraq, and whether or not he's fallen in love.

'It's good,' he says.

'What is?'

'This. The exhibition. Your work. It's good.'

Just this one word, from him, and she is entirely happy. She finds herself grinning.

'It's clearly just what you should be doing. You've really found yourself.'

He speaks like he's reading her palm. Over near the door, the young woman he'd been speaking to catches Billie's eye, and smiles. Billie nods and smiles back at her. And then thinks, is that his girlfriend?

'They keep looking over,' she says.

'Oh, yeah. I told them I was coming to talk to you.'

She doesn't make sense of this for a moment. 'I'm sorry?'

'I told them it was you. The artist. The exhibition, remember?'

'Oh.'

She feels like there's a bubble in her chest. It's difficult to breathe round. It's making her giddy. Her dad's red eyes, his request. Ciaran's one word, *good*, and how happy she is.

He touches her arm. 'What is it, Billie?'

'It's too much.' She shakes her head. 'It's silly, I know, but I'm just not up to this.'

'I understand.'

'I'm going to go home.'

She straightens up, then hesitates, not knowing what to do with her wine glass. He stands up too, takes it off her.

'You'll tell Norah, will you?' she says. 'And, oh God, have her tell Alexis that I'm sorry. I'm ill! Say I'm ill. Oh, and she can't sell the Matty picture.'

'I'll be right back.'

'Okay.' Then, 'Why?'

'I'll see you home.'

They walk. Heading south through the evening streets, they pass loud boys in suits and girls in floaty dresses who move through the city on an entirely different plane, giddy with drink and summer. Exhaustion and peace and the cool air and Ciaran's presence there beside her make her feel cut adrift from everything, as if her feet land a millimetre above the pavement. They walk along, talking. His travels and hers. Photographs and paintings. Caravaggio and ridiculous relationships and his venomous loathing of Luke, and the failure of any sleep to be quite as refreshing as that slept on Norah's sofa, and Billie there with coffee in the morning.

'It's been far too long,' he says.

'What can I say? I've been busy.'

He laughs. There are new creases at the corners of his eyes. His fingertips brush the back of hers. She glances up at him, smiles.

'It's good to see you,' she says.

He smiles back. 'It's good to see you too.'

He catches up her hand.

'This okay?'

'Yes.'

Connected and distinct, his hand wrapped warm around hers, their footsteps fall into easy synchronicity.

After a while, he slows to a halt, and she sees that they're at an Underground station, the steps open down into the dark.

'Shall we take the Tube?' he asks.

Two girls pass, arm in arm, maybe seventeen years old, and they're singing to themselves, to the open street, the city, happy and oblivious.

He swings her hand just slightly, gently.

She smiles. 'I'm liking the walk really quite a lot.'

'I'll walk with you then, if you'd like that,' he says. 'As far as you want to walk.'

This makes her lean in, up on tiptoes, and kiss him on the lips.

Holmedene Avenue, Herne Hill, 7 July 2005

She stirs at the sound of the blackbird singing in the rowan tree outside her window. She doesn't really wake; she is aware of herself, the tangle of the duvet round her right foot, the press of her shoulder into the mattress, the twist of her nightshirt round her thighs. Ciaran lies beside her. She feels him breathe. After a while, she looks at him, the softness of his sleeping face. Then he opens his eyes, dark, unfocused. He puts his arm out, and she shifts herself closer. They lie, almost sleeping, her leg resting over his legs, his arm around her shoulders. Soft.

She thinks, I have to get up. Then after a while she says, 'I have to get up.'

He mumbles something. He pulls her in closer. They lie together. A car passes the end of the street, heading down Half Moon Lane.

'I have to get up.'

'Mmn.'

She peels herself from him, lies on her back. 'God.'

'What is it?'

'Work.'

He rolls onto his side to look at her. 'Do you have to?'

'I've got this meeting.'

'Ugh.'

'With my boss. About my contract.'

'All right.' He slides his arm out from underneath her. 'You'll need coffee.'

As he gets out of bed she watches his body for a moment, the twists of muscle and the sheen of his skin as he pulls on yesterday's shirt over his boxers.

'D'you know,' he says, looking round the chaos of the room, the stacks of books and leaning canvasses, clothes slung in a heap in the armchair by the window, her easel standing on tiptoes in the rubble of paints and artboxes and folders, 'I really love what you've done with the place.'

She laughs. He smiles at her, heads out of the room. She hears his footfalls on the stairs and the quiet below as he potters round, opening cupboards, boiling the kettle. At least Norah isn't up yet, to tease them, to be all *I told you so* about it.

She rolls onto her front, looks sideways out towards the window, watches the way the light whitens the ancient hare's skull on the windowsill, catches on the silver of the old toffee tin where she keeps her strange and broken things. The things she'd loved for their ugly mysteries.

There comes a point with everything when the thing itself is no longer necessary, like a seed is used up as a seedling grows. Time for a clearout perhaps, she thinks.

Later, though. She'll do it later.

For now, she lies there, the cool cotton beneath her cheek. She closes her eyes and the redness there flares and streaks with other colours. She wants him to come back, get back into bed beside her. She should get up. Coffee, shower, clothes, run for the train; but her body will not move, doesn't want to. Train to Victoria, Circle line to Edgware Road. Walk – run – from there. If she gets up and showers now she can make the meeting. But time ticks on and she doesn't stir. The blackbird is singing in the rowan tree in the front garden, and the light through the blinds is soft and early, and she just listens to the birdsong, and Ciaran moving around in the kitchen. She hears him coming back up the stairs, and he's there. He sets the cups down on the heap of books and newspapers by the bed. Leans in and kisses her.

'How much do you want the contract?'

She pulls a face. 'Need it.'

'Ah, well.'

He sits down on the edge of the bed.

'There you go.' He offers her a mug. 'Careful.'

She blows on it, sips, winces.

'I did say careful.'

'The thing is though,' Billie says, 'I've already left it a bit late.'

He looks at his watch. 'Yeah. Maybe.'

'I really hate being late.'

The bird sings. Her hands are hot round the mug.

'I suppose I could call,' she says. 'Say I've come down with something.'

'Better than just turning up late.'

'She can't sack me for being sick, can she?'

'Nope.'

'I'll call her.'

He takes the cup off her, sets it down. 'Later.'

'Yes, later.'

Later, in the kitchen, she will switch on the radio while she makes further coffee, as he slices bread for toast, and just as she is saying something to make Ciaran laugh they will hear the news. They will hear about the dazed and bleeding people stumbling through the dark. The broken bodies left behind. The bus twisted like a crushed can, the wounded and the dead. And the selflessness, the fierce instinctive kindnesses of ordinary people. She will see herself, a different version of this morning, as it would have been without Ciaran in it. A crowded carriage. Arm linked round a metal pole, she is racing through the dark, towards an important meeting which doesn't matter now at all, swaying towards the moment of explosion, of the world's collapse.

She will grip the edge of the kitchen counter, the breath knocked out of her.

He will put his arms around her, and she'll turn to him, and they'll just stand there, listening, holding each other. Listening.

She will shake her head, and mumble into his chest, and darken the blue cotton with her tears.

'Billie,' he will say. 'Billie, love, seriously, you are right where you should be.'

But for years to come, as she moves through the city, she will find herself stepping round empty spaces on the pavement, because they seem somehow occupied. She feels like she is the ghost walking over other peoples' graves. It occurs to her: there is no particular reason for me. It makes her reach for her phone, and call Ciaran, and talk for ages about nothing much at all.

Later, there will be a wedding in the local register office, and a party after at the Commercial Hotel, and her dad will drink too much and dance with Ciaran's sister, and Matty's daughter, a crumpled flowergirl, will fall asleep on her father's lap. Later, Billie will struggle through a difficult pregnancy and birth, and discover a vital, urgent love for her little girl, who inherits Madeline's pensive frown and uses it when considering Stickle Bricks or unfamiliar food. And there will be inevitable struggles: her work, and Ciaran away for his work, and the baby's sometimes overwhelming needs, and worries about Matty and their father's failing health. There will be illness, and there will be death, and through it all there will be love.

But for now, the blackbird still sings outside the window. Now, there is just the kiss, and the taste of coffee, and the clear strong knowledge that this, however long or brief, is happiness.